## "Some things are still private, sir, one's thoughts especially so."

"But if you want to kiss me again," she added, feeling suddenly and strangely shy but determined, "you may."

"May I?" Dev raised his eyebrows. "I will admit that I enjoyed your kiss when we were here before. But others would say that I'd taken advantage of you."

"They would be wrong," Robina said. "I kissed you first. I wanted to know how it would feel, and now I want to know if it feels the same way whenever one kisses a man. I do trust you with my virtue, Dev."

"Do you, Robby? You should not be so trusting. Sithee, I'm not certain I can trust myself. You're a mighty tempting wench. But there are rules."

"Bother the rules," she said. "Do you not *want* to kiss me?"

"Aye, sure, I do," he responded, pulling her roughly into his arms.

Uncertain now, but curious, she looked up and tried to gauge his mood. But he allowed her no time for that before his lips claimed hers, hot and demanding.

As he held her close, she heard him moan quietly in his throat.

"A fast-paced, action-packed story...Filled with passion, danger, Scottish allure, treason, and love. The romance and passion sizzle off the page...Ms. Scott has yet again created a dazzling story with a bigger-than-life hero and a feisty heroine. A must-read."

—MyBookAddictionReviews.com

## THE LAIRD'S CHOICE

"Wonderfully romantic...[a] richly detailed Scottish historical from the author frequently credited with creating the subgenre."

—*Library Journal*

"Splendid scenery...Atmosphere abounds in this colorful romance."

—HistoricalNovelSociety.org

"A fine piece of historical romance fiction."

—TheBookBinge.com

## HIGHLAND LOVER

"4½ stars! Excellent melding of historical events and people into the sensuous love story greatly enhances an excellent read."

—*RT Book Reviews*

"With multiple dangers, intrigues to unravel, daring rescues, and a growing attraction between Jake and Alyson, *Highland Lover* offers hours of enjoyment."

—RomRevtoday.com

"[An] exciting, swashbuckling tale...will grab your attention from the very beginning...Ms. Scott's unique storytelling ability brings history to life right before your eyes...If you are looking for a great Scottish romance, look no further than Amanda Scott!" —RomanceJunkiesReviews.com

"The latest Scottish Knights romance is a wonderful early-fifteenth-century swashbuckling adventure. As always with an Amanda Scott historical, real events are critical elements in the exciting storyline. With a superb twist to add to the fun, readers will appreciate this super saga."
—GenreGoRoundReviews.blogspot.com

## HIGHLAND HERO

"4½ stars! Scott's story is a tautly written, fast-paced tale of political intrigue and treachery that's beautifully interwoven with history. Strong characters with deep emotions and a high degree of sensuality make this a story to relish." —*RT Book Reviews*

"[A] well-written and a really enjoyable read. It's one of my favorite types of historical—it's set in medieval times and interwoven with actual historical figures. Without a doubt, Amanda Scott knows her history...If you enjoy a rich historical romance set in the Highlands, this is a book to savor." —NightOwlRomance.com

"[A] gifted author...a fast-paced, passion-filled historical romance that kept me so engrossed I stayed up all night to finish it. The settings are so realistic that the story is brought to life right before your eyes..."
—RomanceJunkiesReview.com

## HIGHLAND MASTER

"Scott, known and respected for her Scottish tales, has once again written a gripping romance that seamlessly interweaves history, a complex plot, and strong characters with deep emotions and a high degree of sensuality."

—*RT Reviews*

"Ms. Scott is a master of the Scottish romance. Her heroes are strong men with an admirable honor code. Her heroines are strong-willed...This was an entertaining romance with enjoyable characters. Recommended."

—*FreshFiction.com*

"Deliciously sexy...a rare treat of a read...*Highland Master* is an entertaining adventure for lovers of historical romance."

—*RomanceJunkies.com*

"Hot...There's plenty of action and adventure...Amanda Scott has an excellent command of the history of medieval Scotland—she knows her clan battles and border wars, and she's not afraid to use detail to add realism to her story."

—*All About Romance*

## TEMPTED BY A WARRIOR

"4½ stars! Top Pick! Scott demonstrates her incredible skills by crafting an exciting story replete with adventure and realistic, passionate characters who reach out and grab you...Historical romance doesn't get much better than this!"

—*RT Book Reviews*

"Captivates the reader from the first page... Another brilliant story filled with romance and intrigue that will leave readers thrilled until the very end."

—SingleTitles.com

## SEDUCED BY A ROGUE

"4½ stars! Top Pick! Tautly written... passionate... Scott's wonderful book is steeped in Scottish Border history and populated by characters who jump off the pages and grab your attention... Captivating!"

—*RT Book Reviews*

"Readers fascinated with history... will love Ms. Scott's newest tale... leaves readers clamoring for the story of Mairi's sister in *Tempted by a Warrior*."

—FreshFiction.com

## TAMED BY A LAIRD

"4½ stars! Top Pick! Scott has crafted another phenomenal story. The characters jump off the page and the politics and treachery inherent in the plot suck you into life on the Borders from page one."

—*RT Book Reviews*

"Scott creates a lovely, complex cast."

—*Publishers Weekly*

# Devil's Moon

# AMANDA SCOTT

*Devil's Moon*

## BORDER NIGHTS

WITHDRAWN

FOREVER

NEW YORK   BOSTON

Copyright © 2015 by Lynne Scott-Drennan
Excerpt from *Moonlight Raider* copyright © 2014 by Lynne Scott-Drennan

Forever
Hachette Book Group
1290 Avenue of the Americas
New York, NY 10104

www.HachetteBookGroup.com

Printed in the United States of America

First Edition: March 2015
10  9  8  7  6  5  4  3  2  1

OPM

Forever is an imprint of Grand Central Publishing.
The Forever name and logo are trademarks of Hachette Book Group, Inc.

The Hachette Speakers Bureau provides a wide range of authors for speaking events. To find out more, go to www.hachettespeakersbureau.com or call (866) 376-6591.

The publisher is not responsible for websites (or their content) that are not owned by the publisher.

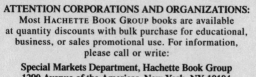

*To Kevin*
*for always making life interesting*
*Don't do this one again!*

*How foolish are mankind to look for perfection*
*In any poor changeling under the sun!*
*By nature or habit, or want of reflection,*
*To vices and folly we heedlessly run.*

—James Hogg, the Ettrick Shepherd

*Author's Note* _____

For readers' convenience, the author offers the following brief guide:

**Adam's ale**—water

**Auld Reekie**—the devil

**Borderers**—people who live in the Borders on the Scottish or English side

**Buccleuch**—Buck LOO

**Castle steward**—manages domestic concerns; collects rents, keeps accounts

**Castle warden or constable**—acts in place of its owner in owner's absence

**Clish-maclaver**—gossip

**Fitchet**—the slit in a lady's gown that allows her to reach her pocket, purse, etc.

**Haugh**—HAW (k) = low-lying meadow beside a river

**Hawick**—HOYK (almost two syllables)

**Himself**—refers to the laird or lord of the manor

**Keekers**—eyes

**Kist**—chest, box, chest of drawers (can also be a coffin, but not in this book)

**None**—the clerical midday hour, about 1:30 to 2:00 p.m. in springtime

**Pliskie**—mischievous, full of tricks, wily

**Sike**—a narrow rivulet that may flow only in spring-time and early summer

**The Douglas**—refers only to the "current" Earl of Douglas

**Wheesht**—As in "Hold (or Haud) your wheesht"—Be quiet.

# Devil's Moon

# *Prologue* ⸻

*Coklaw Castle, the Scottish Borders, July 1403*

The night was black. Not a star shone, and the damp, clinging mist was as cold as mid-November. The castle's tall, square keep rose above its outer wall, although the two appeared as one solid density against the night sky.

Armed with a shovel and dirk, the thickset man known as Shetland Jamie felt his way to the crest of a low rise thirty yards southeast of the wall. He thanked God for the darkness and blessed the mist that hid him. He heard no sound from the wall walk above.

The siege laid by Henry Percy, the powerful English Earl of Northumberland, had been in effect for fifteen days, but his army had not attacked for a sennight, so the Scots inside the castle no longer feared an assault. Doubtless, the earl meant to starve them out.

Jamie had worried about his shovel making noise, but yesterday's misery-making rain had softened the ground, so the downpour had been good for something beyond easing the army's stink. Moreover, the heavy mist had muffled the night bird's call he'd heard a short while ago, so it would doubtless muffle any sounds he made.

Jamie had studied the rise from the day he'd first recognized the stunning opportunity that had presented itself to him. Now, following an image in his head of what he had seen earlier, he soon found the pile of rocks he'd left to mark his spot.

Cautiously resting his shovel on a shrub, he gently set down the crockery jar that held the most precious part of his burden, out of the way but where he could find it again.

Dawn remained distant, and the English tents and siege fires lay to the south, beyond the crest of a nearby hill. Northumberland's tent was the finest, of course. The Percys were wealthier than God, and Shetland Jamie's family was poorer than dust.

But God knew all and willed all, did He not?

Jamie believed that God had provided this chance and had willed the idea into his head. A wise man recognized opportunity when it came his way, and he knew that he'd have had to be blind *not* to see this one. The others had left him alone, guarding that fine tent for just a few minutes, but that had been enough.

It would mean hanging if they caught him, but if they didn't, he'd be far better off than he was now. God had paved the way for him tonight, too, with the darkness and mist.

As he pictured numerous possibilities that the future might hold for him, he quietly shifted the pile of rocks out of his way. He would bury his treasure for the nonce and take good care that no one suspected what he'd done.

Northumberland's son, the formidable Hotspur, was here at Coklaw, too. He had said that the siege might last for a month but that, when they went, they would go quickly.

Hotspur always moved quickly.

Nevertheless, the siege was the oddest Jamie had seen. They had lobbed some of the earl's new cannonballs at the curtain wall, and one had even struck the keep wall inside. But they'd done almost no damage. The siege, he thought, would be a long one.

Nevertheless, the earl was Coklaw's rightful owner, because the previous year, after Northumberland's victory at Homildon Hill, England's king, Henry IV, had awarded him all lands belonging to the Scottish Earl of Douglas. But even the Percys were not powerful enough to wrest those lands from the iron Douglas grasp. Everyone on both sides of the line knew that the Douglases could raise ten thousand men in a blink.

As a result, Northumberland was irked with King Henry, and Hotspur was tired of fighting wars for a king who didn't pay his debts. The plain truth was that the Percys had come to sympathize strongly with the Welsh, who also resented Henry's treatment.

Jamie cleared a space between plants for his hole and began digging. The ground was workable, but he did have to feel for rocks with his shovel or dirk to avoid clanging the shovel's metal blade against one.

After a time, he knelt to test the result of his labor. The hole was deep enough, but its sides were still rough, so he used the dirk's blade to scrape the sides out more. He had wired the jar's lid on, to keep it in place.

Satisfied at last, he laid the jar in the hole, used his hands to push the dirt back in, and stood to tamp it down. Knowing that rain and settling would form a dip, he made a hill of pebbles, twigs, leaves, and rocks on top. He would look again in the morning to be sure that nothing remained to suggest that anyone had dug there.

Standing with shovel in hand, he listened, but even the night birds were silent. He felt as if he were the only one in the world who was still awake.

Retracing the path he had taken earlier, he followed the curving hillside toward the English encampment. Soon, he saw the glow of low fires ahead—more fires, he noted, than when he'd left. The mist was thinner, too, and he could see more men moving about than should have been up so late. Had they missed him and raised an alarm?

As the thought crossed his mind, two burly shapes emerged from the nearby mist.

"Jamie, be that ye?" a familiar voice muttered, as the shapes became two men muffled to the eyes.

"Aye, Rolf," Jamie muttered back. "Be summat amiss?"

"Sakes, man, we been looking all over for ye. Where ye been?"

"Damned if I know," Jamie said, glad he'd planned for such questions. "I went seeking the latrine, and I been seeking me bed ever since."

"Well, stir your stumps, man. The Scottish Duke o' Albany's on his way wi' an army to end our siege, so we're making straightaway for Wales."

*"Wales!"* He glanced over his shoulder, back the way he had come. "But—"

"We're to aid the Welsh rebellion. So hie yourself, or they'll leave ye behind."

"We're leaving *now*?" Jamie fought to keep the panic from his voice.

"Aye, Hotspur means to make Carlisle afore dawn."

An icy chill settled over Shetland Jamie. He hadn't even had a chance to count his treasure. Now he might never see it again.

# Chapter 1 _____

*Teviotdale, the Scottish Borders, Easter Sunday 1428*

Although the waning, nearly full moon had slipped behind a cloud that gave it a silvery halo but dimmed the rugged landscape below, the five riders on the ancient drove road saw their way easily. Their sure-footed horses were accustomed to moonlight rides.

Somewhat hampered by their booty—a pair of softly lowing cows and four nervous sheep—the small party traveled slowly downhill, northward, through a cut that men called "Leg o' Mutton," due to its shape. White Hill lay behind them, and the shadowy Witch Crags peaked in the northeast distance.

The sixth and seventh members of their party acted as sentinels, the sixth riding the western hill crests that separated the cut from Slitrig Water, flowing swiftly northward toward the town of Hawick. The seventh man rode near the timberline of the eastern hills, skirting their rocky heights.

The slope below those heights, to the party's right, boasted patches of dense shrubbery and scattered trees near its base, denser woodland above, with grass and rugged crags from the tree line to the top. A gurgling stream ran alongside them to their left.

The western slope of the cut was neither as high nor as steep as the eastern one, although the Slitrig side of that west ridge was steeper. Foliage on the cut's east slope was thicker than the trees and shrubbery to the west.

Familiar with every cranny and dip in those hills, the riders knew they would be home within the half-hour. Other than an occasional nightjar's call and the soft chuckling of the stream, the night was still.

The large man riding his sturdy roan next to the leader's big, powerful black heaved a sigh. "Nowt to boast of in this lot o' beasts," he muttered in near disgust.

"We did not lift them to boast of it, Sandy," the leader muttered back. "We took them to feed our people and because the Turnbulls likely stole our kine first."

"'Tis true, that. But chance beckoned us to take more. Had Rab been—"

"With luck, they won't miss a half-dozen beasts," the leader interjected curtly. "The last thing we want is a feud with the Turn—"

A shout drew their attention to the west slope. Light from the moon, emerging from its cloud, revealed a rider pounding downhill toward them.

"That be Shag's Hobby!" Sandy exclaimed unnecessarily.

Turning in the saddle toward the riders behind them, the leader said clearly but without shouting, "Jeb, you and Ratch hie those beasts into the woods. Keep them still and yourselves out of sight. Dand, get Hobby's attention and wave for him to follow us. We'll be riding apace, but be ready to slow before the next turning. Shag will see us from the east ridge and will follow when he can."

Sandy protested. "Sakes, me l—"

"Silence!" the leader snapped. "I told you, Sandy, call me nowt tonight save Bean. And if you're thinking we should ride home like madmen, you're daft. You ken fine that Hobby's haste means riders are coming. We must make anyone who sees us now believe that we're nowt save innocent travelers."

Sandy shook his shaggy head but urged his mount to a faster pace. Then he said, "I doubt ye'll be tellin' that tale if them riders catch us."

"Haud your wheesht! We're nobbut a mile from Coklaw. If Jeb and Ratch keep our beasts hidden and quiet, we'll be just four innocent riders."

"*If* them wha' come didna already see us *wi'* the beasts—"

A shout came from Hobby, now more than halfway down the west slope: "A dozen riders coming up yon road through the pass! Likely they're after us!"

Waving for him to follow, the three remaining riders gave spur to their horses.

~

Twenty-four-year-old Sir David Ormiston of Ormiston, riding from Hermitage Castle in Liddesdale to Hawick for the night, crested the drove road pass above Leg o' Mutton and, in the increasing moonlight, saw three riders racing toward the cut's narrow end. A fourth man, nearing the base of the slope below, shouting as he rode, gave Sir David to understand that the three had set watchers to guard their passage.

The shouted warning amused him. The group was small, and although he scanned the east slope for more

watchers, he saw none and had no interest in the horsemen, raiders or not. He acted for the fifth Earl of Douglas
and had business with him in Hawick.

Jock Cranston, the captain of his fighting tail, drew
rein beside him. "D'ye think they be reivers, sir?"

"If they are, they are unsuccessful ones. Do you see
any beasts?"

"Nay, but they may be just heading out. Or mayhap
they're English."

"A mere four men or five if they have a second look-
out yonder?" David shook his head. "The three were in a
pelting hurry when I topped the hill, but they've slowed
and—"

He broke off, stunned. The moon, abruptly freed of the
cloud that had dimmed it, beamed brightly down on the
leader's horse, turning its black hide glossy and revealing
a big diamond-shaped white star between its eyes when it
tossed its head.

"I know that horse!" Sir David exclaimed. "But who
would dare—?"

Louder shouts from below interrupted him.

"They're fleeing," Jock muttered. "'Tis gey strange, if
ye ask me."

"I'm going after them," Sir David said. "You and Coll
bring the others more slowly, Jock. I don't want *us* to look
like raiders. If I'm right, that lot is heading for Coklaw,
so I mean to learn who the bangster is that dares to ride
Black Corby."

"Aye, that could be Rab Gledstanes' Corby," Jock
agreed. "And we ken fine that Rab isna riding 'im. Whoever the lad be, he rides like he kens the beast well."

"Corby is even better trained than my Auld Nick is,"

Sir David said curtly. "But if that chap runs him into a rabbit hole, or worse, he'll answer to me, by God."

"Ye could be mistaken, sir."

"Bring the lads, Jock. I'm away."

"Wi' the deevil in ye, too," Jock muttered loudly enough for him to hear.

His only reaction was to smile grimly and spur his horse after the riders below.

The road he followed was safe enough, and Auld Nick was agile. But Sir David also knew that the speed he was demanding from him was such that his crusty father, and likely others, would deem it reckless.

Nevertheless, he wanted to catch up with the riders before they could vanish. A thought tickled his mind about who *might* be leading them, but he dismissed it half-formed as daft and fixed his attention on the path ahead.

Glancing back as he forded the stream that tumbled down the center of the cut, he saw his men following more slowly. The riders ahead had disappeared around a curve before he'd ridden halfway down the slope.

Auld Nick was willing, though, and the moderate pace that his master had set earlier from Liddesdale had not taxed him. The stallion was eager to make speed.

Although the moon was bright whenever the scudding clouds allowed it, the light it cast was too dim to read tracks from the saddle of a galloping horse. Sir David did not try. Instinct and the unique black stallion made him confident that his quarry would race to Coklaw Castle, midway between the end of the cut and the river Teviot.

A quarter-hour later, the castle's huge square stone

tower loomed ahead, pale gray in the moonlight. He saw no sign of the riders or their horses, but he knew Coklaw. Its stables and yard lay inside the wall, and the gate was swinging shut.

"Hold the gate, Clem!" he shouted, recognizing the lad shutting it.

Clem waved, and Sir David slowed Auld Nick. "My men are right behind me," he said to the lad. "Stay here to admit them. Someone else can look after Nick."

Riding more sedately into the stableyard, he saw another lad in breeks, boots, leather jack, and a knitted cap trotting across the yard from the stables.

Sir David shouted, "Here, lad, come see to my horse!"

The boy failed to heed him, but another one, no more than eleven or twelve years old, darted from the stable, shouting, "Aye, sir. I'll see to him for ye."

He did not recognize the youngster. "Do you know who I am?"

The boy's eyes flared like a nervous foal's. "Aye, sir. Ye be Dev—that is, Sir David Ormiston."

"Auld Nick will be hungry. You're not afraid of him, I hope."

"Nay, sir. I'm no afeard o' any beast. I'll gi'e him oats and hay."

"Good then. I'm going inside."

The boy's eyes widened more. He glanced warily toward the stable and back at Sir David. "I could send some'un tae tell Old Greenlaw ye're here."

"Don't trouble yourself. If your steward's not snug in his bed, he ought to be."

"Aye, but—"

"Never mind, I know the way," Sir David said, striding

toward the tower's postern door, the one the other lad had used.

⁓

Shutting the postern door, the person who had dashed across the yard ran up the stairs, muttering, "Lord, preserve me. There's no time! That was Dev, and he saw me. He thought I was one of the lads, but he must *not* find me still up."

There was no time to lift the heavy bar into its brackets, let alone to bolt the iron yett across it all to make that entryway impregnable. It did not matter, though. Dev would use the main entrance.

*"Just hurry, Beany, get upstairs."* Puffing, then startling at the sound of a crash downstairs—the door, the damned door, crashing back against the wall—

*"He's inside, not out front!"*

Heavy, hasty footsteps pounded up the steps below.

*"The landing's yonder. There's the door, push it open. Close it…doucely, doucely! Throw the bolt and get rid of your dirk. Hurry!"*

No time. Hide the dirk! Would the bolt hold? Footsteps on the landing!

*"He's here, Beany. You're for grief now, and it serves you right."*

The latch rattled. A deep, familiar voice growled, "Open this door!"

"I will not! 'Tis the middle of the night. Go away! You've no business here."

The door crashed open. The big, dark-haired man filled the doorway. Even in the dim light of a moonbeam through the small window, anger blazed from his eyes.

Without hesitation, Sir David strode to the breeks-clad figure in the middle of the room and snatched off the knitted cap.

A cloud of tawny hair cascaded to her waist.

He'd been angry first because of the horse, but despite his brief suspicion earlier, he was furious now. Grabbing her by the shoulders, he gave her a rough shake. "What demon possessed you to take such a mad risk? *Raiding!* On a horse as recognizable as Corby?"

"Faith, did you find our beasts and take them for yourself?"

His mouth gaped, but it was the last straw. Gripping one slender arm, he turned her toward her bed, sat on it, pulled her across his knees, and gave her a smack on her leather-clad backside hard enough to make her screech. "That one's for Rab," he growled before smacking her harder. "That's for Black Corby." Then, with the hardest smack, he snapped, "And *that* one is for me."

Livid with anger, nineteen-year-old Robina Gledstanes struggled unsuccessfully to free herself. "Damn your eyes, Dev Ormiston, let me go! May God curse you from here to your satanic home in Hell! Release me, *damn you*!"

"Such pretty language," he said sardonically. "Mind your tongue, Beany, or I'll give you a few more smacks."

"*Don't* call me Beany," she said grimly. "Only Rab..." Her twin's name caught in her throat, but she swallowed it and said, "Only he could call me that. Moreover, I learned my pretty language from him—*and* from you, Dev."

Resting his big hand on her backside, he said evenly, "I doubt that Rab would accept that as an excuse any more than I do for such curses flying from your lips."

*"He's right about that, you wee vixen."*

A shiver shot through her, and she sighed. "Just let me go, Dev, please."

He released her then, and she stood, resisting the urge to rub her backside. She would not give him the satisfaction of knowing how much it stung.

"Put on some proper clothing and meet me downstairs," he said as he got to his feet. "I have much more that I mean to say to you."

"I won't," she retorted. "You have no *right* to call me to account, Dev."

"You'll do as I say, or by God, I'll strip those breeks off you myself and take leather to you."

"You wouldn't dare!"

He sighed. "You know better than that, Robina."

*"You damned well should, Beany. Dinna be daft!"*

Angry, unexpected tears welled in her eyes at the sound of that persistent voice. It was so clear that it was as if Rab stood right behind her, watching them . . . and taking Dev's side against his own sister—as usual.

She stared at the floor, fighting the tears, willing Dev to leave.

Instead, he said softly, ominously, "Besides, Robbylass, who would stop me?"

"I will," said a small but firm voice from the doorway.

Startled, both of them whirled and saw a towheaded

boy standing there with a raised dirk in his hand. The weapon was longer than his arm.

~~~

Dev found himself displaced when Robina pushed him aside to confront her nine-year-old brother, exclaiming, "Benjy! Whatever are you doing out of bed?"

"Sakes, who could sleep wi' such a din in here? What's Dev doing here anyway, Beany, and why were ye a-screeching like a banshee?"

"Give me that dirk," she commanded. "And remember to offer it hilt first."

The little boy obeyed her, saying, "Ye ken fine I wouldna hurt ye."

"I ken fine that you belong in bed," she retorted.

"I'll take him," Ormiston said, moving her aside and taking the dirk from her hand as he did. "You put a dress on, Robina. I'll meet you in the hall."

"Where did ye come from, Dev?" the boy asked, looking up at him.

"From Hermitage Castle," Ormiston said. Then, with a hand to Benjy's shoulder, he added quietly, "But you should address me as Sir David, you know, or 'sir,' not Dev."

"Hoots, nae one else here calls ye aught save Devil Ormiston. But Beany and me call ye Dev, though, just as your own lads do and our Rab did."

Benjy's voice faltered on the last three words.

Urging him gently across the landing to his bedchamber, Dev pulled Robina's door shut behind them, hoping it would stay put despite its broken latch and bolt. He said, "D'ye still miss him sorely, laddie?"

"Aye, sure, don't you?"

Pausing to be sure of his own voice, Dev said, "I do, aye. But it is our duty to get on with our lives. I know it's hard, Benjy, but Rab would want us to be strong."

"Even Beany?"

"Beany *is* strong," Dev said, wishing she were less *head*strong.

"But ye're sore vexed with her, aye? I heard ye a-skelping her."

Dev pulled back the covers on the boy's cot. "In you get now," he said.

"Dinna be wroth with Beany," Benjy said. "She gets sad, too, just like us."

∽

Robina finished twisting her long hair into a plait and declared herself presentable enough in her simple kirtle and bare feet to avoid further censure. She had heard Benjy say they always called him Dev and wondered what Devil Ormiston would say about that.

*"Likely nowt,"* her twin said. *"He's too wroth with you. Mind your step when you go down, and listen meekly to what he says. Don't challenge or sauce him!"*

She grimaced, knowing that Dev was waiting for her, because she had heard him go downstairs. Before that, she had heard the hum of his voice in Benjy's room and Benjy answering him, but that was all.

Her backside still stung. Although she had known Dev for years, she had never known him to be as angry as he was now. Sakes, what was she going to tell John Greenlaw to explain her broken door?

*"You'll think of something."*

She would. Meantime, Rab's advice was good if only she could make herself follow it. Unfortunately, Dev's nature, and her own, compelled her to defend herself in every way against the man.

Not only was he the handsomest creature to stalk the Borders but he also seemed to think he was the smartest one and the finest ever to ride a horse, wield a sword, or... sakes, to do anything! But he had no *right* to lift a hand to her.

Entering the hall, she saw that he had lit torches and candles and was on one knee now, putting peat chunks on the fire he had stirred to life.

He straightened when he saw her, and she saw that he looked tired.

He moved closer, eyeing her narrowly, and she marveled again at how blue his eyes were, even by candlelight. She could tell that he had been traveling, because he had not shaved. The dark growth appeared to indicate the lack for days, but on him it looked good.

He frowned. "What?"

The single word surprised her. She had expected him to begin ranting the moment he saw her.

"You said you had much to say to me, but I hope you won't say that I must not call you Dev. I always have, after all."

"I don't mind it," he said quietly. "It seems as if the only people who call me David now are the women in my family, Archie Douglas, and my father. In troth, I tend to answer most easily to Dev."

"Are you still furious with me?"

"I am. Come and sit down."

"I'd rather stand, thank you."

His mouth quirked into a near smile. "You deserved every lick."

Grimacing, she said, "I know that *you* think so." She nearly added that Rab thought so, too, but she did not want to have that conversation with Dev—not now, not ever.

"I think you know that I'm right, too," he said. "What *were* you thinking?"

"That our people need food," she replied. "You know that the raids have begun again, and the Douglas does naught to stop them."

"I thought you were sending for your aunt Clara and Jarvis to stay with you."

She shrugged and then wished she had not when his dark eyebrows snapped together again. To divert him, she said, "You know that you and your men cannot stay here tonight, Dev. Greenlaw would have an apoplexy. You'll have to ride on."

"I know. I'm expected at the Black Tower before dawn."

"You told Benjy that you'd been at Hermitage," she said. "With Douglas?"

"Nay, he's in Hawick, and I've matters to report to him. But we are not going to talk about me, Robina. What became of your aunt and your cousin?"

"I don't want them. Coklaw survived the siege of 1403, so it's impregnable. Greenlaw protected it then and can do so again if he must."

He drew a deep breath, and when she saw his hands fisting, she took a hasty step back. He shook his head—at himself, she knew—and his hands relaxed.

"You know I'd never use my fists against you, Robby. But what do you think would have happened if, instead of my men and me, those chasing you tonight had been a raiding party? What if English raiders had followed you here?"

"We'd have barred the gate and the doors, of course. I told you!"

"Think, Robina. Clem hadn't shut the gate yet when you ran across the yard and in through the postern door. You didn't have time to bar that door. And Greenlaw is asleep. The risk you took to go raiding, as I am certain now you did, is intolerable. I promise you, I'll see that you don't endanger yourself so again."

"You can't promise any such thing, Dev. You do *not* have the right!"

"You said that before, lass. You'd be wise to recall my reply."

The shiver that shot through her did not dampen her anger, but much as she'd have liked to walk away, she could not seem even to look away. Frustrated but determined not to let him see how much he unnerved her, she returned his stare and drew a deep breath.

When his gaze shifted briefly to her breasts, she realized her error in deciding not to waste time putting on her shift before donning her kirtle.

~

She had turned into a beauty, to be sure, Dev decided, albeit not for the first time. The thought renewed his concern for her, though, and his temper stirred again. Returning his gaze to her face in time to catch her nervously licking her lips, he knew she understood how much her escapade had angered him.

"See here, Robby," he said, "you don't need me to tell

you how much danger you courted tonight. Your own good sense should tell you that."

"Would you send *your* men on a raid and not go with them?" she asked.

He said curtly, "Lass, when I organize a raid, I do it because the Douglas has ordered one, and *he* does not go with us."

"Well, don't tell me you've never led one. I know you have, and Rab did, often."

"That's different. You're a woman, Robina, much as you try to ignore that fact."

"Rab would never have let our men go without him, nor would our dad when he was alive," she insisted. "We cannot keep all our stock inside the wall, nor do we have enough men left to guard them. Therefore, the English and our neighbors help themselves whenever they please. We just took some of our own back."

"*Just* your own?"

She shrugged again, making those enticing breasts undulate beneath the soft pink material of her kirtle. He had noticed that the garment was surprisingly low-cut and that she had not bothered to wear a shift.

The kirtle boasted a hastily laced red bodice, which jutted her breasts invitingly toward him. If Rab saw her now, he'd rise out of his grave to teach her propriety.

Grimacing at his own conduct, Dev realized he could hardly condemn her lack of decorum after staring as he had. If he expected her ever to accept his authority, he'd be daft to admit he'd noticed the way her nipples tried to thrust themselves through the thin fabric.

"Would you have stopped here if you hadn't seen us?" she asked then.

"No," he said. "The hour is late, and they're expecting me in Hawick. Also, I had a message from my father, complaining about my long absence, so I'm for Ormiston as soon as I've reported to Archie and slept."

Her gaze met his again as she said, "So, say whatever you still want to say to me, Dev. Then, you can be on your way."

He stepped close enough to put his hands on her shoulders again, gently this time. "I've shot my bolt for tonight, Robby," he said. "But don't do it again."

"Do you think I'm witless, Dev?"

He nearly smiled then. "I do not," he said. "You are impulsive and headstrong, and you don't give a thought to safety. If anything, you're too clever for your own good. Does Greenlaw know what you were doing tonight?"

He saw her swallow and then eye him measuringly. Her thoughts were as open to him as they could be. But she knew him, too. He did not need to speak.

With a wry and rather wary look, she said, "I don't suppose it would do any good to say that he does know."

He shook his head. "I should have given you another smack for Greenlaw."

"I'm thankful you didn't," she admitted. "But I almost wish you could stay. I…I have questions…about Rab and…" Swallowing visibly, she fell silent.

"I told you how he died," Dev said. "He saved my life and doubtless others, too. I don't know what more you would *want* to know."

"I'm glad you were with him, Dev, and could hold him whilst he died. I forgot to thank you for that when you brought his body home to us."

He didn't remember telling her he'd held Rab in his

arms, but he had, so he must have told her. "You were too distraught to put such thoughts into words then, lass. I wasn't thinking clearly that day, myself."

She looked as if she were about to ask another question, but she didn't, and he decided that the less they talked about Rab, the better they would both feel.

"Go to bed, Robby," he said, stepping back. "I'll return as soon as I can. Meantime, try to imagine what Rab would say to you about tonight and what he most likely would have done had *he* seen you riding through that cut instead of me."

"I don't have to imagine it," she said, scowling. "I know exactly what he thinks...thought...and what he would say and do. But he cannot—"

"If you mean to say that he can't do anything about such behavior now, you'd be wiser to recall that I can," he interjected bluntly.

She stuck her tongue out at him then and danced quickly away as she said, "Goodnight, Dev. I expect we won't see you again for months."

He could have assured her that he would return much sooner, but he thought it was better for now to let her think as she liked. She would find out soon enough that he had decided to make his presence felt at Coklaw even while he was away.

That was little enough for him to do, in view of his promise to Rab.

# Chapter 2 _____

As soon as Dev had gone, Robina hurried up the stairs, trying to put his stern image out of her head so she could think straight.

*"You would do better to recall what he said to you, Beany. You ken fine that he never makes idle threats."*

"I know," she muttered. "But he doesn't understand how things are here."

*"He understands enough,"* Rab said. *"He kens you fine, too, so you must do no more raiding."*

"Not whilst he's anywhere near Coklaw, certainly," she agreed. "However, he has duties elsewhere now, so he won't be back for a while. Meantime, we have wool to shear and cows to give us milk, butter, and cheese."

*"You underestimate Dev, lass. He'll return long before you expect him."*

"You forget that he has to go to Ormiston Mains to see his father."

*"Ormiston's nobbut ten miles away. And I doubt he'll stay long."*

"Don't be daft, Rab," she said tartly in her normal voice.

*"Wheesht, lass! Do you want to wake Greenlaw or his Ada?"*

Well aware that the steward and his housekeeper wife slept in a room at the top of the stairs, she murmured, "Dev said his father sent for him. Ormiston hasn't seen him since before what you call the 'wee skirmish at Chesters' six weeks ago that got you killed. I doubt that Dev's family will let him leave again soon."

She had reached her landing, and Rab did not argue the point, making her wonder if her maidservant, Corinne, was in her bedchamber. Someone, thinking Robina might want her, might have wakened the maid. But the room was empty.

Deciding that Rab agreed that Dev's family would keep him as long as they could, she undressed and got into bed. Her backside still stung, so she decided that if her twin was right and Dev returned too soon, she would find a way to get her revenge.

*"I'm not wrong, Beany. I know Dev better than you do."*

"You do, aye," she muttered grimly. "During the past few years, you spent more time with him than with me or anyone else at Coklaw."

*"And you are…or were…jealous of our friendship, lassie. You took few pains to hide it, but there was nae need of such. Wherever I am, I carry you with me, just as you carry me with you. We've been in each other's thoughts since the day we were born and 'tis likely we always will be. But be kind to Dev. He'll make you a better friend than an enemy. He'll also look after you and Benjy for me."*

"I don't need looking after, least of all by Devil Ormiston," she said firmly.

*"'Tis a wee bit late to protest, I fear."*

"What do you mean?"

She heard only silence.

"Rab?"

In the torchlit yard, Jock Cranston nodded in reply to Dev's lifted eyebrow.

"They were raiding, sir," Jock said. "I sent two of our lads back toward the cut quiet-like, and they met three more of their party with four sheep and two cows that they'd lifted. The men wouldna tell me *where* they'd lifted them, but that's what they'd done."

"Aye, I learned as much myself," Dev said. "I'm going to leave you and Jem Keith here whilst I'm away, Jock. Don't stir coals with anyone, and don't let Jem do so, either. I just want you to keep an eye on things here. Greenlaw, the steward, is a good man, as we know, but the best Gledstanes men-at-arms rode with Rab."

"Aye, and four o' them was killed at Chesters when he was."

"And then I gave leave to others to visit their families after we buried him," Dev said. "If they have not reported back yet, send for them. Those Percys at Chesters got nowt from their ambush but the deaths of a few good men. But if they know who Rab was, they may now hope to seize Coklaw."

"Aye, sir. Does Greenlaw know ye're a-leaving me here?"

"No, but you need say only that I thought you might be useful to him. I shan't be away long, but my father has as good as summoned me home, so something may be amiss. If it is aught to delay me, I'll get word to you. Meantime, there is one other thing."

"Her ladyship?" Jock said in a carefully even tone when Dev paused.

"Just so," Dev replied.

"I did wonder, sir. Black Corby be gey finicky about who rides him."

Just thinking of the danger she had flirted with on her mad raid made Dev's blood run cold. Grimly, he said, "You will keep such conjecture to yourself, I know, Jock, but you know her ladyship almost as well as I do. If you see her taking the bit between her teeth…" He paused, then added, "Keep a close eye on her."

With an uneasy look, Jock said, "I'll do me best, sir."

"That is all I ask," Dev said, knowing that where Robina was concerned, he could ask no more of any man, save himself. "I'm away then."

Summoning his other men, he mounted and led them out of the yard. Heading westward to the nearest Slitrig Water ford, they wasted no time. Even so, it was two hours after midnight when they rode up the hill to Hawick's stockade gates.

Shouting, "A Douglas!" Dev identified himself to the guards, and the town gates opened. The Douglas's Black Tower loomed ahead on his right with only two faint lights above the ground floor. Torches lit the front entrance and the archway into the stableyard.

Dismounting in the yard, Dev turned his horse over to Pony Eckie, his equerry, and walked back around to the main entrance.

The porter admitted him, saying, "How many be wi' ye, Sir David?"

"Seven to sleep inside," Dev said. "I expect the Douglas is asleep by now, aye?"

"Aye, sure, sir. He doesna keep late hours. The chamber ye used when last ye was here be open for ye, if ye want it. Your men can sleep in the great hall."

Thanking him, and telling him to send his squire up when he came in, Dev went on up to the cell-like room he had used many times before. It boasted only a cot with bedding, a washstand, and a straw pallet leaning against one wall.

The cot was uncomfortable, but he welcomed it.

He didn't wait for his squire, Coll Stitchill, but divested himself of his weapons, boots, breeks, and jack. Then, in his shirt and netherstocks, he lay down and assumed that he would be asleep before Coll came in.

Instead, his thoughts drifted back to Robina. She had seemed the same, as headstrong as ever and as sure of herself and her right to do as she pleased. Now that he reviewed their meeting in his mind, something seemed awry, but he had no idea what it was. It was not her fury. He had deserved that for several reasons.

He had seen her only briefly when he'd escorted Rab's body home for burial, and he knew he had been a bit short with her then. The last thing he'd wanted to do was to give her a clear picture of how Rab died. That he had flung himself in front of Dev and two other men, engaged with opponents of their own, and had taken a blow likely meant for Dev, was something that he would tell her eventually though, because she deserved to know how heroically her twin had behaved.

At the time, she had greeted him stoically and without a tear, saying only, "This is your fault. You promised when you first took him from us that you would keep him safe."

Her words had cut through him like so many knives, shredding him to his soul, because she was right. He had made her that promise. He'd been a damned fool to say such a thing, but that was four years ago. He had wielded authority over other men for only weeks then and, he knew now, had been dangerously cocksure of himself.

He would not make such a promise again to anyone. One could never predict what would happen in battle... or in life, come to that.

He heard the door open and Coll's soft movements as he prepared for bed, but Dev kept his eyes shut.

Drifting, he was semiconscious when a stray thought brought him fully awake again. What had struck him as awry earlier was that, except for that catch in her voice the first time she had said Rab's name that night, she had shown none of the lingering grief that one might expect. Nor, and even odder, had she shown much surprise, grief, or other emotion the day he'd told her that Rab was dead.

She had simply looked at him and said, "I know he is."

That was also when she had said it was all Dev's fault.

He had never heard that she had what Highlanders called "the Sight." So how, he wondered, could she have known of Rab's death before he'd told her? He had heard of mothers knowing that their sons had died before word reached them. He had never heard of a sister who had. However, Robby also knew that Rab had died in his arms, although he could not recall telling her so. Perhaps twins were different.

That was the last thought he had before Coll woke him soon after dawn to tell him that the Douglas would see him as soon as Dev had broken his fast.

The next thing Robina knew, the bed curtains were rattling back and Corinne was bidding her a cheery good-day. The maidservant's irrepressibly curly black hair stuck out as usual all around the edges of the white veil she wore, and her light sky-blue eyes twinkled when her gaze met Robina's.

"Is it morning already?" Robina muttered, sleepily blinking. "I cannot have slept more than a few hours."

"Aye, they told me what time ye got back," Corinne said as she took a fresh, russet-brown wool kirtle from the nearby kist and shook it out. "What happened to yon door?"

"Never mind what happened to it," Robina said. "It was my fault. Can you get one of the lads to fix it, so that I need not tell Greenlaw?"

"Aye, sure. Will ye get up the noo, or d'ye want me to go away again?"

"No, I'll get up," Robina said. "Did they tell you what beasts we brought back?"

"Two coos and four sheep, and one o' the ewes be lambing soon, Shag said. And," Corinne added with her cheeky grin, "there be two new menfolk in the yard as weel, mistress. One o' them's young, and a gey handsome chappie, too."

"What?" Robina sat up. "What new men?"

Corinne shrugged. "I dinna ken exactly who they be, but the younger one's called Jem Keith, and the older one thinks he's cock o' the yard. He doesna give orders, but our men hop when the chap says 'hop.' And Greenlaw likes 'im."

Robina frowned, trying to imagine who the two men could be. Awareness came with a jolt. "May Auld Reekie fly away with the villain," she muttered.

"D'ye ken them, then?" Corinne asked, laying the kirtle out at the foot of the bed.

"No, but I can guess who foisted them onto us," Robina replied. "If I am right, you'd be wise to keep away from both of them. And don't let either of them fix my door."

Corinne nodded, her eyes twinkling again. "Aye, then, I'll stay away from the old one for sure. I've seen him afore, I think. Mayhap when we buried the laird."

"Corinne, I mean what I say. Stay away from them *both*."

With a roguish smile, Corinne said, "Now, m'lady, ye ken fine that I try to behave as ye'd wish. But I canna help m'self. When a handsome laddie takes interest in me—"

"Good sakes, *has* he? Already?"

Corinne's eyes twinkled again, and a reminiscent smile touched her lips. "He said I'm the sweetest morsel he's ever clapped his keekers on. And then he said—"

"Enough!" Robina said, stifling an unexpected bubble of laughter. "I know you attract men like flies to a honey pot, Corrine, but in troth, I think you do so willfully. Only last week, I saw you in the yard, kissing Shag's Hobby."

Corinne shrugged and moved to the washstand to pour water from the ewer into the bowl. As she watched the water level rise, she said frankly, "I like kissing handsome men, mistress—or kind ones, or any ones, I expect. 'Tis how I were born. Me mam's mam were a tavern wench, after all."

"And no better than she should have been, I know," Robina said, having heard the excuse before, often. "I also know that your granddad was a French soldier who came to the Borders with others of his sort to help old King Robert's army invade England. But, Corinne, that was forty years ago."

"When the Frenchmen first came, aye," Corinne agreed. "But they was here for years, and me granddad stayed after the others left, 'cause he'd married me granddame. By then, he said, he spoke the French tongue with so strong a Scottish brogue that he doubted France would take him back. And though he were born noble, as a younger son, he said, he had more chance to better hisself here, 'specially if he could win hisself a knighthood."

"But he never did, I know," Robina said, swinging her legs out of bed to let her bare feet adapt to the chilly air before touching the floor. "Even so, if I thought *you'd* been behaving like a tavern wench—*truly* behaving like one—"

"In troth, mistress, I dinna ken what that means," Corinne confessed. "Me mam said that mostly it meant that me granddame enjoyed the laddies afore she met Granddad. Mam said she'd explain more when I were older, but she died afore then, and I came here."

Since Robina was also unsure of exactly what behaving like a tavern wench meant, she said, "Do not encourage the new man, Corinne. Faith, but I'd liefer you encourage no young man unless you mean to marry him."

"But Hobby be a handsome chappie, and he thinks I'm sweet. As for Jem Keith…" Pausing, she added, "See you, m'lady, Hobby left to visit his mam. Also, how will I know I want someone or that he might want me if I dinna encourage them all to flirt wi' me?"

Robina could think of no good answer to that, so

she told Corinne simply to behave herself, then dressed swiftly and went downstairs to break her fast. Afterward she hurried outside to see what men Dev had left to guard her.

~

When Douglas's steward escorted Dev to the inner chamber beyond the hall dais, the wiry, thirty-eight-year-old, dark-haired earl sat behind a big table there. He had several documents before him, a stick of red wax, and his heavy seal in a polished oaken box.

Douglas looked up when Dev entered and the steward announced his name.

Dismissing the steward, Douglas looked speculatively at Dev. His dark eyes glinted, and a thin smile appeared. "Welcome back, Davy-lad," he said in his customary evenly measured tones. "How did you find Hermitage?"

"As well-run as you had expected, my lord," Dev said. "Forrest did say he could use more men, though. It seems the Percys or men like them are bent on mischief again."

They discussed some additional provisions and weapons that the constable at Hermitage had requested. Then, abruptly, Douglas said, "Did ye have cause to visit Coklaw on your way or returning, lad?"

"I looked in briefly last night, sir," Dev said. "All seemed to be well, although rumors of incipient trouble are ever flying."

Douglas cleared his throat but remained quiet for a moment or two.

Knowing that the earl disliked making decisions, Dev wondered if trouble existed of which he was unaware. At last, he said, "Have you heard otherwise?"

"Not yet," Douglas said, meeting his gaze again. "I do find it worrisome, though, that a tower as close to the borderline as Coklaw is—less than a day's march, I'm told—has lost its laird and can provide nae one suitable to take his place. I'm thinking of putting one of my own captains in charge there."

Exerting every fiber of his being, Dev strove to conceal his dismay.

⁓

Robina easily recognized Jock Cranston, but seeing him in the stableyard shocked her, because he was the captain of Dev's fighting tail. Jock had always ridden at Dev's side if Rab or another noble leader did not ride with him.

Without hesitation, she walked up to him and said sternly, "What are you doing here, Jock? You should be with Sir David."

"Aye, I should be, m'lady," Jock said as a wry smile creased his thin leathery face. "Likely, he'll find hisself in trouble without me, but he told me to stay here and keep young Jem Keith wi' me. I dinna ken if ye've met Jem."

"I need not meet him now, Jock. I have all the protection I need. In fact, I am beset with protectors."

"Nay, then, m'lady," Jock said quietly. "Ye lost four o' your best men at Chesters, including his lordship's equerry, and others o' them be still wi' their kin. I had your Sandy send for those men when he awoke, so likely I'll be here only till Sir David returns."

She nearly told him that she had no need of Sir David, either, but she held her tongue. Her battle was with Dev, not with Jock, who was only obeying orders.

With an inner sigh, she wondered exactly what orders Dev had given him and this Jem Keith person, who flirted with vulnerable maidservants.

*"The truth, Beany, is that you resent any interference at Coklaw, which is why you never sent for our nosy aunt and that greedy son of hers. Not that I don't agree with you about keeping them away, but…"*

Ignoring Rab, she wondered just how much trouble Jock might cause her.

Deciding to test the man, she said lightly, "I suppose I must thank you for looking after us, Jock, but I won't keep you here now, talking. Sithee, I walk outside the wall each morning. We can talk more later, if you like."

"I'll tell your Sandy to send a lad or two with ye, m'lady."

"I'd only send them back," Robina said firmly. "I like to walk alone, and it has been relatively quiet here of late. I'm just going into the west forest, so I shan't be long."

Turning away, she strode toward the gate, fully expecting him to say she must not go. Hearing only silence, she waved at Ratch, who currently manned the gate.

He grinned as he opened it. "Mind yer step out there, me lady," he said. "We dinna ken how many lads Devil Ormiston brung wi' him last night. Mayhap he left some o' them outside the wall, too."

Smiling, she said, "If he did, I can cope with them. But pass the word that no one is to make trouble for Jock Cranston whilst he's here, Ratch."

"We all ken better nor that, m'lady. But ye must have a care, too," he added with a straight look. "Them Turnbulls may ha' men out a-seekin' their beasts, and Jock kens that as well as we do. He saw for hisself what we brung home."

Although that detail alarmed her, because what Jock knew Dev would also know, she returned Ratch's look with ease. "Jock wields no authority over me," she said softly. "Come to that, I doubt he will risk angering me."

"I was no thinking o' Jock," Ratch said. "I was thinking o' his master."

Feeling a tingle at the base of her spine reminiscent of the muscles clenching there when Dev had warned her that he'd meant what he'd said, Robina rolled her eyes anyway and said, "Sir David may be angry. But he won't murder me."

Ratch looked skeptical but swung the gate wide, and as she hurried through the opening, she assured herself that none of the men would betray her to Dev.

*"You like to think so, Beany, but you're daft if you think Jock Cranston won't tell him all he kens when Dev returns. Sakes, if Corinne tells Jem Keith about your door…"*

"Oh, hush, Rab," she muttered. "I don't care if Dev is angry with me. He can't get angry about the door, because he broke it. And I won't let anyone confine me inside our wall. I've rambled over our hills almost daily since I was small, and we'd hear about any English raiding party long before they arrived. You know we would."

As usual, when there was naught that he could say, Rab kept silent.

Even so, she knew he was right about one thing. Jock *would* tell Dev if he learned that she had done anything of which Dev might disapprove.

"Beany, wait!" Benjy shouted behind her. "I'm going with ye!"

~

Knowing that the Douglas, despite a generally mild temperament, would take no more kindly to dissent than his forbears had, Dev managed to avoid blurting his dismay at the earl's notion of installing his own man at Coklaw.

The last thing Rab would want was a Douglas running his castle.

Forcing calm into his voice, he said, "I doubt that you need to worry about losing Coklaw to the Percys or other English ruffians, my lord. Recall that when Northumberland besieged the castle twenty-five years ago, he failed to breach its walls."

"Aye, but that was then. The Percy cannon are more effective now."

"John Greenlaw is as skilled a constable as I know," Dev said. "He held Coklaw then, and he says the castle is still impregnable. I believe him. Moreover, although the English still intrude on our lands, we're keeping closer watch than ever. We'd hear of any large party, let alone cannon, heading toward Carter's Bar or Carlisle, and they'd never dare try to approach the area through Liddesdale."

Douglas was silent for a time before he said, "I'll think more on the matter, but I cannot say that I agree with you. Perhaps you'd like to take your men and have another look at our defenses throughout the Middle March."

"I am at your disposal, my lord, although I've had word from my father, desiring me to visit Ormiston. He said only that it had been long since I was home, but such a summons from him is unusual. It should take only a day or two of my time."

"Certes, you may have leave to see if aught is amiss. Look in at Scott's Hall on your way back, though, and see if Wat Scott can spare men for Hermitage. If he does not want to lead them himself, he can appoint you to do so."

"Aye, sure, I'll talk to him," Dev said. He knew that Walter Scott, Lord of Buccleuch and Rankilburn, just two years older than himself, would likely agree and have men to spare. However, he also knew better than to say so before discussing it with Wat.

Taking the earl's nod as dismissal, Dev left the chamber. When he spied his squire at a nearby table with some of his other lads, he nodded toward the door and kept walking. Coll and the others quickly followed. They had already taken the gear and weapons to the yard, and their horses were ready and waiting.

Mounting Auld Nick, Dev set a fast pace, and an hour and a half later, Jedburgh's six bastille towers loomed into view. The towers had taken the place of Jedburgh Castle two decades ago, after the Scots had routed the castle's English occupants and razed the fortress to prevent further English occupation.

Skirting the town and heading toward Jedburgh Abbey, Dev and his men forded Jed Water in the shadow of the abbey's arches to the accompaniment of its hundred-foot clock-tower bells, pealing the midday hour of None.

Continuing northeastward along the Teviot, they reached the village of Eckford an hour later and forded the Teviot before its confluence with Kale Water, which flowed into the river from the south. A short time later, the Teviot curved sharply northward toward its own convergence with the river Tweed.

Ormiston Mains lay straight ahead. Its tall peel tower

perched atop a grassy knoll overlooking the Teviot to the east and south. In the distance behind them, the riders could still see the village of Eckford edging the Teviot's south bank.

At Ormiston, they dismounted in the yard. Leaving Ormiston's grooms and his own men to attend to their horses, Dev headed for the tower entrance. Before he reached it, his sister Fiona, her long dark hair flying loose in tangles, ran from the nearby kitchen annex and flung her arms around him.

"I feared you were never coming home again, Davy!" she exclaimed, hugging him.

Nine years his junior, thoughtful, often still childlike but with a mind of her own, she was his favorite of his two sisters. Gellis was three years older than he was and had always been too bossy and self-absorbed to please him. But Fiona was sweet and generous.

"You look like a shaggy bairn," he said, holding her away to look at her. "How are you going to attract a husband if you don't keep yourself tidy?"

"Faith, sir, if you came home only to scold me, you may take yourself off again," she said. "I heard naught save criticism from Kenneth and Lucas when they were last here, although they, like you, are too lazy to present eligible men to me. I *don't* want to hear the same song from you, Sir Knight. As for Father—"

"David, come in," his father called from the doorstep, interrupting her. "It is time to dine. One of the lads told us you were coming, so we have waited for you."

Setting Fiona aside, Dev strode to meet him. Shaking hands, he said, "'Tis good to see you, sir. I hope your summons doesn't mean that aught is amiss here."

"Nay, nay," Ormiston said, urging him toward the stairs. "We've seen you too rarely of late, that's all. Moreover, my son, I've decided it's time that you married."

~

### The English Borders, Near Alnwick

Old man Jamieson coughed and coughed, gasping after each bout until Chukk thought he'd cough his innards out. When he lay back at last, Chukk mopped his brow with a wet cloth.

"Can I fetch ye summat else, Da?"

The only reply being a slight shake of the gray head, Chukk shut his eyes, wondering if God had time to listen to prayers from the likes of him. After all, God had said, "Thou shalt not kill," and he had killed so many times he'd long since lost count.

"Lad." The word wafted to him as no more than a breath through the stillness.

Opening his eyes, Chukk saw that the rheumy gray eyes had opened, too, showing more awareness than they had for two days or more.

"Aye, Da, I'm here."

"Ye…mun get home…to *Hjaltland*."

"Northumberland's been our home for most o' me life," Chukk reminded him.

"I put by some…gelt for ye." The gasping voice grew stronger. "I'm spent, lad. I'll niver see Lerwick again. But ye'll find our kin and tell them wha' happened. Tell them…we didna drown. That we niver…made Bergen."

"I dinna ken how to get there," Chukk protested. "Nor do I speak the Norn."

"Wi' gelt, ye can do as ye please."

"Aye, but we ha' nary a farthing to spit on."

"I do…nae farthings, b—" The word caught in the old man's throat, making him cough again. The bout was shorter. Chukk wrung out the cloth and laid it gently on the old man's clammy brow.

"Da, rest now. There'd be nowt for me in Lerwick even an I *could* get there."

"'Tis Percy gelt…good silver. I'll tell ye where it be. But ye mun promise me…here at me deathbed…ye'll go…home."

As sure as he could be that the old man had lost his senses, Chukk promised anyway. He spoke the words that would bind him before Shetland Jamie said what he needed to say and exhaled his final breath.

# Chapter 3

"Where ye going, Beany?" Benjy demanded, running to catch up with her. Tigtow, Rab's black-and-white sheepdog, loped at his heels. The dog had attached itself to Benjy after Rab's death, as if it knew that its master was gone forever.

"I'm going for a ramble as I do each fine morning," Robina replied. "But I cannot take you with me today."

"Cannot or will not?" the boy asked, raising his eyebrows in the same way that Rab always had when he'd asked her such questions.

Fighting an unexpected urge to cry, she said, "You may decide which it is, but I need time to myself today. My temper is uncertain, and I think better when I'm alone."

"But—"

"Don't fratch with me now, laddie," she said firmly. "I'll take you with me tomorrow. We can go wherever you like then."

Benjy looked at the clouds overhead, thicker than they were at this time the day before. "It will likely rain tomorrow," he said with a frown.

"If it does, we'll do something else and go for a ramble

together Wednesday or Thursday. Meantime, you think about where you'd like to go."

"I know where," he said quietly.

"Tell me."

"I want to go up Sunnyside Hill to the graveyard. I...I want to visit Rab."

The tears welled in Robina's eyes then, and an ache captured her heart, but she ignored both. Looking past her little brother to the open gateway, where Ratch stood watching, she knew that taking Benjy with her would be unwise.

English raiders were unlikely, but it *was* likely that the Turnbulls of Langside might be looking for two missing cows and four and a half woolly sheep. She would go alone today if only to reassure herself that no danger lurked.

She knew their estates and she knew their people. She would soon know if anyone had seen strangers in the area or aught else of interest.

Barring a full-scale raid, no one would harm her. But Benjy was now Laird of Coklaw, and any enemy able to recognize the boy might view him as a useful pawn, political or otherwise.

Such likelihood was small, but she dared not ignore it.

"We'll go tomorrow if we can, I promise," she said, giving Benjy's shoulder an affectionate squeeze. "But you must go back now."

"If it is dangerous for me, then it's dangerous for you, too, Beany." Before she could assure him that she could look after herself, he added in the firm tone that always made him sound older than his years, "You had better take Tig with you."

"I will, thank you," she said. "Perhaps you'd like to visit the stable and see the beasts we lifted last night. Don't make a song about the lifting, though."

He gave a boyish snort at that. "You say that as if I *would*."

She grinned. "I know you won't, but you should know that Dev left two of his men here to guard us. They know about the beasts, and so does he."

"But they let you come outside the wall?"

"They have no authority here, Benjy, not over us."

He gave her a speculative look that, from an adult, she might have thought mocking, but he did not argue. Instead, he held the flat of his palm out to the dog, and said, "Stay with Beany, Tig. Guard her."

Then, squaring his shoulders, he walked back to the gateway.

Ratch stood aside to let him in, waved again at Robina, and shut the gate.

*"You'd best hope you don't run into trouble, Beany. Tig can be fierce, but he's no proper escort. Sakes, you may be putting* him *at risk."*

Ignoring Rab, she eyed Tig thoughtfully.

The shaggy sheepdog sat looking at her alertly, his mouth slightly open as if he smiled. His dark brown eyes sparkled with his anticipation of a run.

"All right, Tig, let's go," she said with a sweeping gesture westward.

The dog dashed ahead of her and then ranged back to be sure she was coming. As they set out toward the hills separating Coklaw from Slitrig Water, she sighed and felt herself relax for the first time since Dev's arrival the night before.

The midday meal at Ormiston Mains was noisy and plentiful. Servants and the Ormiston men-at-arms ate at trestle tables in the lower part of the great hall, but screens on the dais provided some privacy at the high table for Ormiston, Dev, and Fiona.

"Where is your maidservant, Fiona?" Dev asked her.

"Eating with the housekeeper," Fiona said. "I wanted you and Father to myself today. You are all the protection I require, Davy, so do tell us all you did whilst you were away. I know about that dreadful ambush at Chesters and that Rab..."

She paused, her cheerful demeanor faltering.

Recalling that Rab had enjoyed a light flirtation with her, Dev said quietly, "We all miss him, Fee. I visited Coklaw yestereve and saw his sister and their little brother. They are alone there now but for servants and their steward."

"It is so unfair," she muttered. "I recall thinking how sad it was that both of his parents had died, leaving him with such heavy responsibilities for his years."

Remembering that Rab had left most of those responsibilities to others while he honored his duties to the Douglas, Dev said, "He was gey young to die, to be sure, but the lad who just inherited those responsibilities is only nine years old."

"Mercy," Fiona said. "Rab's sister is his twin, is she not?"

"Aye," Dev said, suppressing a sudden urge to smile when an image of the scowling Robby flashed into his mind's eye, hands on her hips, furious with him. "Her name is Robina. Rab called her Beany."

"I don't think we have met," Fiona said. "Tell me about her."

"She is grief-stricken at present. I expect she worries about the future, too."

"Faith, I would," Fiona said. Looking from Dev to her father and back, she said, "Losing Mam was horrid. One's grief never goes away, either, not entirely. I cannot imagine losing all of my family save one brother. Especially if it was Kenneth," she added with a wry twist of her rosy lips.

"Fiona," Ormiston said sternly. "You know better than to speak so."

"Yes, sir," she said automatically. "I apologize, but Kenneth is not my favorite brother. I do not think it is solely my fault that that is so, either."

"I expect I'm your favorite," Dev said, winking at her.

She raised her dimpled chin and said, "Aye, perhaps, for today. Unless you lose your temper."

"Have I ever lost it with you?"

Fiona laughed. "Mercy, I'm not going to answer that with Father sitting here, having just taken me to task for speaking disrespectfully of Kenneth. But I will say that I'd rather have you roar at me, Davy, than lecture me to death and then declare that it is your duty to report my transgressions to Father."

"Sakes, is that what Kenneth does? He used to call me an odious scruff, but other than that, he rarely spoke to me."

"Well, I am glad he lives up near Peebles, and I hope Father lives forever."

Both men chuckled at that statement and their conversation continued amiably.

When Ormiston had finished eating, he said, "You have your duties to attend, Fiona, so we will excuse you. David, we can talk in my chamber."

Thus dismissed, Fiona stood, grinned at Dev when he stood up beside her, and then, on tiptoe, she kissed his cheek. "I'm glad you're home," she said. "I know you can't stay long, but do come again soon."

"I shan't leave before morning at the earliest, Fee," he said with a teasing smile. "Douglas gave me leave to see to family matters, so the length of my stay must depend on why Father sent for me."

Smiling again, she took her leave, and Ormiston gestured toward the end of the dais, where a stout, carved door led into his private chamber.

Robina strolled in the hilly forest with Tig for a peaceful hour and then spent the rest of her morning attending to her usual chores. By midday, her bedchamber door boasted a new latch and a strong bolt, and Corinne assured her as she helped Robina tidy herself for the midday meal that she had asked Shag to fix it.

"He did it straightaway, too, mistress, and asked me nae questions."

Nor would the usually stoical Shag ask her any, Robina knew. It was not the first time he had fixed something for one of the twins without a word said to anyone.

She spent the afternoon with Ada Greenlaw, Coklaw's plump, gray-haired housekeeper, who had decided that it was time to begin spring cleaning.

"We'll must air mattresses soon, mistress, and turn out every kist and cupboard," she said firmly when Robina entered the small room near the kitchen, where the house-keeper discussed household matters with her minions and her mistress.

"I am sure you have everything in hand, Ada," Robina said with a smile. "What would you like me to do?"

The housekeeper remained sober. "I did ha' a list for ye, m'lady, but I been a-watching our young master still moping about. I'm thinking now that the best thing ye could do wi' your time is to keep that wee laddie busy."

"Benjy won't take kindly to supervising housework," Robina said. "He is aware that he is the new laird, you know."

Mistress Greenlaw did smile then. "Aye, he's a one. I fear he thinks being Laird o' Coklaw be superior to being King o' Scots."

"Aye, well, Rab felt the same," Robina said.

She listened for Rab to deny her statement or at least to comment. When he did not, she became aware that Mistress Greenlaw had spoken.

"I'm sorry, Ada," she said. "I let my thoughts wander. What did you say?"

"Only that we miss our young laird fierce, m'lady. I expect ye were feeling it then, too. Our Rab could be a bit capernoited, time to time, but he bade fair to become as fine a man as your dad and your granddad."

"Perhaps," Robina said, aware that her twin could certainly be impulsive, even reckless, but unwilling to agree with anyone else regarding either trait. "I know that everyone misses him, but together, we can look after things at Coklaw until Benjy is old enough to take charge here."

"Aye, sure, we can," Ada said. But even a listener with weaker insight than Robina's would have discerned the doubt in her voice.

"I think Benjy might enjoy relaying some of Green-law's orders to the stables and yard," Robina said. "He would learn much by doing so, too. I shall ask Greenlaw if he will do that, unless you think he might object."

"He'd be glad to teach the laddie all he kens," the housekeeper said. "Our Benjy mayn't be as willing to learn, though."

"Perhaps, but I think Greenlaw should begin teaching him. I wish he would teach me more, too. Then, I could help teach Benjy."

The housekeeper's lips tightened. "Good sakes, m'lady, ye ken fine that Greenlaw doesna think it suitable for a woman to take charge of a castle, especially one as close to the line as we be and wi' so many estates to look after."

"I don't want to take charge," Robina protested. "I just want to *know*."

"Ye should be looking for a proper husband then. May-hap ye'll choose one who will teach ye such things."

"I don't want a husband either, Ada," Robina said tersely. "I know that Greenlaw thinks a husband would keep me out of trouble, for he has told me so. But *I* think a husband would *create* trouble. He'd want to run everyone and everything here. How would Greenlaw like that after being in charge for twenty-five years?"

"Truth be, m'lady, I think he'd welcome someone else taking hold here. When your da were alive, although he and your mam were at Gledstanes as much as they was here, and sometimes more, Greenlaw knew that if he were doubtful o' summat, he could ask your da. Wi' the young laird, he could talk things out and sort them in his mind whilst he did. Even when he had to persuade Master Rab that *his* way were best, he said talking to Master Rab helped him think."

"Talking to me could also help, then," Robina said doggedly.

"If ye mean to discuss Master Benjy wi' him, ye might tell him how ye feel, too, then," Ada said reasonably.

"I'll see him at once," Robina said. "Then I'll collect Corinne and some of the other maids and begin turning out kists. With clouds gathering overhead, as they are, I doubt we'll be putting mattresses or pallets out to air for a while."

No sooner had Lord Ormiston shut the door to the inner chamber than he said, "I meant what I said about marrying, David, but I thank you for not mentioning it at the table. It is not a suitable subject for us to discuss with Fiona."

"She should be thinking of her own future, should she not, sir? Have you anyone in mind for her?"

"I am not ready to part with that lassie yet," Ormiston admitted with a rueful smile. "However, you are fast gaining age, my lad, and I've decided on the perfect wife for you. Kerr's youngest, the lady Anne, is of a suitable age and should make you an amiable wife."

Feeling his stomach clench, although he'd not seen the wench in months, Dev gathered his wits and said, "Am I to understand that you've made Kerr an offer?"

"Nay, nay, for you are old enough to make your own arrangements, although I shall be happy to aid in the negotiations. I know Kerr better than you do, after all. I did write, inviting him to bring his wife and Anne for a visit at Beltane. That will give you a chance to get to know the lass and her family better than you do now."

Wise enough in the ways of his father to know he had set his mind on Anne Kerr as his good-daughter, Dev said, "I ken fine that you believe any son of yours is worthy to marry any noblewoman in the land, sir. However, it does occur to me that Kerr might have other plans for his daughter."

"I keep my ear to the ground for such news, as you must know, lad. I have heard nowt of any such plan, let alone one for that lassie to marry a knight of the realm."

"A landless knight, however, and a youngest son," Dev reminded him.

"Surely, the King or Douglas..." Ormiston paused, his native intelligence clearly, Dev thought, overcoming such hopeful thinking.

"I doubt that Jamie Stewart will bestow land on me," Dev said. "And since Douglas knighted me more or less because he felt obliged to and did not include a promise of land, I expect I'll be making my own way for some time yet. Where would you have us live?"

"We'll discuss that with Kerr, of course," Ormiston said, recovering his aplomb. "He'll dower the lass well, I'm sure. How long will Archie Douglas await your return?"

"Not long," Dev said. "When I begged leave to come here, he bade me stop at Scott's Hall on my return to ask Wat to provide additional men for Hermitage."

"I see. Then you must ask Archie for leave again at Beltane. I've invited the Kerrs to spend a sennight with us. I'm hoping Lucas will visit us then, too."

"I think Lucas would be a more eligible husband for the lady Anne than I would."

"Lucas has his sights set on someone else, I believe,"

Ormiston said. "He has been spending much of his time at Dunbar."

Dev raised his eyebrows. "Has he?"

Ormiston nodded, and they discussed other such matters for a time before Ormiston said abruptly, "I hope you don't object to Anne Kerr, David. Having received my invitation, Kerr will likely be thinking just as I am."

"Which is why I don't feel as if I *can* object, sir," Dev said. "But Anne stirs no warm feelings in me. She is too compliant and demure, as if she has no thoughts of her own. A frown stirs her tears, although I swear I've done naught to distress her."

"Then you must teach her to behave as you want her to behave."

"Is that what you did with Mam?" Dev asked with a slight smile, remembering some lively disagreements.

Ormiston smiled warmly. "Your mother was different."

"I'd like my wife to be different, too, sir. I could go so far as to admit that Anne bores me daft, but I would never be so rude as to say so."

"That is wise of you," Ormiston said with a sardonic look.

"I have little taste yet for marriage," Dev said, feeling desperate.

"You have time yet to get used to the idea."

Dev stifled a sigh. Beltane, the first of May festival, was three weeks away.

Learning that Benjy was in the stable with Tig, "helping the lads," Robina deduced that both would enjoy themselves for a while longer and went to look for Greenlaw.

"He and that Jock Cranston and our Sandy went to look at the fold on the Ormiston estate wi' an eye to keeping them other three sheep awa' from the one about to drop her lamb, till after we shear 'em," Ratch told her.

The estate adjoining Coklaw Mains to the east was called Ormiston. Robina had deduced only after meeting Dev that the estate must have belonged to an earlier Lord Ormiston. When her grandfather acquired Coklaw, the Ormiston estate, another to the north called Orchard, and one near Gledstanes called Hundelshope had all come with it.

Thinking about Ormiston made her wonder if Dev was home yet or still in Hawick, attending to duties for Douglas. Not that it mattered where he was, she assured herself.

After the midday meal, she collected Benjy and asked him if he'd like to learn more about his estates from Greenlaw.

"Aye, sure," the boy replied. "'Tis me duty now, is it no?"

"Do you want to talk to him about it, or shall I approach him first?"

"You can tell him," Benjy said. "But tell him we'll be busy tomorrow. Dinna forget you're taking me with you to Sunnyside Hill."

"I'll remember, love."

"I'm having wheat sown in that haugh near the river's curve," Ormiston said late that afternoon. "Perhaps you'd like to walk down with me and have a look at it."

"Aye, sure, sir," Dev said, hoping that Ormiston did not mean to press him further to marry Anne Kerr. Just the thought of spending his life with her made him queasy. However, a landless man was of little interest to most fathers seeking husbands for their daughters, so Kerr might prove to be an ally, despite his long friendship with Ormiston.

His mind eased by that hope, Dev turned his attention to the weather, noting that the clouds were thicker than yesterday and more threatening.

As they walked down toward the river, Ormiston said casually, "I'd like you to ride the bounds with me tomorrow, David. I ken fine that you think you'll gain nowt from me, but you should know all you can about these estates. The Fates take a strong hand in men's lives, and third sons *have* inherited titles."

Tuesday morning when Robina went downstairs, she found Benjy at the high table, nearly finished with the remains of what looked like a large repast. She was glad to see it. The boy had neither eaten nor slept well since they had buried Rab.

"Oh, good, you're up," he said. "I told them to bring you some Adam's ale, and I put sliced beef on your trencher. I was about to send a lass to fetch you."

"You're in a hurry then," she said. Taking the stool beside his, she picked a roll from the basket in front of them and tore off a piece to butter.

"I want to go and get back before it rains," Benjy said. Straightening on his back-stool, he waved for the lad serving the high table to remove his trencher.

"I looked outside," Robina said. "The clouds are rather high to rain today."

"Perhaps," he said, watching her take her eating knife from its sheath on her leather girdle to cut her meat. "But clouds can swoop low before one expects them to, Beany. Prithee, eat quickly."

"I've barely begun," she said. "Strive for patience, love."

"Was Rab patient? Was our father?" Benjy gave her another, more direct look. "Come to that, Beany, are *you* patient?"

Her mouth twitched, making him grin.

"I thought not," he said, pleased with himself.

"I do strive to be patient," Robina said. "And we must both try harder now than ever, love…especially with each other."

"Aye, but we'll walk up the hill straightaway when you finish, though."

"Yes, Benjy, but you go fetch a jack first. 'Tis cold out."

Agreeing, he ran from the dais, and Tig darted out after him from under the table, leaving Robina to finish her breakfast in peace.

She had brought her own warm cloak downstairs with her, so she was ready to go when Benjy returned. Not until they emerged onto the timber stairs overlooking the yard and she saw Jock Cranston talking to Sandy did it occur to her to wonder if Jock might try to keep her from taking Benjy with her.

Deciding to behave again as she normally did, she headed for the main gate with Benjy beside her and Tig cavorting gaily around them.

Wiry, dark-eyed Shag was at the gate and opened it as they approached. He glanced at Benjy and then looked steadily at Robina but made no comment.

Thanking him for fixing her bedchamber door, she

added, "We're going up Sunnyside Hill to the graveyard, Shag. I expect we'll be back for the midday meal."

"I expect so, too," Benjy said fervently. "I brought only one apple to share."

Shag smiled at him. "Ye should take a fishing pole, Master Benjy. Then ye could catch your dinner from one o' the burns and cook it over a fire."

Benjy gave him a look and said quietly, "Mayhap I will do that another day, but ye should call me 'laird' now, Shag."

Shag looked at Robina, who returned his look but kept silent.

"Aye, sir," Shag said, "if that be what ye prefer."

~

Dev and his father spent the morning together, riding over the estate while his lordship pointed out improvements he had made and discussed his plans for the future. He did not mention Douglas, the Kerrs, wedding plans, or Coklaw, making Dev begin to wonder at such uncharacteristic restraint.

Since he thought he had made it plain—however tactfully—that marriage was not even on his list of hopes for the near future, he had expected his father to press harder about marrying Anne Kerr as they rode.

Lord Ormiston usually knew what he wanted, why he wanted it, and how he planned to get it. He was not one to let grass grow under him once he'd made up his mind, either. However, that morning, he had actually, proudly, pointed out how *well* his grass was growing everywhere that he wanted it to grow.

As hours passed, and conversation continued on the same tedious lines, Dev began to feel distracted, frustrated, and bored. He understood his father's desire that all three of his sons know his plans for Ormiston Mains, but the subject failed to interest Dev.

Having known since he had begun to know anything about the world into which he was born that he would inherit naught from his father beyond mementos in which his elder brothers took no interest, he felt little concern for the family's estates.

Accordingly, he was relieved when at last, with their tower in sight, Ormiston abruptly changed the subject. "You mentioned at table yesterday that you had stopped at Coklaw," he said. "Had you opportunity to judge how things are fixed there? Is John Greenlaw still in charge?"

"He is," Dev said. "I also left Jock Cranston and Jem Keith there, because some of the men who took leave after the ambush at Chesters had not yet returned."

"'Twas a good notion," Ormiston said. "As isolated as Coklaw is, and as close to the borderline as it lies, it is forever vulnerable to attack and *must* be well guarded."

"Douglas agrees with you. He's thinking of putting one of his own men in charge there to protect the place against attack or another siege."

"Is he?" Ormiston frowned thoughtfully for a long moment but then said only, "No doubt that *is* the wisest course."

Dev felt a strong urge to deny its wisdom. But he realized before he spoke that he could provide no evidence to prove that Archie and Ormiston were mistaken.

# Chapter 4 _____

Robina waited until the gate shut and they were well away from the wall before she said, "Benjy, I think you must give some thought to what you expect now of our people. A man gains respect not by demanding it but by earning it. If you recall, John Greenlaw and Sandy called Rab 'Master Rab' long after Father died."

"I was nobbut seven then, but they should ha' called him 'laird,' aye?"

"Perhaps they should, but it did not trouble Rab when they called him Master Rab, and after a time, they did call him 'laird.'"

Benjy did not answer, and Tig had run on ahead. They walked in silence for a time and then discussed other things until they reached the graveyard on a grass-covered northeast knoll overlooking the vale below. A simple wooden cross that Sandy had made and stuck into the dirt mound was the only marker for Rab's grave. They had had no time yet to have a stone carved for him.

Benjy gazed at the mound of bare earth. "At first it made me sad to come here," he said. "But now I feel closer to Rab when we do. I wish he were closer to the castle, though, so I could visit him more often."

"You might be sorry if Coklaw is besieged again," she said. "Some raiders destroy nearby graveyards when they attack. You would not want that to happen to Rab's grave."

"Nay, but this is too far. I want to visit him every day."

She was about to explain that he could come up as often as he liked but nearly jumped out of her skin when Rab's voice sounded right behind her:

*"He can't come here often or alone most of the year, Beany. It's too far. Also, in winter, I'll lie under mounds of snow. I'd like to watch him grow, though. What we need is a carved stone or marker near the wall where he can visit me."*

It was all she could do not to whirl and scold Rab for startling her. Instead, her fruitful imagination converted his suggestion into a more practical idea.

"Benjy," she said as they turned toward home after briefly visiting their parents' graves, "you know my favorite tree—that big oak in the woods?"

"Aye, sure," he said. "West o' the gate, beyond the tower clearing."

"I go there whenever I'm angry or sad. As ancient as that tree is, I'm sure that more than one spirit dwells there, because no matter when I go or how I feel, it always makes me feel better. You could visit my tree and talk to Rab there, or—"

"Could we find a tree that's only Rab's?" His eyes sparkled with enthusiasm.

"That's a grand idea," she said. "We'll find a sapling, dig it up, and replant it where you can see it from your window. Then it would be Rab's tree forever."

"I like hawthorns when they grow into trees and are

not just part of the shrubbery," he said. "Mayhap we could make a hawthorn grow into Rab's tree."

Nodding, she said, "They live a long time, but even if that one dies, we can plant a new one in its place. Then Rab will always know where you expect to visit him."

"We'll do that," Benjy said with a decisive nod.

"We both have chores to do this afternoon," Robina reminded him. "But we can find a site and a good sapling tomorrow morning if you like."

He said eagerly, "I know just where it should be. There's a rise outside the wall, on the side of the clearing where the sun comes up. I can see it from my window, and it lies near where the woods begin again, too, so our hawthorn will be amongst friends."

Smiling, Robina said, "You're a good, thoughtful lad, Benjy. We'll have a look at that site straightaway, but I'm sure it will do."

Benjy seemed pensive as they made their way back down and spoke again only to point out his chosen site.

When they reached the gate and Shag opened it for them, the boy went to him and, looking up into the older man's eyes, said, "I been thinking about what I said to ye, earlier, Shag, and I want to apologize. Ye should call me whatever seems fitting to ye, I think."

"I thank 'e, sir," Shag said. He looked at Robina and raised an eyebrow.

Aware that he was asking if she had told Benjy to apologize, she shook her head.

Shag smiled then and said, "I'd like to shake your hand, sir."

Solemnly, the boy shook hands with him.

⌒

At Ormiston that evening, after Fiona retired, her father and Dev moved to the end of the table nearest the fire to enjoy their excellent claret.

Men in the lower hall diced or chatted and drank ale, but the dais privacy screens were up. After a time, casually, Ormiston said, "I've been thinking about Archie Douglas."

Reaching for the jug, Dev said, "Have you, sir?"

"You did say he might put his own man at Coklaw, did you not?"

"So he said," Dev agreed, pouring more wine into his father's pewter goblet and then into his own. "I mentioned that Greenlaw has proven his ability to keep the castle safe and reminded Archie of the Percy siege years ago."

"What did he say to that?"

"That he would think more on the matter before making a decision."

"Then there is still time," Ormiston said. Leaning nearer, he added, "Sithee, you serve Douglas. You also know Coklaw and its family. *And* you know Wat Scott, and Wat may support an idea that has occurred to me. I've been mulling it over, and the longer I do, the better I like it. You are the right man to take charge there."

A startling, even terrifying, vision of himself married to the decorous, ever sensitive Anne Kerr and living at Coklaw with Robina arose in Dev's imagination so swiftly that he could not stifle a mirthful snort.

"I see no humor in my suggestion," Ormiston said dourly.

"I beg your pardon, sir," Dev said dutifully. "But if Archie had had me in mind for the position, he'd have said so. Moreover, I cannot imagine Anne Kerr living at Coklaw."

"Agreed," Ormiston said, his manner still stern. "But I do agree with Archie that in these perilous times, Coklaw must have someone in charge other than its aging steward. We don't want the Percys seeking again to seize such parts of Teviotdale as they believe are theirs. And, the last thing the Gledstanes will want is a Douglas moving in with them."

"Rab did ask me to look after them," Dev admitted.

"When was this?" Ormiston demanded. "You've told me little about what happened near Chesters."

"I don't like talking about it," Dev said quietly. "Rab died in my arms, and he knew he was dying. A dozen Percy men ambushed a near dozen of us, attacking us from above with lances. It was damnably close quarters, and we were fighting with axes." He swallowed hard, staring into his goblet, the images still painfully clear in his mind.

Ormiston, an experienced warrior himself, kept silent.

Drawing breath, Dev went on, "Rab saw a chap with a lance aimed at me and, by urging Black Corby between us, he was able to knock the lance up and away. But he was so intent on the lance that he failed to see the dirk in the man's other hand. The dastard got Rab in the neck, knocking him off his horse and beneath the melee."

"Young Rab was a reckless lad but an honorable one, and courageous," Ormiston said. "I'm sorry we've lost him, but I'll be ever grateful to him for saving you."

"I expect I'll be grateful one day, too, sir. At present, I grieve his loss too keenly to feel other than selfish when gratitude stirs, and deeply indebted."

"I do understand that," Ormiston said. "What happened then?"

"Auld Nick and Corby went for the lancer's horse, and two of my lads got to us. That was damned fortunate, because I'd flung myself off Nick to aid Rab. But it was too late. He was losing blood too fast, and although Jock and the lads routed the ambushers, I couldn't stop the bleeding. Rab could barely speak, but he told me not to fret, that he'd always known his life would be short. He worried about Benjy and Robina, though, and Coklaw. He...he made me promise to keep them safe."

"That settles it then," Ormiston declared. "You must tell Douglas about that promise. In fact, you must leave for Scott's Hall in the morning. I'd go with you, but you'll do better, I think, on your own."

"What about Anne Kerr?"

"We'll discuss that later," Ormiston said glibly. "I cannot tell them not to come for Beltane. However, I will think more about Lady Anne."

A disturbing memory fluttered in Dev's mind that one Coklaw estate was called Ormiston. "With respect, sir, are you thinking that I might marry Robina instead?"

"You could do worse," Ormiston said. "But we'll think no more of bridals. You are old enough to serve as Robina's guardian, and Benjy's, for now."

Angry words leapt to Dev's tongue, but he swallowed them, knowing that defiance would only arouse his parent's ire. It would do himself no good, either. He'd be wiser to bide his time and devise calmer arguments.

"Archie is gey contrary," he said. "He has a hard time making decisions and tends to go counter to what anyone else suggests to him."

"If you have learned that much about him, I warrant you can easily parley with him," Ormiston said with a speaking look. "Ask Wat Scott what he thinks about it when you see him. He has a wise head on young shoulders, does Wat."

Dev stifled a grimace. Wat Scott could think and say what he liked. Robina's opinion would be a flat negative, and she would not hesitate to express it.

Nor, he reminded himself, could he expect Douglas to appoint him to the post. He was, after all, the newest and least experienced of Archie's knights.

～

The site Benjy had chosen for his tree being suitable for the project, Robina agreed Wednesday morning to help him find a good sapling. So, after breakfast, they made their way painstakingly through the thick hawthorn border that separated the castle clearing from its adjacent woodland.

Benjy was particular, and since the hawthorns would not flower for another month, he found it hard to make a choice, but Robina possessed her soul in patience, knowing that the matter was important to him.

"There are too many plants that look healthy and strong," he said at last. "I dinna ken which is best."

"I remember Mam telling me that plants, like most people, prefer to stay near where they were born," Robina said. "Mayhap you should choose the best one that lies nearest the rise you chose for its new home."

"I know just the one, then," he said, nodding. "I'll show you. Then I'll tell Sandy to send a lad out to dig it up for us and replant it."

"Don't you think, since it is going to be your special tree to honor Rab, that we should do the work ourselves?" Robina asked gently.

He looked at her, grimaced, and said, "I didna think o' that."

"Well, now that you have, what *do* you think?"

With a sigh, he said, "That ye're right, Beany. I think Rab's spirit be more likely to stay in a tree that we planted ourselves."

"I agree," Robina said. "But you may run and shout at whoever is on the gate to send out two shovels and a spade for us. Then meet me at the rise."

He ran toward the gate, and Robina heard him shouting as she returned to the rise he had selected and studied it. A narrow sike flowed nearby, and low hawthorns grew beyond it at the perimeter of the clearing. Benjy had chosen well.

He joined her minutes later, lugging two shovels and a spade.

"I should have said to ask for a rake, too," she said. "This ground is covered with twigs, weeds, and other debris. But we can scrape it clear with our shovels. Then I'll prepare your sapling whilst you pull up any weeds around where we'll dig its hole."

He showed her his sapling, one of the first he had liked, which amused her. It looked sturdy enough to survive and small enough not to have widespread roots, so she set him to weeding and carefully dug a trench around the sapling. When the trench was deep enough, she looked again at the sky.

She had been eyeing it all morning, because the gathering clouds had lowered and darkened more swiftly than usual. However, if it did rain before they finished digging the hole, the trench water would protect the sapling and soften the dirt in their hole.

Although Benjy was eager and worked hard for a time, his shovel was heavy, and he soon tired. Robina continued digging the sapling's hole, and when next she looked at her brother, he and Tig had curled up together amid the hawthorns and were fast asleep.

Smiling, she returned her attention to the hole. She had shortened the skirts of her kirtle and shift by tucking them up under her leather girdle. So, despite work that warmed her, she soon noticed that the temperature was fast falling.

The likelihood that they would finish that day looked smaller and smaller.

Whenever her shovel struck a rock, she dropped to a knee, picked up the spade, and uncovered the rock carefully to avoid unnecessary damage to the shovel. Then the blade scraped another object, one that she discovered was a strange reddish-brown color and smooth. Using just her hand, she cleared enough dirt away to recognize it as crockery.

Although she suspected that the rise must be an old midden and would reveal only broken bits of things, she took care not to break what she had found until she could see what it was. To her surprise, it began to look as if someone had thrown away a crockery vase or jar. She glanced toward Benjy.

*"Dinna tell him yet, Beany. Learn more about it first!"*

A flash of lightning overhead and an explosive thunderclap at nearly the same time startled her and warned that time was short. Benjy's cry of distress told her that the thunder had startled him, too, and wakened him. Tig stood guard beside him, glowering at the sky.

Benjy scrambled to his feet, but Rab was right. She would not tell him, not yet.

With a second blast of thunder, the clouds burst, unleashing a torrent of rain.

Soaked before she could think, Robina swiftly scooped a layer of dirt over her discovery. Then, just as swiftly, she set rocks and pebbles in the hole and tried to shovel her dirt pile farther away so it would not wash back in.

"Come on, Beany, afore we drown!" Benjy shrieked, grinning. "It must be nearly time to eat, too, so I'll take the spade if you can carry the shovels. Hie in, Tig!" he shouted to the dog, as he took off running.

Robina needed no further urging, but she feared that, despite her efforts, the hole would fill with dirt again before they returned.

Dev was midway along the Borthwick Water trail when the cloudburst struck and a wind began to blow. He and his men carried oilskins, but he loathed wearing one. He had expected the rain to begin with a sprinkle.

Two of his men had donned oilskins earlier, but the rest scrambled for theirs now as he did. He wore his steel bonnet, but his head was the only part of him not immediately soaked. He could barely see two feet ahead, but he knew that Auld Nick would remember the way. They had been to Scott's Hall many times, and Nick was smart. He would keep to the oft-traveled path unless Dev commanded otherwise.

At their usual pace, the Hall was a half-hour away.

However, the trail quickly became slick with mud, so they had to take care, lest one of the horses injure itself or slip off the trail into the fast-flowing Borthwick Water.

He loathed any rain heavier than mist, but he and his men had ridden in all elements. They knew he'd get them out of the downpour as soon as he could and would not want to hear any grousing unless he was doing it.

By the time he could make out the Hall gates through the gloom ahead, he was silently muttering imprecations to God. Why had a perfect being not created rain to water trees and plants without making men miserable?

The gates opened as they approached, and the watchman on the wall walk—doubtless near drowning, too—waved them in.

Dismounting beneath the stable's overhanging thatch, Dev gave thanks that the wind no longer blew rain into his face. He had begun to aid his equerry with Auld Nick when he heard a shout and recognized Wat Scott's deep voice.

Seeing his host descending the stairs of the keep to the cobbled yard, Dev said to his equerry, "I must go, Eckie. Tell Coll to see to himself before he looks for me."

"Aye, sir, and I'll see that his pony gets dried and fed, too."

Turning toward the central one of the three towers composing Scott's Hall, Dev realized that Wat wore only a linen shirt, leather breeks, and his rawhide boots. Nevertheless, he was grinning like a dafty and tilting his face to the driving rain.

His brown hair, already soaked, looked black, and his deep-set eyes gleamed with childish delight before, briefly, he shut them. Then, looking at Dev and extending a hand, he said, "You look miserable, Dev-me-lad. Don't you love the rain?"

"You know I don't," Dev said. "I'm glad to be here, though, even if I have to suffer your notion of wit. Take me to your fire, sir, so I can dry myself. I'm soaked to the bone."

"Aye, anon," Wat said. "Geordie, put these lads in the east tower when they've tended their horses, and have someone build up the fire there. They'll want to dry out. Some may welcome dry clothing, too, if you can find any."

"Aye, laird, I'll see to it," Geordie Elliot, the captain of Wat's fighting tail, said as he emerged from the stable. "Auld Nick looks well, Sir David," he added when Dev reached to shake his hand. "Ha' ye misplaced Jock Cranston?"

"Jock's attending to other business for me, Geordie. It's good to see you."

"Come along, you rain-feardie," Wat said with another grin. "I warrant I can find dry clothes for you, too, if you brought none with you."

"I brought other clothes, but they'll be as wet as I am, despite the oilskins. The wind was fierce before we reached your glen."

"Let's go in, then, and get you dry," Wat said. Leading the way upstairs past the hall entrance, he stopped at a bedchamber that Dev had used before. Wat gestured for him to enter and then followed him in.

Seeing towels and a pile of dry clothing awaiting him on the bed, Dev shot his host a wry smile. "Are you always prepared for soggy visitors?"

"One of my lads saw you from his post on the east hill yonder and rode to warn us," Wat said as he shut the door.

"Before I ask what brings you, Dev, I want to hear more about that fracas at Chesters. I was shocked to hear of Cousin Rab's death and surprised by how fast they buried him. Due to my own duties, I had not seen him for an age, but I know the two of you had become fast friends."

"Aye; he was five years younger, but we understood each other from the start, and he soon became my second-in-command," Dev said, stripping off his wet clothes.

He described the ambush at Chesters and Rab's heroism. "I'm here today only because of him and Black Corby," Dev added. "I won't forget that. I saw him home again afterward, and if his burial was quick, it was because I could not stay and Greenlaw was too upset to attend to it."

Nodding, Wat said, "You were wise to act swiftly then. I should warn you that Gram will want to hear all about Rab's death, and his burial, too. So will her sister, the lady Rosalie Percy, who is visiting us. The Gledstanes are their cousins, too, after all."

An involuntary smile touched Dev's lips at the thought of Wat's paternal grandmother, Lady Meg Scott, a woman as strong and determined in her way as Ormiston was in his. When Wat's people referred to Herself, they meant Lady Meg, rather than Wat's mother or his wife, Molly.

"If Lady Meg demands details, or even my head, I am certainly not man enough to defy her," Dev said, reaching for one of the towels. "She won't want to hear the worst of it at suppertime, though, with others at the high table."

"Nay," Wat said. "Nor will Aunt Rosalie want to hear the details."

"You called her Rosalie Percy," Dev said, briskly drying himself. "I know that Lady Meg's mother was a Percy and that Meg has sisters, but I've never met Rosalie."

"She is Gram's youngest sister. She married Richard Percy, who died in Wales a few years ago. Rosalie barely knows her two sons, because he fostered them elsewhere in England when each one turned eight. So when he died, she returned to Scotland and stays a portion of each year with her siblings and their families. You'll meet her at supper."

"Before then, I should tell you that I've been to Hermitage for Archie Douglas," Dev said, setting aside the towel and reaching for a pair of dry braies. "His constable there wants more men. He fears the Percys may attack Liddesdale."

"Unlikely," Wat said. "They seem content to raid Scotland by way of Carter's Bar and the fells. Still, I expect Archie sent you to see if I'd provide more men for Hermitage."

"He did," Dev agreed, tying the cord of the braies at his hips. "He said something else, too." He paused, reaching for the breeks that lay on the cot.

By the time he looked back, Wat's eyes had narrowed. "What did he say?"

"That he might put one of his own men in charge at Coklaw."

Wat was silent long enough for Dev to fasten the breeks. "I'd wager you can guess what I think about that," Wat said then. "My father traded half of our Murthockston estate for half of Branxholm, and I mean to exchange the other half for the rest of it. It suits me fine to have Gledstanes at Coklaw, but I don't want a Douglas living next to Branxholm."

"Likely, you'll want one of your own people at Coklaw then."

Wat shook his head. "Archie wouldn't agree to that," he said. "He'd fear that I'd want to add the Coklaw estates to mine own. I'd never do such a thing to a nine-year-old laird and a cousin at that, but—"

"What would you think of my taking that post?" Dev interjected.

Wat raised his eyebrows. "Did Archie suggest that?"

"My father did," Dev said dryly. "He thought you might favor such a solution and that I should suggest it to Archie. But . . ."

He paused because Wat was nodding. "Archie might agree to that, because he won't want to displease Ormiston. How do you feel about proposing that solution to him?"

"Damned uncomfortable," Dev said frankly. "It isn't that the notion lacks appeal, but my father as much as admitted that he has an ulterior motive."

Wat grinned. "Robina? Sakes, that would suit me just fine, although . . ."

". . . Robina is likely to hand me my head in my lap," Dev said.

"That *is* what I was thinking," Wat said.

Eyeing him warily, Dev said, "I've no interest yet in taking a wife."

"No one is suggesting that we summon a priest, my lad. But if Robby could be persuaded to accept you as warden of the castle . . ."

"When Rab lay dying, he did make me promise to look after Robby and Benjy, and Coklaw," Dev said, suppressing his dislike of being maneuvered into such a situation, even by Rab, his own father, and Wat.

"Certes, that's a fine point to make with Archie," Wat said, nodding. "I can see that it's true, too, by your so-reluctant demeanor, and so will he."

Dev nodded. "It is true, but I did not tell Robina."

"You've seen her, then."

"Aye, when we buried Rab and again, briefly, Sunday night on my way back to Hawick from Hermitage."

Wat eyed him as if he expected more, but Dev wasn't about to tell him how or where he had first seen Robina Sunday night.

Wat said, "How is she?"

"As you might expect. Rab was her twin, after all."

"Was she glad to see you?"

"Not exactly," Dev admitted, sitting to pull on socks and boots that felt a bit snug. Sensing Wat's speculative gaze on him, he held his breath, waiting for him to ask why not.

"I'll ride to Hawick with you," Wat said at last. "If we put it to Archie together, I warrant we can persuade him that it's the best course for all concerned."

Feeling much relieved, Dev said, "You do have a knack for persuading others."

"I do, aye," Wat agreed bluntly. "Are you ready to go down? They'll be serving supper soon, and Sym Elliot will have told Gram, Molly, and my mother that you are here. They will doubtless be at the table before us."

Dev was ready, so the two went downstairs together and found the women waiting as Wat had predicted.

He had failed, however, to predict their response to their plan for Coklaw.

The rain having continued to pour all afternoon, Robina spent her time indoors with the housekeeper and Corinne, attending to housekeeping tasks.

Benjy escaped to the stables, declaring that he'd be "helping the lads see to the ponies." Privately, Robina hoped the "lads," including Jock Cranston, would recall that he was Laird of Gledstanes and Coklaw and not just a pest, getting in their way.

The three women were in the boy's bedchamber when Mistress Greenlaw declared her belief that they had finally found all of Master Benjy's cast-offs and mending, and added as she picked up a basket of clothing from his cot, "I do suggest, m'lady, that you consider finding a lad to look after Master Benjy's clothing for him. Not only because he is now the laird, but also because I found two pairs of his soiled braies, one set of netherstocks, and a good shirt under his cot."

Robina considered the suggestion. "'Tis true he has a title now," she said. "But he should learn to look after himself and his belongings before turning those duties over to anyone else. Neither Rab nor I had personal servants before we were thirteen, Ada."

"Ye wasna, either o' ye, master of Coklaw yet, neither, m'lady."

Robina glanced at Corinne, who continued to fold the garments before her as if she heard none of their exchange.

*"Och, aye, she hears, as do I, but I don't know about this, Beany. We learned to do what servants could do for us, to learn how such things should be done."*

Sending Rab a silent curse, wishing yet again that he were at hand in the flesh, to deal with Ada Greenlaw...

*"My flesh lies six feet underground, lass."*

"I know, I know," she muttered without thinking.

A hastily stifled gurgle from Corinne warned her belatedly to collect her wits just as Ada said, "I ken fine that ye ken the facts, m'lady, but that gets us nae forwarder."

Flushing warmly, Robina realized that the housekeeper thought she had been commenting on her previous statement. "I did not mean to be rude, Ada," she said. "But Benjy should learn the proper way of doing things before he orders servants of his own about. Laird though he is, he is ill-prepared for such responsibilities. However, if you or Greenlaw had someone in mind for the position..."

"I do not, m'lady," the housekeeper said stiffly. "Nor has Greenlaw suggested such a thing. I but spoke me mind to ye."

"And I am grateful to you for your advice and your candor," Robina said sincerely. "Prithee do not think otherwise. I don't know how we would get on here, Ada, without your wisdom and experience to guide us."

Her sensitivities visibly assuaged, Mistress Greenlaw nodded. "I'll just take this basket o' laundry down then, so Mary and Gert can get on with it." With that, she carried the basket in her usual stately way out of the room and down the stairs.

Exchanging a look with Corinne but making no comment and hearing none, Robina finished her portion of the folding. When she looked around to be sure they had done all they could, Corinne said to her with a grin, "Ha' ye seen the new lad yet, mistress?"

"Which new lad?"

"That Jem Keith I told ye aboot, the one Sir David left here wi' Jock Cranston. I dinna ken how ye'd miss seeing such a fine, strong chappie."

"I am sure he is a good man, Corinne, but I expect Jock and Sandy have kept him busy. Also, I have been out with Master Benjy these past mornings. Prithee, finish up here and then order me a bath. After all our turning out of kists and such, I feel as if I've bathed in dust. If it would not shock everyone, I'd run out into the rain to get clean again."

"If ye did, ye'd likely see that Jem-lad," Corrine said. "I doubt that a wee bit o' rain worries the likes o' him. He's one as kens what he wants."

Robina decided that she'd better have a look at Jem Keith if only to judge whether he should be flirting with her always flirtatious but hopefully still innocent maidservant.

It was raining harder than ever, though, so she decided she'd be wiser to see if Benjy had come in yet. If not, she would send someone to fetch him. The boy caught cold too easily to be out long in such weather.

# Chapter 5 ⎯⎯⎯⎯⎯⎯⎯⎯⎯⎯

The Scott women and Lady Rosalie were on the dais when Dev and Wat entered the hall. Lady Meg stepped forward to meet them with her usual grace and the big smile that Dev had hoped to see. It altered her plain features amazingly.

"Sir David," she said, extending her right hand in a natural but nonetheless regal manner, "we welcome you. It has been long since your last visit."

"'Tis my misfortune, madam," he said, returning her smile. "Meantime, you continue to look well, I am happy to say, and grow ever more beautiful."

"You are kind, sir, or a scandalous rogue," she replied with a touch of tartness. "I have never possessed the smallest claim to beauty."

"Blethers," he retorted. "You have the most charming smile I have ever seen. I look forward to seeing it whenever I come here and would be sadly disappointed if you failed to reward me with it."

"Now who is talking blethers?" she demanded, but even her eyes smiled now. "Not that I dislike compliments from handsome young men, you understand, so you must not stop offering them. But I forget my manners," she added abruptly. "I believe you have never met my sister Rosalie, so I shall present you to her as soon as you make your greetings to Molly and Lavinia."

Turning to Wat's beautiful tawny-haired wife with an apologetic smile—although he knew that, like everyone else at the Hall except Wat, Molly usually deferred to Lady Meg—Dev greeted her with pleasure and then spoke to Wat's mother.

Lavinia, dowager Lady Scott, was a fading, fragile beauty who looked nearly as old as Lady Meg despite being two decades younger. After exchanging brief pleasantries with her, he dutifully turned his attention to the lady Rosalie Percy.

He saw little resemblance to Lady Meg in her prettier, more stylishly-garbed sister, although she boasted the same slender, softly rounded figure as Meg's. But, although he deduced that Rosalie must be nearing fifty, the abundant hair beneath her simple veil was darker than Meg's and still lustrous. Also, despite being a widow and having borne two sons, Rosalie's twinkling eyes and flirtatious smile revealed a less dignified personality.

Dev suspected that she usually found life more amusing than not.

Wat cut their conversation short by declaring that supper was ready to serve, so Dev hastily greeted his host's two younger sisters. Fair-haired Janet was a year younger than Robina. Bella was twelve, had dark hair, and was rather pert. Dev liked them both.

Privacy screens separated the dais from the lower hall, where a buzz of low-voiced conversation continued throughout the meal.

Dev sat at his host's right, and Molly Scott sat next to

her husband with the three older ladies next. Janet and Bella sat beyond them.

Menservants had no sooner served everyone and withdrawn than Lady Molly leaned forward and said to Dev across Wat, "I'm told you've come from Ormiston, sir. I hope your family is well."

"They are, my lady," he replied, leaning forward to see her. "I saw only Father and Fiona, though, and stayed two nights with them."

"You rode there from Liddesdale, did you not?"

"I had been at Hermitage, aye," he said, feeling Wat's steady gaze on him and wondering what else Molly had heard.

Tucking a stray tawny curl back under her veil, she said, "Did you stop at Coklaw on your way, or did you go straight on to Ormiston?"

"I did look in briefly at Coklaw," he admitted.

"How are Robina and Benjy getting on?" she asked gravely. "I have met them only twice, but I grieve for them both. They must sorely miss Rab."

Conscious of Wat's shrewd gaze, Dev said, "They seem to be getting on as well as one might expect, my lady."

Lady Meg put her head forward to see him past Molly and said, "In my opinion, they should not be there alone, as they are. Do you not agree that Robina would be wiser to remove to Gledstanes and take Benjy with her?"

"Coklaw is their home," Dev said tactfully. "They have never lived anywhere else. I doubt that we could dislodge either of them if we tried."

Wat said, "Douglas said he might install one of his own men there, Gram. He fears that Coklaw is vulnerable now, that the Percys might try to besiege it again."

"Blethers," his grandmother said. "The Fifth Earl of Douglas is..." Visibly catching herself, she went on in a musing way, "That first siege was no more than a successful ruse to add a few Douglases to Northumberland's army before he joined the Welsh rebels. Recall that he held the fourth Earl of Douglas hostage then. Even so, Northumberland had no hope of tearing Teviotdale from the Douglas grasp just because England's Henry IV had offered it to him. No Percy can match the combined Douglas and Scott power." To Wat, she said, "Do you *want* Archie to put his own man in charge at Coklaw, love?"

"You know I do not," Wat said. "I mean to persuade him to put Dev in charge of Coklaw, instead. He's exactly the right man for the position, because he knows the castle, the area, and the Gledstanes."

"Aye, but if Robina stays there, you cannot do that," Lady Meg said flatly.

"I agree," Molly said, with a glance at Lady Meg and another at Wat. "Only think how it would look, sir," she added hastily. Then to Dev, she said, "Truly, Sir David, you would damage Robina's reputation and your own, as well. You cannot want to do that."

"Moreover," Lady Meg said, "Archie cannot be so daft as to put a handsome young knight in charge of Coklaw whilst Robina is unwed. Such a warden must be older, and preferably married, someone who can look after Robina and Benjy properly."

"I see no such necessity," Wat said. "Robina merely needs a chaperone."

"But finding someone suitable would take much time," Molly said.

Dev looked at Wat just as Wat was exchanging a look

with his grandmother. Watching them closely, Dev saw Wat flick his gaze slightly past her.

Lady Meg raised her eyebrows. Then her lips quirked into a half-smile.

"Will it answer, do you think?" Wat asked her lightly.

"You'll have to ask her."

"Ask whom?" Rosalie demanded.

Wat smiled and said bluntly, "You, Aunt. Since you expect to be here for several months, would it not amuse you to stay with Robina until we find someone else?"

"It is more a matter, I should think, of whether it would amuse Robina," she said, cocking her head musingly. "She barely knows me, sir. A year ago last November, when I visited, was the first I'd seen of her or Benjy, because they were born after I left Scotland."

A lad entered with a fresh jug of wine and moved to refill Wat's goblet, but Wat stopped him, saying, "Take that into the inner chamber. We'll be in shortly."

Dev felt himself tense. Things were moving faster than he'd anticipated. However, he could too easily imagine, and feel terrified by, an outraged Robina either wrapping a Douglas man around her thumb or driving the poor devil mad. On the other hand, that same outrage if *he* took charge at Coklaw stirred only eager, if rather fiendish, anticipation.

⁓

Robina ate supper with Benjy in his bedchamber. Having been shocked to find him there earlier—sound asleep, soaking wet, and shivering—she had quickly wakened him.

"We must get these wet things off you," she said. "Sit up, and I'll help."

His face was ashen. Rubbing his eyes, he muttered, "I

was tired, Beany. I dinna ken why I'm so tired. Sorting tack, looking for cracks and rot, didna seem like work. But…"

"Right now we need to get you warm. You don't want to get sick."

The boy shrugged. "Jem and some other lads ha' been sneezing and coughing this past sennight. I didna get it from them, so I willna catch it now."

*"Ada is right, Beany. Our laddie needs a keeper."*

Hearing footsteps on the stairs and recognizing them as Corinne's, Robina ignored Rab and went to the doorway. "Corinne, is someone bringing my hot water?"

"Aye, mistress, I were just a-coming to set the tub in your chamber for ye."

"We're going to wash Master Benjy first, so be sure it is not too hot for him. He fell asleep in his wet clothes."

"Ay-de-mi," Corinne exclaimed. "I'll tend to the tub. I told them to hurry."

Minutes later, Benjy was in the tub, complaining that he did not need two women to wash him. "I can do it myself, Beany. Ye didna help Rab bathe."

*"That you did not!"* Rab said, startling her by speaking in such normal tones that she looked from Benjy to Corinne, astonished that neither had heard him.

"What is it, mistress?" Corinne asked, quick as ever to read her expression.

"Naught," Robina said. "I was just thinking of what Ada said."

*"I told you, lass, nae one else can hear me. But unless you're willing to keep your door ajar all night, lest he sneak out as you and I used to do, you'd best find someone to share responsibility for his safety."*

"I thought o' Mistress Greenlaw, too," Corinne said, fetching a towel. "When she said that about our laddie having some'un o' his own—"

"What are you two talking about?" Benjy demanded. "You should not ignore what I say to you. Prithee, recall that I am your laird."

"So you are, my love, and Rab did bathe himself," Robina said, smoothing his damp hair. "But Rab was grown, and you are a boy who needs to get warm. So, let Corinne dry you whilst I put fresh bedclothes on your cot. Then we'll put you to bed, and you may have your supper on a tray. I'll keep you company if you like."

"I would, aye," the boy said. "You can tell me stories whilst we eat."

She agreed and left him to Corinne's cheerful care while she sent a housemaid to fetch fresh bedding for his cot.

"He fell asleep right on top of his cot, Daisy," Robina said when the maid returned with blankets, sheets, and a fresh pillow. "I've stripped the wet things off, and his pallet is barely damp. If you'll help me turn it over..."

Fifteen minutes later, Benjy was in bed—this time, under the covers.

"I'm going to use your water now," Robina said. "But I'll be quick."

"Aye, ye will, for 'tis likely it be getting cold," he said with a wan smile.

The water was lukewarm at best, but she washed quickly and was glad to be clean again. Donning a fresh shift, a lavender-colored kirtle, and a pair of leather mules, she sent Corinne to ask someone to bring their supper to Benjy's chamber and returned to find her little brother wide awake.

"I thought you might have fallen asleep again," she said.

"Nay, but when do you think this rain will end? I want to plant Rab's tree."

She had been thinking about Rab's tree, too, and whatever it was that she had struck while digging its hole.

⁓

The blasting wind and rattling rain continued all day Friday, blowing and pelting down so hard that even the rain-loving Wat declared it a bad day to travel. "In any event," he said, as he and Dev lingered at the high table with their ale after breaking their fast, "we should discuss our tactics before we approach Archie."

"He has knights much more experienced than I am," Dev reminded him. "I'm not even sure I'm right for the post, but I'll admit, I'd dislike his putting a man unknown to Robina and Benjy in charge there. I worry that Archie might act quickly, too."

Wat shook his head. "If Archie acts fast, it will be the first time. His father always made the decisions, so Archie still hesitates to make his own. Because he left the Scottish army in France, declared himself too sick to go back, and persuaded his father to return in his place, I think he feels guilty that his father died there, making Archie the fifth earl."

"Even so, no one calls him a coward," Dev said.

"They do not, but neither is he a good leader. He cannot make up his mind to order a new shirt without pondering for a fortnight. Moreover," Wat added, "he'll resist taking action at Coklaw without first telling me. I have not won my spurs yet, but I am still one to reckon with in Teviotdale."

Dev smiled. He could only agree with that. If the Douglas could raise ten thousand men in a sennight, it was only because Wat Scott could provide half of them.

"I've been thinking about your aunt Rosalie," Dev said. "She's unlikely to travel whilst this heavy rain continues."

"Or as long as it threatens to rain," Wat agreed with a knowing grin. "But by the time Archie agrees to anything that we might suggest..."

"I was not thinking of Archie but of Robina," Dev said when Wat paused. "I do agree that she ought to have an older woman at Coklaw, besides Mistress Greenlaw, to guard her reputation and, if possible, to keep her out of mischief. But I also think we must warn her before we present her with Lady Rosalie."

Wat gave him a straight look. "*You*, not we, will present her. Gram has known Robby since birth and is right to worry about her reputation. The only wonder is that Robby hasn't already pitched herself into the briars."

Recalling two cows and four wool-laden sheep, Dev clenched his jaw.

"What?" the observant Wat demanded. "Do you mean to say she *has*—?"

"It came to nowt," Dev interjected swiftly. "Just a lark, harmless."

Wat's eyes narrowed, but Dev met the look steadily.

"I doubt that," Wat said at last. "So, if we do persuade Archie to appoint you, Dev, as I expect we will, you must make clear to that pliskie lass that her choices are two. She can accept a suitable married woman or widow—my grandaunt instead of her aunt Clara, if she prefers—or she and Benjy *will* remove to Gledstanes."

Dev nodded. Wat was right. They could not leave her

to her own devices any longer. The area was too dangerous, and Robina was mindless of her own safety.

"I did not expect hesitation from you on this subject," Wat said, eyeing him shrewdly. "Your reputation belies such a reluctance to issue orders."

With a wry smile, Dev said, "'Tis not reluctance to issue the ultimatum that delays me but knowing that she will likely murder me for doing so."

"You admitted that she is out of charity with you, and I begin to suspect this 'lark' of hers as the cause. Do you mean to tell me *how* you incurred her wrath?"

"I do not."

"I see. May I assume that you discovered it and exacted retribution?"

Dev remained silent.

"It does occur to me, you know," Wat went on, "that the usual route from Hermitage to Hawick crosses Slitrig Water at Woodford. Instead, you had to skirt some hills to reach the Hummelknowes ford and Hawick. That likely—"

"Enough, my lord," Dev said more curtly than he had intended. "Unless you order me to explain and give me good cause, I shall say no more about it."

Wat raised his eyebrows, but his eyes gleamed now with humor. "Almost do you tempt me, Dev. I begin to suspect that you care more about our Robby than I knew."

"She is Rab's twin, and I promised him I'd look after her...and Benjy."

He nearly added, "That's all," but the two words stuck in his throat.

Wat awarded him another long look but said only, "As I recall, you can give me a good game of chess."

Surprised by the non sequitur and wondering if Wat was still talking about Robina, Dev cocked his head in silent query.

"The board is on that shelf behind you," Wat said. "We can play here, or we can adjourn with the ale jug to the inner chamber and play in peace. We should have time for several games whilst this rain continues. But I warn you, my lad, I mean to leave as soon as it eases enough to keep us from drowning. It will *not* do to let Archie think too long."

Dev got up to fetch the board and the chessmen. "It won't help our cause if we arrive at the Black Tower looking like men dragged out of a loch, either," he said as he set the board between them and handed the box of pieces to Wat.

"We'll have plenty of time to clean up before he grants us an audience," Wat replied amiably. "Archie likes to keep people waiting, especially men he views as competitors. It makes him feel more powerful."

They enjoyed several chess matches and more than was good for them of Wat's potent whisky before they retired Friday night. The rain continued to drench the countryside through Saturday night and into Sunday, and by Sunday morning, Wat had had a surfeit of inactivity.

"We're leaving in an hour," he said as he and Dev broke their fast soon after dawn.

The women had not stirred, but men in the lower hall had been up for some time. Several still sat at trestle tables, eating or quietly talking.

As a last effort, Dev said, "It's Sunday. Archie may not agree to see us today."

"He'll attend Kirk in Hawick this morning, because the

townspeople like to see him," Wat said. "Besides, time is passing, and it is a splendid day to travel."

Knowing they would be soaked long before they reached Hawick, Dev stifled a groan. He knew better than to argue, though, so they set out an hour later.

He was confident that Wat's skills in any parley would win the day. His feelings about Archie's likely decision to send him to Coklaw, however, remained mixed.

No sooner did that thought flick through his mind than an image appeared there of an elderly, stern-minded, even brutal Douglas knight ordering Robby around. That image made him growl loudly enough to earn a mocking grin from Wat.

"Do you think growling at this lovely, soft mist will diminish it?"

Giving himself a mental shake, Dev grimaced and said, "You'd be well served, my lord, if this *mist* of yours were to summon up a kelpie or two to drag you underwater."

"You may hope, but I think you fear something other than rain or kelpies, my lad. I never thought I'd see the day that mere thought of a small female could make you quake in your—but nay, those are my boots you're quaking in, and that *will* not do."

Dev shook his head, seeing naught to gain by explaining that he'd reacted to his mental image of an angry Douglas knight harming her.

If anyone was going to teach Robby to behave…

~

Benjy had begun sneezing and coughing before dawn Friday morning, so Robina ordered him to stay in bed and kept him there until Saturday afternoon, when he rebelled. Then, ferreting out a Tables board and dice, she bundled him up by the solar wall above the hall fire, drew a table close, and taught him the basic moves for the simple French form of the game that Corinne had learned from her mother and taught to Robina and Rab.

Benjy soon revealed a natural gift for the game's strategy.

During their fourth game, when Robina rolled a double four while his pieces blocked her fourth line, and he rolled a six to win, he crowed, "I thought I'd be years learning to beat you. 'Twas easy, though!"

"The luck of this game depends on the dice, laddie," she said, as delighted as he was that he'd won. "Set your pieces again, and we'll see how much you've learned."

They played until the midday meal and again Sunday morning. That afternoon, he decided on his own to nap. Assuring herself that he had simply exerted himself too much the day before, Robina nevertheless sat with him for a time and realized only after he fell asleep that the heavy rain had eased to a drizzle.

The respite pleased her, and its timing would allow her to get out into the fresh air, if only long enough to retrieve the crockery jar she'd found.

⌁

The Douglas had welcomed Dev and Wat's late-morning arrival cheerfully. "I hope ye've come to tell me that ye'll provide men for Hermitage, sir," he said to Wat.

"I can provide a score if you need them, my lord," Wat replied.

Dev kept quiet and let Wat work his magic with Archie, hoping to learn more about the art of persuasion. Although he paid close heed, he learned only that Wat was persistent and could digest insults, pressure, and other such tactics without losing sight of his goal.

At midday, Archie said he would decide whilst he ate his dinner and that they should take theirs with their men in the hall until he summoned them.

An hour later, after a meeting so brief that they'd remained standing, Dev said to Wat as they and their men rode away from Hawick, "I heeded all that you said to Archie. But I still don't know how you persuaded him. I was sure he'd say no."

"It helps to know your adversary, and I know him well," Wat said. "Like most bad leaders, Archie thinks first of *his* interest and only then of his men's or his clan's needs."

"Even so, he often goes contrary to what anyone else suggests. Is that why you brought my father into it, to explain that it was his idea?"

"Partly," Wat said. "But recall that Archie needs my lads at Hermitage, a fact of which I reminded him when I said I'd send the captain of my fighting tail with them. When Archie said you could lead them instead, that's when I told him that your father had suggested you as the proper person to take charge of Coklaw. I spoke rather doubtfully..."

"So he might think you opposed that notion, yourself," Dev said when Wat paused. "I see. I thought you were just echoing my own doubtful view of the matter."

"Blethers," Wat said flatly as they approached the Slitrig Water ford and drew rein. "Archie did not hesitate to command you to take charge as warden. Moreover, you are the *best* choice, Dev. We know that Robina will refuse to move, and Archie knows he cannot order her to go. He also knows that, by assisting him with his decision, I have accepted a stake in the outcome. So, don't let me down, my lad, or I'll cut out your liver."

"So encouraging," Dev said with a grimace. "I'm glad the rain has eased, because I'll be spending my nights either with the men in the lower hall or, more likely, out in the stable until the lady Rosalie can come to us. You need not fear for Robina's virtue, I promise you, even if her dragons, the Greenlaws, should disappear."

"I'll see that Rosalie arrives soon," Wat promised. "In a day or two if the rain stops. That gives you time to warn Robby that she's coming. In troth, though, I think I have more confidence in you than you do. Just be yourself, Devil, and don't count the cost."

They parted then, and Wat turned westward with his men toward Branxholm.

Dev didn't lack confidence. He knew he could run Coklaw. He just hoped he could find a way to live peacefully with Robby... before she murdered him in his sleep.

Fetching Rab's oilskin, her warm cloak, and a sturdy cloth sack, Robina put on her stoutest boots, donned her cloak and the oilskin, and went out into the yard. Although the drizzle continued, she could trust the oilskin to keep most of her dry.

Fearing she had little time before Benjy awoke and looked for her, she found Ratch and asked him to fetch her a shovel, a small pail, and a spade.

"Sakes, mistress, what d'ye want wi' such t'day?"

"We are planting a tree for Master Rab on that rise southeast of here, and I want to see how much damage the rain has done to our hole. Benjy would finish the job today, but I want him well before he comes outside again, so I'd like to tell him that all is well. In troth, though, I fear the rain will have filled our hole up again. If it has, I must dig out what I can and protect it better, lest we get more rain."

"Sakes, mistress, show me what ye need, and I'll send a pair o' lads to do it."

"I cannot allow that, Ratch," Robina said. "Sithee, the graveyard is too distant for Benjy to visit by himself, so we decided to plant a tree nearby to make Rab seem nearer, but we want to plant it ourselves. Just fetch me the tools. I shan't be long."

He nodded and, in minutes, she was listening to him shut the gate behind her.

As she had expected, rainwater filled the hole and had washed dirt and debris from her pile in with it. The damage was not as bad as she had feared it might be, though.

Kneeling on part of Rab's oilskin and arranging the rest to keep the drizzle off her, she used the pail to scoop as much rainwater and soupy muck out of the hole as she could. Then, she spaded out the heavier mud until she reached her layer of pebbles.

The rain-washed air smelled crisp and bracing, so she took her time and was glad to be outside after days of confinement. In the end, she used her fingers to free the jar. When at last she wriggled a hand under its bottom end, its weight surprised her. The mud was reluctant to release it, but at last, with a sucking sound, it let go.

Only then did she see that the jar's cap was tightly wired in place.

*"Beany, don't let anyone else see that until you discover what's in it."*

"I know," she murmured. "I just wonder how I'll get that lid off."

*"Don't use your dirk, and be careful. That wire looked rusty."*

The drizzle allowed her to wash off most of the muck, but nothing about the jar suggested what its contents might be. Slipping it into the cloth bag and carrying it under her oilskin to the nearby shrubbery, she set it under some overhanging hawthorn, where no one on the wall could see it. Then she dragged dead branches from the thicket to the hole, piling them there and hoping they'd keep dirt from filling it again before the rain stopped.

She was trying to decide if she'd done enough when her eye caught movement to the west. Turning sharply, she saw riders approaching, eight or more.

One of the leaders carried a banner. It was rain-soaked and wrapped round its pole, but she suspected that Dev was returning.

"Is it not just like the man, to return when I least want him," she muttered as she dropped the few branches she still carried, bent down, and scooped up the jar in its sack. Tucking it inside her cloak, under her left arm, she gripped the oilskin closed with her right hand. Then she strode to the gate, shouting as she went for someone to open it.

When Ratch obeyed the shout, she said as she passed him, "Prithee, have someone fetch those tools for me. Riders are coming, and I must not greet them as I am."

"I believe ye," Ratch said, his eyes atwinkle. "Ye look like ye rolled in the mud."

Smiling but saying no more, she hurried inside, hoping that if it *was* Dev, he would not dare to confront her in her bedchamber again. Not until she had hidden the jar.

Despite the hilly terrain, Dev had set a fast pace, so he and his men had reached the first hilltop providing a distant view of Coklaw and its surrounding vale less than an hour after leaving the Black Tower. Dev's oilskins kept him relatively dry, and his usual energy had long since overcome the lethargy that the rain had caused at Scott's Hall.

Despite lingering concerns for Robina, he was eager to reach the castle. He had commanded men many times in the field, but he had never taken charge of a stronghold, let alone one that had played a strategic role in Border history.

It would be a challenge, but he welcomed new challenges.

Benjy would be another one. The boy had idolized Rab and was unlikely to look fondly on any man attempting to take his place. They had also lost their father not long ago, and although James Gledstanes had spent much of his time away from Coklaw, even more after his lady wife's death, Benjy doubtless still felt his loss keenly, too.

And John Greenlaw. What, Dev wondered as they followed a track down through the forest, would Green-law think of Dev's assuming his most important duties at Coklaw? Greenlaw was getting on in years but was not much older than Ormiston was, and the man was an excellent steward.

Emerging from the woods to see the tower again, much nearer, he spied an oilskin-draped figure sitting or kneeling on a slight rise southeast of it. As he watched, the figure rose to its feet, looked toward the castle, and then turned away from it. Hurrying to the dense hawthorn thicket that ringed the clearing, the figure bent again and dragged branches from the shrubbery into a low pile.

Although the stiff oilskin covered the person from tip to toe and revealed nowt of its shape, its movements suggested a female. She was alone, outside the wall, so Dev's first thought was that it could not be Robina.

His second thought was a more cynical one, that he was foolish to assume any such thing. It could well be Robina, because the men of the household had already shown that they wielded no authority over her.

The figure gathered its tangle of branches and dragged them toward the place that Dev had first caught sight of her.

Watching her move, he became more confident that it was Robby. But what the devil did she think she was doing?

He urged his pony to a faster pace.

Coll, bearing Dev's banner beside him, shot him a look of surprise, but Dev ignored him. She was looking right at him now. The oilskin revealed little, but he was as certain as if she stood two feet away that it was Robina.

Either she had recognized him or the sight of oncoming riders had disturbed her, because she strode back to the shrubbery and bent to scrabble under a bush. Then, she gave him only her back view as she hurried toward the opening gate and inside.

⁓

Nearly running up the main stairs, Robina passed the hall archway only to hear Ada Greenlaw's voice: "M'lady, ye're no taking them oilskins upstairs, are ye? Ye'll drip all over everything."

"I'll leave the oilskin here on the landing, Ada. Riders are coming, and I'm filthy, so I must hie myself upstairs and get out of my wet clothes."

"I wonder who it be," Ada said, bustling toward her, but Robina did not wait. Clutching the jar beneath her cloak and praying that Ada would not demand the cloak as well, she hurried up the stairs.

"Corinne be helping Daisy in the scullery," Ada shouted up the stairs after her. "I'll send her to ye directly."

"Thank you," Robina shouted back, grateful to know that Corinne was not ahead of her on the stairs or in her bedchamber.

*"I warned you that he'd return sooner than you expected."*

"Is it Dev?" she muttered. "Can you be sure?"

*"Now, that would be telling. You'll see soon enough."*

Nearly consigning her brother to a place much warmer than the castle, she recalled, flushing hotly, that, considering his present state, the curse might be unwise.

At that thought, she heard his soft laughter.

*"Certes, but you're a one, lass."*

Wishing again that he were alive but reaching her bedchamber in apparent safety, she hurried inside and shut the door behind her.

Looking for a place to conceal the jar until she had enough time and privacy to examine it closely, she saw only her clothing kists and the washstand. Then she recalled that, while they were sorting and cleaning, they had put four extra blankets in the large kist in the near corner by the head of her bed.

Flinging off her cloak, she knelt by the kist, unfastened its leather hasp, raised the lid, and slipped the jar under the folded blankets. She had barely fastened the lid shut again when the door opened and Corinne entered.

"What be ye doing, mistress?" she asked, entering and scooping Robina's cloak off the floor. "Mistress Greenlaw said ye wanted to change your dress."

"I want my lavender kirtle," Robina said. "But I've been mucking about in the hole for Benjy's tree, so what I need first is soap and water."

"Ye'll no find any kirtle in that kist. We put them blankets in that one. Your kirtles be in the one by the washstand. But if ye want hot water—"

"If the ewer is full, I'll use that," Robina said. "Riders are coming. I think that perhaps Sir David is returning."

"So soon? The man left less than a sennight ago."

"He said he'd return when he could," Robina said. "I did not expect him this soon, but I cannot think who else it could be."

Corinne's eyes widened. "It could be raiders!"

"In daylight without warning? I doubt it. They carry a banner, but it was soaked and drooping."

"Aye, then, but ye're in much the same state," Corinne declared, shaking her head. "Ye've mud all over your boots and your skirt. And this cloak be a sight, too."

"Don't scold; just help me," Robina said, dragging the

wet kirtle off. "If it is Sir David, he'll want to see me, and I don't want him to condemn my appearance."

"Wash your face then, whilst I fetch out a clean shift and your lavender kirtle," Corinne said. Hesitating, she added with a frown, "Ye dinna think he's come to take Jem Keith and that Jock Cranston away, do ye? I'd no mind seeing Jock go, but…"

"Corinne, Jem Keith serves Sir David, not us." But it was likely, she thought, that Dev *had* come to collect his men. As she hastily washed, she told herself firmly that she would be glad to see him depart as soon as he had collected them.

That thought stirred her twin's chuckles again. *"You must like Dev, Beany. You think about him too often for one who dislikes him."*

She had to press her lips together to keep from replying aloud, but her thoughts surely made her opinion of Rab's teasing clear to him.

"Ye should wear your white veil," Corinne said, shaking out the kirtle.

"You know I don't cover my hair unless I must," Robina said tartly. Realizing that her irritation was with Rab, not Corinne, she added, "I don't mean to snap at you. I just wish I knew why Sir David has returned so soon. He left his men here because he thought we had too few. We haven't hired more in the meantime."

*"Dev made a promise, lass."*

Robina had her shift on, but a rap on the door startled her as she stepped into the lavender kirtle. Hastily slipping her arms into its sleeves and yanking it up, she held its unlaced bodice together with her free hand, extended the other to Corinne to button the sleeve, and said crisply, "Who is it?"

"It's me," Benjy said, pushing the door open. "I woke up."

"Then go back to your room, wash your face, and tidy yourself," Robina said. "I think Dev has returned. If he has, he will take supper with us."

His eyes lighting, Benjy dashed back across the landing to his chamber, leaving her door and his own ajar.

Robina hastily tied her bodice laces, while Corinne moved toward the door to close it, but stopped when a female voice said from the landing, "Dinna shut it, Corinne. Sir David be here, and Greenlaw says to tell her ladyship they be in the inner chamber."

"Ye're blushing, mistress," Corinne said with a grin as she shut the door. "Are ye sure he doesna interest ye just a wee bit? He's a fine, strong chappie hisself, I'm thinking."

Grimacing, Robina said, "I'm hot from hurrying. Prithee, help me with my hair."

~

Dev had no sooner dismounted in the yard than Greenlaw strode from the stables to meet him with Jock Cranston and Jem Keith following him.

"Ye're back gey soon, lad," Greenlaw said, shaking his hand. "Come inside wi' me. I've a few things I'd like to say to ye, and some questions I want to ask."

Realizing that the steward had learned about his previous Sunday night's visit—and had likely gleaned most of the information Monday morning, soon after he discovered he'd acquired two new men—Dev wondered if Greenlaw meant to take a high hand with him.

Whether he did or not, he knew he'd have to tread lightly until he revealed that Douglas had appointed him Warden of Coklaw. He knew, too, that he deserved to hear whatever Greenlaw was likely burning to say to him, especially if the older man knew that he'd skelped Robina... in her bedchamber.

Robby would not have told him that, Dev assured himself, only to recall Benjy's innocent disclosure that he'd heard Dev "a-skelping her." He didn't know the boy as well as he knew her.

He remained thoughtful as he followed Greenlaw— still muscular and solidly built despite his gray hair—into the inner chamber and shut the door behind them.

"Ye must ken fine that I've learned near all there is to ken about your visit last Sunday night, sir," Greenlaw said, moving to the center of the room.

Feeling his way, Dev said, "I agree that my visit came at a late hour, but it was fortunate that I came this way."

"Aye, it was, although I'm glad ye didna run into our lads whilst they was a-gathering them sheep and cows. I'm told they'd returned afore ye arrived, but..."

When he paused Dev said carefully, "I did learn about the raid, aye."

"Your lads will no ha' talked about it elsewhere, though, I'm thinking."

Dev relaxed. "They will not. The reason I count the visit fortunate is that I learned Monday that the Douglas was thinking of putting his own man in charge here."

"Why? The late laird and his da trusted me. Does the Douglas *dis*trust me?"

"No, John. He understands that if Coklaw were to suffer another siege, you'd defend it as fiercely as you did before. His concern is that, with a nine-year-old laird known to be here, Coklaw might become a target for Percy mischief."

"So who's he putting in charge, then?" Greenlaw

demanded gruffly. "I doubt folks hereabouts will take kindly to any Douglas at Coklaw."

"How do you think they'll feel about an Ormiston?" Dev asked gently.

"An Ormiston? But your father—" He broke off, then smiled. "Sakes, lad, are ye telling me the Douglas ha' put ye in charge?"

"Will it vex you sorely if I say that, yes, he appointed me warden here?"

Greenlaw drew a breath and let it out. With a rueful smile, he said, "I canna tell ye how worrit I ha' been, sir, that he'd send someone like hisself, or worse. Ye've relieved me mind of a crushing weight."

"I'll try to deserve your confidence, John, and I'll welcome your wisdom and support. I hope I can also earn her ladyship's support."

"That's as may be, sir. That 'un has a mind of her own and does as she wills."

"I hope you'll let me know when I go amiss here," Dev said. "We may not always agree, but I'll always listen to your advice."

"Me wife did say that Lady Robina would like me to begin teaching young Benjy what his duties as laird will be. I expect ye'll want a say there, too, aye?"

"Aye," Dev said, smiling. "Come to that, if you have advice to offer *me* and can weave it into what you tell the lad, you may help me save face from time to time."

Greenlaw nodded. "I think we'll get on well, sir."

"I mean to do all I can toward that end. Now, I had better see her ladyship."

"I already sent for her, sir. She...um...needed a few minutes to..."

"...to wash off the mud?" Dev suggested. "I saw her outside the wall when we came over the hill. She should not have been out there all alone as she was."

"Her ladyship often goes out alone," Greenlaw said evenly. "She has since she were a bairn. She knows the country and our people gey well."

"I do recall Rab saying the same thing," Dev admitted. "When we were together, she often rode with us."

"When Master Rab were home, sir, they were nearly always together."

"I see that I must make no hasty decisions," Dev said.

"I'm glad you've come to us, Sir David. You'll doubtless want to leave the household to Mistress Greenlaw and her ladyship, and you can leave daily management of the estates to me. Ye'll also want to see the accounts, I expect, and to meet our tenants."

"I want to learn all you can teach me," Dev said.

"Aye, good, then. We've a month yet till Whitsun quarter day, so ye've nae need to think about that yet. However, although Sandy is a fine warrior and has done his best to train our lads, Master Rab always did so afore we lost him."

"I can set Jock Cranston to training them with Sandy to aid him, then," Dev said. "Jock is gey skilled himself and a good instructor." The door opened rather abruptly then to reveal Robina, so Dev added, "We'll talk more anon, John, thank you."

As Greenlaw moved toward the doorway, Dev remembered Lady Meg's concern for Robina's virtue. It occurred to him, too, that she would be less likely to fire up in Greenlaw's presence. "Don't leave, John," he said. "Stay whilst I talk with her ladyship."

If Greenlaw gave him an odd look, Robby's expression

was odder. Her plump lips parted, and her beautiful green eyes widened.

"Prithee, my lady, sit down," Dev said. "I have something to tell you."

⌒

Robina stared at Dev, wondering what right he thought he had to give orders to her steward. When she looked from one to the other, Greenlaw avoided her gaze.

"What is it, sir?" she asked bluntly. She had never called him Dev in front of anyone except Benjy or Rab, but neither did she want to address him formally as Sir David, or let him loom over her. He was up to something.

He met her gaze and said just as bluntly, "It is useless to try softening this. Archie Douglas has named me Warden of Coklaw."

"But he cannot *do* that! Benjy is Laird of Gledstanes and Coklaw. Does the Douglas think he can seize our home?"

"No, nor would other barons allow that," Dev said more gently than she had expected. In her experience, the man usually matched tone for tone.

*"Aye, but that gentle tone is the one that should make you tread carefully."*

She remembered Rab warning her about that before, so she said evenly, "I suppose I do not know what a warden does, exactly."

"He takes charge of a castle or other fortress when its owner is absent or unable, for reasons of youth or incapacity, to do so," Dev explained.

"Then Greenlaw is already our warden," she said, looking from one to the other.

"Nay, m'lady," Greenlaw said when Dev gave him a nod. "I were nobbut your da's squire years ago, when I had charge during the siege. Afterward, he named me his steward. In ordinary times, I look after the household and such. Your da and Master Rab, and their men, like our Sandy, ran the stables and looked after what crops and stock we have. A warden acts over all, in place of the laird."

"I see." She looked at Dev. "Does that mean you'll be living here? Permanently?"

"It means I'll be living here as much as any laird with men to lead might," he replied. "However, Lady Meg and the other ladies at the Hall feared for your reputation. So until you have a suitable companion, I'll sleep in the stable loft."

"Nay, then, ye canna do that, sir," Greenlaw said, looking shocked. When Dev frowned, the older man added hastily, "I beg pardon, sir, but if I may explain?"

Dev gestured for him to continue.

"Sithee, sir, your proper place as warden is in the master's chambers. It wouldna be right for ye to sleep elsewhere, certainly not under the stable thatch. As to her ladyship's virtue, I'd wager that she can protect herself. But Mistress Greenlaw and I both sleep in this tower, and near everyone in the Borders kens us. Nae one will concern themselves wi' her ladyship's repute whilst we live here."

"I understand that many folks know your reputation, just as you know that her ladyship has nowt to fear from me. But Lady Meg insisted that she have someone of rank to bear her company. In fact…" He hesitated, looking speculatively at Robina.

"In fact," she said grimly, "you have already selected

someone. Who? Aunt Clara? Or, now that you have sealed my fate, am I even allowed to inquire?"

*"Beany, behave yourself!"*

Dev frowned as if he'd like to demand the same thing, and she would have loved to smack them both. That being impractical, due to the death of one and the proven ability of the other to retaliate in kind, she met Dev's frown and matched it with one of her own.

He smiled then. "Is that how I look? Forgive me, Robby. I'm new to this position, but I'll learn quickly. You do know Lady Meg, aye?"

"Aye, sure," she said. "But if you're going to tell me that you persuaded her—"

"I would not be so brash," he said. "The woman terrifies me, and in this instance, the boot is on the other leg. She decided that you should have her sister, the lady Rosalie Percy, to stay with you for a time. Mayhap you know that Rosalie is visiting at the Hall."

"I know she did so a year ago November and again last summer," Robina said. "She spends a quarter or so with each of her three siblings, so I expect she is spending springtime with Wat and Molly now. I like Cousin Rosalie, but I *don't* need her."

"Nevertheless, she is coming," he said. "So, unless you want to tell Lady Meg and Rosalie yourself that you won't have her, you will welcome her."

She began to object but his gaze caught hers, and she saw the flint in his eyes.

*"You don't want to fight this one, lassie. Trust me, you will lose."*

Robina exhaled, gritted her teeth, and tried to think of something to say that would not sound like utter capitulation.

The inner chamber door banged back against the wall, and Benjy stepped into the doorway, grinning. "Dev, you *are* here!" he exclaimed. Running to him, he added joyfully, "I'm so glad you've come back!"

Dev caught the boy when he leaped at him, and swung him up to look him in the eyes. "I'm glad to see you, too, laddie, but I heard that you were sick."

"It was just a wee cold and a bit of the catarrh," Benjy declared, hugging him. "I'm mostly all better now."

"Did they make you sniff onion with mint and mustard?" Dev asked him. "My mam used to do that. It smelled odious, and I don't think it helped much."

The boy's eyes widened. "Robina gave me honey in a bit of claret, that's all. It tasted sweet and made me sleepy."

"Well-watered claret," Robina said. When Dev smiled, she relaxed, giving thanks for Benjy's entrance. Under ordinary circumstances, she would have told Dev exactly what she thought of his issuing such orders to her. But with Greenlaw watching, and Rab's hasty warning, the thought of drawing the wrath of all three...

It occurred to her that having another woman in the tower, a much older woman, might be beneficial. At least, Cousin Rosalie would not fling orders at her.

Dev had noted the wary look Robby gave him before Benjy burst into the room. He was sure that, just before then, she'd been about to rip up at him for what she doubtless perceived as his determination to rule her or ruin her life. With two sisters, he'd had many such accusations hurled at him, at his older brothers, and more rarely, at their father.

So, Dev decided as he put Benjy down, the boy had timed his entrance well.

He would avoid a fight with Robina as long as he could, but he had no doubt that the first time a decision of his went against her wishes, a fight would be necessary.

Touching Benjy's shoulder, he said, "Have you eaten your supper, or do you mean to bear us company at the high table?"

"I haven't eaten yet." Benjy looked at Robina. Then his jaw set. He said calmly, "I will join you at the table."

Dev looked to Robina, too, but she smiled and said, "I do agree that he seems well enough to join us. However," she added with a minatory look at the boy, "you will go straight to bed the minute I see you yawning, sir."

With a lopsided, wary smile, Benjy said, "Aye, sure, Beany."

"Suppose you go and see if they are ready to serve us," Dev suggested. When Greenlaw looked about to speak, Dev stopped him with a slight gesture.

Benjy was already running to the doorway. When he disappeared through it, Dev said quietly, "I know you might have saved him the task, John, but I need a moment without him." Turning to Robina, he said, "Does Benjy usually sup on the dais? I don't recall his joining us there before, but I don't want to disturb his usual customs."

Smiling naturally at last, she said, "He has been supping with me and Corrine since Rab..." Her eyes clouded. Swallowing, she went on more briskly, "It might not be suitable when we have company, of course. You should know, though, that he does try to exert his lairdship inappropriately from time to time."

"As he should," Dev said. "My brother Kenneth has

acted the lord over the rest of us since he first understood what it meant to be my father's heir. Father snubbed him often when we were small, but it had little effect. Ken still does it, but Father evidently thinks it's good for him to acquire and polish a lordly manner."

She nodded. "Our father gave Rab a good measure of such freedom, too, but I was less tolerant." Giving him a straight, rather teasing look, she said, "I soon learned how to get even with him when he tried acting the lord over me."

As she was speaking, she gave an odd start, as if someone had pinched her.

Frowning, Dev said, "Is aught amiss, lass?"

She shook her head but would not look at him.

"Robina, what is it?" he asked more sternly.

~

*"Serves you right, Beany. If you jump every time I speak, you're soon going to have to explain yourself to him."*

"Robina, look at me."

Forcing herself to focus on the impatient, now irked Dev, she struggled to recall what he'd asked her. "Naught is amiss, sir, truly," she said. "I thought I heard something, but I expect it was only Benjy, chattering to someone near the doorway."

He gave her an even sterner look. But, after a long pause during which she kept silent, he said, "John, where exactly do you and Mistress Greenlaw sleep?"

"At the top of the main stairs, sir, under the ramparts. We both sleep lightly."

Recalling the night Dev had chased her to her bedchamber, Robina nearly smiled at that assertion.

Apparently, Dev was remembering, too, because one corner of his lips twitched, and his stern gaze slid away from her as he said, "Then I *will* take the master's chambers, since you think it would cause talk if I do not."

"I do think it would be best to begin as you mean to go on, sir," Greenlaw said. "We all know that Lady Robina stands in no danger from you."

"I'm certain of that," Robina said, glaring at Dev.

Holding her gaze again, he said gently, "As long as you behave yourself."

A chill touched her spine then, but irritation stirred, too.

⁓

Dev had just congratulated himself on getting the last word, when Robby's chin came up and her mossy-green eyes narrowed and took on a catlike yellowish tint. "I trust you won't interfere with the running of this household," she said icily.

"I won't. But it would not astonish me if Lady Rosalie should make a number of suggestions or take command of it herself, come to that."

To his surprise, she smiled. "How well do you know her ladyship?"

He shrugged. "I've just met her."

She grinned then. "I thought so," she said.

# Chapter 7

Robina excused herself and Benjy from the high table soon after the boy had eaten. Her feelings about Dev's taking charge at Coklaw remained mixed. The news had shocked her, and she was still trying to accustom herself to it.

That Rab seemed to welcome Dev's arrival was irksome.

*"You'll soon be glad he's here."*

"Will I?" she retorted, glancing toward him to see only the wall beside her.

"Who ye talking to?" Benjy asked over his shoulder as they went up the stairs.

"Myself, laddie. Sometimes I like to enjoy a conversation with the one person who always understands what I'm talking about."

"Are ye saying I'm nobbut a dolt, then?"

Hearing amusement in his tone, she said lightly, "I am not, and you know it. I think I must be as tired tonight as you are, though, so I'm going to go to bed, too."

"It seemed to me that Dev expected ye to go back downstairs."

*"It seemed so to me, too, Beany."*

Robina thought they were both right, but she was not ready yet to talk more with Dev. She wanted to examine the jar and see if she could open it.

She said, "Dev has been traveling hither and yon for a sennight, Benjy, so he must be sleepy, too. Besides, he did not say that I *should* go back down, so I'm going to bed as soon as you are tucked up in your cot."

Corinne was straightening the coverlet on Benjy's bed when they arrived and greeted them with a grin, saying, "I've shaken out his bedclothes, mistress, and smoothed his cot. He's a restless sleeper, our laddie," she added, ruffling his hair.

"I can get myself ready for bed," he said, stepping away from her.

"Can ye now?" Corinne said, exchanging a smile with Robina. "We'll just see about that, won't we?"

When Benjy frowned, Robina said, "He's feeling much better, Corinne, so he won't need you. I'm for bed myself, though, so unless you've already brought up my hot water, prithee shout for someone to fetch some to my chamber."

"Aye, sure, mistress," Corinne said.

*"Benjy should have a lad to look after him. He's too old to be coddled so."*

For once, Robina agreed with Rab. But, suspecting that Dev would say such needs of Benjy's fell within his purview now, she would ask him about it first.

⁓

Downstairs, Dev waited at the high table, wondering if Robina would return. He had already decided that it was unlikely. If she knew he'd seen her on the rise, under that oilskin in the drizzle...

He was more than curious about what she'd been doing, which made him wonder if it was his well-honed suspicious nature that made her behavior, in retrospect, seem furtive, or something more than that. She *had* hurried inside when she saw him.

Asking a lad to remove the privacy screens, he watched as men in the lower hall laid out pallets, diced, played other games, or talked together. But his thoughts stayed with Robina. "Likely, she hurried inside only because of the rain," he muttered.

Motion to his right drew his attention to Greenlaw stepping onto the dais. "If ye'd like, sir," the steward said, "I'll show ye to the master's chambers. Your man likely has all in readiness there for your comfort by now."

"Sit down, Greenlaw," Dev said, pushing out the nearest back-stool with a foot. "I've decided that you and I should meet briefly each morning to discuss aught that might need my attention. Do you know of any such thing that I should see to straightaway?"

Greenlaw's lips twisted wryly. "We ha' lost stock since the young laird's death, sir. Likely some o' our greedier neighbors ha' taken advantage o' his loss, when they ought to be grieving wi' the family."

"You know as well as I do that Borderers' thoughts rarely linger on death," Dev said. "It occurs too often hereabouts to dwell long on each loss."

"Aye, so I should tell ye, sir, that young Benjy has set his heart on planting a memorial tree to our Rab on a rise not far from the gate."

"That rise to the southeast?"

"Aye, sir. But if ye're thinking he ought not to dwell—"

"Nay, nay," Dev said hastily. "Benjy is still a bairn,

whatever else he may be. As long as I have a say here, he will enjoy his childhood as much as he can whilst learning his future duties."

"I'll say nae more about that, then. As to the stock..."

Resigned to hearing more about Coklaw's losses, Dev decided that at least he now knew why Robby had been creeping about in the rain. Since Benjy had been in bed, sick, she had simply been seeing that his memorial to Rab was safe.

She was a good and loving sister, so it likely *had* been no more than his own too-suspicious nature that had made her actions seem furtive.

⌒

As soon as Corinne departed for the night, leaving a lighted candle on the stand by Robina's bed, Robina got up, slid the bolt on her door into its slot, and opened the blanket kist. The jar lay under the four blankets where she had left it.

Taking it out and moving near the candle, she examined the jar. It seemed ordinary, about eight inches tall. Her two hands could encircle it with her thumbs and forefingers overlapping. The top end and its crockery cap were a bit smaller. Such a jar might contain water or wine, or barley. Whatever it held now did not slosh; it rattled a little.

The wire crisscrossed the cap and wrapped under the lip of the jar, where it flared wider. Whoever had wired it shut had twisted the wire ends tightly. Also, as Rab had noted earlier, the wire was rusty. She would need a tool of some sort and gloves to protect her hands. Such items were stored in the tool shed by the stable.

Since she could do no more that night and was ready for bed, she tucked the jar away again, unbolted the door so Corinne could get in, in the morning, and went to sleep.

Waking at the sound of the latch, Robina saw bright light through the shutters and knew the clouds had broken at last and the sun had come up.

"'Tis a fine soft day, mistress," Corinne said with a smile as she moved to the washstand with a can of hot water for the ewer.

"I'll wear my old drab kirtle, the one I decided not to cut up for rags," Robina said. "I'm going to see how the hole for Benjy's tree looks this morning, and it will be muddy."

Her chamber windows, no more than two arrow slits, looked westward over the wall toward Slitrig Water and Hawick. With the shutters open, she saw blue sky with drifting white clouds. The hills and forest beyond the wall wore a soft gray blanket of ground fog, but the storm had moved on and the fresh air beckoned.

Dressing quickly, she strapped on the narrow belt bearing her small dirk in its sheath, over her shift, before she donned her kirtle. Then, she adjusted the belt so she could reach the dirk's hilt through the kirtle's right-hand fitchet.

Plaiting her hair by herself to save time, she left Corinne to make the bed and tidy the bedchamber, peeked into Benjy's empty room, and hurried downstairs.

No one was on the dais, so she took a roll from a basket on the high table and a slice of cold beef from under the nearby platter's cover. Rolling the beef into a narrow tube, she bit off one end as she turned toward the main stairway and finished it before she reached the outer door.

Stepping into the misty yard, she glanced at the sky

and drew a deep breath of the rain-freshened air. Then, tearing off a chunk of her roll, she raised it to take a bite and heard a familiar shriek of anger. Scanning the yard, she saw Benjy in the grip of a total stranger. The boy fought to break free as the man dropped to a knee, hauled him across the other one, and began to belabor his backside.

Flinging her roll aside, Robina snatched up her skirts and flew down the steps.

Dev was talking with Shag at the gate when he heard Benjy cry out and turned to see Robina running toward Gyb Christie, one of the men-at-arms from his tail. Gyb had the boy across his knee and was giving him a sound skelping.

"What's that dastard think he's a-doing to our Benjy?" Shag demanded.

Dev barely heard him. He was running after Robby, wondering what demon had possessed her to take on a man twice her size, instead of shouting for help. *By heaven,* he thought, *when I get my hands on her...sakes, on all three of them...*

The man punishing Benjy faced the northwest corner of the yard with his profile toward Robina. He hadn't seen her yet, because he had his attention fixed on the boy, who was still screeching with pain and indignant fury.

Putting her hands out toward the lout's nearer muscular shoulder, Robina shoved hard and skidded to a halt as he went over sideways and Benjy scrambled away.

Hands on her hips, Robina snapped, "How *dare* you strike my brother!"

"By heaven, ye pliskie bitch, ye need a lesson more than he does," the lout said, leaping to his feet faster than she had expected.

Swiftly reaching through the fitchet in her skirt for the dirk's hilt as she stepped back, she said angrily, "You have no *right* to touch him."

"Hush your gob, lass! By heaven, I'll teach ye wisdom if nowt else."

He reached for her but paused when Benjy shouted, "Dinna touch her! I'll see ye hanged an ye do!"

"Hoots, I'll finish wi' ye later, ye ill-deedit skemp," the man retorted, turning back toward Robina, who now had her dirk in hand.

*"Beany, don't be daft!"*

"I vow," she muttered grimly, ignoring Rab, "you will *not* touch him again. Nor will you touch me. If you are wise, you will go about your own business."

"I like a fierce woman, but I'll no ha' ye playing wi' knives, lassie," the lout said, grinning now. "Gi'e me that 'un afore ye hurt yourself."

His hands moved, but she stepped back on her right foot, holding the dirk low as she did. Then she swept it back farther to gain momentum as he reached to grab her other hand, still held out obligingly closer to him.

As he pulled her toward him and she moved to thrust the dirk toward him, a grip of iron clamped hard around her wrist, startling her and throwing her off balance. Keeping her gaze fixed on her adversary, she saw his eyes widen just as Benjy's had. His insolent grin returned a split-second later.

She had time only to note those facts and hear him say, "Thank 'e," before a solid fist flashed past her ear to his square jaw and sent the man flying backward.

His feet left the ground before he crashed down and lay still.

Shifting her attention from the man on the ground to the one still gripping her right wrist in a viselike left hand, her startled gaze met Dev's furious one.

He released her, reached down with his left hand, grabbed the man's jack, and hauled him to his feet as if he weighed no more than a good-sized salmon.

"Can you stand by yourself, Gyb?" Dev asked quietly.

"Aye, sure, master," the lout assured him, looking wary.

"Good," Dev said. Letting go of him, he knocked him down again, moving so quickly that neither his victim nor Robina saw the blow coming.

"*This* is the lady Robina Gledstanes," Dev said grimly as the man, Gyb, struggled to sit. "That lad you were skelping is her brother, Benjy, Laird of Gledstanes and Coklaw."

"I didna ken," Gyb replied from the ground. Blood streamed from his nose.

"You will henceforth treat them both with the respect due to their rank," Dev went on. "You will also, if you have further complaints about anyone here, make those complaints to her ladyship, respectfully, or to me. Do you understand me?"

"Aye, sure, sir," the man said, sitting now and bloody. "But ye canna blame a man for thinking she were nobbut a dairymaid or housemaid. Just look at her."

"I thought you said you understood me, Gyb," Dev

said, his voice quieter and gentler than ever. The look in his eyes was like ice-covered flint.

Robina understood then, exactly, why men called him Devil Ormiston.

So did Gyb. "Aye, master," he said hastily. "I do understand, I swear."

When Dev continued to hold his gaze, Gyb cleared his throat, got awkwardly to his feet, and turned to Robina.

"I'm that sorry, m'lady, I didna ken who ye were," he said humbly. "It'll no happen again, I promise ye. I hope ye can forgive me error."

"She does," Dev snapped before Robina could speak. "Now, go and tell Jock that I want to see him, and see that you keep busy and out of my sight until my temper cools. That may be some time yet."

"Aye, master, I'll keep clear." With that, Gyb hurried to the stable.

Benjy fairly danced with glee. "By the Rood, Dev, ye showed *him!*"

Turning a look on the boy nearly as flinty as the one he had shown Gyb, Dev said with surprising calm, "Go inside now, and wait for me at the high table. You and I will talk more about this. Meantime, give thought to how your own behavior may have caused the trouble, so we can discuss that."

Nodding, Benjy turned toward the keep entrance.

"Benjamin," Dev said, "a nod is not a proper reply to a command."

Turning back, his face reddening, Benjy said, "Aye, I'll think on it, Dev."

"Have you not still forgotten something?"

Grimacing and shooting a rueful look at Robina before

meeting Dev's gaze again, Benjy said quietly, "Yes, sir, I forgot."

"Take care that you do not forget again. You may go in now."

Seeing a glint of tears in the boy's eyes as he passed her, Robina forgot everything else. "If your other men behave like that brute, I don't think much of them," she said. "As for telling him that I've forgiven him, you can both think again. I'll decide who deserves my forgiveness, not you."

"Have you finished?"

Something in his tone stirred a tickle of caution, so she said, "Yes."

"Good, give me that dirk."

"I won't," she said. "Rab gave it to me, *and* he taught me how to use it."

"Blethers," Dev retorted. "He might have given it to you, but I'll wager you plagued him witless to make him do it. Whatever he taught you, I'd also wager any amount you like that he never thought you'd draw that dirk against a warrior like Gyb. *What* did you hope to accomplish by thrusting it at him?"

"I…" She paused. She had visualized such an encounter often, because Rab had told her she should plan for when she might have to use the dirk—or the smallsword that he had also given her. He had said she should do whatever she could to divert her opponent so she could strike true. "Rab said—"

"If Rab suggested that you could kill a man—"

"Not kill, just wound," she said indignantly.

"Aye, sure, much better," he growled. "Make the man angrier."

The sarcasm in his voice fired her temper again.

"Sakes, do you think I'd *want* to kill anyone?"

"I know you don't." His voice was quieter, and his sweeping glance told her that he had remembered the others in the yard. "That you *don't* mean to kill makes your actions *more* dangerous," he went on. "By Heaven, if Rab were here, I'd..."

The look that crossed his face then told her two things: that Rab was fortunate not to have to face Dev just then and that Dev felt guilty and deeply saddened again to have thought such a thing, even for a moment.

She reached out to touch him, but he said brusquely, "We'll continue this discussion inside."

"Sir," Jock Cranston said, striding toward them, "Gyb said ye wanted me?"

Robina snatched her hand back without touching Dev. As he told Jock that he had indeed sent for him, she remembered that her purpose in coming out had been to see how soon she and Benjy could finish planting Rab's tree.

She glanced yearningly at the gate.

Dev said, "Jock, I want you to make clear to Gyb how near he came today to the hanging tree. He took it on himself to skelp young Benjy, and when her ladyship intervened, he had the temerity to threaten her."

Jock grimaced. "I did see that some'un gave him a clout or two."

"I did," Dev said. "Her ladyship might well have gutted him had I not."

Jock's bushy eyebrows soared upward then. He glanced at Robina and back at Dev. "I'll see to it, sir. D'ye want him flogged?"

"No, but put the fear of it into him and keep him out of my way."

"Aye, sir," Jock said. With a nod to Robina, he returned to the stable.

"I cannot go in yet," Robina said. "I have things to do first. Also," she added hastily when Dev frowned, "you told Benjy that he should wait for—"

"Benjy can go on waiting," he said curtly. "It will do him good to wonder what I might do. But if you want to keep that dirk, Robina, you'd best stop trying to defy me. We have a few things we must settle between us straightaway."

She cocked her head. "Will you let me keep carrying my dirk after we talk?"

"No, but I'll let you keep it after I see that you understand why you must *not* carry it." He waited a beat, then added, "Defy me, and *I'll* keep it."

Tempted to tell him that Rab had given her a small-sword and taught her how to use that, too—as proof that Dev should trust her with her weapons—she thought again and decided to hold her tongue. Dev would likely confiscate the sword, too, if she mentioned it.

It occurred to her only as they approached the main entrance that she had not heard a peep out of Rab since he had shouted at her not to be daft.

What if Dev was right? She *had* plagued Rab into teaching her, but she knew that he had taught her well.

Dev struggled to keep his temper. He wanted to put Robby across his knee again for her foolhardiness, but when memory of doing so before stirred his cock to life, he wondered if such thinking was not just as foolhardy. As Warden of Coklaw, with the Scott's Hall ladies concerned for her virtue, he dared not let his temper or any other emotion-driven impulse, or reflex, rule him.

Gesturing for her to precede him up the timber stairs, he said, "We'll use the wee room off the hall landing, where Rab stowed visitors until he could see them when his men or others were in the hall."

She obeyed silently. When she reached the entry, he leaned past her to open the door, thinking he ought to assign someone to act as porter. "Did Rab not have someone to tend this door?" he asked her as she stepped inside.

"Aye, sure, when he was here," she said. "We had a porter whilst Father was alive, too. After he died, whenever Rab was away, we had little need of one. We rarely had visitors other than on quarter days, and if Benjy or I went outside, we could open the door for ourselves. In the event that we did have a visitor, someone from the yard would escort him to Greenlaw. Dev, really—"

"Go on up," he said. "I don't want to talk here."

With a sigh, she went up to the little room across from the great hall and looked around as she stepped inside, as if she'd expected someone else to be there.

The room was stark. A wide table with a back-stool behind it faced the door. Another stool faced the table, and two three-legged stools sat against the south wall, at Dev's left. A long arrow-slit there and a second one over the table admitted daylight.

Shallow steps jutted from the west wall to the archer's narrow platform, which served at present to hold a jar of quills, a tinderbox, candles, and other items within reach of anyone sitting behind the table. The only ornamental feature was a rectangular, intricately carved wooden box at the near edge of the table that held a penknife, an inkpot, a silver seal, and sticks of red wax. Its lid lay nearby, inner side up.

"Sit down if you'd like," Dev said.

"Are you going to sit, too, or tower over me and bellow?" she asked.

Irritation stirred. He did not think he ever bellowed. He had certainly not intended to bellow at her. But the look in her eyes was one that he had seen many times before on both twins and his sister Fiona. Robina was testing him. He relaxed, amused, and gestured toward the nearby back-stool. "Sit, fierceling."

To his dismay, her eyes brimmed with tears.

⁓

Robina turned abruptly away toward the back-stool, raising an arm to dash away the sudden, unexpected tears. More streamed down her cheeks, though, and the last thing she wanted was to let Dev see her cry.

The room was silent. She'd been glad when they came in that she and Ada had tidied it, because others, not to mention herself and Benjy, often left things there that they meant to take elsewhere later. None of that mattered now.

She felt Dev gently touch her shoulder. "Robby, I'm sorry," he said. "Perhaps we should have this discussion later."

She shook her head and drew a breath. "It's not your fault," she said, her voice still unsteady. "It's just..." Her voice caught.

"It's just that Rab used to call you that when you were sulky or trying to wrap him round your thumb," Dev said. "I should have recalled that before I spoke. But when you looked at me as you did then, you looked just as he did when he wanted to change a subject or coax a man to do something he didn't want to do. It amazes me how much you can look like him despite being half his size and female."

"We were twins, after all," she murmured.

"Aye, sure, but he was big, brawny, and hard-muscled. And you are...not," he finished lamely, as though he knew he might be overstepping the bounds.

"Perhaps you had better just say what you want to say to me," she said. "I don't want to sit unless you do, and Benjy *is* waiting."

"Very well," he said. "Put plainly, I don't want you to carry your dirk because it gives you a false sense of safety. The worst you could do to any man with that weapon is to cut him. But, in a fight with anyone larger, you are the one most likely to get hurt. I'll ask you to believe that I know what I'm saying. I have taught weaponry to many men and lads, including your reckless brother."

Although she knew she had lost the argument, she said quietly, "Rab did teach me how to use it."

"I'm not questioning that," Dev said. "I do question the likelihood that he expected you to defend yourself with it against any angry or malicious man, let alone a warrior. Did Rab say you were skilled enough for that?"

Much as she would have liked to, she could not claim that Rab thought she could take *him*, let alone Dev or any other warrior, in a fight. His teaching had made her confident that she could defend herself, though. Without that...

"I see," Dev said. "I mean what I say, lass. You may keep the dirk because he gave it to you, but you are not to carry it. Someone attacking or capturing you could take it and use it against you. Neither of us wants that."

"Is there anything else?" She winced then at the echo of her words, knowing that she had sounded sullen or as if she were trying to deflect him again.

But he said more gently than she had expected, "Just this: I think you recall that Gyb mistook you for a milk-maid out there, Robby. That kirtle you're wearing does look fit for the ragbag."

"Are you going to tell me how to dress now?"

"No, I'm going to make sure that every man out there knows who you are and that he is to treat everyone at Coklaw with due respect. Nevertheless, you wore only that thin pink kirtle when we met in the hall last Sunday night, and now this ragged one. So you are either in desperate need of new clothing or sadly careless about your appearance. Lady Rosalie will notice such things when she arrives—"

"Must we have her?"

"We must. Don't interrupt me or try to change the subject again. If you have more suitable garments, you would be wise to wear them. If you lack such clothing, tell me, and we'll do something about it."

"In troth," she said, "I rarely think about what I wear, because I so seldom see anyone who makes me think about it. Doubtless you are right, though. I disliked hearing your man say that about me. But, if you mean I should have new dresses made, I think you will find that we are short of gelt at present. I do have better garments than this one, though. I wore it because Benjy and I were going to go and see if it might be possible to plant his tree for Rab now."

His lips thinned, and she suspected that he disliked the very idea of the two of them going outside the wall.

"Is there aught I should know that you have not yet told me?" she asked him. "Has someone reported raiding parties in the area?"

He shook his head. "If anyone has, I've heard nowt of it. Nor has Wat. I was just thinking that I must talk with Benjy first, and then briefly with Greenlaw. But then, unless the laddie irks me again or the two discussions last long enough to take us to the midday meal, I'll go with you. I'd like to help."

To his chest, she said, "Benjy and I agreed that we should do the work ourselves. Our graveyard is too far for him to go there alone, so the tree is to be in memory of Rab and a place where Benjy can visit him."

"You, too, I expect. Do you not *want* me to help?" he added bleakly.

Her rueful gaze flew up to meet his. "I did *not* mean that. I wouldn't... Oh, my wretched tongue! Now I'm the one who didn't think. Well, I did, but I was thinking that you meant you needed to guard us, and I—"

"Never mind, Robby," he said. "I ken fine what you think about that. I don't want to be your jailor. If I worry about your safety, it is because it is my duty now to do so and because I promised Rab that I would."

She gaped at him. "You *what*?"

# Chapter 8 _____

"Sit, Robina," Dev said testily. "If you don't, I'm liable to shake you. I'd like to promise I won't do anything so physical, or bellow, but we have to be able to talk to each other without fearing that we'll break something if we say the wrong thing. I know you weren't expecting any of this, but you simply must—"

"We'll get along better, Dev, if you stop giving me orders," she interjected.

Instead of sitting, she stepped away from him toward the wall. Taking advantage of his frowning pause, she added, "You told me that Douglas appointed you Warden of Coklaw. You said not a word about Rab having aught to do with—"

She broke off with an odd look on her face.

"What is it?" he asked.

"I remembered something," she said. "Naught to do with you," she added hastily. "But you should have told me straightaway. I could have explained that we need no more protection. With the Greenlaws and our people..." She spread her hands. "Truly, sir, Rab cannot have meant for you to live here."

"I told you the truth about Archie," he said. "Perhaps

I should have told you earlier that Rab made me promise to look after you, but I've had only two chances, and neither seemed appropriate. I thought the news would just stir more coals between us."

"Perhaps," she admitted. "But you were wrong not to tell me. Good sakes, sir, you should have told Benjy *and* me! When, exactly, did Rab extract this promise from you?"

"Just before he died," he said quietly. "You know I was with him then."

"Aye." The color had drained from her face, and he was sorry to awaken those memories, but he steeled himself to deal with the immediate problem. "You've changed the subject again," he said. "But you should know that Rab insisted. I'd have promised him anything then, Robby. But I agree with him that you and Benjy need someone other than your people to look after you."

"So, the Douglas just happened to appoint *you*?"

"No, he was going to appoint one of his cronies. He told me so, himself. I assured him then that the Greenlaws were enough, but he disagreed, because Coklaw is too close to the border. Would you liefer have a kinsman of his in charge here?"

She shook her head. "But if that's what he wanted, why *did* he send you?"

"Wat Scott suggested that I was the best man for the task, because you know me and I know Coklaw," Dev told her. "But it was my father who suggested that I talk to Wat, because he was sure that he would not want any Douglas in charge here."

"Because Branxholm lies so near us, aye?"

"Aye."

"So you rode to the Hall, Wat agreed, and now you are our warden."

"I was going to the Hall, anyway, on Archie's orders," Dev said. "And I was not as quick to agree as you suggest. Nor did I think Archie would agree. But Wat was persuasive, so here I am. Do you dislike it so much that you want me go?"

She looked thoughtful, as if she expected him to say more or, since she was looking distantly past him, almost as if she expected someone else to speak.

Rab kept quiet, and Robina wondered if he was afraid that Dev, having been so close, too, might hear him if he spoke. She had hoped that Rab would say he'd never expected Dev to live with them. But she also wanted to know if Rab had referred to that exchange with Dev when he'd said, *"Dev made a promise, lass."*

At the time, she'd thought he meant only that Dev would return soon.

Dev was waiting for a response to his question, and the truth was that if Douglas had put one of his cronies in charge of the castle, she would have had no choice. He was Coklaw's liege lord, and although he lacked legal right to seize the castle, he did have the right—as primary protector of the Scottish Borders—to put his own man there when Coklaw's rightful laird was only nine years old.

Accordingly, she met Dev's solemn gaze and said, "I wish you'd told me this before, but I'll admit I made it difficult. I don't like having anyone here who thinks he can order me about, but I don't want anyone else doing so.

"I don't dislike *you*," she added. "I dislike anyone other than Father or Rab interfering in what I do. After all, I've managed this household without interference since I was twelve. Next, I expect it will be Cousin Rosalie."

"I thought Greenlaw and his wife managed it," Dev said.

"Greenlaw looks after the accounts and supervises the menservants, and Ada supervises the maidservants and such details of the household as she and I deem necessary when we talk each day. Naturally, Father oversaw everything whilst he was alive. After he died, everyone deferred to Rab and to me when Rab was not here."

Dev regarded her silently for a long minute. His demeanor seemed relaxed now, rather than tense or angry, but she sensed that he was trying to think how he might, without force, compel her to accept his authority.

*"Sakes, you menseless wench, you're not thinking properly."*

So, Rab was still speaking to her, but she didn't want to hear it. She knew what Dev would say. Biting her lower lip, she dared to hope that he might—

"Do you recall how Greenlaw defined my position here?" he asked quietly.

"I do," Robina said with a sigh. "You stand in the place of the laird. In other words, you are now the person to whom everyone must defer, including me."

He nodded, watching her. "That is how it is and how it will be. I won't defer to you just because you want to do as you please. Nor will I always confer with you before I make a decision. However, I do understand your dislike of the situation."

"Do you?"

"Aye, you've made that clear. Will it help if I say I do not mean to interfere with the household? You and Mistress Greenlaw know much more than I do about what stores you have, what you need, and what maintenance is required. It all seems well run to me. I'll expect you to warn me before you make major changes and to tell me what you need."

Relaxing, she said, "We'll do that."

"You mentioned Lady Rosalie," he said. "I expect we'd both be wise to wait and see if she does expect to take over before— What?"

Robina shook her head ruefully. "I was spouting words, sir. I doubt she'll try any such thing. Just wait till you meet her. I adore her."

His lips thinned, pressed together.

"Truly," Robina said. "She is the merriest person, but I warn you, she, too, is accustomed to taking her own path. She told me last time she was here that she enjoys being a widow, because she can make her own decisions. If someone upsets her, she just moves on to the next kinsman until things sort themselves out. I'm glad she's coming."

Dev gazed morosely at her while flinging silent curses at Wat and Lady Meg. Did either one think he would find such a woman helpful in curbing Robby's impulses?

"You look stunned," she said. "You need not, for you will like her, too. Men always do, except perhaps her brother, Simon. She says that he is domineering but that she has wound him round her thumb since she was a child...nearly always."

Dev found that information less than reassuring, but he was not one to fight his battles before time. His lips relaxed into a smile, and he said, "Then perhaps we will rub along together in peace and charity."

Robina chuckled, and he was glad to see the light in her eyes when she did. She said, "It would be better if we could, but I fear we'll raise storms for a time yet. I'll agree to talk them out, if you will."

"I will," he said, "if you can acknowledge that I'll have the final word."

Rolling her eyes, she said, "I know that. Don't expect me always to be graceful about acknowledging it, though."

"You'd be wise to remember that I mean what I say, Robby."

"So do I, sir," she said, laying emphasis on the last word.

He pressed his lips together again but this time to keep from grinning at her.

The door opened, and Benjy looked in. "I thought ye must ha' forgot me, Dev. They'll be serving our dinner anon. Mayhap ye'll want to wait till after—?"

"Nay, laddie, we'll talk now. Robina and I have finished, and she needs to change her dress. You and I can talk here whilst she does that."

Benjy looked at Robina then, searchingly.

With a glance at Dev that told him she understood the look as well as he did, she said, "Nay, laddie, Dev did me no harm. You should know, though, that he is taking charge here, to help look after Coklaw and us."

He'd meant to tell Benjy himself, but he was willing to give Robby the last word, especially since she cast him a wary smile as she left the room.

Robina went hastily upstairs to change the ragged kirtle for something more suited to the high table. At least Dev had not *ordered* her to change it. Although she could not say that she had won any major points in their argument, she realized that she had enjoyed crossing verbal swords with him. In truth, she had made *some* good points of her own.

She hoped he wouldn't be too hard on Benjy, although without knowing what the boy had done to stir Gyb's ire, Dev had likely made no decision as to his fate. She would just have to trust Dev.

Finding Corinne awaiting her in her chamber, Robina unlaced her kirtle bodice as she said, "I'll wear the pink one now."

"Aye, sure, mistress," Corinne said, taking the kirtle from the kist where it lived and shaking it out. "Did ye finish planting our Benjy's tree?"

Her tone was too casual, and Robina knew that any news flew swiftly through the castle. "You know we did not," she said. "Did your friend Jem tell you all about it?"

"Well, it were Daisy as said ye'd come back in wi' Sir David after ye knocked that Gyb over. She said Sir David were looking as fierce as a man could look. So—"

"I see," Robina interjected with a stern look. "If you were hoping to learn more about what happened…" She let the words hang between them.

"Nay, mistress," Corinne said hastily. "I'll just fetch a brush for your hair."

Satisfied, Robina said, "I expect you also know that Sir David is warden here now."

Corinne nodded. "Aye, Daisy said Mistress Greenlaw told her, 'cause Greenlaw told Mistress Greenlaw. I'll wager ye're vexed about that, too."

"In troth, Corinne, I am more relieved than vexed. But if I hear from anyone else that that is how I feel, I swear I'll dismiss you to the scullery."

"Ye'll no hear a peep about aught ye say to me, mistress," Corrine said earnestly.

"You'd be wise to see to that," Robina retorted. "A promise is like an unpaid debt, Corinne. You pay the debt by *keeping* your promise."

Her words echoed in her own ears as she finished dressing. She had as much as promised Dev that she would deal honestly with him. Could she keep that promise while still keeping secrets from him?

⁓

"Sit there, Benjy," Dev said, gesturing to the stool that Robina had rejected.

Benjy sat gingerly and watched him so warily that Dev wondered what Rab might have done in such an instance.

Dismissing the thought, he reminded himself that he had taken responsibility for the boy's upbringing. "I want to know exactly what happened this morning, laddie," he said. "Why did Gyb punish you?"

Benjy swallowed visibly, making Dev recall how his own, then much larger and more physically powerful, brother Kenneth had made him feel when Ken towered over him with strap in hand, demanding answers to unanswerable questions. Unanswerable, that was, if one were usually honest but cherished one's skin.

Accordingly, he drew out another stool and sat facing

Benjy, who straightened on his own stool and looked right at him to say, "I been a-thinking on it like ye said, sir. But I dinna...do not know why he skelped me."

"Just tell me what happened."

"I do ken that. He came out o' the stable and yelled at me to start mucking out stalls. I said I wasna one o' the lads as did such and I were a-waiting for me sister. Then he cursed and said I'd best get me backside inside or he'd make me sorry. I said he shouldna speak so to me, and that's when..." He paused, swallowing again. "Did I do wrong, sir?"

Dev hesitated. This was harder than he'd expected. Benjy was, in fact, Laird of Coklaw, and the sooner the men all understood that, the better. Even so...

"I cannot say that you did wrong," he said at last. "But I'd like you to think about what Gyb saw in the yard this morning."

When Benjy frowned, Dev added, "I'm not saying Gyb was right. He was dead wrong to lay a hand on you. But he saw a lad wandering in the yard who looked able to help with the chores. Sithee, he mistook you for a stable lad, so he yelled at you."

"He didna need to shout," Benjy said, raising his chin in much the same way that Robby did when she gathered her dignity. "We dinna...do not shout at our people here at Coklaw. Me da didna like it, nor did our Rab."

"I'm glad to know that," Dev said. "I will explain that to Gyb and to any other of my men who need telling."

Benjy looked more cheerful. "Then ye're no still vexed wi' me?"

Dev shook his head. "However," he said, "I will tell you something that I learned when I was your age. My father is Ormiston of Ormiston, a gey powerful man. So, I thought his name and title would protect me whatever I did. When something similar to what happened this morning happened to me, I had no sister at hand to aid me. I could not sit for a sennight, and when I bleated about it to my father, he said that if I wanted our people to treat me with respect, I should avoid telling them that they must do so. Instead, I should behave respectfully to them and *show* them the behavior I expected *from* them."

Benjy was quiet for a moment, thinking. Then he said, "Beany said summat o' the sort to me t'other day. I thought I understood her then, but today was different. In troth, sir, it's hard to ken what a laird should do, time to time. I'm thinking our Rab should ha' stayed alive till I were more grown up."

It took Dev a moment to swallow the lump in his throat before he said, "I think I can help you learn the things you should know."

"Aye, I'm glad ye've come to us. I ken fine that *ye'll* ken what to do."

"Then shall we go and see if Beany has come down yet? I'm starving."

"Me, too, but ye'd better no call her Beany, 'less ye want your eyes scratched out."

"I'll try to remember," Dev said with a smile. "Meantime, you need not call me 'sir' all the time. You may still call me Dev if you like."

"Good, then let's go find Beany, Dev."

⁓

Robina reached the hall just as Dev and Benjy stepped onto the dais. Dev had his hand on the boy's shoulder, and as they took their places at the table, Benjy looked up at him with a reverent expression that she had seen before only when he'd looked at Rab.

The sight jolted her, but she hastily scolded herself. Her little brother needed masculine guidance, and he could do much worse than to choose Dev as his hero.

*"That's right, Beany. Moreover, you'd be a fool to be as jealous of Dev where Benjy is concerned as you were of Dev and me."*

"I was not jealous but lonely, even when you deigned to take me with you," she muttered, surprising herself with that sudden awareness but silencing Rab.

Hurrying, she took her place just as Corinne approached from the service stairs.

"Beg pardon, m'lady," the maidservant said with a wary smile. "Mistress Greenlaw said I were to sit by ye the noo. She said it'd look better to them in the lower hall to see ye with a female by ye, now that Sir David be taking the laird's place."

"Thank you, Corinne, but I shan't—"

"Thank you, Corinne," Dev echoed. "Mistress Greenlaw is right. You will attend her ladyship until the lady Rosalie Percy arrives."

"Lady Rosalie *Percy*?" Corinne looked agape at Robina.

"*Cousin* Rosalie has visited us before," Robina said, stifling annoyance. "I doubt you have met her, since she has not stayed overnight, Corinne. She is Lady Meg's sister, who married a Percy cousin of *their* mam's. She will be staying with us for a time."

Robina could see that Corinne was bursting to demand more details. But then the maid looked past her, likely at Dev, and silently took her place beside Robina.

Sensing that Corinne was uneasy in the unfamiliar role, she murmured. "Just do as I do."

Dev said the grace, and as soon as they sat down, Benjy began pelting him with questions about his boyhood.

Robina took the opportunity to say, "Corinne, you may accompany me to table until Rosalie arrives. However, you need not expect to become my shadow."

Corinne's eyes widened. "Nay, m'lady, I'd never expect that."

Aware of silence on her right, Robina turned to see that a platter now sat beside her, and Dev was waiting to serve her. She wondered if he'd heard their exchange.

His eyes began to glint, then to twinkle.

"Shadow?" he murmured.

"You know I'd never tolerate that," she muttered back.

"I do, and I won't burden you with a keeper unless you prove that you need one."

"Except for Rosalie," she said with a sigh.

"Sakes, lass, you said you like her. Don't judge the end before the event."

"Is that an ancient Roman maxim?" she demanded. "My father could spout one for nearly any occasion, but I do not recall that one."

"That maxim was according to David Ormiston," he said. "Come to that, though, my father is also fond of them, so I may have heard its like before."

To avoid talking more about Rosalie, she encouraged him to tell her about his father. She soon learned that Ormiston and James Gledstanes had had much in common.

When they finished eating, Dev suggested that they plant Rab's hawthorn tree.

She said, "It will be muddy out there. I should change back into my old kirtle."

"You don't need to," he said lightly. "Benjy and I will do the work. You need only direct the proceedings."

"Aye, that's a good notion," Benjy said. "Dev loved Rab, too, Beany, and you already did most o' the work, a-digging yon hole."

She opened her mouth to argue but saw the expectant gleam in Dev's eyes in time to lift her chin and say, "You are both too kind. I just hope the work doesn't wear you out."

She also hoped that Dev would slip and cover himself in muck.

~

Dev watched the play of emotions on Robby's face and realized he could almost read her thoughts. He had annoyed her again. That was plain, but she had thought better of challenging him, which augured well for the half-truce they had agreed to. Something in the way she eyed him now, though, warned him that he'd better watch his step.

Outside the gate, Benjy ran to the rise and skidded in the mud, waving wildly as he fought to keep his balance. Succeeding, he turned and grinned at them.

Dev muttered, "I'll wager you hoped I'd be the one to slip, and more calamitously."

Looking startled, she said with a saucy grin, "It would serve you right!"

"Would it?" he said softly, holding her gaze.

Color rose in her cheeks. Her chin jutted upward. "Aye, it would," she said and strode away to join her little brother on the rise.

Noting that she neared Benjy warily and raised her skirts, Dev smiled.

Honoring their decision that, although he could help them, no one else should, Dev carried their tools. Handing the spade to Benjy and assessing the hole, half-filled with mud and debris from the rain, he said, "Perhaps you will clear away those new weeds, Benjy, whilst I dig the muck out of this hole. Beware of flying mud, though."

"The sapling he chose stands yonder, Dev," Robina said, pointing. "I dug a trench around it, so you need only dig underneath to move it."

"Good," he said. "You seem to know what you're doing here, too, lass."

"I watched my mother and helped her when I was small. Few things grow well here, but the hawthorns flourish."

"Was it your lady mother who circled the clearing with them?"

"I think so, although my granddame may have begun it. Mam thought the hawthorns would keep the forest from creeping nearer, but my father doubted her and called them a damned nuisance. They do need much trimming and pruning to deter them from creeping closer. I think they have kept the forest at bay, though."

He nodded, thinking her mother was right, that the dense hawthorn thicket did keep sapling oaks and beeches from rapidly multiplying. But the clearing kept enemies from creeping too close, so the hawthorn itself would frequently need pruning back.

He began digging out the mud and soon hit a layer of pebbles and small rocks. "This must be where you stopped digging," he said to Robina.

"Beany said the rocks would mark that spot," Benjy said. "She dug a grand hole, but the clouds burst on us, and we had to run, so she put the pebbles in."

"A good notion," Dev replied, noting that Robina looked oddly relieved. Catching her eye, he raised his eyebrows.

She shrugged, watched him for a few moments, and said, "Your leathers and boots are covered in that mud, sir. I know that you travel as light as Rab did, if not lighter, and most of his clothing will be too small for you."

"I thank you for your concern, my lady, but I sent one of my lads back to Ormiston from Hawick to tell my father that Archie had appointed me warden here. My lad will gather what I'll need and return by week's end."

"Then I hope your squire can keep you tidy until then. Greenlaw can help, too. You must know that he served as my father's squire for years before becoming steward here."

Their conversation continued on such harmless lines until Benjy's tree was firmly in the ground, and the boy expressed his approval of the result.

Agreeing that the sapling looked splendid, Robina ruffled his hair as she added, "But you, my lad, must rest. I heard you coughing, and we don't want you sick again."

"Och, Beany, I'm no a bairn. A wee cold in the head willna kill me."

"That's true," Dev said. "But, if you want to grow as tall and strong as Rab, you'll need lots of rest. So go now and tell them to open the gate. We'll bring the tools."

When Benjy had obeyed, Dev said, "I'd like to see more of the area, Robby, the nearby woods and such. If you think they'll be dry enough, we might take a walk. You can tell me aught that you think I should know."

"I must see Benjy settled first," Robina said. "If I don't put him to bed, he'll engage in some activity that he means to do for just a moment and not sleep at all."

"Could not Corinne—?"

"He has declared himself too old to be coddled by a maidservant."

"I see," Dev said thoughtfully. "You know, I think Ken had a lad to look after him when he was about Benjy's age. Did not Rab?"

"Not until he turned thirteen. But Ada did suggest one for Benjy, and I have been thinking about it."

"It's a good notion," Dev said. He told her what Benjy had said about how hard he found it to know how a laird should behave.

"Poor laddie," she said. "I remember Rab's reaction when our father died and he suddenly found himself the laird. We were just seventeen."

"Aye, and Wat Scott was but four-and-twenty," Dev said. "He told me the sudden burden terrified him. He was sure he'd never do as well as his father or grandfather had."

"I'll meet you in the hall as soon as Benjy's asleep," Robina said.

*Chapter 9* ─────────────

Robina took Benjy upstairs and tucked him into his cot. Telling him that the sooner he slept the sooner he would wake up, she went quietly out of the room.

Crossing the landing, she entered her own chamber, relieved to find it empty.

Experience assured her that, without orders to the contrary, Corinne would keep busy elsewhere until it was time to help prepare her mistress for bed. Robina did not change clothes for supper at Coklaw unless special company arrived or some mishap occurred that precluded wearing the clothes she had worn all afternoon.

Shutting her door and bolting it, she went to the blanket kist and took out the jar. Having found a small iron crow such as men used to pry bent nails out of wood, she wrapped the lower part of the jar in a towel from the washstand, put the crow's claw foot under the stiff wire, and pried carefully to avoid breaking the jar.

The wire moved more easily than she had expected, since it had easily withstood her efforts to pry it up with her fingers.

Certain that she had found the right tool but unwilling to linger lest Dev come in search of her, she returned the jar, along with the crow, to the kist. Then, taking her pink and moss-green shawl from its hook, she flung it over her shoulders and hurried downstairs to find Dev on the hall landing, waiting for her.

"You were faster than I'd expected," he said.

"Where do you want to go?" she asked. "The Ormiston estate?"

"Not today. I've been up Sunnyside Hill only once, but it must have some fine views of the surrounding area. Have we time to go and return before supper?"

"Aye, sure. Benjy and I went up and back in a morning without hurrying."

They set out at once, and Robina easily kept up with Dev's long stride, although she knew she was taking at least a stride and a half for each one of his.

They walked mostly in silence, and she enjoyed the calls of the birds and squirrels.

Grinning when Dev pointed to a tiny rabbit just before it hopped out of sight behind a bush, she recalled how much she had missed Rab when he was away. No one else at Coklaw had delighted in such simple sights as she did.

They neared the summit much faster than she and Benjy had. By then, most of the clouds had drifted eastward, so the sky was blue with just a few scattered white ones in it.

She felt warm with the sun still well above the horizon. But, knowing that a chilly breeze would greet them at the top, she was glad she had her shawl.

Cresting the hill, they paused and stood silently, looking at the graveyard ahead with its low fence around it. The ends of it met at the lych-gate, in the shelter of which the men had set Rab's shrouded body before burying him.

Memories and images swooped over Robina, catching her off her guard.

⁓

Dev saw the sadness engulfing her. "Do you want to go back?" he asked quietly.

She shook her head. Then, straightening her shoulders, she went to the lych-gate, opened it, and walked into the graveyard.

Dev followed her, noting that the rain had settled the earth mound atop Rab's grave. Grass was even beginning to grow there. It came to him then that, having told Corinne to keep close to Robina, he ought to have brought her with them. Perhaps, though, it was only his eerie sense of Rab's presence that had stirred the unwelcome thought.

Some guardian he was proving to be, but they were there now, and that was that. With a mental shrug, he returned his attention to Robina, who had stopped with her back to him at the edge of Rab's grave.

Hearing an odd squeak from her, something akin to the distant scream of a rabbit in a hawk's talons, he looked more closely. Her shoulders were shaking.

Moving swiftly to her, abandoning all thought of propriety, he put his hands gently on her shoulders and drew her unresisting body close against his. Noting that the top of her head was a few inches below his chin, he murmured, "There's no harm in grieving, Robby. I'll wager you haven't shed a tear since he died."

She shook her head and, through her sobs, said in a gasping tumble of words, "I was too angry with him for dying and with you for *letting* him die."

He had known that, because she had flung similar words

at him when he'd brought Rab's body home. Hearing her say so again now brought a new stab of pain, though.

Then she turned abruptly and, when his hands came to rest on her shoulders again, she looked up at him with tears streaming down her face. "Oh, Dev, I vowed *never* to say that to you again! I *know* it was not your fault, but I couldn't help thinking, over and *over*, that if only you'd not taken him with you. If only..."

She gave way to her tears then, her body heaving against his, and he held her close, damning propriety and all who would say he must not hold her.

⁓

Helpless in the flood of tears, Robina feared she must have lost her senses to have said such things to him, let alone to succumb to her increasingly selfish emotions right before him as she was now. Despite what she had said, Dev did not deserve her anger; yet she had no one else to whom she could freely express her feelings, let alone do so in such a humiliatingly undignified way.

He remained quiet, unmoving, and he held her close. With her cheek against his warm jack, she could hear his slow, steady heartbeat. She felt as if he'd enfolded her with his body, taking her into a safer place than any she had known since her father died and Rab had ridden off to serve the Douglas.

"Go ahead and cry yourself out, Robby," Dev murmured to the top of her head. "This is a good place for it. The creatures won't mind, and the breeze won't tell."

Suddenly, it was easier to stop, and she remembered similar times in her distant past when the simple permission to cry had dammed up the torrent.

Drawing a long, shuddering breath, she tilted her head back to look up at him. "I've rained all over your jack, and I don't know what came over me, but you're right. It is the first time I've let myself cry for Rab."

"I thought so," he said. "I think you have had a hard time of it here."

"I cannot control my thoughts," she admitted. "They tumble about in my mind, all mixed up. One minute I'll be furious with everyone, the next I'll be sad or terrified that I'll start crying and won't be able to stop. Then I remember that everyone else is sad, too, and that a sensible Borderer does not dwell on death."

"Blethers," he said. "Lady Meg said much the same thing when I was at the Hall, and I nearly told her to her head that often one does dwell, that it's simply human to grieve. It is *not* an offense against nature."

Robina's watery chuckle surprised her as much as it must have surprised him. "I'd like to be there if you do tell her such a thing to her head," she said in a voice that sounded, to her, almost normal. "She'd snatch *you* baldheaded."

"I'd deserve that if I spoke so uncivilly," he said in that same quiet tone.

She looked at him more searchingly then. "Dev, I do know that it was not your fault. You did what you had to do, as Rab did. Men fight to keep us safe, and men die because of it. Please don't think I do blame you."

"Robby, you said nowt to me that I've not said to myself many times. Everyone says 'if only' in times of tragedy, whether they admit it or not. It is natural to be angry, too, even—or especially—with the one who died. You must not think you are alone in thinking such things.

I have cursed Rab for his heroism more times than I have praised him."

With that, he kissed her lightly on the forehead. When he continued to hold her and look into her eyes, she didn't look away. The moment lengthened until, without thinking, she raised herself on tiptoe and touched her lips to his.

It was as if a flaming bolt shot through Dev. Never before had he felt such warmth spread within him or such yearning. His body ached with it.

Without thinking, let alone considering consequences, he tightened his arms around her and took what she'd offered him.

She melted trustfully into him, the warmth of her body adding to the heat of his own, and let him capture her lips. He teased and tantalized them with his and with the tip of his tongue until her lips moved eagerly under his and she moaned in his arms. Then a bird whistled from a tree beyond the graveyard fence.

Common sense restored itself, or his natural sense of survival awoke.

He growled, low in his throat, and released her.

She smiled and stepped back. "I'd wager that that whistle means Rab is watching," she said lightly.

"I hope not," he said, trying to keep his own voice light. "If he has access to lightning bolts up there, I'd liefer he not fling one at me."

"Faith, do you think he would object to a friendly kiss?"

Startled to hear her define it so, he said, "Do you think he would not?"

"Well, he might not approve of you licking my lips as

you did," she said. "But it felt good, and you have made me feel much better than I did. I'm all warm inside and, and tingly. I've not felt so before."

"If it were possible for Rab to watch us, I doubt he'd be as pleased about what I did as you seem to be."

"Do you *not* believe he watches?"

He hesitated, reluctant to speak the truth lest he upset her again.

"You don't," she said. "Well, I know that he does, Dev. I can feel him here. I feel his presence often, and I know—"

"Robby, I think it is good that you feel as if Rab watches over you, but..."

Again he hesitated, and she stepped into the void, saying, "You believe he is just cold and dead in that grave, aye?"

"That is what I think," he admitted. "But none of us really knows the answer to that mystery, nor will we until we are dead ourselves."

"I do know," she said firmly. "He *is* watching us, and since he made you promise to look after us, I'm sure he's glad you're here, even if he did see you kissing me. He knows, as I do, that you were just trying to make me feel better. And you have, Dev, but I think we should go back. Benjy will likely have wakened from his nap and will be looking for us."

"Aye, then," he said, looking at the little bird. It whistled its clear, high *pee-ew* and leaned precariously on a slender branch—its distinctive red, white, and black head down below its feet now—as if it were determined to keep them in sight.

Dev told himself firmly not to be a fool, that if Rab

were going to flit about, watching to see that his twin and Dev behaved, he would do so as a hawk or an eagle.

He would *not* do so as a wee goldfinch.

⁓

Walking back down the hill toward the castle, Robina could still feel Dev's lips against hers and the warmth that had spread throughout her body when he'd kissed her. She wondered what Rab would say about it. It had been all she could do to speak lightly of him. She did not believe for a moment that he would ignore what they'd done.

However, she saw that Dev did feel guilty about the kiss. He'd given her such comfort that the last thing she wanted him to suffer was guilt. But, if he thought that Rab could see them, perhaps what he felt was not guilt but merely something other than what she had felt. Surely people didn't all feel the same sensations when they kissed.

She had kissed no one but Benjy for so long that she did not recall how it had felt. Her father's hugs had comforted her, and so had Rab's. Come to that, Rab had kissed her on the mouth whenever he had come home or was leaving again. She had always felt happy that he was home or sad that he had to go but had never felt such warmth as this.

She would think about that. Meantime, she resolved to repay Dev for his kindness by being as amiable as possible.

They chatted with each other and with Benjy at supper, but she bade Dev goodnight when she rose to take Benjy up to bed.

"Come back down when you get him settled," Dev said. "We can talk more."

"We left Benjy all afternoon," she said. "I should spend some time with him now, tell him a story, at least. Then, perhaps I will."

A half-hour later, though, when she left Benjy in his cot and saw that Corinne had not come upstairs yet, she went into her own bedchamber, shut the door, and bolted it. Then, she took the jar and the iron crow out of the kist.

Sitting cross-legged on the floor with the jar in her lap, she used the crow to pry the wire end away from the lid, turning the jar until she could get a firm grip on the wire. Whoever had wired the lid to the jar had made sure that it would stay in place. Both ends of the wire wrapped under the jar's lip, crisscrossed its top, and then wrapped again under the lip. At last, though, the lid fell into her skirt.

When it did, a handful of blackened coins spilled over it, clinking merrily.

Staring at them in stupefaction, she knew they were likely silver and wondered how much they were worth. Picking up the jar, noting that it was still nearly full, she rejoiced to think how helpful so much gelt could be in providing for Coklaw and its people.

Her next thought was that she must tell Dev straightaway.

*"Nay, dinna be daft. Recall that Lady Rosalie is a gabster, and a damned Percy. Once she hears of such a find, the news would fly through the Borders on both sides in a twinkling. We don't even know how the jar got there, Beany. You must tell no one!"*

Rab was right, she decided. Quickly returning the coins to the jar and securing the lid with its wire but wrapping it only once around after crossing it over the top, she rewrapped the jar in its towel and slipped it back into the kist.

She would return the iron crow to the tool shed in the morning.

Hearing a rap at the door and Corinne's voice, she went to let her in.

"Why did ye bolt it?" Corinne asked as she strode in with Robina's hot water.

"I wasn't sure Benjy was asleep yet," Robina replied glibly. "He came in without knocking the other day, and I think he's getting too old for that."

The excuse sounded weak to her, but Corinne nodded as she poured the water from the can into the ewer.

"Men," Corinne said. "They be intriguing creatures, even as bairns."

"Sometimes," Robina said, wondering if Dev would come looking for her.

"That Jem Keith be gey fascinating and a gey good kisser. But I dinna think he's as bonny a laddie as our own laird were."

"My father or Rab?" Robina asked, although she knew which man it was. She had had to curb Corinne's flirtations with Rab.

*"And without due cause, I'd say."*

But the look on Corinne's face belied his words. Looking rapturous, she said, "Och, mistress, ye ken fine which one I meant. I shouldna say it, but our Rab were the bonniest man in the Borders, I think, *and* the best kisser."

A strong suspicion struck Robina that Corinne and Rab had been even better acquainted than she'd known.

*"Don't go putting wicked thoughts into your own head, Beany. And tell the lass she should not speak so of me."*

Robina wished she could confront him face-to-face to

see if he spoke the truth. Since she could not, she ignored his command and prepared for bed.

The next day, Tuesday, passed peaceably. She saw Dev only at meals.

Someone had discovered that, thanks to the storm, debris had blocked a drainpipe for the castle wellspring's outflow, now flooding the yard's lower end. Dev and Sandy, taking charge of clearing the pipe, spent that day and Wednesday morning seeing to it.

Then, Wednesday afternoon, the lady Rosalie arrived with an impressive entourage.

~

Dev was in the yard, talking with Greenlaw, when a hail from the wall walk announced the visitors and Shag opened the gate. The party rode in, two by two. A man about Dev's age and a lad that Dev knew led with the Scotts' star-and-crescents banner.

Behind them, Wat rode beside the lady Rosalie, who rode a fine-looking gray palfrey. She wore a stylish green kirtle under a matching cote-hardie with short tippets from which her arms in their knuckle-length sleeves emerged, an outfit that Dev thought any duchess might wear with pride.

Behind Rosalie, Janet Scott rode next to an older, gray-haired woman in an engulfing gray houppelande.

A dozen armed riders trailed behind them, Wat's entire fighting tail.

The man riding beside the banner-carrier immediately dismounted and moved to the palfrey's head.

Wat grinned at Dev as he dismounted. "Don't look so alarmed," he said with a knowing glint in his eyes.

"I promise we won't *all* stay for days. I brought Jannie along to visit with Robina. I'm sure Robby won't mind sharing her bed tonight. And, as promised, I brought my saintly aunt Rosalie to lend consequence and propriety to this establishment."

"*Saintly*, you say? Pay him no heed, Sir David," Lady Rosalie said with a twinkle in her eyes. "He and Janet, and his men, stay just overnight, and I brought only my attire-woman, Potter, and my equerry with me."

"Have you supplies enough to feed us all?" Wat asked. "Or shall I send Geordie and one of the other lads out to bring in a few rabbits?"

"We can feed you," Dev said, shaking his hand and nodding to Janet, who was allowing Lady Rosalie's equerry to help her dismount.

"Cousin Rosalie!"

Turning, Dev saw a smiling Robina hurrying toward them from the keep. She wore the rose-pink kirtle again with the pink-and-green shawl that matched both the dress and her moss-green eyes. The kirtle was shabby, but its color suited her and if the shabbiness distressed her, she gave no sign of it.

Rosalie opened her arms, and Robina hugged her warmly.

"I like your fine dress, madam," Robby said, standing back again and looking the older woman over from tip to toe. "What a beautiful bright green!"

"It is good, is it not?" But Rosalie was eyeing Robina, too. "Meg said you would need new garments, my dear. And, if I may judge by that kirtle, she's right. But Wat assures me that even such a village as Hawick can produce a proper mercer, a haberdasher, a seamstress, and mayhap even a ladies' shoemaker."

Robina looked at Dev, who willingly nodded. He hoped she understood that he would approve anything she needed, especially clothes more suited to her station in life. He was sure that she hadn't given a thought to new clothing since her father's death.

He walked with Wat as they shepherded everyone inside. "My thanks for bringing her ladyship so soon," he said. "I feared she might wait until the roads were dry."

"Nay, she is all eagerness and will enjoy taking Robby in hand."

"Aye, perhaps, but will Robby enjoy that?"

Wat eyed him in much the same way that Rosalie had eyed Robina. "How are you getting on here, Dev? I hope you have *not* had to sleep in the stable."

"Greenlaw ended that notion," Dev admitted. "Since I stand in the master's place, he said, I must have the master's chambers. He and his Ada sleep at the top of the main stairway, and he assured me that they are light sleepers."

Chuckling, Wat said, "I won't ask you if *that's* true."

"Did you come straight here from the Hall or did you go first to Hawick?"

"Straight here," Wat said. "There have been raids east of here on the usual routes, so I thought I'd better get Rosalie settled in before she heard about them."

"Then I'm doubly grateful," Dev said, hoping the raids *stayed* well east of them.

⁓

"You have a ladies' solar here, do you not?" Rosalie asked Robina after Ada Greenlaw had taken Potter to show her where her mistress would sleep.

"That is where we are going," Robina said, casting a

glance back to see that Janet was right behind Rosalie on the stairs. "I use it rarely myself except to do mending, but we can be cozy there. Have you not seen it before, Cousin Rosalie?"

"Nay, you did show me a little of the keep when I visited shortly before your father died. After we dined at your high table that afternoon, I returned to Scott's Hall with my steward, Len Gray."

"He is no longer with you, though," Robina said, vaguely recalling the man.

"Oh, no, Len has family in Fife and returned to them last year. I decided then that, besides my dear Potter, I required only an equerry to see to our horses and to arrange for the additional men and ponies we need when I travel."

"Do you still enjoy moving about so often?" Robina asked.

"I do. I recall this stairway," she said. "You and I talked for a time in that room across from the hall. Rab and Wat were out looking at sheep or some such thing."

"What a sorry hostess you must have thought me!" Robina exclaimed.

"Naught of the sort," Rosalie said. "You were but seventeen then, I think. You turned eighteen the following April and have just turned nineteen, I believe."

"Aye, my birthday fell on Easter Sunday this year, not that we make much of such days anymore. Nor did I want anything made of it," she added softly.

"I was so sorry to learn of Rab's death," Rosalie said as Robina opened the door to the solar. "You must miss him sorely."

"I feel as if I've lost part of myself," Robina admitted.

Forcing a smile, she added, "*You* must not feel sorrowful, though. I'd liefer you make me laugh."

Returning her smile, Rosalie moved to sit in the cushioned window embrasure, so Robina drew two stools closer to it.

Janet, shutting the door, said, "Wat said that some men call Sir David 'Devil Ormiston,' because he has a devilish temper. I have never experienced it, myself, but I did worry about you, Robby. Is he difficult to live with?"

"He can be a tyrant," Robina said frankly. "But I have a temper, too, and so did Rab, so temperamental men don't frighten me."

Rosalie raised her thin, arched eyebrows. "Take care that you do not defy Sir David too often, lest he wash his hands of you *and* Coklaw. You must not risk that unless you'd welcome one of Douglas's minions here."

"Sir David won't abandon us," Robina said.

"Are you so sure, my dear, that you'd *take* that risk?"

"There is no risk, because he will not leave us," Robina said. Although she said it to defend Dev, she realized that she meant it. She *was* certain. Dev's sense of honor and his dedication to duty were too strong for him to abandon her or Benjy.

# Chapter 10 _____

Dev and Wat Scott had gone outside to talk about well-spring blockages. As they discussed the various problems and possibilities, Dev glanced around the yard and realized that he had not seen Benjy since their visitors' arrival.

Nor did he see him now, but as his gaze met Sandy's, the older man made a slight gesture. Following it, Dev saw the boy sitting in the shadow of the stable's overhanging thatch, leaning against the wall with the shaggy dog Tig's head resting on his lap. At first, Dev thought that both boy and dog were asleep, but when one of the stable lads strode past them to the nearby trough with a pail, Benjy turned his head to watch.

"Sakes," Wat said, "is that young Benjy? I saw him just before Christmas, and I vow he was but half that size then."

"He's nine and growing fast," Dev said, catching Benjy's gaze and motioning for him to join them.

Pushing Tig aside, Benjy scrambled to his feet and ran to them. "I didna want to interrupt you," he said with a smile. "Me stomach's starting to growl, though, so I'm thinking we may be nearing suppertime."

"Make your greeting to his lordship, Benjy, or do you not remember him?"

"Aye, I remember," Benjy said, looking up at Wat and extending his hand for him to shake. "You're the Lord o' Buccleuch and Rankilburn, sir. I saw you arrive, but I wasna sure what to do wi' so many visitors, so I thought I'd best keep out o' the way."

Resting a hand on the boy's nearer shoulder, Dev said, "You acted wisely, laddie. Mayhap you will also prefer to eat your supper in the lower hall."

Benjy looked up at him with wide eyes. "Are ye vexed wi' me, then?"

"No, no, I just thought you might liefer sup with some of the younger lads."

"I'm the laird, and Buccleuch and them others be my guests, aye?"

"That is true," Dev said, ignoring Wat's smile. "However, if you will recall—"

"—that ye stand in me place till I'm grown, aye. But ye did say ye'd teach me how to go on, so I should sup wi' me guests and learn whilst they're here, aye?"

Wat bit his lower lip. His eyes danced with merriment.

Continuing to ignore him, Dev met the boy's solemn gaze and said, "You are right, Benjy. His lordship will sit at my right hand, and you may sit at his."

"Good," Benjy said, nodding. "Will we go in now?"

"Shortly," Dev said. "You might want to go up to your chamber first to brush your hair and wash your face."

As they watched him run off, Wat chuckled and said, "That one may prove to be more of a handful than Robby."

"I doubt it," Dev said. "He is much less likely to defy me or to challenge every word I say."

"Does she do that?"

Aware that he had spoken as bluntly and impulsively as he had learned he could safely do over his years of friendship with Wat, Dev called himself to order but said honestly, "She has not yet defied me, exactly. But she *has* declared that she means to choose her own path, and she frequently challenges me."

"That does not surprise me, but you make me feel blessed," Wat said. "My sisters rarely challenge me. In fact, only one person at the Hall states her own mind with regularity and the supreme confidence that she can do so with impunity."

"Lady Meg," Dev said with an appreciative smile.

"Aye, Gram always says what she thinks, although to give her her due, she is usually right when she disputes my opinions. Even so, she has accustomed herself to the fact that I've stepped into my father's shoes and mean to fill them."

"Always?"

"Mostly," Wat said, grinning. "She does tend to support nobles who dislike his grace's notion of instituting a rule of law throughout the land," he added as his grin faded. "Not that she thinks they're right, but she does say that after Jamie Stewart's long captivity in England, he should have waited to get on friendlier terms with his nobles before deciding to impose English notions of law on all of Scotland."

Dev raised his eyebrows. "What do you think about that?"

"We Scotts have always supported the rightful King, and I support Jamie," Wat said quietly. "I don't mean to alter that position, and Gram knows it. We do agree that all Scots should be able to cross a nobleman's land when they must without fearing that their ignorance of his private laws might see them hanged."

"I believe that, too," Dev said. "I also agree with Lady Meg and my father that his grace ought not to impose new notions on us without due discussion. If he dismisses his supporters' concerns, he may one day find himself with no supporters."

They continued to talk while they walked inside. As they crossed the hall toward the dais, still chatting, movement on the dais drew Dev's notice.

Corinne stood at the ladies' end of the high table, alone.

"Who's the pretty, dark-haired wench?" Wat asked him.

"Robina's personal maidservant, Corinne," Dev said. "Robby doesn't change for supper, and Corinne *has* been sitting with us at meals, but..."

Corinne smiled uneasily as the two men stepped onto the dais.

"Is aught amiss?" Dev asked as he moved to his customary place.

"Nay, sir," Corinne said, relaxing and smiling in her usual cheerful way as she looked from him to Wat and back again. "Her ladyship were still in the solar wi' her cousins, and I didna like to interrupt them to ask if I should eat in the kitchen or here wi' her. So I thought I'd wait here and ask her."

Dev started to tell her that Robina would not need her but said instead, "I suspect that she may not need you, Corinne. But you *should* ask her."

Corinne's eyes twinkled, and her smile grew mischievous. "Just what I thought m'self, sir," she said.

Beside him, Wat made an odd sound in his throat, but Dev ignored it.

~

Entering the great hall to see Corinne flirting with Dev and Wat Scott, Robina hesitated in the archway, causing Lady Rosalie and Janet nearly to bump into her. Hastily begging their pardon, she strode forward, intending to tell Corinne what she thought of such behavior. Really, the woman was soaring above herself!

Over the noise of people in the lower hall taking their places at the trestle tables, she heard from just over her right shoulder, *"Wheesht now! You're jealous again. You must know that as well as I do."*

"I am not!" she retorted indignantly, turning her head toward the voice.

"What's that you say, Robina?" Lady Rosalie asked. "In troth, my ears must be failing me, for I could not detach your words from the other chatter here."

But Dev was smiling at Corinne. And Corinne's cheeky smile was one that *no* maidservant should bestow on the master of the castle.

Robina gritted her teeth.

"Robina?"

Startled, she turned to Lady Rosalie and said ruefully, "Forgive me, cousin. I was thinking aloud. Prithee, blame not your ears but my bad manners. Janet, when we reach the table, Cousin Rosalie will sit next to me and you will sit by her. But I've not asked yet how long you can stay. Must you leave when his lordship does?"

"Wat means to leave in the morning. I wish I could stay longer, though."

Robina grinned. "I'd love it if you could. Coklaw and Rankilburn are near enough that I think we should see each other much more often than we do."

"'Tis a good notion, that," Rosalie said, evidently overhearing their exchange easily enough. "You can help me furbish Robina up, Jannie. You have excellent taste yourself, and I expect you know the haberdasher in Hawick."

"Aye, sure," Janet said. "The mercer, too. Do you need furbishing, Robina?"

"Evidently," Robina said dryly, casting another look at Dev and Corinne.

⁓

Wat nudged Dev and murmured, "Your primary charge is shooting arrows at you with her eyes, my lad. Have you done aught to deserve them?"

Following Wat's gaze, Dev saw the three ladies approaching the dais but saw naught in Robby's demeanor to justify such a description.

Then she looked right at *him*. Her eyes flashed angrily.

Glancing at Corinne, he noted with relief that she had not heard Wat's comment. Her attention had riveted itself to the approaching women.

With a wary glance at Dev, she moved hastily past him to meet them.

"Well, my lad?" Wat said. "What did you do?"

"Nowt of which I'm aware," Dev said. "She does have a temper, though."

"That much I do know," Wat said dryly. "Nevertheless, I've staked my gelt on you," he added as he turned with a smile to speak to his grandaunt.

Behind Wat and Rosalie, and Lady Janet, who stood now beside Rosalie, Dev saw Robina talking to Corinne. Corinne's face was scarlet. She shook her head.

Rosalie moved past Wat then to greet Dev.

Smiling, he said, "I thank you for coming, madam. I hope they have made you comfortable."

"Potter will have everything in hand, sir," she said. Gesturing toward the plump, gray-haired woman stepping onto the dais in a blue gown and houppelande, she added, "There she is now. I trust you won't mind if she sups with us. I like to keep her nearby."

"Then it will be as you wish," Dev said, noting that Benjy had run into the hall and was heading at speed for the dais. "As you will see if you look yonder, you are also to be blessed with our young laird's presence. He reminded me that I'd promised to show him how a laird must behave. Quite a task, you'll admit, for one who is not, himself, a laird."

"You are now," she reminded him.

"In essence, aye," he agreed, shifting his gaze to Janet, whose air of easy dignity as she greeted him reminded him of Wat's lovely wife, Molly.

With luminous blue eyes and hair the pale yellow of bedding straw, Janet would soon be drawing a host of suitors if she was not doing so already.

As Lady Rosalie moved to stand behind the back-stool next to the one at his left, he said, "Pray, take your place beside me, madam."

"That is kind of you, sir, but—" Catching his direct gaze, she said, "Thank you, sir," and stepped to the nearer seat. Then, however, and firmly, she said to Janet, "Leave the one by me for Robina, dearling."

"Aye, sure, Aunt Rosalie. That way, we can each talk with her more easily."

Shifting his attention to Robina, now just a step away, Dev saw her eyes flash sparks again. But she made no comment. Moving silently and with her customary grace and regal posture, she took her place between Rosalie and Janet.

"Stirring coals, Davy?" Wat murmured.

"Your grandaunt's age and rank entitle her to that seat," Dev retorted.

Wat leaned closer to whisper, "If you value your hide, don't *ever* refer to her grandauntness or her age within her hearing. You missed a verbal lashing just now only because she had turned to speak to Robina."

Grimacing, but knowing he should have spoken more quietly, Dev shifted his stern gaze to the lower hall. When an expectant hush fell, he said the grace-before-meat, nodded to the waiting servants, and took his seat.

Dutifully, he talked with Rosalie until a lackey brought the meat platter and held it so Dev could serve her and himself. When the lad moved on to the other ladies, Dev turned back to Wat and saw that he was chatting with Benjy.

"Me brother Rab said you're a good master, m'lord," Benjy said. "I mean to be a good one, too. May I ask you another question?"

"Aye, sure," Wat said. "I remember how hard it was to take my father's place so unexpectedly. So if I can ever help, you need only send for me, and I'll come. If I'm away, my people will know that such a request must be fulfilled at once."

"Aye, well, we have Dev for now, so 'tis likely I willna

need to trouble you. But if aught happens to him..." The boy paused.

Wat touched Dev's foot with his own but did not look his way, so Dev knew he meant only to be sure he'd be aware of the exchange.

Taking care not to draw Benjy's attention, Dev continued to listen.

"Benjy," Wat said gently, "do you *expect* something to happen to Dev?"

"Well, me da's gone, your da's gone, me mam's gone, and now our Rab's gone," the boy said. "So I think it likely that Dev will go, too. Do not you, sir?"

"We all go sometime, Benjy," Wat said. "That is how God wills it. But sickness took your mam, and your dad's injuries in battle years ago likely hastened his death. My father had lived a good, successful life, but Dev is young and strong. Moreover, he's here at Coklaw, rather than out fighting other warriors, as he was when those ruffians killed Rab. I think Dev will be here for some time yet. Even so, if you need me, you send someone to fetch me. Do you understand?"

"Aye, sir, and I thank you."

Dev returned his attention briefly to the ladies' side, only to have his gaze collide sharply with Robina's narrowed eyes. Between them, Lady Rosalie attacked the food on her trencher with single-focused fervor.

He wondered then if Robby's irritation stemmed solely from his having seated Rosalie next to him, or from something else as well.

Rosalie certainly knew that her rank entitled her to the seat. She was also a guest, while Robina—mistress of the household and acting hostess or not—was merely the sister of the current laird and his predecessor. Had Rab or their father been alive, either might have asked her to sit by him. But, in all likelihood, both would have acted as Dev had and put the widowed baroness in the seat of honor.

However, Dev did not mean to let Robina go on eyeing him like a sullen bairn. He held her gaze with a steely one of his until Janet spoke to her and Robby turned to reply.

Dev returned his attention to his supper. He would speak to her later.

~

"That shade of pink suits you, Robby," Janet said. "I know Aunt Rosalie dislikes that kirtle, but one of your new dresses *must* be that color."

Having been wondering if Dev was as angry with her as he'd looked—and, if he was, whether she'd be able to explain her own anger to him—Robina felt nonetheless a touch of warm amusement, and relief, at Janet's comment.

Looking her in the eye, she said, "You are being tactful, Cousin Janet. You should know, though, that we recently turned out every kist and cupboard in this keep, and I have but four kirtles in various colors and conditions left."

"*Only* four kirtles! No gowns?"

"Four kirtles—brown, pink, lavender, and green. However, Dev has condemned the old green one to the rag-bag. I kept it for cleaning and mucking about, so I expect that henceforth, I shall have to ruin one of the others to please him."

"So he does require pleasing," Janet said with a smile.

Robina shrugged. "Men always want deft handling, do they not?"

"Aye, they do," Janet said with a low, soft chuckle that reminded Robina of the sound a contented hen might make.

It made Robina smile. "Don't you have to treat his lordship deftly?"

"Especially when he is *being* 'his lordship' instead of plain Wat," Janet said.

"Even so, he is not *Devil* Ormiston," Robina said.

"Nay, for 'Devil' suggests a fiery temper. Wat is... that is, his temper, is icy. His voice chills one to the bone, and he speaks in such a measured way that he makes one quake like a jelly. Worse, he continues speaking in that manner until one writhes inside and wants to promise anything to make him stop."

"Mercy," Robina said, glancing to her right. She saw only the back of Dev's head, because he was talking with Wat.

Benjy stood, clearly ready to depart, and she nearly made a motion to stop him. But he looked at Dev, cocked his head as if to say something, then sat down without speaking.

Deciding that Dev had reacted as she had to his getting up before his guests had finished eating, she turned back to Janet and said, "Does Wat often get angry?"

"Not with me," Janet said. "He has scolded me only twice in my life that I recall, but I've taken good care ever since to avoid stirring more than a chilly look. He is, by nature, a charming and kindly man, Robby. Usually, he reserves his wrath for those of his men or others who grievously offend him or one of his family."

"I think I prefer Dev's temperament, even so," Robina said. "He ignites into a fury, and he may wreak vengeance on whoever lit the flame. But that flame burns quickly and then is gone as if it had never been."

Memory of her sore backside having reminded her for

nearly a day afterward of what Dev had done to her the night they lifted the Turnbulls' beasts brought a warm flush to her cheeks. But if Janet noticed, she said naught of it.

They continued to chat in a friendly way until Lady Rosalie said, "I think we should remove to the solar, do not you, Robina? I brought some lengths of fabric with me that I'd like you to see."

Resigned to the fact that she was to be "furbished," Robina smiled and said, "Aye, cousin, I do think we should excuse ourselves."

Rosalie spoke quietly to Dev and rose. Dev and Wat stood, too, and Robina saw Wat make a gesture to Benjy, who leaped to his feet. When she moved to follow Rosalie, however, Dev stepped in front of her.

"Wait for me in that wee chamber across the landing," he murmured with a wry smile that, combined with his tone, struck her as being implacable rather than friendly. "I must have a word with Wat, and then I want to talk to you."

A chill slithered up her spine, but she straightened it and said with forced calm, "I hope it will not take long, sir. I must not abandon our guests."

In reply, he stepped silently aside to let her pass.

Aware that Janet, right behind her, had heard him, and feeling fire in her cheeks, Robina swept past him and followed Rosalie toward the landing.

~

Smiling at Janet, Dev said, "I shall bid you goodnight, my lady. I expect I shan't see you again until morning, but I hope you are enjoying your stay."

"I am, thank you, sir. I only wish I might stay longer.

Robina did say that she'd like that, too, but perhaps you will not permit it, or my lord brother may not."

"I've no objection, so let us ask him," Dev said, wondering if Robby had urged Janet to make the request. Whether she had or not, the lassie was welcome, so he turned to Wat and said, "Your sister and Robby have agreed that Janet should stay a few more days unless you object to that. Do you?"

Wat hesitated, gave Dev a long look, and shifted his gaze to Janet. "If you recall, Jannie, we did promise Mam and Gram that you'd return on the morrow. Moreover, I believe, you brought clothing for only one night."

"I brought two kirtles, one gown, slippers, and boots, sir, as well as two clean shifts and my cloak. I would fare well here, I promise you."

"Nevertheless, you won't want to break your promise to Mam or Gram, or to disappoint Bella." When her face fell, Wat waited a beat, as if, Dev thought, he expected more debate.

However, Janet remained silent, so Wat said, "I expect we'll return in a sennight or so. Then, perhaps you may stay longer."

Hugging Wat, she said with a smile, "That will be wonderful, sir. Tomorrow you'll wish you'd let me stay, though. You could depart much earlier without me."

He chuckled. "That is undeniably true. Enjoy yourself, lovey."

Bidding them both goodnight, she hurried from the dais.

Watching her, Dev said sagely, "You can easily bring both Lady Lavinia and Lady Meg round your thumb, can you not?"

"I can, but 'tis true that we promised. Moreover, my

friend, it occurred to me that you have enough on your trencher now without adding my sister to your burdens. We'll return in a week, earlier if you need us...or me."

Thanking him with unexpected relief, Dev told Wat to make himself comfortable in the inner chamber until his return and followed Janet from the hall.

At the landing, he watched her round the first curve above him before he opened the door into the room across the way and shut it behind him.

"Cousin Rosalie said I was not to be alone with you," Robina said then.

She stood near the south end of the wide table, facing him. Her left hand rested near the carved wooden box containing the penknife, sealing wax, and seal. From behind her, mote-ridden rays of the lowering sun through the arrow-slit streaked golden highlights in her hair, giving her an undeserved halo.

"Doubtless," she added when he remained silent, "Rosalie would say you should at least leave the door open."

"We'll have this talk without an audience," he said, his voice carefully even. "You ripped up at Corinne before supper, and you're angry with me, too. I want to know why."

When her cheeks darkened, he said, "Come now, Robby. You're rarely so reticent about sharing your thoughts. Tell me."

Pressing her lips tightly together, she glowered at him as if his statement of the simple facts had made her angrier. Then, straightening her shoulders and raising her chin, she said, "I shan't trouble you by explaining what I said to Corinne, sir. She is still innocent in the ways of men, though, so you should not encourage her to flirt with you. Nor should Cousin Wat."

Dev had all he could do not to laugh at her description of the forthright, obviously man-hungry Corinne. He'd seen the maidservant in the yard with Jem Keith. She flirted as naturally as she breathed and was as enticing and amiable a lass as he'd ever met. But Robby *was* an innocent. He would have to tread cautiously.

Or…perhaps not. He had been about to offer her a dismissive platitude when a second thought struck him, one that he was nearly certain would irk her. It might also reveal more of the truth than she wanted to reveal.

Accordingly, he said, "Are you saying that you believe Wat and I were flirting with your maid and the sight made you jealous, Robby? Is that it?"

Her jaw dropped, her eyes flashed, and for a long moment she remained speechless, staring at him. "Jealous!" she squeaked at last. "Me? Are you mad?"

"Do you think so? In troth, if I'm wrong, it much relieves my mind, because jealousy in a woman is most unbecoming. Her temper becomes uncertain and shrill. Her eyes lose their luster; and her lips grow chapped and ugly because, in her foolish misery, she chews them. Also, more times than not, she fails even to ask the chap if she has cause to *be* jealous. In this instance, *you* certainly have none."

Her mouth had fallen open again. She shut it. Then she said tartly, "I was thinking of Corinne's welfare, not of you or me."

"Blethers," he said. "You were jealous."

"I was *not*!" As she snapped the words out, she scooped up the wooden box with her left hand and hurled it and its contents at him. Her aim was uncannily accurate, too, especially as she had thrown the damned thing with her left hand.

Dev caught the box inches from his face with his left hand and the stoppered inkpot, when it lurched out of the box, with his right.

He let the lid and the other items crash to the flagstone floor.

After the clatter, silence fell.

⟶

Aghast at what she had done and hoping to avoid the likely Devilish consequence, Robina stepped hastily back, anxious to put the table between them.

"Stand right where you are," Dev ordered curtly.

Her legs threatened to fail her, so she obeyed, resting her hand on the table again to steady herself. What demon had possessed her to throw *anything* at him?

Then, to her shock, he smiled. "If you can shoot as accurately as you throw," he said, "I'd be a damned fool not to give you a bow and a quiverful of arrows."

"Father and Rab taught me to shoot *and* to throw," she said. Her voice felt shaky, so she cleared her throat. "I should *not* have done that."

"No," he said. "But I'm glad I had the privilege of seeing that throw. Pick up the penknife and the other things now, and don't *ever* do that again."

She did not reply but picked up the box lid and the wax sticks, seal, and penknife while he crossed the room to return the box and its inkpot to the table. He stood there, waiting, until she put the other items where they belonged.

She hesitated then, staring at the carving on the lid, grateful that it had not cracked, and seeking the will to face him again.

He put a hand to her shoulder. "Look at me, Robby."

She did, exhaling and squaring both shoulders to brace herself. But when her gaze met his, her mouth curved of its own accord into a weak but rueful smile. "I've never thrown anything at anyone before," she said. "I was so *angry*. Even so..."

"We'll say no more about that," he said quietly. "I do want to say one thing, though, and you would be wise not to rip up at me until you hear me out."

"I wouldn't dare," she muttered.

"Ah, Robby, if only I could believe that," he said, shaking his head. "However, the next time you rebuke a servant—or fly out at me in anger—consider first how much more you can achieve by doing so privately."

She nodded. "I do know better. Father was always respectful. He tried to teach me and Rab, but"—she swallowed hard—"but we both have such fiery tempers that..."

"I understand about fiery tempers," he said.

She looked away, bit her lip to keep from smiling at the understatement, and then looked back at him to say, "By my troth, Dev, I *will* strive to remember."

"Then I will, too," he said. He held her gaze, and suddenly, she could almost feel his warm lips against hers again. Then, hastily, he added, "Meantime, I expect you should rejoin Rosalie and Janet before one of them comes looking for you."

"I must see Benjy to bed first," she said.

"I'll see to the laddie," Dev said. "I want a word with him, too."

"Mercy, what has *he* done?"

"That, Robby-lass, is between Benjy and me. But don't worry; I'm not angry with him. I just want to get to know him better."

*Chapter 11* ———————————

Robina felt Dev's gaze until she rounded the first curve in the stairway. Glancing back, she listened for his footsteps and was relieved to hear none. The landing for the laird's chambers lay ahead, with her own room and Benjy's above it.

A peek into Benjy's room revealed only his neatly-made cot, so he had likely run outside to enjoy the improving weather and longer-lasting daylight.

The solar was above, in an angle with two chambers flanking it. The one that shared its landing had been Rab's. The other had a half-landing two steps higher.

Above, under the ramparts, were the Greenlaws' room and some smaller ones that shared a narrow central walkway.

Entering the solar, she found Rosalie and Janet chatting and joined them, pulling some of Benjy's mending from the basket there before she sat down.

Reaching for a pile of multicolored fabrics on a table near the window seat, Rosalie said, "Before you begin sewing, my dear, I want you to see these fabrics. I brought things for Janet and Bella, as I always do, and I thought of you when I saw these, especially this lovely saffron-gold silk. It will make up into a splendid gown for you to wear for Beltane."

"Mercy, madam, I cannot afford such fine goods," Robina said, eyeing them with quiet envy.

"Faith, I bring them as gifts. One cannot make up for years of neglect—"

"But you lived in England with an English husband," Robina protested. "Truly, madam, no one here *expected* you to visit us, let alone to bring gifts. I'd wager that, in those days, it could have cost you your life to come here."

Rosalie shrugged. "I disagree, but I understand why you'd think so, living as near the line as you do. At Elishaw, we were almost as often on the English side as the Scottish, because the line so often changed, but my mother was English, so I had cousins on both sides. Then my brother, Simon, declared for Scotland, so Elishaw is Scottish now."

"Even so, madam—"

"My name is Rosalie," she said. "If you must be formal, call me 'cousin' or Cousin Rosalie. 'Madam' always makes me think of older women like my mother," she added with an impish grin.

As if she were not an "older woman," herself, Robina thought, suppressing a smile as she agreed. Then, noting a twinkle in Janet's eyes, she knew that Janet felt the same fond amusement and returned her attention to the fabrics.

"I hope you won't be difficult about these, my dear," Rosalie said.

"I am not so ungrateful," Robina said. "It is just…"

"Just consider the greater likelihood of attracting suitors if you dress becomingly," Rosalie said when she paused. "I know that Sir David agrees with me. Janet and I can help you with your hair, too."

"What's wrong with my hair?" Robina demanded, and was instantly sorry. "Pray, forgive me, cousin. I *am* grateful and I welcome your advice. But—"

"But you are tired of being told what to do, aye?" Rosalie said. "I knew the instant I mentioned Sir David that I'd taken a misstep," she added. "I vowed I would *not* do that, that I would be the soul of tact and discretion . . . not that I have ever attempted either virtue successfully. But one does imagine that one ought to try."

Robina smiled then, recognizing a kindred spirit.

⁓

Dev found Benjy in the yard, playing a form of hoodman-blind with stable lads, who were all older and larger than he was. They wore hoods and were trying to capture a hoodless Benjy, who carried a string of small, noisy bells in each hand.

As Dev watched, Benjy wadded the bells in both hands, slipped silently between two of his would-be captors, and skipped away from the milling group. All of them were reaching out blindly, grabbing each other, and likely thought the boy was standing still.

Instead, he ran lightly and silently in his bare feet to the far side of the yard, where the sheepdog, Tig, lay alertly watching him. Bending as if to pet the dog, Benjy wrapped both strings of bells around Tig's neck. Then, with a sweep of his arm, he sent the dog running around the group of older lads and watched with delight as they stumbled over their feet and tried to catch Tig.

Benjy saw Dev then and grinned. Motioning the dog back to him, he snatched at the bells, caught one string, and waved the dog around again with the remaining one.

Shaking the string in his hand, Benjy dashed toward the gate, away from Tig. Half of his opponents moved toward the boy. The others followed the dog.

Then Tig rejoined him, and Benjy collected the second string and signaled for the dog to lie down again.

Dev motioned for the boy to join him.

Nodding, Benjy headed straight through the lads who were seeking him, ringing his bells as he went.

One of them—Dev thought it was Shag's son Hobby—reached out and caught the boy's tunic. But Benjy had untied its laces and easily slipped out of it.

"Here now, ye young deevil, that be cheating!"

"'Tis not; ye ha' to catch *me*!" Benjy shouted back, only to run full tilt into one of the others, who held on to him.

Laughing, Benjy surrendered. "Your turn to be prey now," he said cheerfully to his captor. "I'll take your hood."

"The sun has set, Benjy," Dev said. "Time to come inside and let these lads finish any chores they have left and get to bed themselves."

"Aye, sure," the boy said, handing the hood back to the lad and running to Dev. "That was fun," he said, grinning.

Ruffling his curls, Dev said, "It looked like fun, but that lad was right. You did cheat when you gave the bells to Tig."

"I know, but our Rab said that if a man needed to catch a breath, that was one way to find time for it, if the dog would cooperate. Tig follows my signals."

"I saw that. You and Rab have trained your dogs well, but come along now. I'm going to walk upstairs with you. I have something I want to discuss with you."

"Are you vexed wi' me then?"

"No, just curious about some things."

"Tell me what they be as we walk, then."

Dev almost told him that they should talk privately but realized that they could discuss one subject, at least. He said, "I was wondering if you might like a lad to help look after your things, the way my man, Coll, looks after me."

"But Coll is your squire, is he not, and squires dinna look after bairns. Also, Beany said I must learn to look after me own things."

"She is right. However, I doubt there is any rule against your having some help whilst you learn such things. You are rather old for women to be tucking you up at night, changing your bedding, and helping you dress, are you not?"

"I am *that*," Benjy said with feeling. "When our Rab was here, he'd tell me stories after I was in bed," he added with a sigh. "He told me about great battles, and about heroes like William Wallace and the Bruce. Beany tells me tales o' wee folk and funny things that our mam and dad or Rab used to do. I like both sorts, but I dinna need anyone to put me to bed. I ken fine how to get m'self there."

"I know some tales that I could tell you," Dev said when they reached the landing outside the boy's door and Benjy opened the door.

Turning with a grin, he said, "I'd wager you ken some good ones, too."

"I do," Dev said, following him in and shutting the door. "I might think of a short one now to tell before I return to Lord Buccleuch. He awaits me downstairs, likely plotting to defeat me again at chess, but there is another matter I want us to discuss first."

"That *does* sound as if ye're vexed," Benjy said, eyeing him doubtfully.

"I'm not, I promise. In fact, the boot may be on the

other foot, laddie, because I overheard something you said to his lordship."

Benjy frowned. "What was it?"

"You said you expected that I'd leave here or die, as your mam and dad and Rab did. You were speaking to his lordship in confidence, but I kept listening. Perhaps you would liefer I had not, Benjy, but I want you to know that I mean to stay here and see that you and Robina—and Coklaw—keep safe."

"I ken fine that ye mean that, Dev," Benjy said solemnly. "But men dinna choose their deaths, do they, or their bounden duties."

"That's true," Dev admitted. "But I promised Rab as he lay dying that I'd look after you and Coklaw, and see that you grow into a good man and a good laird. You're right to think of duty, and you know I owe mine to the Douglas and his grace, the King. The likelihood of either demanding service from me right now, though, is small. His grace is in the North, trying to tame his cousin, the Lord of the Isles, and will be there for some time. The Douglas sent me here and expects me to keep Coklaw from the greedy English."

"What if you do have to fight?"

"Then I'll arrange for my father and the Scotts to send men to look after you here. In any event, I'd like you to put your trust in me, Benjy. I don't insist that you do so, because one has to earn trust by being trustworthy. But do think about that, will you?"

"Aye, sure, Dev. I didna ken that ye'd promised our Rab whilst he were a-dying. But if a man makes such a promise, he must keep it, aye? Did ye swear as a Borderer?"

"Aye, laddie, I did," Dev assured him.

"Then that's how it will be. If ye think I should have a lad to help me look after me gear, I'm willing. I dinna think Beany will mind if I tell her that I'll learn to do it all m'self, too. So, now will you tell me a story?"

Robina spent the rest of the evening with Rosalie and Janet in the solar. Rosalie's woman, Potter, joined them when she came to ask when her mistress wished to retire and stayed because Rosalie asked her to help them advise Robina.

Squirming while the attire-woman looked her over from tip to toe, Robina held her tongue when Potter said, "As ye'll likely agree, mistress, her ladyship should confine her hair more tidily. Them plaits be too heavy and come loose too easily. She's still a maiden, so she need not wear a veil, but some nice netting would—"

"I'd liefer you not discuss me as if I were a plant to prune," Robina interjected then. "Nor do I want to stuff my hair in a net. I like it as it is, because I can tend to it mysel—"

Catching Janet's dancing gaze and the slight shake of her flaxen head, she broke off, saying, "You are all determined to make me miserable."

"Not miserable, dearling," Rosalie said. "But if you want a husband, you must—"

"I *don't* want a husband," Robina said impatiently. "I have Benjy to look after, and I love it here at Coklaw. Nor have I met anyone with whom I'd liefer spend my life. Men are too quick to command and rarely heed anyone save other men of their rank or higher."

"I won't argue that with you," Rosalie said. "But I can

assure you, dearling, a married woman has more freedom and power in her home than a sister does. I know, because I was a sister first and then a wife. As a widow with a generous portion, I make my own decisions now. Imagine how glorious it is to do that!"

"You have told me that before, cousin, and almost does that persuade me. However, I cannot seek a husband merely to murder him so I may join your company."

With a burst of laughter, Rosalie said, "I am so glad I decided to come to you, my dearling. You cannot imagine how many times I wanted to murder Richard Percy."

From then until Robina and Janet retired to their beds and Rosalie to hers, she entertained them with tales of life in England. Many of her tales drew laughter, but several made Robina wonder how she had stood it for so long.

After Robina dismissed a contrite, nearly silent Corinne for the night and shut the door behind her, Janet said from her side of the bed near the wall, "I did not like to ask whilst Aunt Rosalie was with us, or your Corinne, but did Sir David tell you?"

The question stopped Robina's breath in her throat, but Janet's calm gaze reassured her enough to say as she climbed into the bed beside her, "Tell me what?"

"I thought he had not. I asked if I might stay longer and told them that you'd like me to do so, but Wat said no."

"Mercy, why?"

"We did promise our mam and Gram that we'd return tomorrow. But I saw Wat look at Sir David first in that tentative way one has when one is considering another person's wishes or needs before answering a question."

"Well, if Dev dared to say no—"

"Nay, for I asked him first, and he said he had no objection. He did give me a look, too, then…almost the same look that Wat gave him."

Robina chuckled. "He likely wondered if I'd put you up to it."

"Do you think so? In troth, he seemed most sincere. Wat also said we will likely return soon, though, and I can stay then. That is the good news."

"It is," Robina agreed.

Despite being unaccustomed to sleeping with another in her bed, she slept well and awoke the next morning determined to show the well-meaning Rosalie that she could be compliant. Accordingly, when Corinne entered cheerfully with their hot water, Robina said, "I'd like you to brush my hair this morning, Corinne."

The maid's expressive eyebrows shot upward. "Aye, sure, mistress," she said. "But if ye're no going to do it the usual way, what will I do with it?"

Looking at Janet, whose pale gold tresses lay in their usual smooth, silky sheet to her waist, Robina said, "What do *you* think she should do?"

Cocking her head thoughtfully, Janet said, "You have long, thick, unruly hair, but I think that if she were to plait it carefully and wrap it round your head like a crown or a chaplet, it might look quite regal and gey becoming."

It sounded to Robina as if it would be horrid, heavy, and uncomfortable. However, having vowed to herself to accept Janet's advice, she did.

When Janet left to visit the garderobe, and while Corinne was still arranging Robina's hair, Robina asked curiously, "How does a woman *draw* men's notice, Corinne? I expect I should know that if they mean to plague me to seek a husband."

Corinne stared at her in surprise before her eyes began to twinkle. "Aye, well," she said. "I do ken more about that than about arranging hair, mistress."

◦

Dev went downstairs early to see his guests off, only to discover that Wat was still abed. He came down a short time later and said, "I decided to indulge myself and would wager that Jannie has made no appearance yet, either. The lass has no sense of time."

"Nevertheless, she's welcome here whenever she likes," Dev said, amused.

"I know that, but you know women." Regarding him more shrewdly, Wat added, "That is, you don't, of course, not as well as I do. Gellis has been married for a decade or more, has she not?"

Dev nodded. "I do remember what it was like to live with her, though."

"Perhaps, but Fiona adores you. Bella adores me, too. But I expect when she gets older, she'll exert herself to wind me round her thumb, as Jannie does."

"Sakes, Bella does that now," Dev said, grinning.

"True, but it's less worrisome when the 'woman' won't see her thirteenth birthday until October. However, I was not thinking of my sisters."

"Molly has you wound round her thumb, too."

"I can hold my own with Molly and my sisters, just as you do with Robby. However, I still have to contend with Gram and my mother."

"Aye," Dev said, knowing better than to comment on either one. "You do have more to contend with than I do, my lord. I acknowledge my blessings."

They were halfway through their meal when feminine voices from the stairs alerted them shortly before Janet and Robina entered the hall together.

Dev stared at Robby and heard a gasp beside him from Wat.

She wore a clean lavender-colored kirtle, but in place of the leather girdle she usually wore, she had knotted a purple-and-yellow striped ribbon round her hips with only her eating knife in its soft leather sheath attached to it.

But her hair was what had stirred his astonishment. Somehow, she had created two much tighter plaits and coiled them into a massive crown atop her head. The effect was rather alarming, although her face, looking almost pixyish beneath the mass and undeniably beautiful, also looked a bit more feminine and less like Rab's.

Beside her, Janet beamed.

Dev glanced at Wat, who likewise stared but got to his feet and moved to greet the two young women. Reminded of his manners, Dev stood, too.

Robby avoided his gaze and smiled at Wat. She lowered her lashes then, doubtless to watch her skirts as she stepped onto the dais. When she looked back up at Wat, she fluttered her lashes rather oddly.

Dev wondered if she had got something in her eye.

⁓

Covertly watching Dev through her lashes as she smiled at Wat, Robina decided that he had not even noticed the new way Corinne and Janet had arranged her hair.

She liked the new ribbon that Janet had given her to wear with the lavender kirtle. The hair was another matter. There was, she thought, too much of it to pile atop anyone's head. Errant strands escaped. Some were long enough to tickle her neck and cheeks, so she kept brushing them off with one hand or the other. Each time she did, Janet gave her a stern look, but Robina could not abide the tickling.

"By my troth, Robby," Janet muttered as they took their seats, "you *will* get used it, but do stop flicking your hands as if you were shooing flies. Gram would swiftly condemn such behavior. She certainly did so when I did that."

"But your hair is smooth and tidy," Robina protested. "This…"

"It is most becoming and one of the current styles of fashion."

Robina clenched her teeth. But Tad, the lad who helped serve the high table, was approaching with their breakfast, so she held her tongue.

The men, having finished eating, excused themselves. As they did, Wat said, "I trust you have sent your bundle down already, Jannie."

"Aye, I just have to wash my hands and fetch my cloak after I eat," she said.

"We'll be waiting outside with the horses," he said.

"Men," Janet said with a sigh. "You would think that *one* of them would notice how well you look this morning."

Robina shook her head. "Dev…that is, Sir David, did notice the other day when he thought I'd dressed like a maidservant, Jannie. But I doubt he'll offer me compliments now that he is the warden here at Coklaw."

"Och, aye, I forgot about that," Janet said. "Mam and Gram *were* concerned about your reputation."

"Aye, Dev said as much when he told me that Rosalie was coming."

When they'd finished eating and Janet had collected her cloak, Robina walked out to the yard with her to bid her farewell, with mixed emotions.

She understood why Wat had insisted they keep their promise, but she would miss Janet's company. Even so, the jar of coins called to her, and she hoped it was safe in its kist. Corinne or Ada might take a blanket or two out to exchange for others due for an airing. Surely, they would not take all four at once out, though.

Dev and Wat stood with the horses, and Benjy was with them, too. Minutes later their guests rode through the gateway. When the gate shut again, Benjy darted into the stable, shouting that he had promised to help Jem Keith.

Dev put a warm hand to Robina's back, between her shoulder blades. "I'll walk in with you," he said. "I expect you'll miss Janet."

"I will," she agreed. "Although we live only fifteen or sixteen miles apart, we have rarely spent time together. While my father was alive, we spent our holidays at Gledstanes with cousins in Peebles and other kinsmen."

"'Tis often the way of things," he said, guiding her toward the steps. "We make plans to visit kinsmen who live at some distance and assume that we can see the nearer ones anytime. But time passes swiftly."

"True," she said, smiling.

He looked at her then and smiled back. She felt an impulse similar to what she had felt on Sunnyside Hill just before she had kissed him. Briefly, she wondered how she had dared, but when his smile reached his eyes, she wanted to do it again.

Truly, she thought, it was as if he were two different

men, one stern enough to send chills up her spine, the other too attractive for her own good.

～

Her smile was like the sunrise—sudden, sparkling, and lighting up the world—and Dev was glad to see it. It warmed him all through, in more ways than one might expect. It was, he decided, a fortunate thing that the lady Rosalie had come to Coklaw to protect her.

～

Chukk watched from shrubbery on an east-facing hillside as the Lord of Buccleuch and Rankilburn departed from Coklaw on a well-muscled bay. A young fair-haired woman in a brown cloak with its hood thrown back rode a dun-colored horse beside him. His fighting tail, two-by-two, followed them.

He had heard that Buccleuch was there, so it was good that he was leaving. The fewer people at Coklaw, the better.

Although the sky was clear, the ground remained muddy, and thick ground fog had risen each night, covering the hills and lower areas till morning.

His hiding place was high enough to provide a panoramic view eastward, and had the hills around Ruber's Law not been in his way, he might have seen all the way to Jedburgh. The river Teviot flowed to the north, and from the hillcrest, he had seen the town of Hawick two miles to the northwest. Southwest of him, his men waited in the maze of rugged hills above Liddel Water, yet well away from Hermitage.

He had come to Coklaw alone, so he dared not let them

catch him. He had wanted to see how it looked by daylight, to plant his bearings firmly in his mind.

The castle was starkly visible, its tower keep thrusting skyward surrounded by a solid stone wall. He saw figures on the wall walk, ever watchful. He could also see the grassy rise southeast of the wall in the wide clearing that surrounded it. Doubtless, watchers also watched from nearby hills, but anyone who saw him would likely take him for a shepherd, perhaps seeking lost sheep.

If he could watch Coklaw for a time without drawing notice, he might learn something useful or see a way to get close enough to dig. Digging quietly enough would not be easy, either. Even at a distance, he could see grass and weeds growing on the rise.

He'd need a shovel or at least a sharp spade. Today, wanting to look like a shepherd, he'd brought only a shepherd's crook and a dirk with him.

Perhaps the dirk would suffice if he could get close enough, unseen.

Until he knew more, he'd keep watch and see what he could see during a day's time...or over the next few days, if he could stay hidden.

His men would wait. They knew better than to abandon him.

# Chapter 12 _____

Robina had little time in the next few days to miss Janet or do aught save accede to Lady Rosalie's wishes. They spent Thursday afternoon looking through clothing kists that Ada had stored away after Robina's mother died.

When Robina protested, Rosalie had scoffed. "Do not think I mean for you to wear any of these, dearling. They are long out of fashion. But we may find use for some of the fabrics. In troth, you may be surprised by what we find."

Fortunately, in Robina's view, moths had ruined some of the fabrics, and most were sadly thin. Moreover, since Robina had inherited her father's coloring, rather than her mother's flaxen hair and pale complexion, Rosalie declared the soft pinks and pale blues that Lady Gledstanes had favored too insipid for Robina.

"At least, now we can have someone turn them all into useful rags," Rosalie said briskly Friday morning as they broke their fast. "We can also visit the shopkeepers in Hawick today with a good conscience."

They set out after breakfast with Rosalie's equerry, Ned Graham, and an escort of six riders, led by Jock Cranston.

Robina would have preferred having Sandy in charge, but when Dev said she could take Jock and three of his men, or he'd go himself, she agreed to Jock. She was certain that, with Dev and Rosalie advising her, she'd want to murder one if not both before day's end. Jock would offer no opinions about how she should dress or wear her hair.

Rosalie had arranged Robina's hair herself that morning in two long plaits, looped, twisted together at Robina's nape, and contained in some black netting of Rosalie's. "We'll find lighter netting more suited to your hair at the haberdasher's, dearling," she said when Robina grimaced. "But you must accustom yourself to dressing like a lady."

Robina had been tempted to take a few coins from the jar to spend but Rab had warned against it: *"Rosalie would surely ask where you got them!"*

Having survived a productive day in town, she nearly lost her temper the next morning when Rosalie insisted on plucking her eyebrows.

"I do not agree with the current fashion of shaving one's front hair, let alone one's eyebrows," Rosalie said, clamping her tweezers onto one errant hair and yanking it out. "We do want a well-defined arch, though, so don't wince like that unless you want me to pluck too much in error. Sir David said only this morning how much you remind him of your twin brother. But, I vow, he will not say so if we can tame your eyebrows. I shall dab a touch of pomatum on each when I finish, to lay them flat."

*"Sakes, what's wrong wi' twins looking like twins?"*

Since Rab had seldom spoken to her in recent days, Robina jumped at the sound of his voice and nearly got the tweezers in her eye.

"Do sit still," Rosalie said. "I vow, you are as twitchy as Benjy. Did you see how Sir David stared at you last night? I think he has begun to see how feminine you can be."

*"He's got nae business staring at you at all. Tell him to stop."*

Suppressing her annoyance, Robina said, "Good sakes, madam, why should I want him to notice me that way? Does he think me *un*feminine?"

*"God bless us, you like the man!"*

Mentally retorting that she did *not* like Dev, Robina fought to conceal any outward display of her shock.

Rosalie shrugged. "You may not care about such things yet, dearling," she said. "But he *is* a man, and one can often judge how others will react by the way those nearest one do. You have likely drawn no such interest before now, as busy as you've been seeing to Benjy. But you won't want to continue seeing to his needs after the laddie takes a wife. Only think how horrid it would be to live here at Coklaw with a much younger good-sister giving the orders, whilst you look after her squalling bairns."

"Have mercy, madam! That *cannot* happen for at least a decade."

"Blethers, many men marry at fifteen and can legally marry younger," Rosalie said. "Benjy is nine, so that is just six years away. He will begin taking interest in girls sooner than that, too, horrified though he may be now by the thought. Worse, you have just turned nineteen, more than old enough to be married, Robina. By the time Benjy begins seeking a wife, if you *don't* have bairns of your own with a man of your own…"

*"Mayhap even twins of your own,"* Rab chortled.

Robina's head began to ache. She liked Rosalie and enjoyed her company, but there were times when she feared that the woman would drive her mad.

Sunday afternoon, Robina declared as she arose from

the table after their midday meal that she meant to ride into the countryside to clear her head, only to have Rosalie and Dev say in chorus that she must not.

"Not until I can arrange a suitable escort," Dev added. "Jock Cranston and Rosalie's Ned heard in Hawick that the raiders have been raiding again."

"East of us, aye," Robina told them, fighting to keep her temper. "But if any were near enough to stir trouble here, I've heard naught of it."

"Even so," Dev said, "you must not ride out alone."

"Then come with me," she said impulsively, adding a belated smile.

Caught off guard for once, having expected her to argue more, Dev realized that Robby was truly unconcerned about raiders. Moreover, he wanted to ride with her. He waited for Rosalie to speak, but she turned away to say something to her woman, and Robby did not invite her to ride with them. "Very well," he said. "I'll go."

When they reached the stables and he found that Sandy had bridled Black Corby for her and had strapped a Borderer's flat leather saddle to the stallion's back, he snapped, "What the devil do you mean by this, Sandy?"

"The laddie needs exercise, sir, and since Master Rab's equerry died in that fracas, as I thought ye knew, none o' the lads here can ride him," Sandy said, surprised. "Her ladyship did send earlier to ask that I fetch him out for her."

Robina said, "You know I can ride him, Dev, and he needs exercise. He's had almost none since you arrived, due to the rain and..." She bit her lower lip.

"...and due to my presence and your knowledge that

I'd object," he said, giving her a stern look. "If he needs exercise, one of my lads or yours can see to it."

Sandy opened his mouth, but Robina forestalled him by asking sweetly, "Which of your lads do you like least, sir? Or have you forgotten how Rab trained his horses? Recall that the men who attacked you did not steal Corby, *and* that you had to lead him home."

Nettled, he said, "Do you think I could not ride him?"

"In troth, I don't know," she replied, meeting his gaze. "You ride as well as Rab did, if not better. *Have* you ridden Corby?"

"No," he answered honestly. The truth was that he'd have liked to try the stallion's paces, but Rab had never allowed it. Memories of things that Rab had told him about the horse began coming back to him.

"I expect you could teach him to mind you if you exerted the patience to do it," Robina said thoughtfully. "However, if you expect to beat him into submission..."

"I don't," Dev retorted. "Rab evidently taught him to accept you, though."

"Do you want to test me, to see if I can manage him?" she asked with a soft but teasing smile.

Sandy looked down at the ground, doubtless hiding his own smile, but Dev knew when he'd lost.

"Stow your mockery, lass," he said. "He's no horse for a lady, but I know you can ride him. I've seen what Corby can do when he loses his temper, though. That was the first thought I had when I saw that you meant to ride him."

"He never loses his temper with me, but I'll forgive you for your lack of confidence in us," she said. "Prithee, Sandy, give me a leg up."

Freezing Sandy in place with a look, Dev said, "Let

me, Robby." Making a stirrup with his hands, he hoisted her up, watching as she arranged her skirts and settled herself astride. In the process, she revealed that although she was barefoot, she wore the damnable breeks again, under her skirts.

"What the...?"

Grinning, she said, "I do possess *some* modesty, and riding astride is more comfortable with them. One can never get one's skirts underneath one just right."

Stifling a chuckle, he easily imagined that skirts, although useful for padding, could create problems for a rider.

The stallion stood as if rooted until she patted its neck. It acknowledged the pat with a toss of its glossy head, a snuffling snort, and a prancing shuffle or two.

"Corby is eager to go," Robby said. "You do still mean to come with us?"

"I do," Dev said, seeing with relief that Jock was leading Auld Nick out. The two stallions were well acquainted and well mannered unless bad manners were commanded or the order of the day, such as in battle.

"I thought we might ride up Sunnyside Hill," Robina said. "It will be good exercise for them, and we can see how Rab's grave has fared since our last visit. Then, if we ride down the other side, we can let the horses out on the flatter road home."

He agreed and let her lead. For a time, he scanned the surrounding country as they rode. But the woods grew thicker, and birds and other forest creatures began to chatter to each other, so he relaxed and let himself enjoy the day.

He also admired Robina's light hands and natural posture, as well as Corby's quick response to her slightest gesture or command. She was, he decided, much safer on Corby than she would be walking alone in the woods. Aware that he'd be unwise to say so, he watched silently and admired.

As they passed through a clearing that gave a view to the west, he felt a strange prickling that he recognized as the sense of someone watching him. Looking westward, he saw only the range of hills that separated them from Slitrig Water.

Robina looked, too, making him wonder if she sensed the same thing.

"What is it?" he asked her.

"Naught," she said, glancing over her shoulder at him. "I've been breathing in the fresh air and enjoying what one might call the peaceful clamor of the woods. The path from here on is wide enough for two horses, though."

Accepting the tacit invitation, it occurred to him that he ought to have had one of the lads ride behind them. Rosalie would likely say something about that, although she had not objected when Robby invited him.

He'd been grateful to the older woman for letting him handle the situation, but he was sure she would disapprove of the two of them riding alone together.

As he urged Nick up beside Corby, Robby smiled at him, and her smile warmed him as it always did.

"Art glad you came?" she asked.

"Aye," he said. "How far out do your watchers stay?"

"They are not just ours, sir. Watchers are everywhere hereabouts, so word spreads quickly when English raiding parties creep northward."

"So you knew raiders were coming when your own stock was lifted?"

She grimaced. "Those were Scots, I'm sure, not English—a small party, too."

"Were the cows and sheep you lifted your own, then?"

"I don't know. We just took what we needed."

"From the same people who took yours."

She was silent, and when he glanced her way, he saw that she was nibbling her lower lip, staring straight ahead.

At last, she turned and looked at him. Wetting her lips, she said, "You know how it is, Dev. One takes what one needs. I think the Turnbulls took ours, but one cannot be sure unless one catches them at it. No one saw them that night, but the tracks led to Langside. We needed a good cow, and wool to trade, so..." She shrugged.

He winced, certain she could not know the risk she had run. Scottish Borderers did take from their neighbors as often as they took from the English, but anyone who caught a raider could lawfully hang him, or her.

"Don't say what you're thinking," she said. "The day has been pleasant so far, and the graveyard lies just ahead."

He kept quiet, but his thoughts were busy. Somehow he had to teach her to have more concern for her own safety.

~

Watching Dev, Robina was grateful for his restraint. They reached the graveyard soon afterward and dismounted to look at the grave. She sensed Rab's presence strongly as they stood there, but he kept silent, too.

"What is it, Robby? Art sad again?"

Startled, she said, "Not sad, just pensive."

"I think you have been pensive since I arrived, or longer," he said. "Keeping secrets, or thinking about Rab?"

Uncertain how to reply, since the truth was unaccept-able, she realized that silence was just as bad. Dev would surely suspect that she was keeping something from him.

She would have liked to tell him about the jar of coins, but Rab's warning was sensible. And, in truth, whether Dev was currently master of Coklaw or not, the money belonged to Benjy, not to Dev.

The thought was disheartening, and she wished Rab would recall that he had trusted Dev. Confiding in him should be not only safe but sensible.

Rab, however, remained as silent as his grave.

"We should head back down," she said with a sigh.

"Keeping secrets then," Dev said grimly. "Don't you trust me?"

"Oh, Dev, no, don't think that," she said, putting a hand to his arm, shocked that he had so nearly guessed her thoughts. "I know I've been a bit difficult, but—" Break-ing off when he grinned, she said bluntly, "Do you think that was funny?"

He shook his head and bit his lower lip.

"Damnation, David Ormiston, do you dare to *laugh* at me now?"

"Nay, nay, I'm striving mightily *not* to laugh or to say what I'm thinking."

"Just *what* were you thinking?"

"That when you refuse to tell me what *you* are thinking and then say that I'm mistaken to suspect a lack of trust, you make me want to kiss you one minute and put you over my knee the next. But, by heaven, if you swear at me again, I'll—"

"I won't swear," she said hastily. "But neither will I tell you all I think. Some things are still private, sir, one's thoughts especially so. But if you want to kiss me again," she added, feeling suddenly and strangely shy but determined, "you may."

"May I?" He raised his eyebrows. "I will admit that I enjoyed your kiss when we were here before. But others would say that I'd taken advantage of you."

"They would be wrong," Robina said. "I kissed you first. I wanted to know how it would feel, and now I want to know if it feels the same way whenever one kisses a man. I do trust you with my virtue, Dev."

"Do you, Robby? You should not be so trusting. Sithee, I'm not certain I can trust myself. You're a mighty tempting wench. But there are rules."

"Bother the rules," she said. "Do you not *want* to kiss me?"

"Aye, sure, I do," he responded, pulling her roughly into his arms.

Uncertain now, but curious, she looked up and tried to gauge his mood. But he allowed her no time for that before his lips claimed hers, hot and demanding.

As he held her close, she heard him moan quietly in his throat.

⁓

Dev heard his moan, too, and realized that she had bewitched him. He wanted her in every way—other than marriage, of course, he reminded himself brutally. He suspected, though, that her invitation had just been an attempt to avoid answering his question about the secrets she was keeping from him.

The pliskie lass needed a lesson, and he needed release for his own emotions or whatever it was that inflamed his body, if only to show her the dangers of tormenting men... one man, at least.

Thrusting his tongue into her mouth and finding it hot inside and yet softly yielding, he pressed his lower body tightly against hers, letting her feel his desire.

She was too short, but a flat-topped boulder sat nearby. Without warning or sign, he lifted her to stand on it and did so without releasing her mouth.

For once in her life, she did not fight him but wrapped her arms around him and held him as tightly as he held her.

Raising a hand to her nape, he felt the thickly coiled plaits and wished he could pull them loose, unplait them, and let her unruly hair fly free.

Her tongue danced against his, as if she knew just what to do, thus stirring him to wonder if she had done such things before, and with whom. Was that why she had begun to dress differently and to do such odd things to her hair?

He stroked the plaits with his fingertips, and caressed the soft nape beside and beneath them while he raped her mouth with his tongue. She tasted minty, so he knew she had rubbed mint leaves against her teeth when she'd cleaned them.

His body yearned for hers, but he dared not even muss her hair, since neither of them could redo it, and anyone seeing her afterward would guess what they had done. Instead, he forced his hand down between her shoulder blades, encouraging her soft breasts to press against his chest.

Seconds later, without thought for consequence, he slid a seeking hand to her side and up to cup the nearest breast.

Hearing her gasp and deducing that no man had done

*that* to her before, he brushed her nipple with his thumb and rubbed it a little, drawing a stronger gasp.

To his delight, she pressed closer, as if she would rub both breasts against him. His cock strained for release from its confinement.

The two sensations, together, brought Dev abruptly to his senses.

His inner devil had nearly overcome him, and it was a wrench to thwart it. But he knew that if he did not stop at once, he would not stop at all, so he gripped her firmly by her upper arms and stood her back a little atop the boulder.

Her eyes were glowing with desire and something else…curiosity perhaps. If that was so, his awakening conscience suggested, mayhap it *had* been only feminine curiosity that stirred her to invite another kiss.

Pushing that thought away, he eyed her warily, wondering what she would say.

~

"Why did you stop?" Robina demanded.

"Because this is neither the time nor the place for such activities. Nor is it wise for the Warden of Coklaw to kiss and fondle the lassie he has sworn to protect."

"But I invited it," she said. "And I enjoyed it. You did, too, I think."

"Our enjoyment is irrelevant," he said. "It was wrong of me, and you are not always wise. Moreover, I suspect that your invitation may have been merely another attempt to avoid answering my question."

"Was it? I own, I've forgotten the question. Did you ever truly ask me one?"

"The subject was secrets," he said, giving her a stern

look. "I sense strongly that you are keeping things from me, Robby. You react oddly to things I say, and to things that others say. At times, you seem to ignore us all, as if you don't hear us speak."

"If I do that, I apologize," she said sincerely, suspecting he referred to instances when Rab had spoken to her. She could not recall if he'd ever spoken to her while she was with Dev, but she did recall more than once that she'd wished he would and he had not.

"I don't want an apology," Dev said. "I want an answer. What secrets are you keeping from me?"

"Not one," she said evenly. It was not a lie, exactly. She was keeping at least three secrets that she could think of offhand: the jar of silver coins, Rab's warnings and advice to her, and her ambivalence about Benjy having a manservant. She had not been able to think of anyone who might suit such a post.

"I won't press you," Dev said in a tone that made her avoid his gaze. "But whatever it is, you'd be wise to tell me before I find it out for myself."

Her relief that he would drop the subject only added to the guilt he'd made her feel. Even so, she could not just blurt out that she'd found a jarful of silver coins. Nor could she bring herself to tell him about Rab.

They rode silently until they reached the grassy flat, when Dev suggested they let the horses run. Robina immediately urged Corby forward, and he was soon in full gallop.

She wished that the wind in her face would blow away her guilt before she had to face Dev again, or that she could think of something to tell him that would not make him suspect that she'd lost her mind.

Dev watched admiringly as Robby pulled away from him on Corby. Most Border women rode well, but she was exceptional. She rode as well as any man he had ever watched and better than many of them. Her hands were light, her seat on the horse made her look as if she were an extension of it, and her hands and knees were so deft that she seemed to be communicating with the stallion mentally.

He indulged his enjoyment, watching her until she glanced back over a shoulder and grinned, clearly challenging him, and urged Corby to a faster pace.

"Well, Nick, shall we show them?" he asked. Nick's ears twitched, which was answer enough. They followed the track around the hill to the north side, and when the tower came in sight, he urged Auld Nick to his fastest pace.

The two stallions were almost neck and neck when they neared the castle clearing and she slowed Corby. Dev reined Nick in, too.

Robby met his gaze with rosy cheeks and pure delight. "I haven't done that for far too long," she said, grinning again.

"Not since Easter night, at all events," he retorted.

She grimaced. "Are you going to throw that up to me forever?"

"No," he said, smiling warmly. "I said what came into my head, with no ill intent."

"Then, as a reward, I'll tell you one thing that has been on my mind, which is whether Benjy is old enough to have a servant of his own. That's not a secret, because we did mention it briefly the day we finished planting Rab's tree. You agreed with Ada and Corinne then that it was a good notion, but I still have mixed feelings about it."

Dev nearly told her that he'd already discussed it with Benjy and had begun arranging for such a lad, because the boy's need had struck him from the outset. But the good angel that perched on his shoulder from time to time to warn him against such direct statements nudged him before he spoke.

He said tactfully, "I do think Benjy is old enough."

"Aye, perhaps, but I know of no one who might serve him who would not need as much training as Benjy does."

"I saw someone the other night, whilst Benjy played hoodman-blind with some of the older lads in the yard. One lad seemed to keep an eye on him as much for the boy's safety as for sake of the game. I thought then that my squire might train him as an aide, so Coll has taken him in hand. But..."

"But that is an excellent idea, sir. Coll takes good care of you. Who is it?"

"A chap called Ash Nixon."

"Aye, Ash is a sweet-tempered lad. He must be twelve or thirteen, too, a good age to look after Benjy without seeming to be his minder."

As they approached the gate, already opening to admit them, Dev glanced at her. She looked pleased with herself, smiling a secret little smile.

His temper stirred. So she thought she had outwitted him, did she? He'd just see about that.

# *Chapter 13* _____

Despite the way Dev had set her so abruptly back on her heels at the graveyard, Robina thought that, for once, she had managed him deftly. Or perhaps Rosalie was right and he did think she looked too much like Rab and was unfeminine. However, she decided with an inner sigh, Dev ought to be satisfied now that she had revealed the secret he'd suspected her of keeping. That would benefit Benjy, too.

Dev let her dwell in that happy state until they returned and went inside. Assuming that he'd go into the hall or the inner chamber, and meaning to go to her bedchamber, Robina gave him her sunniest smile.

"Thank you for a pleasant afternoon, sir," she said. "I hope you enjoyed it, too."

"I did," he replied evenly, but the flintlike look had returned to his eyes.

"I...I mean to order a bath," she said. "I must wash my hair, too. It takes a long time to dry and longer for Corinne to arrange it to Cousin Rosalie's liking."

"That is one thing *I'd* like to discuss," he said in a more affable tone.

"Prithee, not now, and not in that wee room again."

"I agree that that room is too small," he said. "Also, someone might interrupt us there. We'll talk in the inner chamber."

His tone remained affable, but the look in his eyes daunted her. Much as she'd have liked to defy him, she knew she'd be wiser to submit. She had held her own with him before. She could do so again.

The trestle tables were already up in the lower hall. The dais was empty, but someone had begun laying the high table for supper. Dev stepped ahead of her to open the inner-chamber door, followed her inside, and shut it.

Taking matters into her own hands, Robina turned to him and said, "Did I understand you correctly, sir? You want to discuss my *hair*?"

"Among other things," he said.

"You said that, aye. But I must tell you that I've received so much unwanted advice about my hair and my clothes, *and* my behavior, that I'm likely to fly out at the next person to criticize me, even you."

"I'm just curious to know what has stirred you to such a pitch that you seem to be changing everything about yourself."

"Faith, as if you were not one who said—more than once, I believe—that I must learn to be more femin…that is, to behave more like a lady!"

"Behavior is one thing, Robby. Attire and hair arrangements are other matters. Did Rosalie persuade you into all those plaits looped about your ears today?"

"'Twas Janet first, with my plaits twisted into a crown, which I could not bear," she said grimly. "Then Rosalie told Corinne that we should try twisting them at my nape instead. That was better, but today she asked Corinne to do it this way. She said I should wear a veil, too, but I don't like to wear things on my head."

"Then don't," he said, as if it were that easy. "Do you hate all the garments that Rosalie is having the Hawick seamstress make for you, too?"

"I like the clothes better than what they've done to my hair," she admitted. "Rosalie gave me some lovely saffron-colored silk that Mistress Geddes is making into a gown much like a kirtle, although it is to fasten behind. The bodice will have fancywork, and its sleeves will have silk-covered buttons. Rosalie assures me that the dress will suit any formal occasion, although I don't know when I'll attend one."

"Beltane is coming," he reminded her. "Things are not all so bad, then."

"I'd liefer not complain, but I'll tell you how it has been," she said. "Sithee, I don't know what is fashionable and what is not, so I feel as if I must listen to everyone and try to please everybody except myself. I try to follow Rosalie's advice, especially. But when I look in a mirror, I don't see *me* anymore."

Dev bit his lower lip, and his eyes gleamed suddenly with humor.

"What?" she demanded, feeling her temper awaken despite her relief that the hard look had left his eyes. "You are laughing at me again, Dev, and I won't have it. All these plaits feel as if imps are pulling my hair all day. Rosalie said I'd get used to it and that I must accustom myself to dressing like a lady. Corinne says—"

"Never mind what they say," Dev interjected. "Ignore them, Robby. They are all daft, even Janet. You were perfect as you were, even in those damned breeks and that too-big-for-you leather jack. Why, you are so beautiful that if I were in any position to wed, I'd have asked you to marry me straightaway."

"What's this I hear?" Lady Rosalie exclaimed as she pushed the door open and strode in, beaming at them both. "*Marry*! How wonderful! Prithee, forgive me for intruding at such a tender moment, but I could not be more delighted. You are perfectly suited to each other. I own, though, I dared not hope that *this* could happen until much later on. But this is utterly splendid!"

"Oh, no, Cousin Rosalie!" Robina exclaimed. "It is not what—"

"*Not another word!*" Rab snarled in her ear, silencing her.

As she stood, agape, Rosalie said, "Blethers, dearling, I heard the man. And, if he wants to marry you straight-away…" She shifted her gaze to Dev, adding, "Surely, you did not propose to her like that only to say that you meant naught by it, sir. I've seen how you look at each other whenever you're in the same room. You were made for each other."

~

Fighting to collect his wits and noting that Robby was still agape—as if some powerful force had muted her—*and* that Tad and another serving lad were peering wide-eyed at him over Rosalie's shoulder, Dev drew breath and decided on diversionary tactics.

Dismissing the lads with a wave, he said mildly to Rosalie, "Did you have a reason for coming here, madam?"

"I did, aye," she said, "although I cannot think now what it—I vow, sir, your proposal has muddled my brain.

Oh, aye, Greenlaw sought you earlier, but you had not returned from your ride. Evidently, a messenger came here earlier from Ormiston. One of the maidservants told me that she thought she'd seen you come in here, so I meant just to peek in to see if she was right. Then I heard—"

"Is aught amiss at Ormiston?" Dev demanded, knowing she might chatter on until she ran out of breath.

"Nay, for the messenger rode on to Hawick. He came only to tell us your father will arrive on Friday. He'll be delighted to learn of your betrothal, I'm sure, so we could plan the wedding for Saturday. 'Tis the eve of Beltane, when new home fires are lit, so 'tis the ideal time for a wedding. Buccleuch has a new priest, too. Since Coklaw lacks one, and since I must send word of your betrothal to Scott's Hall, perhaps you would like..."

She paused then, eyeing Dev hopefully, but he was still collecting his wits.

⌒

Her twin having fallen silent after his outburst, and Dev now silent himself, Robina said, "By my troth, Cousin Rosalie, I do not see how you—"

"Don't quibble, lass," Dev said quietly. "I did give her cause. But, my lady," he added, facing Rosalie, "I think you inferred more than either of us meant to say. In any event, you will agree that Robina and I have much to discuss. I'd be obliged if you would put off sending word of any kind to the Hall or elsewhere until we have talked again."

Rosalie frowned but said, "I'll leave you two to talk. But you must realize, sir, that if what I heard was not what you meant to say, you have no business being alone with her. I suspect it's not the first time you've taken advantage this way, either. Do you deny that?"

"No, madam."

Robina stifled a gasp, fearing that he might try to explain *why* he had been privy with her at other times. But he said no more.

Rosalie nodded. "I'll leave you alone then, but I suggest that you talk quickly. People are gathering in the hall for supper, and when they see the pair of you emerge together, *they* will talk."

Robina watched her go and waited until the door shut behind her before she said, "She'll send Ned Graham to tell Lady Meg, Dev. I feel sure of it."

"It doesn't matter," Dev said, putting a gentle hand on her shoulder. "To think that I feared we might be overheard in the wee room and thought no one would hear us in here. Robby, two of the serving lads were right behind her."

"Do you think she did it purposefully?"

He grimaced. "I'll admit that I'd like to think so. It would make me feel less of a dolt. But I've seen enough of Rosalie to know that she says what she thinks and is not one who listens at doors. She *is* impulsive enough to draw a conclusion and act on it without due reflection, though."

"Then what are we to do?"

"I'll do whatever you want to do, lass," he said in that same quiet way. He looked steadily into her eyes, as if he expected to see her thoughts.

The look warmed her but also made her nervous. She said, "I cannot make that decision, Dev. I know you don't want to marry me or anyone else."

"It *would* save me from Anne Kerr," he said lightly.

"What has Anne Kerr to do with this?"

"My lord father hoped to announce our betrothal in a sennight or so," he said. "He invited the Kerrs to celebrate Beltane with us and was kind enough to tell me of his plan after he summoned me home."

Robina felt as if her heart had stopped. She could barely draw a breath but managed to say, "But *are* you betrothed? Why did you not tell me?"

"We are *not* betrothed, nor had I any intention to be," Dev said. "In troth, I think Father had gone off the notion himself before I left for Scott's Hall. He'd already issued the invitation, though, so Kerr might be expecting a betrothal. I suggested that my brother Lucas might suit Anne better."

A gurgle of laughter escaped her. "You didn't!"

"I did. The lady Anne is much too staid and cheerless for me."

"Even so, you do not want to marry anyone else, aye?"

"We can discuss that later," he said. "The one thing Rosalie said that *is* true, thanks to her declaration and the two lads who heard it, is that people *will* talk."

"Perhaps I should hang my head and look browbeaten. Then they'd assume you'd just been taking me to task again. That *was* your purpose in bringing me here, aye?"

"Not to browbeat you, Robby, but to try to understand you better. We must discuss this all later, though, because I agree that Rosalie is unlikely to keep her belief to herself. Nor is she likely to admit that she was mistaken about what she heard."

"But if we can keep her from telling Lady Meg and Wat—"

"Sakes, she won't need to send word if she tells her

equerry or anyone else at Coklaw. I'd wager that Tad and Alf have already told people in the kitchen, come to that. You know how quickly such news spreads, throughout the Borders."

She did know. What she did not know was how they could overcome Rosalie's error. She did not want to marry Dev.

*"Then what man* do *you want to marry, Beany? A Douglas? Who could live up to your standards if Dev does not?"*

Rab's question was unanswerable. She did not realize that tears had welled in her eyes until one trickled down her cheek.

Dev brushed it away with a thumb. "Don't cry, lass. I meant what I said. I'll marry you if you want me—nay, if you will *have* me. A man could do worse, *much* worse."

She wanted to smack him. As the thought crossed her mind, her hand flew up, but he caught it easily and held it. "Naughty," he murmured. Then, ruefully, he said, "I'll admit that I provoked it, though. What a *daft* thing to say to you!"

"You should have saved it to use in persuading your father," she said. "What if he hears about it before he arrives? Would he not forbid you to marry me?"

"No," Dev said. Again he looked rueful.

"But if he expects you to marry Anne Kerr—"

"I should not have mentioned that," he interjected, meeting her gaze. "Father knows that I would not agree to that. Furthermore—although I wager this will seal my fate with you—he was the first to suggest that I should be Warden of Coklaw, when I told him that Archie wanted to install someone here."

Robina frowned. "But why, if he'd decided you should marry Anne Kerr?"

Grimacing, Dev said, "Because of your Ormiston estate. Sithee, it was originally one of ours and got caught up in the cross-border land-swapping years ago."

"Is that why you're willing to marry me now, to get the Ormiston estate?" The disappointment she felt nearly overwhelmed her.

"Sakes, lass, do you think so little of me that you can believe that?" he demanded. "Even if splitting Ormiston off from Coklaw made sense, what manner of guardian would I be to take such base advantage of Benjy as that?"

"I...I didn't think of that," she admitted. "I know you would not betray Benjy like that...or Rab."

"Or you," he said, his tone gentle again. "You are just as important as they are."

"I know that you loved Rab as a brother," she said, looking into his eyes again, "and that I—"

"If my feelings for my own brothers are aught to judge by, I cared much more about Rab than that," Dev said. "We understood each other so well from the first time we fought side-by-side that talking was rarely necessary."

"I know," she said with a sigh. "I remember how often you would just look at each other and smile, or how you would both roll your eyes at the same time."

"Usually at something you said that struck us the same way," Dev said. "Rab said once that you were jealous of our friendship, but you need not have been. We both cared equally about you, too, Robby."

"You have told me yourself that I remind you of him, but I am not Rab, sir."

Dev's eyes lit with laughter. "If you were Rab instead

of Robby, I promise you, we would *not* be having this conversation."

"Well, of course not. Even so—"

"Look," he said, "we cannot stand here like this any longer without causing a stir, even if it is only a stir of impatience from those waiting to eat supper."

Pulling a handkerchief from inside his jack, he mopped her face with it.

"At least you haven't blackened your lashes," he muttered.

"Rosalie wanted to. She did pluck my eyebrows."

"Well, don't let her muck about with your hair, or Corinne either. I like it best in a single plait. That's how I've always pictured you in my mind when I've not been here."

"Faith, did I haunt your mind?"

He grinned, shaking his head. "Let us go to supper, you pliskie bairn."

"I'm *not* a bairn."

"True, but believe me, 'tis safer for me to think of you so," Dev retorted.

Her emotions were in such turmoil that she could not think, let alone imagine what he meant by such a statement. However, she lacked energy enough to argue or to demand more answers from him, so she went meekly past him when he held the door for her, and took her place beside Lady Rosalie at the table.

"It is about time," Rosalie said. "What did you decide?"

Dev began to say the grace-before-meat, saving Robina from having to answer at once. By the time he finished, she'd decided to elude the question by changing the subject to one she knew Rosalie could not resist by asking her what new rumors she had heard.

Dev heard Rosalie's question and was glad that Robby managed to avoid answering it. Honor demanded that he let her decide, but he understood, too, that the decision was a burden he should share with her.

Lady Rosalie's misunderstanding unsettled him more than he wanted to admit. He suspected that she might have put him in the wrong on purpose.

Women, in his experience, were always matchmaking. His mother had certainly pressed his older sister, Gellis, to marry and had seemed to think that any man of property would do for her. Perhaps similar thoughts were in Rosalie's mind.

But he was not a man of property, and she must know he was not.

Or did she know him only as a knight and believe that all knights did own property? Many knights did but more did not.

In any event, Robby deserved a man who could take care of her and keep her out of trouble, a man with sufficient wealth that she would never again have to keep her kirtles until she wore them to rags. Never again should she have to put up with well-meaning women who wanted to change her. She should just be herself.

Most women and girls he had met, other than Lady Meg, were too likely to agree with whatever a man said. Such women bored him. Robby rarely agreed with what any man said, and *she* was never boring.

She knew her own mind, and when she disagreed with him, he could always see that she had reason. Not always good reason, perhaps. He was able to visualize a stream of occasions when her so-called reason for whatever she'd done had led to strong argument between the twins.

He had often sided with Rab but not always. Heaven knew Rab could be as reckless as Robby could, and more so. Dev remembered thinking that *he* had been the voice of reason then, and sanity. He grinned at the thought. Devilish sanity, perhaps, which at least once had stirred Rab to try to knock him on his backside.

Unsuccessfully, but he and Rab, grappling wildly, even furiously, had ended in a horse pond, thanks to a fierce shove from Robby. All three had laughed...afterward.

Recalling her suggestion that he'd agreed to marry her because she reminded him of Rab, he smiled. He had scoffed, even laughed at the image that had leaped to his mind then of Rab in a wedding gown, repeating his vows.

In truth, though, he understood what she'd meant, because he had known her almost as long as he'd known Rab and they had all gotten along well together.

So, did he *equate* Rab and Robby in his mind, or in any other way?

"What be ye thinking on, Dev?" Benjy asked. "Ye look powerful vexed."

"Then I beg your pardon," Dev said. "Did you want to say something to me?"

"Only that I ha' been talking wi' Greenlaw about being a laird, and he said I must learn me numbers. A good laird doesna depend on his scribe or some monk to keep his accounts for him, Greenlaw said."

"Not without knowing how to look them over for himself and understand what they mean," Dev said, realizing that he ought to give some thought to the boy's education.

"Greenlaw tells me so much about Coklaw and such

that I canna keep it all in me head. Could you teach me about numbers and accounts?"

"I can, aye," Dev said, hoping he was not overstating the truth. His responsibility for accounts at Ormiston had been nil. So, although he was good with numbers and could read and write, he had not the least notion how one set up the accounts for an estate and had been expecting to learn such things from Greenlaw.

It occurred to him that his father would likely have something curt to say if he were to admit that failing to him. Greenlaw would not.

"I'll tell you what we'll do," Dev said. "I need to learn more about Coklaw's accounts, and since Greenlaw has been keeping them for years, he can teach you and me at the same time. Then I'll know just what you should know."

"Good," Benjy said. "I'd like that. Greenlaw gets hecklesome if I forget."

"I can get hecklesome, too, if you fail to heed what he or I tell you."

"D'ye think I dinna ken that fine, Dev? 'Tis just that some things take longer to stick wi' me than others do."

"I know what you mean, laddie. I'm that same road myself."

⁓

Asking Lady Rosalie to share any new rumors with her had opened a floodgate, so Robina was able to eat her supper in peace, needing only to glance at her occasionally and say, "Art sure of that, cousin?" or "Mercy!"

She could hear Dev chatting with Benjy, although not what they said, and her thoughts drifted back to the inner chamber and Rab's odd behavior, first snarling at her not to speak and then demanding to know whom she would marry if she did not marry Dev. It had sounded as if Rab thought she *ought* to marry Dev. Rab thought the sun rose and set with Dev, though. She did not.

If it weren't for the fact that she and Dev seemed to have been in conflict with each other from Easter night forward, she might have welcomed the idea. She liked him well enough when he was not telling her what she must and must not do, and she knew him better than any other eligible man.

But he was just a friend. A too-domineering friend.

In truth, though, no one was scouring the countryside to shepherd eligible suitors to Coklaw. Nor was anyone likely to, except perhaps Wat or Dev.

"Are you listening to me, Robina?"

Starting guiltily at Rosalie's indignant tone, she fought to recall enough to nod and then said with a smile, "I believe you were describing Jannie's new maidservant, cousin. I hope she finds the woman more acceptable than you do."

"At least Hilda does not flirt with every man at the Hall," Rosalie replied.

Looking directly at her then, Robina said, "I hope you do not tell others that you hold such an opinion of Corinne, madam. That would displease me. Corinne is a good-hearted person who cares deeply about us and is practically a member of our family. She does enjoy flirting, but that is *all* she does."

"Mercy, dearling, I never meant to distress you," Rosalie said, lowering her voice as she flicked a glance past Robina toward Dev and Benjy. "You must admit, though, that the way she goes on about Sir David's man, Jem Keith..."

When she paused, Robina said lightly, "Corinne went

on in much the same way about Rab's equerry, and about Shag's Hobby. She lost interest in Hob only after she clapped eyes on Jem. I've seen them together," she added. "Jem is respectful of her without encouraging her, and she does naught but flirt."

"And kiss," Rosalie said, raising an eyebrow. "I saw that myself."

"Aye, and kiss," Robina admitted. "Corinne says kissing is part of flirting and she enjoys kissing handsome men. She wants to learn how to tell good kissing from bad, so she can avoid marrying a man who can't do it well."

Rosalie glanced toward Dev again and murmured with a dawning twinkle, "Do you *discuss* such things with your maidservant? My dear— What?"

Robina had raised a hand to stop her and was choking back laughter. "Prithee, cousin, who else would you have had me ask? Mistress Greenlaw or one of our tenants' wives? Perhaps if I knew Molly Scott better, or even Lady Meg…"

She blinked, trying to imagine asking the formidable Meg such questions.

Rosalie chuckled, but Robina was undeterred. "Believe me when I say that Corinne is a better source of such information than anyone else I know, cousin."

"Do you mean to tell me that she is not a maiden?"

"Well, of course, she is a maiden," Robina said, although she was not sure about that, thanks to Corinne's comments about Rab. "See you," she went on, "her grandmother was a tavern wench who married one of those French soldiers who came here years ago. Corinne declares that flirting is therefore in her blood."

"I see," Rosalie said. "I also see that I spent too much

time in England, and the English ways must have affected me, because when I was young, if I'd had a maidservant like your Corinne, I would have known much more than I did when I married. Not that my mother—a formidable woman and an English Percy, herself—would have allowed a girl like Corinne to cross our threshold."

"How sad for you," Robina said. "She is the merriest creature."

"Aye, very likely, but you have finished eating, dearling. I expect it is time we excused ourselves to the solar."

Dev, apparently overhearing that remark and thus making Robina wonder what else he'd heard, turned and said, "I mean to take Robina for a walk outside the gates, my lady. As you noted earlier, we have matters to discuss, and we can do so privily there, whilst remaining in view of men on the wall walk."

"Very well, sir," Rosalie said. "Prithee, bring her back in before dark, though. I shudder to think what Meg will say if she learns I've been lax about such matters."

"We won't linger," Dev said, standing. "Do you need your cloak, lass?"

"I don't think so," she said. "The evenings have grown warmer."

"They have, aye," he agreed, giving her a look that warmed her to her toes.

# Chapter 14 _____

Chukk, having returned to the hillside southwest of Coklaw's gate, was slowly, carefully creeping down its slope, hoping no one would see him. He wanted to reach the rise this time and find what his father had buried there.

The weather had been uncooperative since last week's rain, with ground fog from dark till dawn each night. It was, he thought, as if sunny skies in daytime sucked water out of the ground and the ground were trying to soak it back in again.

Before dark, men on the wall walk would see anything that moved if they happened to look that way. After dark, a man might get lost or make too much noise in the dense, nearby woodland, or in the fog. His goal now was to get close enough to see the center of the rise, so that later he could locate it, even in foggy darkness. He carried a sharp spade in a sling on his belt, so he was prepared.

The new moon had not begun to show itself until today, when a scant, pale crescent appeared briefly by daylight. The guards would soon light torches, but even so, the dense fog might conceal him. Whether he could dig up his treasure unheard was another matter.

That morning, he had divided his men into pairs and

told them to scout the area for herds and other potential targets for their raids. Two men on horseback would draw little interest. Six or the full dozen would draw much more.

Cottages littered the Hawick area, many containing loud, curious dogs that ran loose at night. But dogs liked him and none had troubled him.

Although he was a raider, he did not think he was a brutal man by nature. Nor had his father been. They had come from what Shetland Jamie called a gentle island, the largest of the isles that, together, Scots called Shetland. Not that they had always been peaceful.

Naught that the Vikings touched remained peaceful long.

But their own people, according to Jamie, were peace-loving sailors, who wanted only to transport their salted fish, wool, and butter to the Norse town of Bergen, a Hanseatic port, and bring back salt, cloth, beef, and more interesting goods shipped to Bergen from other such ports.

It had been on such a voyage that Jamie's ship had sunk. Jamie, Chukk's mother, and four-year-old Chukk had escaped the sinking vessel in a towboat that washed ashore on the north English coast. Captured by Percys, Jamie had soon realized that they would never get themselves home without help.

Therefore, he had agreed to serve the first Earl of Northumberland, lord of the land. The next thing he knew, he was taking part in the siege of Coklaw and, weeks later, in Northumberland's dreadful losses in the battle at Shrewsbury.

Surviving both events, Jamie returned to his small family near Alnwick.

Now, Chukk lay in shadowed shrubbery beneath scattered beech and birch trees, halfway down the hill's east-facing slope, watching men on the tower wall walk to and fro. Each time the nearest one walked eastward, Chukk moved closer.

The sun had dropped behind his hill but still cast golden rays on the tower ramparts. If darkness came before the fog, he might creep near enough to get a close look at that rise and judge better the chances of digging up his treasure.

~~~

Dev had sharp ears and the ability to listen to more than one conversation at a time, both gifts having proved useful during his years of service to Douglas.

They had also made it possible for him to overhear the exchange between Robina and Rosalie about Corinne. He had ignored Rosalie's idle chatter until Robina spoke, but her defense of Corinne *had* piqued his interest.

He'd nearly laughed aloud at hearing what Robby had learned from the saucy lass.

In truth, though, he'd paid little heed to the maidservant until the night Robby had flung the wooden box and inkpot at him and accused him of encouraging Corinne to flirt with him. *He'd* never flirted with her but he suspected that Rab had. Corinne was an uncommon name, but thanks to their French visitors a few decades past, it was not rare.

Now, though, he was certain that she was one and the same. Robby had described Corinne as "merry," just as Rab had. Rab had also said that his Corinne was free with her favors, although he had not troubled to tell Dev that she was his twin's maid.

As Dev bade Rosalie goodnight and left the hall with Robby, Benjy, and the dog, Tig, following them, he wondered how he and Robby might arrange to talk privately.

He was about to suggest that Benjy should be thinking about bed when he saw that the stable lads had gathered in the courtyard again, this time with a ball.

"There is Ash Nixon now," Robina said when Ash tossed the ball to one of the older lads. Over her shoulder, she said, "Benjy, you like Ash, don't you?"

"Aye, sure, he tells me good stories, ones his da told him when he was my age. I was helping him wi' the horses earlier, but Dev's Coll needed him, so…" He shrugged.

To Dev's surprise, Robby looked at him when Benjy paused, and raised her eyebrows. He'd expected her to tell the boy that they had decided to give him a personal servant but realized she was asking if *he* thought they should tell him now.

Dev nodded, and she said, "How would you like to have Ash help you look after yourself? He could help see that you get your soiled clothes and bedclothes into the laundry and wake you in the morning, and—"

"I'd like that fine!" Benjy exclaimed. "I told ye I'm too old for women to always be a-coddling me."

"Well, Dev thinks it is a good idea, too," Robina said, smiling. "Perhaps we can all speak to Ash, and Ash can begin tomorrow."

"Sakes, if he'll bring my hot water up tonight, he can start then. I dinna need Corinne leaning over me, asking did I say my prayers."

Her eyes alight with laughter, Robina turned to Dev, "What do you think, sir? You and I do have much to discuss, but arranging something like this for Benjy *has* been on my mind, and on Benjy's, too, as you see."

"I should talk to Ash first," Dev said mildly. "Just to be sure the new post will please him. If we all descend on him at once, he may feel obliged to say aye and fear to say nae."

"Sakes," Benjy said indignantly, "why would he say nae?"

"I don't know," Dev said. "Do you think we should just order him to do it?"

He saw Robina open her mouth, but with a look at him, she shut it again.

Benjy frowned and said, "Ye'd better ask him, else I'll be asking him about it m'self after a day or two o' wondering if he might liefer ha' said nae."

"If you'll stay here with Robina and try to look as if you're unaware of what I'm doing, I'll see what Ash has to say right now."

Glancing at Robby, and seeing a speculative look in her eyes as she watched him, Dev made his escape and went to tell Ash that he had a new position.

~

"D'ye think Ash willna want to do it, Beany?" Benjy asked.

"I think he will be delighted to aid you," she said, trying to watch Dev and Ash without looking right at them. "You are the new laird, Benjy. Ash's position here will also be elevated if he serves you."

"Does that mean that nae one else can tell him what to do?"

"Don't forget that Dev rules over all of us, my laddie,"

she warned. "Also, Greenlaw has charge of all the menservants."

His lips twisted wryly, but then he grinned. "I dinna think Dev, nor Greenlaw, will let us forget that, will they?"

Suppressing laughter, she said, "No, Benjy, they won't."

His eyes began to sparkle, and she saw that Dev and Ash were walking toward them. Their conversation, she thought, had been shorter than she had expected.

Ash was grinning. He was a handsome lad with brown eyes, dark curly hair, and long arms and legs, who would likely grow to be as tall as his lanky father was.

"Ash will be pleased to serve you, and he thought you might like to join the other lads in their ball game, Benjy," Dev said. "I explained that he is not responsible for your behavior, so you must remember that. He is only to help you look after your things and yourself. He'll wake you in the mornings and help you prepare for bed...shortly, I think. You are still not completely over your cold."

Benjy nodded, still grinning, and said, "Aye, sir." Then he turned and ran off with Ash to join the others.

"You had already spoken to Ash about this, I think," Robina said lightly.

"I had," Dev admitted. "I thought from the outset that Benjy should have someone besides women looking after him. It is also true, though, that I'd suggested that Coll train Ash for higher service. I like the cut of that lad."

He touched her shoulder then, urging her toward the gate, and nodded at Shag to open it for them.

The sun had dropped behind the western ridge of low hills, but plenty of daylight remained. Robina turned toward the rise, but Dev said, "Let us walk eastward tonight, Robby. Is there not a path through those woods yonder?"

"There is," she said. "I've likely created it myself over the years since I was small. My favorite tree is there, and I visit it often. I'll show you."

"Can they see us there from the wall?" he asked.

She gave him a searching look. "Aye, a bit. Do you not want them to?"

"On the contrary," he said with a wry smile. "I want to know that they can."

In shrubbery near the southwest end of the clearing but too far away to hear their murmurs, Chukk had stopped breathing. What were the two of them doing? Had someone seen him on the hillside or creeping down its slope?

He could do nowt about it now, whatever the man and woman did. They had vanished into the woods, too near him for comfort. And the gate had shut.

Two guards were on the wall at its southwest and southeast corners. With the man and woman outside the wall, the other two corners likely had watchers now, too.

His right cheek lay against the ground, and he was too far from the rise to see it clearly. Nor could he simply pop his head up to see what was what. He'd had to make do by peeking through leaves.

At least, he told himself, they had not brought dogs out with them.

Keeping his eyes on the guards above, he crept forward only when the two he could see looked away from him. His progress was slow, but he was due for some luck. If he could just find the right spot and mark it...

"As I see it," Dev said when they reached the huge, ancient oak that Robby admired, "we have but two choices, to marry or not marry. What we need to discuss is why we might do so and why, perhaps, we should not."

"Faith," she said when he paused expectantly, "do you expect me to start?"

"I'll wager you were thinking it over at supper whilst Rosalie blethered on and on."

She looked up with a mischievous twinkle in her eyes. "What makes you so sure I was not heeding every word she said?"

"You lack the patience, and you jumped nearly out of your skin when she asked if you were listening. The woman clatters like a beggar's claptrap."

"That is a mean thing to say. She is generous and kind."

"Aye, but her blunder landed us in this plight. And her love of clish-maclaver, which *you* encouraged, will likely make it worse for us."

"I don't deny that I encouraged her to share any new rumors she had heard, but I did it to keep her from plaguing me to tell her what decision we'd made."

"At least, she accepts that it is our decision," he said, leaning back against the wide, rough trunk of the oak. "This is a splendid old tree."

"I came here as a child when I was upset or wanted to be left alone. It is easy to climb, and I'd sit in the crook of that big branch up there to think."

"Did no one ever prevent your coming out by yourself?"

"Aye, sure, Father did whenever there was trouble in

the area. He knew I did not roam far, though. I could nearly always hear when someone called."

"*Nearly* always?"

Instead of rising to what was admittedly bait, she gave him a serious look and said, "Why do you think we *should* marry?"

"I did not say we should, only that we ought to discuss *whether* we should."

"Then you *don't* think so. Tell me why not?"

"Robby, don't…" He hesitated, aware that he, not she, was quibbling.

When he paused, she cocked her head in the familiar birdlike way that told him she might keep pressing him to say yea or nae until he lost his temper and either told her what he thought or walked away.

Accordingly, he said with careful calm, "I have not decided anything, lass. I spoke the truth when I said I'd given no thought to marriage because of my obligations to Archie Douglas. However, that was before he sent me here."

"What else do you think?"

"That although Archie did not say how long I'm to remain warden here, he knows Wat wants me to stay. So, unless something changes, I expect I'll be here for some time."

"What else?"

"I told you some of it earlier. I do care about you. I enjoy talking with you—"

"Nearly always," she said, and he was glad to see the twinkle again.

"True," he said, smiling. "But, even when we disagree, you make me think. You see many things the way I do, but you surprise me, too, with thoughts and ideas that have never entered my mind. I welcome that."

"Nearly always."

He straightened then and caught her by her shoulders, giving her a shake. "You can also infuriate me. I'll admit that, too. Will you admit the same thing about me?"

"Aye, sure," she said. "You infuriate me every time you dismiss what I say or prevent me from doing as I please."

"I'll tell you one thing," he said evenly, holding her gaze. "Rab was more likely to understand that I meant well when I disagreed with him and to accept that I knew more about some things than he did."

"Aye, he accepted you as his superior because you trained him, so he turned you into something almost god-like, Rab did. Do you want me to idolize you, too?"

"I do not," Dev said, revolted by the image she'd created of Rab and of her so absurdly imagined self. "As if you *could* idolize me! And, if you think Rab bowed and scraped to my every word and gesture, you've forgotten that he was as stubborn, reckless, outspoken, and care-naught about things as you are…his own *safety* being one of them!"

Hearing his increasingly angry words and overwhelmed by a sudden, clear image of Rab on Black Corby charging in front of the lancer, then falling at Auld Nick's hooves—aware that tears had welled in his eyes, Dev turned sharply away from her toward the tree, furiously fighting to compose himself.

⁓

Stunned by his sudden anger and uncharacteristic tears, and feeling guilty for speaking so rashly, but fighting her emotions, too, Robina drew a breath before she stepped close to Dev and gently touched his arm.

"I should *never* have said that," she murmured.

"Oh, Robby." He pulled her into his arms, holding her so tightly that she could barely breathe. "You can always say what you think to me. It's what I love best about you and always have. I'm just so sorry that Rab died and that I—"

"Dev, don't!" she cried, pushing unsuccessfully against his chest with both hands, trying to free herself from his embrace. "*Don't* say you're sorry that you lived instead. I could not bear that. By my troth, sir, if you are going to carry that burden and see him whenever you look at me—" She broke off, pressing her face and hands against his chest, unable to speak or to breathe properly.

He did not let go of her.

She felt his chest heave with a huge sigh or a sob. Then his right hand gently cupped the back of her head. Its thumb stroked the smooth hair near the centered part that separated the plaits still looped round her ears.

Silence filled the woods around them for a long minute.

Then, quietly, he said, "I was going to say I'm sorry I couldn't prevent his death. We were both warriors, Robby. We knew from the outset that one or both of us might die in battle. I won't deny that I've wondered why Rab died instead of me or never wished that he'd been the one to live. I did wish that, desperately, when I brought him home and saw how devastated you all were. But I knew that wish was futile. God did not grant us the power to change the past. We can only try to make amends when we're at fault."

"Well, you cannot make amends by marrying me."

"Nor have I imagined that I could or that I must. What I will tell you is that I miss Rab almost as much as you do, and I mean to keep my promise to him. If you and I do not marry, I'll do all I can to find you a good husband."

"You will want to approve the man I choose, I expect."

"Would not Rab expect that of me?"

"Aye, he would, but I do *not*," she said firmly. "Nor do I want to talk more about that now. I like you, too, Dev, most of the time. I think Rab approves…that is, that he would approve of our marrying. Likely my father would, too, if he were alive. Rosalie already does, so likely Lady Meg will, and Wat. But this is all too abrupt, too soon, and it demands too much of me."

"I know," he said. "I feel it, too. Especially since my father will also approve."

"Because of the Ormiston estate, aye. But that won't—"

"Don't say it," he warned. "I've told you how I feel about that. Mayhap one day, if we marry and if it pleases Benjy, we can build a cottage on that estate, but only as a place to stay whilst we visit him and his family. That land is his and will remain so. I'm the last person who should covet it, and so I shall tell my father if he raises the issue, as he may."

"It *is* part of your family history, too," she said softly.

"And that is all it is, Robby. I want to make my own family history, and I'm willing…nay, I'd be *honored*… to do that with you if that is your choice. But you must decide, lass. I know that, given time, you will know what you want, one way or the other. I will honor that decision, whatever it is."

She pressed a hand to his chest again, and this time he eased his embrace. When he did, she stood on tiptoe, put both hands to his cheeks and pulled his face closer to kiss him.

Her lips no sooner touched his than, with a moan, he

pulled her close again and kissed her more possessively, thrusting his tongue into her mouth. However, when she darted her tongue to meet his and pressed her body closer, he released her.

"Don't tempt me further, lass," he said. "I have too little control over myself, and I don't want anything to happen that might make you feel *obliged* to marry me. If you come to me, it must be of your own free will."

"Blame Corinne for that kiss then," she said. "I like the way you kiss, and I wanted more of it. She said she wanted to learn how a man *should* kiss. I know now that I want someone like you, who makes me feel it deep inside when he kisses me."

He smiled. "So it's Corinne's fault, is it?" When she nodded, he said, "I'll do all I can to persuade Rosalie to let you think in peace and not urge you to marry me. But we must go in now, Robby. I can see the men on the wall from here. I doubt they can tell what we're doing, but I'd liefer they not start imagining things they might repeat. All we'd need is someone suggesting to my father, Archie, or even Wat that I've abused my power here."

Robina barely heard him. She remembered instead that he'd said she could always say what she thought to him because it was what he loved best about her. Did that mean he loved other things about her, too?

From shrubbery twenty yards from the castle clearing, his view of the rise still obscured, Chukk watched the man and woman go in.

It had grown darker. The guards would soon be lighting torches.

Moreover, he was taking chances that would see him hanged if they caught him. But he could think of no other way to gain his treasure.

His sole hope was to mark the right spot, creep in under cover of the ground fog, and successfully find the right spot. Then he'd have to dig. To accomplish all that would, he suspected, require a miracle of God.

He saw that one of the two men he'd seen on the wall walk had vanished. The other paced for a time and then went round to the east wall.

Deducing that there were only two men on the wall now, and perhaps just the one, Chukk crept closer, stopping only when a watcher returned, and then creeping forward again when the man turned his back.

In this manner, he came to a place where, through the shrubbery, he could see the top of the rise and the small sapling planted there, as near as it could be to the spot beneath which his treasure awaited.

"Da said it were nobbut a foot or two beneath the surface," he murmured.

Chukk did not consider himself a man of intellect, but he knew that a man planting a sapling might easily dig deeper than a foot or two. Most would dig a good-sized hole.

Suspecting that someone had recently found Shetland Jamie's jar, he felt an urge he'd not felt since childhood to cry, kick his feet, and pound the treacherous ground.

Since he could not safely do that, the urge passed, and he eyed the sapling more judiciously. Anyone might have planted it, even the wee laddie he'd seen outside the wall.

The hole might not be so deep, after all.

Dev spent much of Monday riding Coklaw's lands from Hummelknowes near Slitrig Water to the Ormiston estate east and southeast of the castle. He rode with Sandy, Jock, and Shag's Hobby, because two outlying cottars had reported rumors of English raiders and of strangers wandering near their cottages.

The strangers had asked questions and commented that Northumberland was rightful lord of Teviotdale, because Henry IV of England had awarded the Douglas estates to his grandfather. The raiders, men said, were likely thinking of laying siege again to Coklaw.

Dev was certain the rumors were untrue, because whatever the current seven-year-old English King's grandfather had done, the King's warring regents insisted that they wanted peace with Scotland. Even so, he knew better than to ignore such rumors, ever.

After a day spent learning nothing that increased his concern, Dev returned late to Coklaw, spoke with Jem Keith and others who were still up, learned that nothing new had occurred, and retired to bed.

Tuesday morning, when he descended later than usual to break his fast, he learned that Mistress Geddes, a Hawick seamstress, had arrived and begged speech with the laird.

"What the devil does she want?" Dev demanded.

"Mistress Geddes says she's coom tae finish the lady Robina's wedding dress," the lad replied. "We heard summat yestereve about a wedding, sir, but no that her ladyship be the one a-getting married. Be that true?"

*Chapter 15* —————————

Having already discussed the week's meals with Ada Greenlaw that morning, Robina was sitting with Lady Rosalie in the solar, sorting through Benjy's mending, while Rosalie embroidered a pillow cover.

"I vow," Robina said, "most of Benjy's clothing is more fit than mine is for the ragbag. Ash Nixon said he found some of these things in odd places, too."

"I expect most boys are like that," Rosalie said cheerfully. "Just wait until you and Dev have your own, dearling."

Robina ignored the second sentence as she had ignored all such hints for the past twenty-four hours and said, "Benjy needs some new clothing, too."

"I warrant Mistress Geddes will be pleased to make him some shirts and braies," Rosalie said. "She can make him some woolen breeks, too."

A footstep on the landing outside the door was the only warning before Dev opened it and stepped into the room. Had he blown in on a wintry blast, the temperature in the room could not, Robina thought, have dropped more swiftly.

She froze in her place but relaxed when his furious gaze swept past her to Rosalie. "Perhaps, madam," he said icily, "you will be good enough to explain to me what your seamstress is doing here today, talking of gold-silk wedding gowns."

Setting her work aside, Rosalie said matter-of-factly, "I sent my equerry to fetch her yesterday, sir. Robina cannot marry without a proper gown, and you have seen her kirtles. Not one is fit to wear in company, let alone on such an occasion as a wedding. Moreover, tradition decrees that a bride is *entitled* to a new gown for her wedding."

"I asked you to keep your belief in such a wedding to yourself," Dev said. The tension in his voice told Robina that he had exerted himself not to shout.

Looking at her mending to avoid his gaze, she nearly smiled when Rosalie said with surprise, "What would *you* have had me do, sir? One cannot summon up a wedding dress by magic. Cutting and stitching takes time. I did beg Mistress Geddes to sew swiftly and to do the silk gown first, but one cannot expect her to work a miracle."

"I expected only that *you* would keep your word," Dev said grimly.

"But I did," Rosalie protested. "I said naught of bridals to her or anyone else. I strictly told Ned to ask only that she come here to finish the silk dress because her ladyship would need it sooner than expected for a special occasion."

"And what special occasion did you expect Mistress Geddes might imagine taking place hereabouts without her foreknowledge?" Dev asked.

Rosalie shrugged. "There must be many such."

"Blethers," Dev retorted rudely.

The door opened with a bang, and Benjy rushed in, clearly excited but skidding to a halt when he saw Dev.

"Beany, is it true?" the boy demanded when Dev remained silent. "Are ye going to marry our Dev?"

To Robina, every sound in the room seemed to fade away, as if the room and its furnishings held a collective breath, awaiting her answer.

Rosalie and Dev turned toward her with similar, expectant looks on their faces. Benjy's mouth was still agape, his eyes wide and sparkling.

She let her gaze pause a moment on Benjy before shifting it back to Dev. His wrath had cooled. His expression was calm. She sensed only his strength of purpose.

The look in his eyes softened then, warming her.

She said quietly to Benjy, "Dev is willing, laddie, and others are saying that I will marry him. 'Tis a gey important decision, though. One must make it wisely and not let other people's wishes or hopes interfere. After all, when a lady marries, she does so forever. She wants to be sure she's marrying the right man."

"Aye, well, if it matters to ye, I think we'd do fine wi' Dev," Benjy said.

"Your opinion does matter," Robina assured him with a smile. "I must think more before I decide, but I promise I won't think too long."

"Did ye want to talk more about it, then?" Benjy asked solemnly. "Mayhap we could help ye make up your mind."

Flicking a glance at Dev to see him biting his lower lip, his eyes agleam with delight, Robina said gently, "Thank you, love. But I must decide this for myself."

"Aye, then, I'll just go tell the lads to cease their nattering about it till ye do." Nodding with a lordly air to Dev and Lady Rosalie, Benjy left.

When he had gone, Rosalie stood gracefully and said

to Dev, "I will silence Mistress Geddes, sir. I doubt the news has gone any further."

With as regal an air as Benjy's, and more contentment than remorse, she sailed out, leaving Robina alone with Dev, who shut the door and faced her.

Dev eyed Robby warily. She had handled Rosalie's interference better than he had, and meantime, he'd realized something about himself.

He had hitherto believed he preferred gentle, complaisant women to defiant, outspoken ones. His first clue that he might be mistaken was his reaction to his father's belief that Anne Kerr might suit him as a wife. Never had there breathed a more complaisant, obedient woman than Anne... or a more tedious one.

Robby had never been submissive or meek. From their first meeting, she had spoken her mind to him and to Rab without thought of consequence. She would argue with Rab, often fiercely, when they disagreed. Having tried to intervene in one such quarrel between the twins—and only one—Dev had learned quickly that she was willing to fight just as fiercely with anyone when she believed she was right.

Had he been disgusted or scandalized by such behavior?

In truth, as he looked back, he knew that she had surprised and intrigued him. He had also learned that when Rab spoke to her in a certain stern tone of voice, she would heed him. And if Rab informed her, brutally or otherwise, that she had been cruel or rude to someone, she had quickly and most charmingly apologized.

The reverse was also true. She'd exerted more control

over Rab than anyone else that Dev knew with the possible exception of their father and, sometimes, himself.

Realizing that she eyed him now with much the same wariness that he felt, he said, "What are you thinking?"

"Many things," she said. "Thoughts tumble through my mind, one after the other, and get themselves all mixed up."

Leaning against the door, he crossed his arms over his chest, and said, "Fish one out then and tell me about it."

"Aye, well, do you think that Douglas, like Ormiston, hopes we'll marry?"

"Douglas has nowt to do with this," he said firmly, straightening and taking a step toward her. "If you're asking what I'd have done if he *had* suggested it, I'd have considered it as dutifully as any other such suggestion. He is my liege lord.

"However," he went on, "if you want my thoughts, the plain truth is that I've wanted to possess you since I first saw you... not to marry you, mind, just to possess. So, 'tis likely I'd have agreed willingly if he'd *ordered* me to marry you."

"Faith, Dev, one person cannot possess another," she said. "Only a spirit can do that, and I am already possessed by Rab's spirit and have been since his death."

"Have you?" he murmured, stepping closer and drawing her into his arms. "Earlier, you said you wanted more kisses. See what Rab's spirit thinks of this one."

To his delight, she promptly tilted her face up. Their eyes met, and Dev felt something he'd never felt before. He could not have described the sensation to himself or to anyone else. It came and it went in the blink of an eye.

It was as if something had touched or lightly caressed some sensitive spot so deep inside him that he could not

tell what or where it was. He came out of the moment with
a sense of shock, as if all his hair stood on end.

Her lips touched his, and he knew where he was and
what he wanted. Moving one hand to cradle the back of
her head and the other to span the small of her back, he
kissed her lightly and then not so lightly. And this time,
when the tip of her tongue touched his lips, his own
tongue welcomed it inside.

When she pressed her body harder against his, his
responded urgently.

Stroking down her back to her hips, he kissed her more
possessively, urging her passion to match his and delight-
ing when she embraced him more tightly. She closed her
eyes, and he could see her desire in her face and sense it
in her body.

When she withdrew her tongue from his mouth and
gently licked his lips, a memory stirred. He broke off their
kiss long enough to draw a breath, let it out, and wait for
her to open her eyes and look at him. Then he said, "See
here, you aren't just testing me or planning to kiss other
men this way, are you?"

With the most sensual smile he had seen from her, she
murmured, "Would you be jealous if I did?"

"I told you, I don't get jealous. But such behavior can be
dangerous for a woman. Men tend to take such...um...
forthrightness as more of an...an offer than the woman
might intend. From most other women, you'd draw strong
censure."

"Would I?" Her tone was lazy, and he had a strong urge
to shake her and assure her in no uncertain terms that she
must *never* do such things carelessly or with such abandon. Controlling that urge with some effort, he said with

what he thought, under the circumstances, was admirable calm, "Just behave yourself, Robby."

"Is this the Warden of Coklaw speaking now?" When he frowned, she grinned mischievously. "I'll behave, Dev. What else *can* I do? After all, unless I were to flirt with Sandy or your Jem Keith, whom would I kiss? Also, Rosalie has assured us that no one else knows about our supposed betrothal."

He wished he could believe that, but he knew how rumors flew around the Borders—throughout Scotland, come to that. If the King and his contentious cousin, the Lord of the Isles, each sent him felicitations, he would not be astonished.

Smiling at his absurd imagination, he held Robby a little away from him and said, "Just hope that you're speaking the truth and that Rosalie did, too."

However, Wednesday morning, before they had finished breaking their fast, a messenger from Scott's Hall arrived to inform them that his lordship and the ladies Meg, Janet, and Annabella Scott would take the midday meal with them.

~

Two hours later, when Wat arrived with Lady Meg, his sisters, his fighting tail, and two dogs, Robina, Dev, and Rosalie greeted them in the courtyard.

As Robina exclaimed over how much Bella had grown since they'd last seen each other, she heard Rosalie say, "I see that you brought Father Hubert, as I requested, sir."

Noting then that one of the riders was a priest, Robina gave Rosalie a sharp look and then followed Rosalie's gaze to Dev.

His expression must have told her, as it did Robina, that he was angry, because she said hastily, "I recalled your saying, sir, that Benjy needs someone to teach him his letters and numbers. I thought Father Hubert might know someone suitable, but I knew he'd want to discuss the matter with you and that you'd want to meet him. I hope I did not overstep."

"It was kind of you to think of Benjy," Dev said evenly.

Robina wanted to strangle her.

*"Whether she did it for Benjy or to provide a priest for your wedding matters not, Beany. It was thoughtful, and you should thank her prettily."*

More proof, if she needed it, she decided, that Rab wanted her to marry Dev.

Even so, she saw no reason to add to what Dev had said to Rosalie.

As they went inside to the great hall, she expressed a hope to Wat that his lady wife and his mother, the lady Lavinia Scott, were in good health.

"They are," he said with a smile. "Molly would have come, but she is newly with child and still getting sick too often to travel, and Mam prefers to stay home. Both send their affection to everyone here and their felicitations to you and Dev."

"In troth, sir…" Intending to disclaim a need for felicitations, Robina hesitated when Dev caught her eye and shook his head. Recovering rapidly, she went on, "I should exert myself more to visit them. From one cause or another, time passes without notice, and I have been remiss."

"Whatever the cause, we must all do better," Wat said. "We knew we had to put our next visit forward, though, when I heard that you meant to marry on the eve of Belt-ane. We're prepared to stay for a sennight but will leave whenever you like."

Before Robina could think of a reply, Dev said, "You and I can talk more about that, Wat, but your ladies will welcome a rest before we dine. If Robina will take them upstairs…" He looked at her, quizzically raising his eyebrows.

Smiling, she turned to Lady Meg and said, "Would you like that, madam?"

Lady Meg said with a warm smile of her own, "I would, aye. I have not been here in nearly a year, I think. But you must tell me just how all of this came about so… so quickly, dearling."

～

"Come into the inner chamber with me," Dev said to Wat. "Your lads and ours can sort things outside, and I see that you brought Lady Meg's Sym along, so we'll trust him to take control of the high table. I must talk with you."

"I'll go with you if you have a night jar in there," Wat said. "Gram does not approve of men hopping off their horses to relieve themselves at the side of the road when she travels with us, so I am as much in need of relief as my ladies are."

Chuckling, Dev said, "So be it, my lord. On the lower shelf yonder, the covered jar, mind, not the jug above it with the cork in it."

"I do recognize a wine jug when I see it," Wat said dryly as Dev moved to put a fresh log on the hearth fire. When Wat finished his business, he said, "So, what's amiss?"

"Perhaps nowt," Dev said. "But your 'saintly' grandaunt created a dilemma for Robby and me, so I need your sage advice on how things might proceed now."

"Aunt Rosalie has a knack for creating difficulties, but she is a goodhearted woman," Wat said. "Just how did she create this problem?"

Dev explained, and Wat chuckled. "That sounds as if she might willfully have misunderstood. But if you don't want to marry Robina, just say so."

"It's not that I *don't* want to marry her," Dev said. "Robby's the hesitant one, and she feels forced into it now. Had it remained between the three of us, perhaps it would be easy just to say yea or nay. But then Rosalie sent for a seamstress in Hawick to finish a gown they ordered the day after you left, and she sent her man to get you and your priest. She swears she said nowt of bridals, but we both know that people can create a wedding out of nowt save priests and gowns. Add to that the fact that two lads setting the high table were looking over her shoulder when she declared that I had asked Robby to marry me."

"Did you?"

"I did not, but I did say something that Rosalie decided meant the same thing."

"Is Robina unwilling?"

"I'm not sure. I told her the decision is hers to make. She seems to like me well enough when we're not at loggerheads, and she says she'll decide but wants time. She also says it is all too abrupt, too soon, and demands too much of her."

"Completely understandable," Wat said, reaching for the wine jug and pouring claret into two pewter goblets.

Handing one to Dev with a straight look, he added, "How do *you* honestly feel about the whole thing? I ken fine that you've not looked for a wife."

"I told Robby I'm willing, and I am." Grimacing, he added, "Until Archie appointed me warden here, Father wanted me to marry Anne Kerr."

"Anne would not suit you," Wat said. "Moreover . . . But that is irrelevant. If you're behaving honorably because Rosalie put you in this pliskie fix, I *can* help."

"How?"

"As far as I know—and I *would* know—no one else has sought Robby's hand. Since her father's death eighteen months ago, and Rab's more recent one, she has had her hands full, so I've made no effort on her behalf. But she is certainly eligible to wed, and I can provide any number of eligible suitors for her hand."

"She is gey particular," Dev said, slightly nettled. "She knows her own mind."

"She *needs* a husband who will keep her too busy raising children to get into trouble," Wat said bluntly. "Come to that, Ormiston may be willing to aid us in that endeavor. Robby also knows young men in the area, so—"

"She has no interest in any of them; she wants to stay at Coklaw," Dev said flatly. "She would not willingly leave Benjy to marry a man of property elsewhere, and I'd object to any husband of hers raising the Laird of Coklaw. As for my father, I've learned that, despite having invited the Kerrs to spend Beltane at Ormiston, he will honor us with his presence here on Friday."

Wat's eyes twinkled. "Then you'll have a full house, my lad, and more than your share of concerned advisers. I'd advise you to work matters out with Robby as quickly and as privately as possible. I think you're more interested in her than you admit. If she is also more interested..."

When he paused, Dev let the silence linger, wishing he had not tried to explain.

He'd realized the minute Wat suggested finding suitors for Robby's hand that *he* would disapprove of every one of them.

⁓

Staggered by Lady Meg's demand for an explanation, Robina had stared at her, utterly speechless, until Meg said kindly, "Perhaps we might talk later."

With that threat hanging over her, Robina tried to maintain her part in general conversation with her guests while they tidied themselves in the ladies' solar with Potter's help and Corinne's. Rosalie and Meg had moved to the window embrasure to talk.

Twelve-year-old Bella said excitedly, "Tell us about your wedding dress, Cousin Robby! Where will your wedding be? How many guests will come?"

"I've not decided anything yet," Robina said desperately.

"Aye, but will you invite me?"

"Bella, you must not demand an invitation to someone else's wedding, as I am sure you know perfectly well," Janet said quietly but in a tone that carried to her sister's ears over Rosalie's ongoing discussion with Meg behind them.

Lady Meg rose from the cushioned window embrasure, saying mildly, "I think the gentlemen must be growing impatient by now, do not you, Robina?"

"Oh, yes," Robina said with relief. "We ought to go down if everyone is ready."

No one demurring, she led the way with Lady Meg behind her, the others following. When they reached the great hall, Wat met them at the door with Lady Meg's Sym beside him. A lanky man with graying red hair, Sym had served Lady Meg since his childhood. Robina had met him many times before.

Greeting him now with a smile, she said, "I hope all is well with your family."

"Aye, m'lady, Em and Jed be in good health. Jed's here wi' his lordship, and Em looks after our Lady Molly. I see both o' them near every day, which be grand."

Wat said, "Sym will escort my ladies to their places, Robby. I'd like a word with you before we join them, though, if you don't mind."

Noting that Dev stood near the hall fireplace, talking to Jock Cranston and Sandy, Robina said, "Aye, sure, my lord. I hope naught is amiss."

"Nay," he said with a warm smile. "'Tis merely that I talked with Dev, and I want you to know that I understand what happened. I'm sorry my well-meaning aunt put you in such a difficult position. If I can help sort it out, I am at your disposal."

"Are you, sir?" She cocked her head and eyed him searchingly. He was an attractive man, and kind, but one she dared not offend. His smile remained warmly inviting, so she went on, "There *is* one thing you might do, if you are willing."

"Anything, lass," he said, his voice deep with sincerity. "Tell me."

"Will you kiss me? Not a peck on the cheek or a cousinly kiss on the mouth but a real kiss. I want to know if all men kiss the same way."

Wat grinned. "Does Dev know about this desire of yours?"

"Oh, aye, I told him," she said, nodding earnestly.

"And he approves?"

"It is not his business to approve, sir. He has no claim on me other than what Cousin Rosalie thinks she heard. He said I must decide for myself, and I cannot do that without knowing more about kissing. So, if you please..."

She put her hand on his arm, an arm as muscular as Dev's or as Rab's had been. When Wat still made no objection, she tilted her face up invitingly.

"See that his lordship's men find places to set up their tents and hobble their horses," Dev was saying to Jock and Sandy when he saw the ladies enter the hall and noticed that Robby lingered near the archway with Wat. As he watched, Robby tilted her head back and Wat bent to kiss her...on the mouth.

Unable to recall if they had greeted each other in the yard with kisses, he watched in astonishment as Wat put his arms around her and went on with what was clearly much more than a cousinly peck.

Stiffening, but aware that the two men with him were also watching them, and him, he took ruthless control of himself. Dismissing Jock and Sandy to their midday meal, he moved with determination toward the high table.

When he reached it, he saw Benjy near the end, standing next to Wat's priest, who stood beside Wat's place. The lads had set another place beside Benjy, likely for Sym Elliot, who stayed near Lady Meg and often took over for the lad serving her. Swallowing his rising fury, Dev realized he had to tread lightly.

He knew what Robby was doing, because she had told him she wanted to compare men's kisses. But with Wat? Still, if he rebuked her, she would likely ask whom she should choose, if not Wat, and heaven knew what innocent or not so innocent man she would pick next. He had to put a stop to it.

Robina, watching Wat's eyes as they kissed, saw his gaze shift and his eyes widen just before he straightened, gently released her, and said, "Well?"

She smiled and said, "It *is* different."

"Just different?"

"Aye," she said, striving for calm as she looked toward the fireplace and saw Sandy and Jock at a nearby trestle table. Shifting her gaze to the dais, she saw Dev standing beside it at the near end, looking right at her. Without looking away, she said, "Men do kiss differently, sir. I thought they might, but I wanted to *know*."

"*Did* you?" Wat said. Looking at him then, she saw that the amusement in his eyes had turned sober. "Take care, cousin-lassie," he said. "Don't press him too far, or you'll find that you've sown more than you'll want to reap."

"Faith, sir, do you mean Dev? Because he has assured me that he is *never* jealous. I *did* tell him that I meant to kiss other men to learn how it would feel."

"What I mean, Robby," Wat said sternly, "is that Dev is not a man whose temper you want to arouse. You should know that by now. If you look again, carefully, you'll see that he's unhappy about this. Shall we eat now, or do you want to tempt him further?"

"We should eat," she said. Then a new thought occurred to her. "Will Molly be angry if she finds out that you kissed me? Someone may tell her."

"It is kind of you to think about that," he said, clearly amused again. "She might have taken exception to my kissing you, had she seen us without warning. But she will understand your intentions better than most women would. Dev won't, though. You'd be wise to step doucely with him for a time."

Glancing at the dais to see Dev still standing there, clearly waiting for them, she felt a shiver go through her. But she straightened her shoulders and when Wat extended his forearm, she rested a hand on it and let him escort her to the dais.

She saw as they drew closer that Dev *was* angry, perhaps even furious. To her surprise, though, the little chill vanished and satisfaction roared into its place.

"I can see that you two need a moment," Wat murmured when they were near enough for his soft-spoken words to reach Dev.

Dev nodded, his gaze still riveted to Robina. He barely waited for Wat to pass him before he said, "I want to talk to you."

"I can see that, sir," she said, raising her chin. "But our guests await their dinner. We can talk after we have all dined."

She expected him to stop her as she passed. He did not, but before disappointment blossomed, she heard a sound from him that sounded distinctly like a growl.

# Chapter 16 ─────────────

Striding to his place at the high table, Dev faced the gathered company, all of whom were likely wondering if he meant to delay their meal any longer.

Waiting for silence, he said the grace without sparing a thought for the priest at his table and sat down. In the shuffle, as everyone else took their seats, he said to Wat, "Was it necessary to create a scene merely to kiss your cousin, my lord?"

"Cool your wrath, Davy-lad," Wat said evenly. "The lady asked me to kiss her. She said she wanted to learn if men kiss differently or all the same."

Grimacing, Dev said, "Aye, she told me as much, too. Her maidservant put the notion into her head. I told Robby to behave herself."

"I am glad to know she told me the truth," Wat murmured. "She also said you assured her that you are never jealous. She did not mention her maidservant or the part about behaving herself."

"She wouldn't," Dev said with a reluctant half-smile. "As for jealousy, I have neither the right nor any cause for such."

"True," Wat murmured. Then, cheerfully, he looked

past Dev to say, "Here, lad, I'll take some of that beef if Sir David chooses to ignore its presence."

Recalled to his duty, Dev turned to serve Lady Meg from the platter. When his gaze met hers, she smiled.

"I think you and Robina suit each other well, sir," she said quietly.

⁓

No sooner had Dev said the grace than, as everyone sat down, Bella muttered across Janet, "Why were you kissing Wat, Cousin Robby?"

"We're cousins, Bella," she said, leaning close to Janet so neither Rosalie nor Lady Meg would hear her. "I have little knowledge of kissing, so I asked Wat to show me how it is when men kiss women they like more than cousins. He was kind enough to show me."

"I wonder what Molly will think about that," Bella said.

"That, Bella, it is not a subject for you to discuss with her," Janet said firmly.

"Wat said he was sure Molly would understand," Robina said.

"Aye, but will Dev?" Janet muttered in her ear.

"I'll find out after we eat," Robina said. "He wants to talk to me."

"That sounds ominous, but you do not seem concerned," Janet said. "When Wat says he wants to talk to me, I quiver until I learn that I need not."

"Are you two talking secrets?" Bella demanded. "Jannie, you said that talking secrets in front of other people is rude."

"It is rude," Janet said lightly. "Will you forgive us?"

"Do I get to go to the wedding?" Bella asked.

"Bella!" Janet exclaimed, her cheeks reddening.

"If there is a wedding," Robina said to Bella with a smile, "you must certainly attend it. At present, though, naught is settled."

"Well, Aunt Rosalie says there will be a wedding. She also said she might let me help finish your dress, Cousin Robby."

By the end of the meal, Robina's confidence had waned and she understood what Janet meant in saying she quivered before such talks with Wat. Nevertheless, she was glad when Lady Meg rose from the table, said she meant to retire to the solar, and as much as ordered Rosalie, Janet, and Bella to go with her.

Potter, Benjy, Sym, and the priest excused themselves, too, leaving Robina alone at the ladies' end of the table, two seats away from Dev.

Wat murmured something to Dev, who gave a curt nod. When Wat turned away, Dev said tersely, "We will talk in yon chamber, Robina."

His expression was unreadable, but she could still sense his anger. Even so, he was not in a fury, just irked… or something other than irked.

⁓

As Robby walked gracefully into the inner chamber, Dev reminded himself that she was still in his charge. As Wat left, he'd warned him again to curb his temper, but Robby seemed oblivious to it, which, Dev decided, was just as well.

He had often seen her ignore or even take fire from Rab's anger, but he would not allow such opportunities with him. Nor would he allow such flirting as he had witnessed with Wat. To be sure, Wat was amused, but Lady Meg had witnessed the encounter, and so had everyone else in the hall. Dev bolted the door.

"Look at me, Robby," he said then. "I have something to say to you."

"You did not like seeing me kiss Wat, I know," she said, turning. "But surely, even you lack the right to command me not to kiss my own cousin, Dev. So, if you mean to scold, I think you should not."

He nearly told her that the kiss had not looked cousinly to him, but he did not want to fratch with her about that. Nor did he want to lose his temper.

Meantime, she watched him as if she dared him to behave like the guardian they both knew he was.

"I learned something about myself today," he said at last.

Again he waited, hoping she would encourage him to continue.

She was silent, and he knew he either had to say what he was thinking and what he had learned or, perhaps, lose his sole opportunity. But what if ... ?

Finding it hard to swallow, he gave himself a mental shake and said bluntly, "Sithee, lass, Wat promised me that if we don't marry, he will find you a suitable husband, one who will keep you out of trouble and give you lots of bairns."

"*That* is what you learned about *yourself*?"

"No, no, that is what led to my discovery."

"How?"

"Because I realized I'd exert my authority to disapprove of your marriage to any man he chose, no matter how eligible he was or what your feelings about him might be."

A flush reddened her cheeks. The rosiness became her, but he wondered warily if he had shocked her or made her angry. His remaining confidence evaporated. He felt as he had in boyhood, facing unknown but well-deserved censure.

"Why would you disapprove of them?" she asked then, her voice soft, gentle.

"Because I'm a selfish man, Robby," he said, "and apparently a jealous and dull-witted one, too. What did you think of Wat's kiss?"

"He is very handsome."

"Answer the question I asked you."

"He put his arms around me, he is strong, and his clothing has a spicy scent."

"Robina."

She stepped closer, eyeing him as if her gaze might pierce to his soul. "I am trying to think how his kiss compared to yours, Dev. But..." She spread her hands.

"Come here."

"Why?"

"You are begging for another skelping."

She cocked her head. "Am I? Why would you want to do that?"

"Why? Robby, I'm trying to tell you that *I* want you, that the thought of you with any other man made me feel..." He shook his head. "I can't describe it."

"Try."

"Damnation, I can't. Decide! Will you or will you not *marry* me?"

⌐

Robina felt as if the floor had disappeared from under her feet. Whatever she had expected—at best his admission that he had disliked seeing her kiss Wat—she had not expected his demand for an immediate reply to such a proposal. His demeanor had confused her from the moment she'd seen him watching her kiss Wat. She had sensed his anger then and on the dais. Then, after Wat left them, Dev seemed different, less devilish, perhaps uncertain, and otherwise unreadable.

She understood her behavior, because she'd behaved much the same when Rab was angry but refused to tell her what she had done to irk him. She would tease him then until he lost his temper and shouted his thoughts and feelings to her, and to the winds.

She had known that, with Dev, it was a dangerous game. He did not shout when he was angry; he erupted. Then, as she knew, anything might happen.

Expecting next to hear Rab say that she'd just wanted to know she could *make* Dev jealous, she realized he did not need to say it. She knew it was true. She also knew that she'd wanted Dev to admit that he cared about her decision, and he had.

"Robby, will you answer me?"

"I think perhaps I will," she said, meeting his gaze.

"Will answer or will marry me?"

"I think perhaps I'll do both. Kiss me, Dev."

When he pulled her into his arms, she melted against him and lifted her face up to his. His mouth captured hers, and his strong, warm hands moved over her back and sides as if he would memorize every inch of her by touch.

Allowing a few minutes to prove again that his kisses were far superior to Wat Scott's, Robina put her hands against Dev's arms and said quietly, "I don't want to stop, because this feels wonderful, but we're doubtless stirring more talk. Moreover, Cousin Wat may feel obliged to interrupt us if only to see if you've left me in one piece."

"Then you should rejoin the ladies," he said, releasing her with a wry smile. "Will you tell them we've decided to marry, or should I announce it to everyone at supper?"

"Nearly everyone already assumes we're betrothed," she reminded him. "I'll tell my cousins that we've decided to go forward with the wedding on Saturday, as Cousin Rosalie suggested, unless you think we should wait longer."

"No, for everyone is here except my father, and he'll arrive Friday. In troth, I'd liefer have it done and send all of our guests and Wat's priest to perdition. That is, if Mistress Geddes can finish your dress by then."

She smiled. "I think Rosalie would liefer go sleepless than see it unfinished Saturday. Do you still believe that this will please your lord father?"

"I'm certain it will," he said.

"Then, I should go upstairs now," she said. "Someone may come."

"Before you go," Dev said, giving her a stern look and gripping her shoulders again, "I don't ever want to see you kissing Wat or any other man like that again. If you do..." He paused—meaningfully, he hoped.

She grinned. "I ken fine what you'd do, but I'd best not catch you kissing anyone you should not, either, David Ormiston. I may not be able to put you over my knee, sir, but I'd do *something* to make you sorry."

"You terrify me," he said with a smile but only half-teasing.

Tossing him a saucy look, she ran up the stairs, and he watched until she vanished around the next turn.

He loved watching her move. She was nearly always brisk, confident, and capable, but nonetheless graceful.

Recalling Anne Kerr's solemn, demure nature and simpering conversation that bored a man to slumber, he grinned. Although he had initially resented the lady Rosalie's "misunderstanding" and subsequent insistence that a betrothal existed, his betrothal to Robby ended all trepidation about Lady Anne.

Moreover, he was certain that Robby would *never* bore him.

~

The rest of Wednesday passed quickly for Robina. No sooner did she announce her decision to marry Dev than Rosalie summoned Mistress Geddes from the room where she both sewed and slept to inform her that the golden silk gown must be finished at speed.

"We'll all help you cover the buttons, and I'll do some of the bodice ruching if you like," Rosalie added as further inducement.

Janet and young Bella were both to sleep in Robina's bedchamber, with Bella occupying a pallet on the floor. Robina gave the arrangement no thought until the three of them went up to tidy themselves for supper and she saw the pallet with a wool blanket on it that she knew had come from the kist.

"Will one blanket be enough, Bella?" she asked, striving for calm.

"Aye, sure," Bella said, and Robina prayed that the child was right. She could think of nowhere else in that castle full of visitors and servants to hide the jar.

From then on, though, the women, including Bella,

were so busy stitching that Robina saw Dev, Wat, and Benjy only at mealtimes.

Tradition forbade fitting a wedding dress on the bride, so the cheerful little seamstress measured a weary Robina again Thursday evening to make sure that her measurements had not altered, while the other women continued with their tasks.

At last, Mistress Geddes said with a smile, "'Tis a miracle, m'lady. Not only will ye ha' yon lovely gown for your wedding, but two fine new kirtles, as well."

Thanking her, Robina bade them all goodnight, went to bed, and slept until the rattle of the bed curtains and Corinne's cheery greeting woke her.

"The Scott ladies was all up and dressed an hour since, m'lady," Corinne said. "We let ye sleep longer. But Herself says ye must ha' your bath and wash your hair now if ye'd be fit to welcome Lord Ormiston today."

"Ormiston!" Robina exclaimed, sitting up in a blink. "Mercy, I forgot about him!"

Friday afternoon, Dev greeted his father warily and his unexpected younger sister with delight, having no idea what had brought them to Coklaw. While Ormiston dismounted in the yard, Dev aided Fiona, who flung herself into his arms and gave him a fierce hug.

"Is all well at home, sir?" he asked his father, still holding her.

Watching the two of them with a smile, Ormiston said, "Aye, lad."

"You won't have to wed Anne Kerr, Davy," Fiona said, grinning. "Kerr sent word to Father that she is to marry some Elliot man." Then, rather too casually, she added, "Since they couldn't visit us for Beltane, we thought we'd honor Coklaw with our presence, instead. I hope you are pleased to see us and not horrified."

"Never horrified, Fee," he said, hugging her again. "You are both always welcome here. 'Tis good that Kerr doesn't expect me to offer for Anne, though," he added looking from Fiona to Ormiston. "I've offered for Robina, and she has accepted me."

"Godamercy," Fiona murmured, flicking a wary glance at Ormiston.

Ormiston's eyebrows soared upward. "Fast work for a man who had no intention of marrying," he said evenly.

"I do have a tale to tell, sir," Dev said. "But we should talk more privily."

"Does that mean you won't tell me?" Fiona demanded.

"It does," he said. "But you may ask Robby. If she wants to tell you, she will. Meantime, you must both come inside and make yourselves comfortable. We have rather a crowd here at present. Buccleuch arrived Wednesday and brought his sisters and Lady Meg. His grandaunt, the lady Rosalie Percy, has been with us for nigh a sennight."

Ormiston gave him a longer look. "Just when is this wedding to be, David?"

Dev fought a sudden urge to grin, certain that his father would see little humor in the situation. "Wat's priest will marry us tomorrow, sir."

"Tomorrow!" Fiona exclaimed. "Why did you not send for us sooner?"

"Because I'd already received Father's message that he would arrive today."

"'Twas thoughtful of you to wait for us," Ormiston said

with a frown that Dev easily interpreted. He was thus able to keep his temper when his father added, "One presumes that one need not suspect the Scotts had cause to *press* for such a marriage."

"Mercy, why would they?" Fiona asked, looking from one man to the other.

"No one did, Fee," Dev said. To Ormiston, he said mildly, "I won't deny that a member of Wat's party played a role, sir, but none to concern you. Nor am I displeased with the outcome. So let us go in now, and I'll explain it all to you privily. I warrant you could do with refreshment, perhaps some claret to assuage the thirst of your journey."

"And *I* want to meet Lady Robina and Buccleuch's sisters," Fiona said.

They went in, and as they neared the hall landing, he was relieved to see Robby coming downstairs. When their eyes met, she smiled.

He smiled, too, pleased to see that she had arranged her gleaming hair in its usual single plait, rather than any of the fussier styles she'd attempted.

Bobbing a curtsy when he introduced her to Ormiston, Robby said, "I am sorry I missed meeting you outside, my lord. Things here are a bit chaotic, but do come into the hall. Or"—she looked at Dev—"if you want to talk privily with his lordship, sir, perhaps Lady Fiona would like to join the other ladies."

"An excellent notion, my lady," Ormiston said. "I have not seen you since shortly after your brother Benjamin was born, but I shall be delighted to welcome you to our family. David has done well for himself, I think."

"Thank you, sir," Robina said with a twinkle in her eyes.

Nodding, Ormiston said to Dev, "There is an inner chamber beyond that dais, as I recall. Shall we talk there?"

Detecting concern in Robby's eyes, Dev winked at her before he said, "Also an excellent notion, sir. The claret jug and goblets are there."

⌒

Chukk looked down on the increased activity at Coklaw with dismay. Buccleuch was back again, and a new group of horsemen with one young lady had ridden in a short while ago under a banner he did not recognize. There were so many men-at-arms that, had the tents of these new visitors and those of Buccleuch's men not huddled so close to the north and east walls, he might have mistaken the scene for another siege.

The gate stood wide, and men and women walked to and fro. On the east slope horses grazed near a sike flowing northeastward toward the Teviot from the castle.

Chukk had concealed himself that day on a hill north of the castle and opposite the one they called Sunnyside. He had his crook with him and one of his men, a shaggy-haired lad with the ill-got name of Bangtail Joey. No one had challenged them.

"Sakes, we'll find nowt save trouble an we stay here," Joey complained. "There be too many folks, Chukk. What can ye hope t' gain by it?"

"Information is what," Chukk said. "This tower be the closest one o' size to the line hereabouts, less than a day's march afoot, as ye ken yourself."

"Aye, but we're likely to get wet afore we get home again," Joey muttered grumpily. "Jest look at them clouds yonder, a-growing darker as they come."

"The rain may keep away till tomorrow, though raining then would bring ill-fortune for the bride and groom."

"Ye did say ye'd heard that some'un was a-getting married."

"Sakes, near everyone hereabouts be talking about the Warden o' Coklaw marrying the laird's sister tomorrow. Word o' that wedding will ha' got all over the Borders by now, as quick as news flies hereabouts. Ye must pay more heed to such, Joey."

"What do it ha' to do wi' us, though? Tell me that."

"Sithee, yon warden may ha' summat o' Northumberland's, I'm thinking, if we can return it to his lordship, he'll reward us well."

"If that warden o' yours doesna hang us first."

"Dinna fret. I'm sending ye back to move the lads closer. If ye're afeard, just send some'un else t' meet me and take yourself home."

"Nay, I'll stay," Joey assured him. "But what will ye do whilst I'm awa'?"

"Make sure that our prize be here is what."

"Good fortune t' ye then, 'cause if they dinna catch ye, yon rain surely will. Them black clouds dinna be bringing all their kith and kin for nowt."

"Just fetch the lads, Joey. Settle them in that cleuch west o' where we were before. Nae one will stumble on ye there. I'm thinking the rain will keep off till morning, but dinna try to find me 'less ye fail t' see me by Sunday midday."

"Aye, sure," Joey said.

Chukk agreed with Joey about the rain but thought it might provide a gleam of hope. If it did not come tonight, it would come tomorrow.

Then, if the jar he sought still lay buried beneath the sapling, he could figure out how to collect it. If the hole was empty, as he strongly suspected it was, he would simply need a new course of action.

While he waited, he'd have plenty of time and solitude to plan for either option.

# Chapter 17 —————————

Pouring claret into two goblets, Dev handed one to Ormiston and set the jug on the inner chamber table between them.

"Many folks have passed through here today," Ormiston observed as Dev sat in the chair behind the table, facing him.

"They have, aye. News travels fast, as you know, so people have been coming since Tuesday to offer their felicitations. Since Robby decided only on Wednesday to marry me, we told our people to say 'twas nobbut a rumor before then."

"Tell me the whole tale now," Ormiston said.

Dev sipped his wine, taking the time to compose his thoughts. Then he said, "Lady Rosalie began it, sir. I'll not accuse her of doing so willfully. But..."

He went on to explain what had happened and saw that Ormiston, too, was skeptical of Rosalie's "misunderstanding."

Since Dev had accepted his fate more willingly than he'd anticipated, he felt more amusement than empathy as he read his father's changing expressions.

When Dev finished his tale, Ormiston said, "I know

Lady Meg, of course, and her sister Amalie, who married
Westruther. But I've not clapped eyes on their younger
sister. I did hear that she'd married across the line."

"Aye, to Richard Percy, a cousin of Northumberland's
and of her mother, Annabel Murray. He died in Wales
several years ago. Their sons had fostered and married
elsewhere, so Rosalie returned to Scotland, rather than
live with either of them."

"Does she often play mischief-maker?"

Dev smiled. "I've only just met her, sir, but Wat says
she does not. I'd say she's imperceptive, but she may just
be unwilling to admit a mistake."

"Or she thought you'd make a fine husband for Robina."

"Aye," Dev said. "But by my troth, sir, I feel as if I'm
the fortunate one. I thought first that I was just doing
the honorable thing, because I knew the news would
spread no matter what I said or could persuade Rosalie
to admit."

"You were right," Ormiston agreed. "Even someone
claiming an error would just be adding fuel to the rumor.
By the time it passed from one mouth to two ears, it had
become a proposal of marriage, will-ye-nil-ye."

"What I don't know is if Robby agreed to it so she
could stay here at Coklaw until Benjy is of age or because
she truly cares for me."

Ormiston shrugged. "That's of no import now."

"It's important to me."

"Then you must make her care, lad, as any husband
must who wants his wife to think well of him."

They chatted desultorily after that until a rap on the
door announced that supper was ready. Adjourning to the
dais in complete amity with his father, Dev hoped only

that Ormiston would come to like Robby as much as he did.

She soon arrived, leading the other ladies with Fiona. While they went around to the ladies' end of the table, Dev's gaze followed Robby until she and Fiona paused to let Meg and Rosalie pass them and take their places next to his.

Stepping back so Ormiston could greet Lady Meg and let her present Rosalie to him, Dev saw his father's gaze fix on Rosalie in a startled and unexpectedly intrigued way.

Rosalie smiled, and her eyes twinkled. However, she swiftly lowered her lashes, behaving, Dev thought sourly, more like a simpering miss than a woman of her years and experience. The fur-trimmed rose-pink damask gown she wore boasted a deep décolletage, he noted, revealing her plump, inviting breasts.

Shifting his gaze back to Ormiston, only to meet Wat's grin and raised eyebrows instead, Dev recollected himself. People in the lower hall were nearly all in their places. The shuffling ended, silence fell, and he asked Father Hubert to say the grace.

After the meal, Wat stood when Lady Meg did but kept Dev in his seat with a firm hand on his shoulder. Then, in clarion tones, he said, "All who would aid in washing the bridegroom's feet, as tradition demands, step forward without disturbing the ladies as they leave the hall. Geordie, did you fetch the basin?"

"Aye, laird," Wat's Geordie shouted from the rear of the hall.

Trying to stand, only to have Wat clamp steely hands on each of his shoulders, Dev saw Ormiston assisting Rosalie from the dais to follow the other ladies. Two serving lads moved to escort her from the hall, and Ormiston returned to the dais, beaming at Dev.

"'Tis been years since I aided a foot-washing," he said with a boyish grin. "Methinks you'll have the cleanest feet in Scotland if they don't drown you in the process."

"Help me turn him and his chair around," Wat said.

Ormiston happily obeyed, while six men carried a huge tub to the dais.

Dev saw that it held little water and a great deal of mud. A cheering, ever-increasing crowd surrounded them until he began to fear that they *would* drown him.

Just as he thought they'd finished, Wat ordered a second bathing with soap and water, declaring that Dev's feet were still filthy. Hilarity, many riotous wagers, and much wine, whisky, and ribaldry followed. By the end of the night, while those who could still walk aided each other in seeing him "safely" upstairs, the—by then—drink-sodden Dev wondered if he'd survive to see his bedchamber, let alone his wedding day.

He knew no more until the bed curtains rattled noisily open at what he was sure must be hours before sunrise. Coll greeted him then with a too-hearty, nearly deafening "Good day to ye, sir! 'Tis a grand day for a wedding!"

"Doucely, man, doucely," Dev protested, but it came out in a croak. His mouth was dry. Some imp of Satan was playing drums in his head, and his eyes objected to even the gray light from a nearby unshuttered window.

"Ye'll want this," Coll said, handing him a small towel-wrapped bundle. "Sym Elliot brung it from the ice house."

Gratefully leaning against the pillows and placing the cold, damp bundle over his eyes, Dev groaned. "How long till my wedding?"

"Nobbut an hour or so," Coll said, startling him so that he nearly bolted upright before his head reminded him of how foolhardy such abruptness was.

"Fetch me some water, will you?"

Coll handed him a mug. "Sym said t' gi'e ye this, instead. It'll aid ye more than water, he said."

The smell nearly did Dev in. However, he sipped manfully and discovered that the taste was better than the smell. When he'd finished it all, he said, "What was in that?"

"Sym said not to ask," Coll said.

Deciding it would either cure him or kill him, and if it killed him, he'd neither know nor care, Dev lay back again and held the ice-filled towel to his head.

⁓

At nearly the same time, Corinne woke Robina, who had gone to bed much earlier than Dev had. The other women had assured her that she'd be wiser to sleep than to fret about what the men were doing to Dev.

When Robina protested, Lady Meg had said firmly, "You have naught left to do, love. Thanks to Mistress Geddes's skill and efficiency, your dress will be finished by the time we put it on you in the morning."

"But what if it doesn't fit?"

"You cannot try it on without risking the happiness of your marriage, Robby," Janet reminded her. "So leave everything to us now and go to sleep. I'll sleep with Bella in one of the wee rooms upstairs, so you'll have your bedchamber to yourself tonight."

"Aye, dearling; sleep well," Rosalie said. Then, with a knowing smile, she added, "You may not get another chance for some time."

Robina did not know how tired she was until she lay under the covers, but that was the last thought she had until morning.

"I'm famished, Corinne," she said then, sitting up and stretching. "I feel as if I've not eaten for days."

"Ye slept longer than usual, aye," Corinne said. "But ye canna go down yet. Sir David mustna see ye till the wedding, and ye've nae time to eat, anyway. Since ye washed your hair and bathed yesterday and ye'll wear your hair doon yer back today, Lady Meg said I wasna t' wake ye till it were time t' dress."

"The wedding is to be shortly before our midday meal. It cannot be *that* late!"

"Aye, it is, though. It doesna look it because o' the clouds. It looks like rain, m'lady, and that be bad luck on a wedding day."

"Not hereabouts," Robina said. "People in Hawick say, 'Happy be the bride gits a shower on her side.'"

"Perhaps, but ye'll no chance fastening buttons or tying your laces, or looking back as ye walk from the altar wi' Sir David. 'Twould be tempting the devil to do such things. Everyone kens that."

Robina wondered about tempting the devil. Mayhap she would start calling Dev "Davy" as his sister and Wat did. She dismissed the thought as soon as it occurred, though. She couldn't think of him as "Davy." To her, he was and always would be Dev.

The other ladies arrived to help her dress, and shortly afterward, Lady Meg and Rosalie went downstairs. Leading Janet, Bella, and Fiona down more slowly, in her sleek saffron-silk gown, Robina stopped at the hall archway, amazed at the size of the crowd. She prayed that no part of her gown would open to embarrass her before so many.

The ladies had slipped loose white ribbons through the aglets in back where her bodice lacing should be, ribbons that audience members would snatch away when she passed by afterward. The eight silk-covered buttons on each sleeve were undone. And, beneath the gown, the ribbon that gathered it close to keep it on was untied.

Tradition also forbade sashes, belts, or buckles, so she had not worn a girdle round her hips. She had never felt so vulnerable.

All anyone need do, she thought uneasily, was to reach out, grab a sleeve as she passed, and give it a good yank. That would bare her to everyone.

Her silk-shod feet had rooted to the archway's flagstone floor.

Fiona, Bella, and Janet kept silent, but Robina sensed their impatience.

Dev stood on the dais by the makeshift altar, next to the priest, murmuring to Benjy, who stood beside him. Ormiston was next to Benjy, gazing on the lower hall. The men were tall, dwarfing the young laird.

A touch to Robina's shoulder startled her. Turning, she found Wat beside her.

"I'll take you to the dais, Robby," he said with his warm smile. "After all, someone in the family must give you to that devil, so I've appointed myself. Hope you don't mind."

"Only if giving me away means you'll feel obliged to ignore my shouts for aid if he brutalizes me," she replied lightly. Wat's very presence had eased her tension.

With a direct look and no sign of humor, he said firmly, "You know you can rely on me if *ever* you need me, lass."

"I do, sir, and I thank you. You don't think he's a devil, either, I know."

His grin flashed then. "Whether he is, is not, or may become so, I'll back you against him anytime, cousin."

Noting that Dev watched them with a frown, she felt deep satisfaction rather than concern to see it. She smiled at Wat and said, "I think we'd best begin, sir, don't you?"

Hearing his soft chuckle, knowing he'd also seen Dev's frown, she rested a hand on Wat's extended forearm and went with him happily to meet her fate.

Dev watched Robby and Wat approach the dais with her three bride-maidens behind them. Bella walked alone. Jannie and Fiona followed her, side by side.

Although he'd never thought that he was capable of jealousy or understood exactly how the emotion manifested itself, he'd recognized it the instant Wat touched Robby's shoulder with only that beautiful, doubtless sensuous, golden silk between his flesh and hers. To touch her in such a way before Dev could was practically a hanging offense. He wanted to give Wat all he deserved for taking such a liberty.

"A groom usually greets his bride with a smile, my son," the priest said dulcetly.

"Ye *should* smile at her, Dev," Benjy muttered. "Our Beany is gey beautiful, I think. I ha' never seen her in such a splendid gown before."

"Nor have I," Dev said. Catching Robby's eye and detecting a distinct twinkle, he collected his wits. The last thing he wanted on this day of days was to hear her tease him for jealousy that she must easily have perceived.

Nevertheless, having recognized it, he knew he would likely feel it often, because Benjy was right. With her tawny waves unbound, flowing over her shoulders to her waist as they did, she was more than beautiful, and she was about to be his. A wave of masculine pride and responsibility surged through him.

Ormiston, shifting weight, made a slight sound with his shoe. That it drew Dev's notice told him how quiet the hall was. The sea of visitors, servants, tenants, and other guests seemed to hold its breath as Robby and her attendants stepped onto the dais.

Eyes downcast, she approached Dev, watching her step and managing her skirt. The priest stepped forward when she reached her place. Her long, dark lashes flickered then. When she looked up at Dev, his breath stopped in his throat.

Her cheeks were rosy, her mossy eyes limpid. When her lips parted invitingly, he felt his body stir.

"Face me now, my son," Father Hubert murmured.

Dev obeyed and, seconds later, gave thanks that he had only to repeat what the priest said. His wits had abandoned him. His single thought was that Robby was nearly his, in a loose silken gown that blatantly invited sex.

His body stirred again, and he prayed that he wouldn't spend himself before the ceremony ended. The words were a mere buzz, because under the silky golden surface that screamed for his touch, his bride wore at most a thin shift and, irrelevantly, a pair of flimsy silk slippers.

"Have you a ring, my son?"

Startled, Dev took from Benjy's sweaty hand the ring

that Lady Meg had given him the previous day and handed it to the priest. Then, warily, he watched Robby's reaction.

While the priest blessed the ring and then slipped it onto her ring finger, she looked at it and then at Dev, her eyes wide and sparkling. "Where—?"

The priest interrupted her. "Prithee, my children, face your guests."

Hearing him through echoes of Robby's delight and his own gratitude to Lady Meg for her gift, Dev obeyed, tucking Robby's left hand into the crook of his right elbow.

"My lords, my ladies, and all who bless this wedding by your presence, I present Sir David and Lady Ormiston. You may now express your approval and prepare to feast their happiness. And you, Sir David, may kiss your lady bride."

Dev heard that plainly and willingly obeyed.

"Take care that you don't have this dress off me," Robby protested, her lips moving warmly against his. "I've feared it might fall off ever since I put it on."

"I don't want that either, my love," he murmured.

"*What* did you call me?"

"You heard me."

He hugged her closer and saw that some of the ribbons so flimsily linking the aglets at the back of her bodice had nearly freed themselves.

Tugging gently at the worst offender until he could grasp both ends between his first finger and thumb, he managed to tighten it a bit. He saw then that he'd guessed right about her shift being thin. It looked as if it, too, were silk.

His fingers itched to stroke the gown and all that it concealed.

Sitting beside Dev for the wedding feast, Robina waited for the servers to move to others at the table before she said, "How did you come by my mother's wedding ring?"

"You remember it, then. Lady Meg didn't know if you would."

She held out her hand to look at the narrow gold band and the round amethyst nestled in it, feeling again her joy at recognizing the ring when the priest had taken it from Dev. Memories of her mother flooded through her when the priest touched it to her left thumb, index finger, and middle finger, saying, "In the name of the Father, the Son, and the Holy Spirit…" Then, slipping it onto her ring finger, he'd said, "Amen."

It had felt as if her mother were blessing their marriage.

"Of course, I remember it," she said. "Before Mam, it was my Granddame Gledstanes's ring and *her* granddame's before her. But what had Lady Meg to do with it?"

"Your father gave it to her before he died and said that, although it is a Gledstanes ring, your mother wanted you to have it on your wedding day. Rab had agreed, too."

A wary look in his eyes suggested something left unsaid, but she smiled. "Thank you for letting me have it as *my* wedding ring. It was a wonderful surprise."

"What else are you thinking, lass?" he asked. "I keep expecting you to add 'but.' "

Searching his expression and finding only curiosity, she said frankly, "I did wonder if you'd liefer have given me one that marked me as your possession."

To her relief, he chuckled. "And I worried that you'd

expect a ring of mine. I'll think of many ways to demon-
strate that you're mine, sweetheart, I promise you."

That promise, the endearment that accompanied it,
and the warm way he looked at her sent unfamiliar heat
pulsing through her. She felt it from her head, to her heart,
to her toes, in places and ways that she had never known
before Dev came into her life.

Men who had brought instruments began to play
them. Others sang, and in no time, the lower hall became
increasingly rowdy.

She saw Dev turn to Wat and Wat gesture to Sym
Elliot. Sym got up and gestured to Benjy, who followed
him from the dais with a grin. Soon, Jock and other
Coklaw and Rankilburn men began quietly moving
through the hall forming a path of sorts from the dais to
the archway.

"Time to go upstairs, lass," Dev murmured in her ear.
"Whilst our men can still maintain control."

"Nay, my lad," Wat said sternly and loudly enough
for Robina to hear him as he put a hand to Dev's shoulder. "Her ladyship's bride-maidens and the other ladies
will attend her. You will stay with us until she's ready
for you."

$\sim$

"Just who is in charge of this place?" Dev demanded.

Grinning, Wat said, "You are, just as soon as the ladies
have had time to prepare your bride for you. Meantime,
we'll keep you busy. Have some more wine, laddie, but
don't overdo it. You're joining my family, so you *must*
perform well tonight."

Since Dev's own men had joined them and showed no

sign of aiding him, he submitted to the inevitable, wistfully watching Robby leave the hall.

Even with men lining the pathway, she'd already lost most of the ribbons from her gown. He saw her clap a hand to her bodice as if fearing that it, too, would vanish. However, she escaped without further embarrassment.

The singing and music continued, and the songs grew rowdier and more profane until Dev laughed as loudly as anyone.

Then Wat drew his attention to Sym in the archway, gesturing.

"Time to claim your bride," Wat said cheerfully. "We'll come along to see you suitably prepared for her."

"I'd rather prepare myself, thanks," Dev growled.

"Aye, sure, but 'tis our ancient duty to serve you."

"You're enjoying this too much. I missed *your* wedding, so..."

"Nearly everyone missed it," Wat said. "I'd have recommended something similar to you, too, had you given me warning."

Given no say in his doom from then on, Dev reached his bedchamber wearing no more than a grimace. He'd retained a grip on only a tattered shirt that he thought was his.

A grinning Sym stood guard at the door.

When Wat raised his eyebrows, Sym nodded. "The other ladies ha' gone up, sir, and Father Hubert blessed the bed. Herself told him God would forgive his doing it afore her ladyship undressed. I needna tell ye that he said the blessing right quick after that."

"Wise man," Wat said. After a brisk double rap on the door, he lifted the latch and pushed it open. "In you go," he said to Dev. "See that you do credit to your sex, or reap the cost forevermore."

Laughter and jeers from the men below them echoed through the stairwell. Then Wat and Sym gave Dev a push and, to Dev's deep relief, shut the door after him.

The uproar that had accompanied him up the stairs continued.

Bolting the door, he prayed that no one would test the strength of *that* bolt.

# Chapter 18 ————————————

Robina, already nervous, stared in dismay at her clearly naked husband. He faced his bed, with her in it, holding the remains of a shirt strategically before him.

His hair was tousled and his face as red as fury. But he did not speak until she squirmed against the soft new sheet and tugged the coverlet higher over her breasts.

His expression softened, but he still looked strangely unsure of himself.

The ladies Meg and Rosalie had sent Janet and Bella away after letting them help her undress. Then the two older women had plumped pillows behind her to prop her up. But she was as naked as Dev was and felt more vulnerable than ever.

Other feelings stirred, too…a burning anticipation of what lay ahead, an eagerness to learn more about being a married woman.

The sudden clap of thunder startled them both. At the same time, lightning lit the sky outside the open window, and the rain that had threatened since dawn poured down.

It slanted in through the narrow north window a few feet from the bed's head, and through the west-facing window between its foot and the privy-stair door. The master's bedchamber shared its eastern wall, to Robina's left, with the upper half of the inner chamber and the hall below. Dev had come through the door near the southeast corner. The narrower privy-stair door was in the southwest one.

Dev moved quickly, still holding the shirt in front of him, to close the shutters, darkening the room more but giving Robina fine views of his muscular profile and well-formed backside.

When he turned to face her, she clamped her teeth on her lower lip to keep from grinning. Evidently, he could still discern her amusement, because a slow, appreciative smile crept to his face.

She said the first thing then that came to mind: "You look like a mischievous bairn, thinking mischievous thoughts."

"You heard what Wat said. I'm to do credit to my manhood."

"So, even the Lord of Buccleuch and Rankilburn can act the dafty."

"Is that what you think? That this is daft?"

"That is *not* what I said. I said, or as good as said, that Wat is daft if he thinks you need to prove your manhood. I'll tell him so, if you like."

"Move over and let a man climb into his bed," Dev said, striding toward her and casting his shirt aside.

Gasping, she moved hastily away from him toward the wall.

Hearing her gasp and seeing her scoot away, Dev hesitated at the edge of the bed. But, when her steady gaze met his, he climbed in and took her in his arms.

"I wanted to strip that gown off of you myself," he muttered, stroking her thick, wavy hair.

"Tradition rules at weddings," she said. "However, I'm sure we can arrange for you to strip it off me later."

"See here, Robby," he said, turning onto his left elbow so he could more accurately judge her feelings from her reactions. "You sound confident, but I know you've never coupled before. If you're frightened or uncertain, you must tell me."

"Lady Meg explained it to me long ago," she said. "I'd asked Father what married people did and why they slept together. He wouldn't say, and I feared I had upset him by asking. Then, a few days later, Lady Meg came to visit. She was frank."

"She is always frank, brutally so sometimes," he said. Shifting her hair aside to bare her nearer shoulder, he kissed it lightly.

"She said most of it is pleasurable, that but for the first time, she'd enjoyed it."

Her words made his body throb for hers, but he knew he should take things slowly. He said, "I'll make it as pleasurable as I can."

Then, capturing her lips with his, he kissed her deeply and gently stroked her shoulders and arms until he felt her relax. She responded to his kisses eagerly, dancing her tongue against his when it slipped into the softness of her mouth.

When he knew she was ready for more, he eased the sheet and coverlet away from their bodies, baring her breasts, first to his touch and then to his lips. Kissing her, he stroked her body lower and lower until, while he plundered her lips and mouth again, his seeking hand stroked the soft curls at the juncture of her legs.

Her eyes had remained closed, but they opened wide then, and she stiffened. When she gave no other sign of resistance, he began to explore her nether lips with his fingertips. Next, they explored the area within more thoroughly.

His cock was stiff, trembling with its need, but he did his best to ignore it long enough to prepare her as well as he could. When she moaned softly and then muttered, "You're driving my senses daft, Dev. Even so, I can think of naught save what you must do. Prithee, get it done."

"I don't want to hurt you."

"Blethers. If you can make me feel like this, I'll not complain long."

Grinning, he eased himself up and positioned himself to take her. Her request reminded him of his father's advice, years before: "With a virgin bride, 'tis best to get the business done," Ormiston had said. "*Then* teach her about pleasuring."

Robina wondered why Lady Meg had not told her more about the pleasures of coupling. Then Dev withdrew his fingers and pressed something larger into her.

Knowing what it was, she braced herself.

"Doucely, Robby," he murmured. "It will be less painful if you can relax."

She did her best, and he eased his way in. She was glad that Lady Meg had warned her that men soon lost the ability to control themselves, because after moving slowly and carefully for a time, he moved faster and then began to pound into her.

It was over soon after that, and she felt only relief that it was.

She thanked her ladyship then for explaining that men often fell asleep directly afterward. Dev at least waited until they had cleansed themselves and were back in bed. Then he put an arm around her, pulled her close, and silently kissed the top of her head. Lying back, he relaxed and soon began softly to snore.

The next thing she knew it was morning and the rain had stopped.

Mote-ridden sunbeams pierced the shutters. One of them laid a diagonal gold stripe on the opposite wall, across a sampler she'd stitched as a child for her mother.

Thinking she should tell Dev about that sampler, she realized that he'd vanished.

Getting up, she felt a bit sore but otherwise none the worse for their bedding. Already looking forward to the next time, she found the creamy shift she'd worn under the saffron silk gown and pulled it on over her head. Opening the door, prepared to shout for Corinne, she found the maid sitting on the landing step.

Scrambling up with a smile, Corinne said, "I'd wager nae one told ye we'd put your new kirtles in one o' the master's kists."

Shaking her head, Robina said, "Come help me dress. I'm famished."

"Aye, Sir David still be at the high table, but he said to let ye sleep. Everyone will be leaving soon, save for Lord Ormiston and the lady Fiona."

"The Scotts are leaving? Why?"

"Herself did command it," Corinne said.

"Lady Meg *ordered* his lordship to leave this morning?"

Corinne cocked her head thoughtfully. "Mayhap he gave the orders, but it were Herself who said the last thing the pair o' ye'd want were a host o' lingering guests to feed and entertain. That be when Buccleuch gave the order."

Chuckling, Robina said, "I see. I'll miss them . . ." Pausing, she realized that Corinne had not mentioned Rosalie. "Is Cousin Rosalie going, too?"

"Aye," Corinne said. "I think she might ha' stayed, but Herself said ye'd be safe without her now and that the pair o' ye need time alone to know each other better. I think our Benjy will miss Lady Bella, though. He told Ash Nixon she were the only guest who paid him any heed."

With a mental note to have Dev or Coll explain to Ash that he should not reveal Benjy's confidences to others, Robina thanked Corinne and turned her attention to which new kirtle she would wear first.

From the two that were finished—a primrose one, and a new and slightly darker pink—she chose the pink one.

When Corinne asked her to sit so she could arrange her hair, Robina said, "Just brush and plait it as usual. I want no more loops or twists."

"Aye, then," Corinne replied amiably.

After that, Robina was ready in a trice and hurried down to find Dev, Ormiston, and Fiona at the high table, listening to a visibly agitated Benjy.

"What's amiss here?" Robina asked as she approached them.

Benjy turned to her, his face tearstained and white with fury. "Some'un ripped Rab's tree out o' the ground and dug our hole bigger. I told Sandy and them to find the wicked bast—" He glanced at Dev. "I mean, the . . ."

"Villain," Robina supplied gently when he paused again.

"Aye, him," Benjy snapped. "I told our lads to find him and hang him!"

Looking from the boy to Dev, she said, "*Are* they looking for him?"

"Benjy just told me about it, but I expect they are," he said. "I don't know why anyone would do such a thing. But I sent Ash to find Sandy or Jock, so we'll soon know more. The Scotts are upstairs now, preparing to leave. How did you sleep?"

"Soundly," she murmured, her thoughts having flown to the jar of coins in her previous bedchamber. If someone had pulled up Rab's tree to dig deeper—

"Will ye help me put Rab's tree back?" Benjy demanded.

"Aye, sure," Robina promised. "It may be damaged, but we can plant another hawthorn if it is. Rab knows now that it's where you want to talk to him."

"Good, then," Benjy said. "I do talk to him other places, too, but—" Breaking off, he said, "Here comes Tad wi' your breakfast, Beany. Ye'd better sit and eat quick."

She obeyed, exchanging greetings with Ormiston and Fiona as she took her place and then chatting between bites with Fiona.

Tad returned minutes later. To Benjy, he said, "Jock said they couldna find nowt, sir. It rained hard, he said, and the ground be nobbut mud. Whoever dug that hole, Sandy said, must ha' looked a sight after. But the rain washed out all o' his tracks."

Dev said, "We had many visitors, Benjy, and most of them stayed till dark. The culprit might have been someone just acting daft after too much drink."

Benjy shook his head, and Robina saw Ash shaking his, too. "Why do you disagree," she asked the older boy.

"Yon hole be too deep, m'lady," Ash said. "Sandy said

it looks as if someone sought summat else in that hole 'sides a wee tree."

Knowing that if she looked at Dev, her guilty knowledge of the jar would reveal itself, she returned her gaze to Benjy, instead.

To her dismay, he frowned at her and said angrily, "Ye said it were a good place. Ye didna say nowt about some...some *culprit* digging it up."

Tears streaming again, he turned and ran from the hall.

"I'll fetch 'im, mistress," Ash said as he started to follow.

Robina stopped him. "Let him go, Ash. He'll not go far, and I think he'd liefer be alone. If he hasn't tidied his room yet, you might see to that for him. It will likely lift his spirits more than anyone's company would right now."

"Aye, then, mistress, I'll do that," Ash said and hurried away.

Glancing at Dev, she noticed at once that his eyes had narrowed.

Something deep within her quivered at the sight, reminding her of what Janet had said about facing Wat's anger and her own reply, that Dev's could be more dangerous. He was going to be annoyed that she had kept something from him, especially something as valuable as a jarful of silver.

She dared not put off telling him about it any longer.

⁓

Robby had the same speculative look on her face that Rab had always had when he'd done something he knew Dev would dislike or consider reckless. Whatever she had done, he'd soon have it out of her, but he decided they should see their guests off before he confronted her.

She straightened then and said abruptly, "I have something to show you, but I must fetch it, and I cannot show it to you here or discuss it inside the tower."

Dev frowned. "You cannot tell me anything more?"

"I'd liefer show you than tell you," she said. Then, biting her lower lip, she added, "I can think of nowhere inside the keep where the Greenlaws, a household servant, or one of our guests might not intrude. But people are still wandering about here and in the yard, and Wat's men are outside the wall, too, are they not?"

"Aye, they are packing up now, but they set their tents north and northeast of the wall. We must stay nearby, in any event, since the Scotts will depart soon, and we must bid them farewell. If you can safely take your treasure outside, we'll find a place to talk—mayhap at your favorite tree?"

She hesitated. Her expression still revealed her wariness... of him.

Unable to think of a better place in a household or yard teeming with people, Robina said at last, "Very well, I'll meet you at the tree. But we must be certain that no one can get close enough to see us or hear what I say to you."

He nodded. "I'll tell Jock we want privacy. He can keep watch himself, and I'll have him send two lads to check those woods and keep others away."

"Not Jem Keith," Robina said hastily, thinking of Corinne and unwilling to trust Jem, because he seemed too quick to share what he knew with her.

"I'll speak to Jock," Dev said. "But if you fear that one of my men may creep close enough to hear aught I say in a private conversation, be easy, lass. They are all brave men, but not one of them is brave enough for that."

His very tone sent a chill up her spine, and she believed him. Even so, they would have to take care.

"I'll meet you at the tree, then," she said. "I must fetch my cloak."

Dev found Jock in the stable and said, "I'm going to meet the lady Robina by that great oak tree a short way inside the woods west of the gate. We don't want interruption, so find Coll and Eckie and tell them to see that no one in those woods disturbs us. They must keep their distance, too. Send them now, and tell them to let me know when they're in place. If either of them can hear us talking, he is to whistle a warning and move back."

"I'll see to it, sir," Jock said. "Coll is helping Eckie and his lordship's lads wi' their horses, so they're both in the stable. I'll keep watch, too, from the wall walk."

Nodding, then deciding that he and Robby should walk outside the wall together, Dev turned toward the keep to watch for her. Eckie and Coll emerged from the stable shortly thereafter, and he walked to the gate with them.

"Our usual signals, sir?" Coll asked.

"Aye," Dev said. "Just make sure those woods west of here are clear."

He watched them go and stood by the gateway, open now so that Wat's men could come and go. Even so, Shag stood nearby, keeping watch.

Dev beckoned to him. "If you see people heading toward those west woods, discourage them, Shag. Her ladyship and I want to be alone there for a time."

"Aye, sir, I'll see to it," Shag said.

Robby came down the steps then, wearing a cloak that he thought looked too heavy for the day. But it would be cooler and perhaps still damp in the woods. She walked toward him, holding her cloak closed, and he could tell—although most people would not—that she concealed something under the cloak.

"This way, lass," he said when she drew near and he knew that Shag could still hear them. "We'll walk yonder. Shag will shout when Wat comes down."

Robby obeyed silently but looked around as if she expected an enemy to pop up from the shrubbery. He scanned the area, too. Scattered clouds drifted eastward, and a ghostly pale oval moon had risen above the horizon, but no one heeded the two of them.

"We'll be safe here," he said as they entered the woodland and walked to her tree. "My lads will see that we're left in peace."

"I hope so," she said. Eyeing him warily again, she began to open her cloak.

"Wait one more moment," he said, listening for Coll and Eckie to signal him.

She nodded, and seconds later an owl hooted some distance southwest of them. Another echoed it from the north.

"Owls at midday?" she said, raising her eyebrows.

"My lads," Dev said. "Now, let's see this treasure of yours."

She opened her cloak and produced a crockery jar wrapped in a towel. "This is the secret you once asked me about," she said, handing it to him. "Open it, and please don't be too angry with me."

She watched as Dev dealt easily with the wired-on cap. He handed it to her to hold while he peered into the jar. Then, glancing at her with a frown, he poured several coins into his free hand.

"Where the devil did you get this?" he muttered.

"I scraped it with a shovel the day you returned from Scott's Hall."

His expression showed his quick understanding. "In the hole you'd begun to dig for Benjy's tree?"

"Aye, but I don't know how it got there or where the coins came from. My father would surely have told Rab had *he* buried it there. That's a lot of gelt, is it not?"

"It is more than a lot," Dev said. "The silver is tarnished black, so it's been there for some time. Mayhap Greenlaw knows about it."

"I never thought of Greenlaw," she admitted. "I cannot imagine anyone at Coklaw burying it outside the wall, though. Would it not have been more sensible to hide it inside the keep, or to have buried it under a stone in the yard?"

"It would, aye," he said. "What do you expect me to do with it?"

"I don't know, but I knew I had to tell you about it," Robina said. "Sithee, I had it hidden in a blanket kist in my bedchamber. When the Scotts surprised us, I had no time to find another hiding place, so I've lived in terror that someone would need more blankets."

"I'll keep it now," he said. "And we'll keep this between us, Robby, until we learn more about it. Anything buried on Coklaw land belongs legally to Coklaw, so until we learn otherwise, this is rightfully Benjy's property. I agree with you, though, that Rab knew naught of this. If he had, I think he'd have told me."

"Or me," she said with a nod. "He doesn't...didn't know about it."

"We cannot be sure of that," Dev said gently. "It is, however, unlikely that he'd neglect to mention such a fortune to me before he died. At the end, his purpose in exerting himself to talk at all was to see you, Benjy, and Coklaw well protected."

A slight scraping sound above them drew Robina's attention upward. A density of oak leaves on one of the higher branches was trembling.

"What is it?" Dev said.

"A squirrel, I expect," she replied. "But we should go in, and I must keep the jar under my cloak until we are safely in our chamber. I was afraid that if we tried to discuss it there, Coll might interrupt us. But there is a carved box of Rab's on a high shelf there that the jar should fit into. I think it will be safest there."

"Aye, I ken the box you mean," Dev said. Carefully returning the coins to the jar, he replaced its lid and wired it back in place. Then, rewrapping the jar in the towel, he handed it to her.

When he put an arm around her shoulders, she smiled up at him. "Art showing them all that I belong to you now, sir?"

"I'm showing them that I protect my own, Robby."

She had not changed her mind about one person possessing another, even when the other was his wife. But Dev's arm felt natural and right there.

In the oak tree, high above them, Benjy remained motion-less on his branch, praying that if he could not see them, they would not see him. Happy as he was that Dev had married Beany, he felt sad about it, too. In time, Dev would take her away to live with him, and *he* would lose the last member of his family.

When he'd run from the dreadful hole the culprit had left after ripping out Rab's tree, he had headed for Sunnyside Hill. But, recalling that Buccleuch and his family would soon depart, and knowing that Dev and Beany would take a dim view of his not being there to bid them farewell, he'd circled westward through the woods to Beany's tree.

Shortly afterward, when he saw Dev's men, Coll and Eckie, heading toward him, he'd climbed higher so they wouldn't see him and tell him to hie himself back inside the wall. He needed to think.

He'd never meant to listen to Dev and Beany talking, but neither had he wanted to shout down that he was in the tree. Beany would say that he'd climbed too high, and Dev might declare that he ought not to have come outside the wall at all. It seemed simpler then to keep still and wait for them to leave.

Besides, he'd torn the new tan shirt that Beany's seam-stress had made for him.

He knew now that he'd been wrong to keep quiet, and he winced inside at the thought that Tig might have come looking for him and stopped under the tree to bark. Then Dev or even Beany might have climbed up to see why Tig barked, and *he* would never have heard their so-interesting conversation.

For the further sake of his own skin, Benjy waited until Coll and Eckie had followed them through the gateway. Then, climbing down from the tree, he made his way casually to the north side of the wall. There, he helped one of Wat's men tie a rolled tent to his pony's saddle and then walked with him around to the gate and into the yard.

No one heeded him, so he was safe unless he slipped and mentioned what he'd overheard. Benjy hoped he was wise enough not to do such a daft thing.

He *was* wise enough to know what Dev would do if he did.

Dev followed Robby upstairs to the master's bedchamber and looked inside before they entered to be sure Corinne was not there. Finding the way clear, they entered and he shut the door behind them. Taking the towel-wrapped jar from Robby, he said, "I hope you know you can trust me with this."

Meeting his gaze solemnly, she said just as quietly, "I've entrusted you with myself, sir. There's Rab's box, yonder," she added, pointing to the carved box on its high shelf. "I should have told you about the jar at once, but..."

She hesitated as if she was uncomfortable explaining herself to him. Then, in a rush, she said, "I kept it to myself because Rab"—she shook her head—"that is, because Rosalie shares any news or idle talk she hears too easily. I wanted to keep it from her."

"I am not angry, sweetheart, but honored that you did tell me," Dev said as he reached up to take the box from its shelf and opened it. "We will take good care of this until we learn more about it and decide what to do next."

"I should see if Benjy has come in yet," she said after he'd put the unwrapped jar in the box and gently returned the box to its shelf. "The Scotts must be ready to leave, and he should be here to make his farewells."

"Go find him then," Dev said. "I'll be along shortly."

He watched her go, listened for her footsteps heading downstairs, and then bolted the door quietly and took the box down from the shelf again.

Then, bolting the door to the service stairs that connected the chamber with the lower levels, he took out the jar, removed its cap, and poured a handful of the coins into his hand. Laying them out on the table near the west window, he found that they were a mix of English and Scottish coins predating the current kings of both countries. The mixture looked like the sort that Border nobles used to pay their warriors. He recognized marks of Alexander III and Robert I on a few Scottish ones, making some more than a century old.

He also found some bearing the mark of Scotland's Robert III but none showing King Jamie's mark, so whoever had buried the jar had likely done so before Robert III's death in 1406. It was common enough to find English and Scottish coins on both sides of the line, though. People accepted any such as payment, and silver lasted a long while.

Certain that Coll would take no immediate interest in the carved box, Dev carefully returned the coins to the jar, the jar to the box, and the box to its place on the shelf.

Then, unbolting both doors, he went in search of Wat, aware that he had neglected his primary, soon departing guest much longer than good manners allowed.

# Chapter 19 ─────────────

Robina went downstairs, believing she had acquitted herself well regarding the jar of coins. Dev knew about it now, and they might learn more soon.

*"You lied to your husband. He won't react well to that, Beany."*

Nearly jumping out of her skin, she whirled on the stair, because Rab's voice had sounded right behind her. He was not there, not in body at least.

She muttered, "If you mean what I said about Rosalie, I didn't lie. I could hardly tell him that *you* said not to tell anyone else. Where have you been?"

*"With you, lass, always with you."*

"Mercy! I hope not," she said, remembering the previous night with Dev.

He chuckled, and the sound faded to silence when two servants hurried out onto the hall landing and down the stairs ahead of her to the kitchen level.

She went outside and saw Benjy below in the courtyard, holding the reins of Lady Meg's cream-colored palfrey.

Other lads a short distance away held Janet's dun, Wat's bay horse, and another, smaller bay that Robina knew must be Bella's. Lady Rosalie's gray palfrey stood near the stable with Ned Graham.

Benjy watched Robina's approach as if he expected a scolding.

She smiled, although she noted that he'd torn his shirt. "I'm glad to see you, laddie. I had a foolish fear you might forget that Buccleuch and his family will soon be departing."

"Aye, but he sent his Geordie to gather his lads and their ponies outside the gate whilst I were a-helping them pack," Benjy said. "Then Sym said I could hold Lady Meg's palfrey whilst he went inside to speed folks along. They'll take their midday dinner wi' them to eat along the way, so I expect they'll be coming out anon."

"For Sym to trust you with her ladyship's horse should make you proud," Robina said. "He is gey particular when it comes to Lady Meg."

"Aye, he calls her 'Herself,' just as our people were used to call our da '*Him*self,'" Benjy said. "Someday, mayhap they'll call me so, too."

"I think they will," Robina said. Seeing Janet and Bella emerge from the tower with Fiona Ormiston, she excused herself and hurried to meet them.

"You're not leaving already, too, are you, Fiona? I've never had a sister before. I was hoping you'd stay longer."

Fiona grinned. "Father had expected to stay through Beltane. Then, when he learned you were to be married, he said we might stay only until Monday. However, since you and Davy are staying here instead of riding off to an estate of his own, as most bridal couples do, Lady Meg reminded us that you'd be obliged to entertain me and that Davy would have to spend much of his time with Father."

"We would never view such visits as a penance," Robina said sincerely.

"Nay, but we agreed—Father and I—that you should have this time together. So, we are going to Scott's Hall, instead. That way, we'll be near enough for you to visit if you miss us but far enough away, Lady Meg said, to give you and Davy a good excuse to stay away if you'd liefer be alone."

"We'll have to see what *Davy* has to say about that," Robina said.

"You usually call him Dev, I know," Fiona said. "Has he been such a devil to you? Before you married him, I mean," she added hastily.

Robina was shaking her head. "Rab and most of Dev's men called him 'Dev,'" she said. "So, Benjy and I always did, too. I've seen his devilish side, though, and I'll confess that I'd liefer never see it again."

"'Tis likely you're safe," Janet said. "He rarely shows it to women, I think."

"Or to lassocks like me," Bella said cheerfully. "When I have a husband, I hope he is just like Sir Davy."

Robina's startled gaze met Fiona's dancing one as Janet said with her warm chuckle, "You must tell him so, Bella."

Robina smiled at the remark, and Fiona laughed.

Bella's face flushed fiery red, though, and Benjy said, "I dinna think ye should tease her. She doesna like it, and I dinna think Dev would, neither."

Robina looked at her little brother in astonishment, but Benjy was sternly watching Janet, who said promptly, "You are right to object, sir, and it is kind of you to speak up for Bella. I am ashamed to say that I would be the first to condemn such behavior in anyone else." Turning to her

little sister, she said, "I'm truly sorry, Bella. I won't do
that again."

"I forgive you," Bella said. "Likely I should not have
said what I did, either."

Janet hugged her. "You were merely speaking your
thoughts, love. You may always do that to me and to our
good friends Fiona and Robby. I was the one in the wrong,
for teasing you, just as Benjy had the good sense and the
courage to say."

Robina noted that Benjy stood a little straighter. If he
was aware that he'd lost a piece of his new shirt, he gave
no sign of it.

Dev and Wat came outside then with the ladies Meg and
Rosalie. Ormiston followed them with Sym Elliot. Wat's
dogs, hitherto curled in the shade by the stable, leaped up
and dashed with wagging tails to meet their master.

The riders mounted and, amid farewells, bridal wishes,
and promises to meet again soon, Buccleuch's and Ormiston's parties departed together.

Robina watched them go, feeling strangely bereft. She
had enjoyed having the other women there and would
have liked them to stay longer.

⌒

Watching her, Dev sensed her mood and silently put an
arm around her shoulders, drawing her close. When she
leaned closer, he kissed the top of her head and wished
he could scoop her up and carry her upstairs to their
bedchamber.

"D'ye think ye should be a-hugging 'n a-kissing our
Beany out here?" Benjy asked, startling him.

Recovering swiftly, Dev said, "'Tis a husband's privilege

to hug his wife and kiss her whenever he likes, within reason. Did you enjoy your ramble earlier?"

"Ramble?"

"As I recall, you dashed out of the hall in a fury and appeared again only as our guests were preparing to leave. I assumed you'd gone walking outside the wall."

"Och, aye," Benjy said. "I did ramble a bit, and then I went round to watch Buccleuch's men pack their gear onto their ponies. I helped one o' them. Then I helped Sandy and them till Sym said I could hold Lady Meg's horse."

"Mayhap you can find Ash now and think of something to do with him," Dev said. "I want to talk with Robby."

Grimacing, Benjy said, "Talk, aye. I warrant ye'll just be a-hugging and such, then. If I dinna find Ash, I'll help Sandy and them, so ye can do as ye will."

Robina stifled a laugh, and Dev gave her a quelling look. But when Benjy ran off, he said, "Did you detect mockery in that scamp's tone?"

"Perhaps," she agreed. "I also detected some glibness when he described his earlier activities, *and* that he'd torn his shirt. I wonder what mischief he got up to out there."

"We're not going to think about that now. We are going to find Greenlaw."

"Should we show him the jar?"

"Not yet. I looked more closely at the coins before I came downstairs. Some are ancient, some more recent, but I found none from his grace's reign or from those of the fifth or sixth Henrys of England."

"His grace returned from England only four years ago," Robina said.

"Aye, but his reign began in 1406, when his father died soon after the English captured Jamie. The Governor,

Albany, issued Jamie's first coins soon afterward. Therefore, I suspect that whoever buried the jar did so before 1406. What's more, there seem to be many more English coins than Scottish."

She frowned thoughtfully, and he waited for her to demand an explanation.

Instead, she said, "You suspect they have some connection to the siege."

"'Tis a possibility, aye," he said, pleased that she had so quickly followed his thinking. "So much silver amounts to a lordly sum, so I doubt it belonged to a tenant here or in England. Nor would any other lord in the area have reason to bury his money at Coklaw. And, as you pointed out before, for the Laird of Coklaw to bury such a sum outside the wall is too unlikely to warrant further consideration."

"So we approach Greenlaw," Robina said. "He may know naught of the silver, but he will know all about the siege."

~

They found Coklaw's steward in the housekeeper's room with his wife. When Dev said they would like to talk privily with Greenlaw, Robina said hastily, "Mistress Greenlaw must stay, too, sir. She was here during the siege, and we have rarely kept secrets from either of them... not successfully, at all events."

"Ada is fully in my confidence, Sir David, and ye can trust her, too," Greenlaw said. "She's as close as an oyster, is Ada."

Ada knitted silently, and Robina knew that everything was in train for their midday meal, or she would not be knitting. She also knew that whatever Ada was doing, she would not miss a word of what the others said.

Looking at Dev, Robina wondered if he wanted to do the talking. When he gazed steadily back, she said, "We'd like to ask you both about the siege that took place here twenty-five years ago."

"In June of 1403, that was," Greenlaw said, nodding. "Northumberland's army besieged our tower for fifteen days. But they didna breach our wall."

"Northumberland directed the siege himself, aye?" Robina said.

"The first earl, aye, with his son, Hotspur," Greenlaw said. "They tried to persuade me to cede this tower to them. Then, after a sennight, they demanded it."

Ada said quietly, "John told them he'd defend it as long as he had one man to stand by him. They couldna get in, so they dwelt in tents beyond range of arrows from our wall."

"How many were in their army?" Dev asked.

"I canna tell ye that, sir," Greenlaw said. "There was dunamany, though. The laird then—her ladyship's grand-dad, that be—he were at Gledstanes wi' the family. When he heard o' the siege, he hied him to the Governor at Stirling, and Albany gathered an army. Just afore they arrived, the Percys up and fled in the middle of the night. We learned later that they hied theirselves to Wales and got mixed up in the rebellion there."

"We'd heard that England's king were a-coming north, too, wi' more men," Ada said. "But when he heard North-umberland had gone, he followed him to Wales, instead, and we heard later that his men killed Northumber-land's son."

Greenlaw nodded. "Hotspur and his uncle, the late earl's brother, were both killed and some Douglases aided them in that battle, too, and were taken prisoner."

"We want to know more about the siege itself," Dev said. "You had men on the wall, watching the enemy, aye?"

"Aye, sure, sir. We didna make a song about it, though. The English had longbows and a cannon, but my lads popped their heads up oft enough to see what was what."

Mistress Greenlaw said, "They'll be serving the midday meal soon, Sir David. Is there aught in particular that you want to know?"

Dev looked at Robina and gave a slight nod.

She understood it to mean that she should decide what to tell them, so she said, "Aye, there is." To Greenlaw, she said, "I found a jar buried on that rise southeast of the wall when I dug the hole for Benjy's sapling—a crockery jar with silver coins in it. They are tarnished but one can see that they are a mix of English and Scottish coins, more being English. So, we wondered if, during the siege..."

Greenlaw frowned thoughtfully when she paused, and Ada returned to her knitting.

Robina knew then that Ada had naught that she could tell them about the coins but was listening to all that they said.

Turning her attention to Greenlaw, Robina waited patiently to hear what he would say. He looked from her to Dev and then back at her.

⁓

Dev wondered if Greenlaw felt uneasy discussing such a find with him there. After all, the old man knew only that he'd been Rab's friend and was now Warden of Coklaw

by order of the Douglas. If the steward did not trust
Douglas...

Greenlaw cleared his throat and addressed a point midway between Dev and Robby, saying, "I ken nowt o' such
a jar. I can tell ye it didna come from Coklaw or anyone
here. The late master—Master James, bless his soul—
kept nowt from me, knowing that I couldna care for the
place without knowing all he knew about it. Master Rab
and the lady Robina grew up believing as their da did, and
our people all be loyal. How much silver be we talking
about, if ye'll tell me?"

"Much," Robby said, holding her cupped hands apart,
one slightly above the other, indicating the approximate
height and circumference of the jar.

"Then, I'd wager it belonged to them wicked Percys.
Small coins and silver only?"

Dev saw Robby nod when he did. He said, "Silver shil-
lings and pennies."

Greenlaw said, "That be more than I'd expect anyone
hereabouts, other than the Douglas or Buccleuch, to have.
But even a jarful that size wouldna be enough for Northumberland or Hotspur to pay the army they'd gathered to
take to Wales."

"Was it so big?" Robby asked him.

"Aye, m'lady. See you, dunamany Scots joined them,
'cause the Percys were a-taking up against Henry o' England, joining wi' the Welsh rebellion."

Robby looked at Dev, and he nodded. He'd heard as
much, himself.

Greenlaw said, "The current Douglas's father and the
Duke o' Albany, who was Governor of the Realm then,
did both think it were better to occupy Henry in Wales

than to ha' him on our doorstep. We did hear afterward
that Hotspur's army carried a treasure chest to pay their
warriors and to aid the Welsh rebels."

Dev said, "Then you suspect that someone might have
helped himself to it?"

"Men who got close enough to ha' a look at their
encampment said the Percys' tent had guards round it,
day and night, guarding against their own men. From me
own experience of such, I'd say the treasure chest were
inside."

"Aye," Dev said. "'Tis gey unusual for a man to steal
from his liege, though."

"Would someone like that have been able to bury it on
the rise, John?"

Greenlaw shrugged. "They left gey quick, after midnight, m'lady. Had someone taken such a sum, he might
ha' found it easier to hide it here in dark of night than
near their camp. Mayhap he were unable to fetch it afore
leaving."

Dev nodded. Noting that Robby had turned and was
watching him, he smiled at her. "That makes more sense
than any other thought we've had, lass."

"Aye, perhaps, but does it get us any further?"

"Well, to my mind, the likeliest thief was someone
guarding the Percys' tent. If that whole army went straight
from here to the battle at Shrewsbury..."

"They did," Greenlaw said. "And many of them,
including Hotspur, died there."

Dev grimaced. "So, if such a theft occurred, the thief
risked his life to steal the gelt and then fought a battle with
terrible losses. 'Tis likely he was one of those who died."

Robby shook her head. "If he died, then who pulled

Benjy's tree out of its hole and dug the hole deeper?" she asked him. "Someone else knows about that jar, sir."

Dev agreed, but they had learned all they could from the Greenlaws. Suspecting that Mistress Greenlaw was thinking of the midday meal again, Dev said, "I expect we should let these good people get on with their duties, lass."

Thanking them for their help, they left the housekeeper's room and went upstairs. When Robby turned to go into the hall, Dev stopped her and urged her on up the stairs.

"We're supposed to be taking time to ourselves," he reminded her. "They won't be serving food yet for a half-hour or more."

"I don't need to change my dress," she said.

"You may not change it," he said with a meaningful grin. "But you'll likely want to put it back on after I take it off."

"It's the middle of the day!"

"Aye, and a fine time it is for me to learn more about my wife."

⁓

Robina was shocked. It had never occurred to her that her husband might want to couple at any time other than when they went to bed at night. However, just the thought that he *wanted* to couple sent sensations through her body that easily matched much of what she'd felt the previous night.

Her nipples swelled and pressed against the fabric of her shift, as desire coursed through her. By the time they reached their bedchamber, she wanted him to take her in his arms and kiss her again as thoroughly as he had the night before.

Closing and bolting both doors as he had then, he returned to her and reached for the front lacing of her new pink kirtle.

The shutters were open, but the hillsides were distant and no one below could see them. Nevertheless, she felt vulnerable and nearly protested.

Then, she saw the hunger in his eyes, and the fire in her body burned hotter. When his hands, untying her laces, brushed against her tender nipples, she gasped.

He kissed her then as thoroughly as she had hoped, while his fingers and hands remained busy. In a trice, her kirtle and shift slipped down to puddle at her feet. She put her arms up to hug him, but he held her a little away.

"I want to look at you," he murmured.

Her wayward thoughts sprang instantly to Rab. Was *he* watching them?

It occurred to her that if he was, she could do naught to stop him, and that whether he watched or not, God did. All priests said that He saw all and knew all. Since she could do naught to stop God, either, she'd just have to get used to them both watching. The possible presence of anyone troubled her no further after that, because Dev seized every fiber of her being and thought by tweaking a nipple.

"You should pay heed to your husband, my love," he said. "I hope you were not thinking about another man, because I would dislike that."

"Is God a man, then?" she asked, looking up to see how he'd react to that.

His eyebrows rose. "Aye, sure, God is a man. Has anyone suggested otherwise."

"Then I *was* thinking of another man. I wondered if He was watching us."

Instead of chuckling or laughing outright, as she expected, he looked at her more searchingly. "Is that all? You looked... I don't know how to describe it, but you looked as if you were keeping secrets again."

*"I warned you not to lie to him, Beany. You* don't *want to make Dev angry."*

She swallowed. Rab *was* watching, and listening. And she knew that Dev had seen her reaction.

Hoping to divert him, she said, "Do you mean to stand there in your clothes, sir, gawking at me? I'm unaccustomed to standing still whilst someone looks at me as if he would see through my skin to my bones."

"Turn away from me," he muttered, holding her gaze.

To avoid his discerning eyes and because the command sent heat roaring through her, she obeyed. Facing the wall with her sampler hanging on it but conscious only of him watching her, she trembled.

He kept her standing so until she looked over her shoulder at him.

"Have you seen enough?" she demanded. "You are making my skin prickle."

He grinned. "I have not seen nearly enough, lassie-mine, but 'tis a husband's right to look his fill. You may come and undress me now."

"May I? I'd liefer watch you undress yourself."

"Nay, you must learn to do it. Only think if I should be injured and you did not yet know how to undo all my laces and buckles."

She laughed. "Good sakes, I know all about buckles and laces," she said. "I had to help Rab fasten and tie his when we were small. He was all thumbs."

"Then you should excel at the task now. Show me."

He was still smiling, and she was beginning to enjoy herself.

Dev showed her other ways that they could enjoy themselves, and in the days that followed, he taught her more ways that he could pleasure her. They argued occasionally about small things, but he did listen to her. And, if she said something to change his mind, he admitted it far more willingly than Rab ever had.

Dev also showed her how much she could enjoy their coupling. He could stir her passion with a look or a wink, sometimes just by walking into the room.

Wednesday afternoon, while they lingered together at the high table after their midday meal and discussed whether they would ride to the Hall to celebrate Beltane with everyone there or stay home, Coll entered to tell them that two messengers had arrived under a Percy banner and a white flag of truce.

Their blissful interlude thus ended abruptly.

Dev said, "Bring them to me in the inner chamber, Coll. Make sure first that they carry no weapons."

"They don't, sir. We searched them when they arrived. I'll fetch them in."

"You stay here," Dev said to Robina as Coll strode back across the hall.

"I will not," she said, standing when he did. "I have as much right to know what is going on as you do. Moreover, if our men have searched them—"

"You will do as I bid," he replied, fighting to speak calmly instead of reacting as he usually did to defiance. "This is not the time or place to test my temper, Robby.

Having two Percys here is bad enough, white flag or none. I don't want you exposed to such men."

"I disagree, Dev. They're more apt to remain civil if I'm with you."

"Coll and I will keep them civil," he said, no longer bothering to conceal his rising temper. "You will do as I say, or by my troth, I'll carry you upstairs and let them wait whilst I persuade you to stay there."

~

Having already experienced one of his harsher methods of persuasion, Robina grimaced but nodded submissively. "I'll go up, then."

Dev's brow furrowed. "You are submitting mighty quick, lass."

She rolled her eyes. "Faith, you scold me when I speak my mind and you scold when I submit to you. How am I to know the more acceptable course?"

"Obedience is always best," he said sternly.

"Certes, I can understand why *you* think so," she retorted. "Nay, cool your ire, sir," she added hastily when he stiffened. "I won't stay here, but I will go upstairs if you insist."

"I do."

Gathering her skirts in one hand, she raised her chin, gave him a withering look, and left the dais. Crossing the hall to the archway, she maintained her dignity until she was on the stairs. Then, however, she snatched her skirts up with both hands and went lightly but quickly up the one flight to the master chamber.

Bolting the door, she took her sampler from the wall and put her eyes to the laird's squint that it had concealed.

Peering down into the inner chamber, she saw Dev take his place in the two-elbow chair behind her father's heavy oak table.

The scraping sound of the chair across the floor came easily to her ears.

*"Ah, Beany, 'tis a wicked, disobedient wife you are."*

"Hush," she murmured. "Coll is bringing those Percys in. I want to hear."

# Chapter 20

Dev waited until the two men stood before him. The older one, a chestnut-haired man of perhaps thirty, wearing the garb of a peasant or cowherd, carried their white flag. The younger—tawny headed, eighteen or so, dressed in similar style—had relinquished the Percy banner into Coll's care at the door. The lad stood beside his superior with one hand resting atop the other at his crotch.

Coll stayed by the door, armed with his dirk, but Dev could tell that the two nervous men before him wanted only to deliver their message.

"What message do you bring?" he asked the older one.

"Begging your pardon, sir, but who d'ye be? I were told to deliver me message to the Laird o' Coklaw."

"The current laird is nine years old," Dev replied. "I am the Warden of Coklaw, acting in his stead, so you should deliver your message to me."

"May I ken your name, sir, to tell my master?"

"Tell me yours first."

"They do call me Jock o' the Storm, and this be Bangtail Joey."

"I'm Sir David Ormiston of Ormiston," Dev said. "You

rode here under Northumberland's banner. Do you speak for his lordship?"

The younger lad's hands clutched each other over his codpiece as though he feared for his manhood. Under the circumstances, though, Dev decided he'd be wise to deduce little from that.

"I do bring a message from Alnwick," Jock o' the Storm said steadily. "Ye may ken that our fourth King Henry gave all o' the Douglas lands o' Teviotdale to Northumberland as reward for his lordship's victory at Homildon Hill."

"I know that his lordship's grandsire, the first earl, had the temerity to make such a claim twenty-five years ago," Dev said. "He failed to take Teviotdale, though, and I doubt the current earl has enough power to do so. So, what is your purpose here?"

"To ask ye to confer wi' the Douglas. Tell him our master means to ha' what is his and would parley wi' him. Our master will accept payment instead o' land, but if ye dinna agree to one or t'other, we'll besiege Coklaw again."

"So I am to be your messenger, am I? Art too cowardly to ride two miles more to Hawick? Unless his grace has summoned the Douglas elsewhere, he is currently staying at the Black Tower. Did you not know that when you came here?"

The two men looked at each other. Then Jock o' the Storm looked Dev in the eye and said, "I did ken that, sir. But a Scots town be a gey dangerous place for an Englishman. If that be cowardice, so be it. Will ye take our message to Douglas?"

"I will not. Between them, as you must know, Buccleuch

and Douglas can raise ten thousand men in a sennight. Your master would be lucky to raise half as many."

The older man shrugged. "We had over twenty thousand at Homildon."

Dev held his gaze but did not bother to comment. Jock o' the Storm was too young to have aided in the Scottish defeat at Homildon Hill. Moreover, the current earl, Hotspur's son, was a mere shadow of his father or grandfather.

"Be that your final answer?" Jock o' the Storm asked quietly.

"It is," Dev said. "Your white flag will provide safe-conduct back across the line, but I'd advise you to travel swiftly. Keep heading due south and stay clear of Hermitage. Its constable, as you doubtless know, takes a dark view of Englishmen in Liddesdale."

"Aye, we'll keep clear," Jock said. "But ye'd be wise to heed me warning, too, that trouble will follow this refusal o' yours."

"Leave now, whilst you can," Dev said, adding a chill to his voice.

"Aye, then, sir, we're awa'."

Leaving Coll, Sandy, and Jock Cranston to see the two outside the gate and away, Dev decided to attend to his ever defiant, yet ever intriguing wife.

⁓

"D'ye ken who that were?" Bangtail Joey demanded when they were clear of the gate and trotting their ponies southwestward toward the cut. "That were Devil Ormiston! Ye were daft to threaten him, Chukk."

"He's a man like any other man," Chukk said, although he knew better.

"They dinna call him *Devil* Ormiston for nowt," Joey said testily. "Ye told 'im me right name, too, and gave a false one for yerself. Why did ye no call me summat else, too? Answer me that!"

"I didna say ye were a Graham, did I?" Chukk snapped. "I'll wager there be any number o' Bangtails this side o' the line, just as there be south of it."

Joey grimaced but said no more, and the silence continued for a mile or more before Chukk said, "He didna recognize either o' us. That be a good thing."

"What d'ye mean?" Joey asked. "How would he recognize us?"

"I thought ye'd recall him from that fracas near Chesters some weeks back," Chukk said. "That Ormiston chap were wi' the reckless one that the earl's Simon killed wi' his lance. That dead one, they said, were the new Laird o' Gledstanes."

"Aye, well, Himself did tell us to make mischief hereabouts, but I hope it doesna rain again," Joey muttered. "I were a-hoping ye'd take us home soon."

"We need more mischief than a few raids, Joey. You hie yourself back to the lads and find us a new place to shelter, mayhap where we camped at Easter near Langside. Ormiston's men may scour the hills this side o' Slitrig Water, to be sure we've gone."

"What be ye a-doing, then?"

"I'll be a wandering shepherd again," Chukk said. "I've a wee notion under me cantle," he added, patting the top of his head. "But I must hone it some, so I'll think whilst I wander. Meet me in yon lamb's cut early tomorrow—alone. I'll ken more by then about what I mean to do."

Robina heard Dev's footsteps mounting the stairway, but the sampler wanted to tilt. Drawing a breath to steady herself, she adjusted its frame again and stepped hastily down from the stool.

*"He's on the landing!"*

Ignoring Rab, she went to the north window and looked out at the hillside behind the castle just as the privy-stairs door opened in the corner behind her.

Dev was silent, so Robina stayed as she was. If she looked at him, he might see her guilt, and she was sure that he'd be angry with her for spying on him through the squint. But Coklaw was her home, and she had every right to know when someone threatened it. Dev might be the one in charge now, but she would not let him set her aside altogether.

"Are you going to look at me, Robby, or are you going to sulk?"

She turned then but chose to address a point just above his head and said as calmly as she could, "I'm not sulking. Are you going to tell me what they said?"

"Do I need to?"

She looked right at him then but his gaze was steady, his face expressionless. She had discerned no anger in his tone and saw nothing of his mood now, either.

Even so, his question could mean only one thing.

"You know about the squint." In the ominous silence that followed, her stomach clenched and her palms dampened with sweat.

"Coll found it straightaway," Dev said. "We are well acquainted with lairds' squints, lass. They are especially common here in the Borders, where a man knows that a visitor from another clan may be friendly one day and an enemy the next. If he can leave such visitors to entertain themselves long enough to judge how they behave and what they say, he may spare himself much trouble."

"I expect you knew I would watch, then," she said.

"The truth is that I wondered if you knew about the squint. You did not tell me about it. Nor did Greenlaw or anyone else."

"Greenlaw knows," she said. "I don't know who else does. Father showed it to Rab and me years ago." Remembering, she swallowed hard. "He said we both needed to know of it, in the event that something happened to him. He... he also told us what he'd do if he learned that one of us had spied on him or his guests."

Dev shook his head. "If you're feeling guilty, sweetheart, you need not. I didn't give that squint another thought until Coll brought those men into the chamber. Perhaps I should have remembered it when you submitted so quickly."

"You were angry with me then. I did not want to make you angrier, but..."

"...you wanted to know what was happening," he said, finishing her sentence with alarming ease. "I'll admit that your defiance irked me, lass, but you have as much right as I do to use the laird's squint. Does Benjy know about it?"

Surprised, she said, "I doubt it. I did not tell him, but Rab might have." Falling silent, she listened for Rab's voice, expecting—nay, hoping, he would tell her whether he had or had not.

"How old were you and Rab when your father told you?" Dev asked her.

"I don't remember exactly, but..." She thought. "It was

not long after Mam died, because Benjy was a wee bairn. We were ten then, I think, mayhap eleven."

"So your father wanted to be sure that others in the family knew of the squint. And Benjy is the rightful laird now. Moreover, he does not seem to engage much in idle talk."

"That's true; he doesn't," Robina said. "In fact, I was going to ask you to speak to Ash about repeating things that Benjy says to him."

He nodded. "I'll have Coll talk to him. Ash is a good lad, so a hint will be enough. Did you or Rab ever tell anyone else about the squint or use it yourselves?"

She smiled guiltily as she shook her head. "We both knew that Father would react much as I expected you might today. Besides," she added, "it was a trust that he placed in us. We felt important, knowing his secret and keeping it."

He nodded. "Our squint at Ormiston overlooks the great hall. It is no great secret, though, because the hole cuts down through a niche in the stairway wall."

She had naught to say to that, but he continued to look at her as if he waited for her to speak. If it was right for her to know about the squint, he was not awaiting an apology. Once again, though, his expression remained inscrutable.

"You're sure that you're not angry with me?" she said, eyeing him closely.

"I'm sure," he said. "Don't defy me like that again, though. I don't usually react so kindly to such defiance."

"Most men don't," she said. "I should not have spoken to you as I did, though, especially in the great hall with so many ears around. But if you expect me always to submit when you issue orders to me as you do to your men, or even when you simply tell me to do something without due discussion…"

His eyes lit then with humor. "I don't expect such submission from you, Robby, nor would it please me. The thing I liked most about you when Rab first brought me here was your intelligence and the fact that you know your own mind. The trait I dislike most in others, especially other men, is their inability to make a decision. But you should also understand that there may be consequences you will dislike if you defy me or willfully disobey when I command your obedience."

Fluttering her lashes, she looked up at him through them and said, "Mayhap we'll get on better, sir, if you do not command. I *am* persuadable, you know."

"*Do* I know that?" He watched her in a way that sent fire through her body again. "Then, come here to me, naughty one. You must tell me what you thought of our messengers whilst I *persuade* you out of your kirtle and shift."

As she moved to obey him, her body contracted in an area that she had not known it *could* contract. Her breathing quickened, her heart pounded, and her knees felt so weak she was unsure that they'd support her. She realized with an abruptness that shocked her that if he *had* wanted to punish her, all he would have had to do was walk out and leave her standing there so.

Dev was not so cruel. He took his time disrobing her, though, making her ache for release long before he carried her to bed and allowed it.

⁓

Dev awoke to hear the privy-stair door opening. Swiftly, he looked to be sure Robby was covered and then fought to suppress the anger that had flared at hearing the intrusive sound. In his eagerness to enjoy himself with Robby, he'd neglected to bolt the door, so it was his own fault that Coll opened it.

Coll halted on the threshold, one hand on the latch, a cold cresset in the other. When he saw Dev and would have turned away, Dev stayed him with a gesture.

Putting a finger to his lips, he got up and quietly drew the curtain before collecting his braies and breeks from the floor where he'd tossed them.

"How long till supper?" he murmured as he stepped into them.

"Not long, sir," Coll replied as quietly, setting the cresset on a nearby table, along with a twine-tied bundle of fresh candles from a pouch on his belt. "I just came to bring these things up. I didna think…" Pausing, he gave a rueful shrug. "I should ha' rapped on the door, sir. It willna happen again."

"I'm awake," Robby said from behind the curtain. "If you're talking to Coll, sir, prithee ask him to fetch hot water or send Corinne up with it."

Dev nodded, and Coll left the way he had come, closing the door behind him.

"Do you want your shift and kirtle, sweetheart?" he asked.

"Aye, thank you. What was Coll doing here? Is there another message?"

"He just brought us more candles, but supper will be ready soon."

"Why did he think we needed more candles?"

"He brought a cresset, too. Doubtless, he assumes we're enjoying sleepless nights of coupling and might require more light."

Hearing her low chuckle, he grinned as he pulled back the bed curtain and handed her her clothing. He was more amused when she kept the coverlet high until she had both her shift and her kirtle over her head and could pull them into place.

"Don't fret about Coll," he said. "He has waited these past mornings until I shouted, and he'll soon know your needs and Corinne's as well as he knows mine."

Pouring cold water into the ewer, Dev washed his face and hands and donned the shirt and leather jack he'd worn earlier. Then he waited patiently until Coll brought Robby's hot water and she had performed her ablutions.

Supper passed quickly, and despite their naps, she made no objection when he suggested they retire early. She took time only to bid Benjy goodnight before returning with him to their bedchamber. They lay talking quietly for a time.

At last, Dev drew her close, turning her so that her back was against him and they could lie curled together like nested spoons. He felt as if she belonged there.

He soon dozed off, only to waken before dawn and hear her talking to someone.

~

*"Marrying Dev was a good notion, Beany," Rab said as they rode toward Slitrig Water. "He'll look after you now, and God kens fine that you need a man to keep you out of mischief."*

*"I don't get into mischief," she said curtly, leaning forward to urge her horse to keep up with Black Corby. "You must know that I've done only what needed doing to keep Coklaw and our people safe."*

*"You think you can do all that I used to do,"* he retorted. *"You cannot, lass. Dev was right when he threatened to take that dirk away. I must have been mad to give it to you and teach you the few tricks I did show you."*

*"You don't mean that,"* she protested. *"You taught me well."*

*He shook his head. "I let you think so. You and I were too close, too much alike for your safety. Had I realized that you'd imitate me and I'd not be around to rein you in—"*

"What? What are you saying? What do you mean by that? Just because you're a man! Why are you shaking me?" she demanded, trying to push the offending hand away, only to realize that Rab had disappeared and she was in bed with Dev.

"Wake up, Robby? You were talking in your sleep and not too clearly, I might add," he said. His carefully even tone of voice brought her fully awake. "*Who* taught you well, and just *what* did he teach you?"

She swallowed. The remnants of her dream were fading, but she had been talking to Rab. Surely, that would not anger Dev, if she said she'd been *dreaming* about Rab.

"It was Rab," she muttered, trying to collect her scattered wits. "He taught me to use his dirk before he gave it to me. I told you that."

"What sort of dream was it? You said something about Coklaw. Do you often talk in your sleep?"

"Mercy, I don't know," she said, turning slightly to face him. She could see only his muscular shape against the moonlit room beyond him as he leaned up on one elbow over her. "Janet said naught about hearing me talk. Nor did Bella, and I've never slept with anyone else, except our nurse when Rab and I were bairns... and you."

"In this dream of yours, just what did Rab say about your dirk?"

"Naught that he'd not said before. I told you he does *not* object to my having it. Although he did say I should not have tried to—" She broke off. Rab had said that to her after the event in the yard. It had not been part of her dream.

"Should not have tried what?" Dev said. "Tell me. Do you dream of him often?"

"How can I answer you sensibly if you keep flinging questions at me?"

"Choose one, and answer it."

"I don't think I dream of Rab often, but I don't know," she said, choosing what seemed to be the safest question. "I rarely remember dreams when I wake, or if I do, I remember only bits that fade quickly away. Why did you wake me?"

"The boot is on the other foot, lass. You woke me with your chatter."

"I'm sorry," she said. "May I go back to sleep now?"

"Aye, sure," he murmured. "I did not mean to cross-question you. You startled me out of a sound sleep, and I thought you were talking to someone here in the room. Sleep now. Mayhap we'll ride together after the sun comes up."

"I'd like that," she murmured drowsily.

When she awoke to find him gone and Corinne bustling about the room in her usual way, memory of Dev's waking her from her dream swept back into her mind.

Dressing quickly in her old moss-green kirtle, she went downstairs and found him at the high table, finishing his breakfast. When he saw her and smiled, she relaxed. Until that moment, she had not realized she was tense.

"Good morning, sweetheart," he said, standing to meet her. "Do you still want to ride? I thought we might go toward the Ormiston estate today. I'd like to know if anyone saw our messengers heading back to England."

"I must speak with Ada Greenlaw first," Robina said. "I have paid her little heed since the wedding, and I don't want her to think I've abandoned my responsibilities to her. I usually discuss the next few days' menus with her after I break my fast, but I'll meet you in the yard shortly after that."

He agreed and turned to go but stopped at the edge of the dais. She saw Benjy hurrying past the archway at the other end of the hall.

When Dev whistled, the boy skidded to a halt and looked their way.

Dev crooked a finger, and Benjy hurried toward him. His jack had a rip in it, and his shirt looked as if someone had dipped it in muck of some sort.

"What happened to you?" Dev asked. "You look as if you've been rolling in mud."

"Nearly," the boy said, grinning. "Ash is teaching me to wrestle. I got mud in me eye, though, and when he washed it out, he said I'd better change me clothes."

"Go on up, then, and wash your face and hands whilst you're about it. Robby and I are going to ride to the Ormiston estate if you'd like to ride with us."

"Must I? Ash and me were going to help in the stables."

"Aye, then, if you offered to help, you should," Dev said.

Grinning again, Benjy ran off without comment, and Dev glanced at Robby to see that Corinne was serving her breakfast.

Knowing she would likely take longer than she expected, he went outside to give the order for their horses but told Sandy not to keep them standing in the yard. "Have someone bring them out when they see us coming," he said.

With that task done, he returned to the keep. He'd been meaning to visit the ramparts and talk to the men there but had not yet made time for it. Realizing that he'd be able to see the yard from up there and could shout down to let Robby know where he was, he went on upstairs.

Benjy's door was closed, so the boy had likely tidied himself, changed his clothes, and gone outside again.

⌒

Benjy heard the footsteps outside his door and opened it in time to see Dev disappear around the next turn of the stairs. Grimacing, he tiptoed down the stairs, only to hear someone else coming up. Hurrying back to his room, he decided to wait until he heard Dev going down again. He'd been thinking about that jar of coins that Beany had found and wanted to see what it looked like and how much it had in it. If it was his, as Beany had said, he had every right to see it.

He knew exactly where Rab had kept the carved box that Beany had mentioned.

⌒

Robina finished her breakfast and took only a few minutes with Ada to be sure that the housekeeper had everything well in hand. Then, feeling pleased with her efficiency, she hurried upstairs to put on her rawhide boots and fetch her cloak.

Doubtless, Dev had expected her to keep him waiting half the morning.

*"When are you going to tell him about me? He can tell you're still keeping something from him, and he's been more patient than you've any right to expect."*

"I don't know how to tell him," she muttered. "He'll think I'm daft. He won't believe that you speak to me."

*"Aye, sure he will. I've told you things you could not have learned otherwise."*

That was true. He had told her that the ruffians who had taken their stock before had taken more on Easter Sunday. And, when she'd guessed that he meant the thieving Turnbulls of Langside, he had praised her quick wit.

*"I'll tell you now that Dev is no fool. And if he finds out for himself—"*

"Stop, damn you! I don't want to tell him yet. I cannot do it, and I won't!"

*"Och, wheesht now, wheesht!"*

A slight noise above had already warned her that she had spoken too loudly. Looking up, she saw Dev standing on the landing outside their bedchamber.

Wincing, she shut her eyes, hoping that she had imagined him.

When she opened them, Dev was still there.

"Who were you talking to, Robby?"

"N-nobody," she said. "I...I was just talking to myself. People do that, you know, and I...I am..." But she'd said too much. She knew she had.

He knew she was lying. She could see it in his face.

"Come up here," he said. "We'll talk in our chamber."

She tried to swallow, but her mouth was dry. She muttered, "The horses are waiting. We should go."

"The horses are fine," he said. "Come." He pushed open the door to the bedchamber. "This is not the first time I've heard you. And before you insist again that you were talking to yourself, I should warn you that, although I do know people sometimes do that, I've never heard of anyone shouting or *swearing* at herself."

"I didn't do that," she said curtly. When his frown deepened and his jaw tightened, she added impulsively, "If you must know, I was talking to Rab."

# Chapter 21 _____

Stunned by Robina's declaration but well aware of where they were, Dev gestured toward the open door. "Inside," he said. "Now."

She gave him a defiant look but evidently saw that he was in no mood for it, because she remained silent as she walked stiffly into the bedchamber. When she turned to face him, she looked ready for a fight. He did not want one, but he did mean to discover why she had sounded so angry and who had stirred that anger.

"Tell me the truth now," he said, shutting the door. "First you said you were talking to yourself, but you spoke as you would to someone else. It is not customary to shout at oneself, Robby. Last night, you described your dream at first as if it were real, and you have several times spoken of Rab as if he were still alive. That is common when someone is grieving, but now you tell me that Rab—"

"He does talk to me, Dev. I hear him as if he is standing right beside or right behind me. I'm not saying I can *see* him there, but his voice is as audible to me as yours is, and the direction it comes from is just as clear."

"Is he talking to you now?"

"No, but he was. He warns me of things before they

happen. That first night... Easter night, he told me the Turnbulls had lifted our kine. He... he told me to send our lads to get them back or to lift some of theirs in return. When I led them myself, he laughed and said he should have known that I would."

"If that *were* even possible, your twin should think himself lucky to be dead. Because if I got my hands on him..." He stopped, because she was just watching him, not arguing. "Robina, you *know* that the dead cannot speak."

Her lips thinned as if she would debate that fact. Instead, she said with a calm that sent an eerie chill up his spine, "I did believe that, Dev. But I know Rab speaks to me. It is his voice, and it is *not* in my head. I do know the difference, because we always knew each other's thoughts. Sometimes, it was as if we shared one mind. But, at such times, I did not hear his voice; I just knew what he was thinking as if my thoughts were his. He warned me that night that you were after us. That's why I ran upstairs, because he was behind me, shouting at me to hurry. It was just bad luck that you'd recognized me in the yard."

"I didn't," he admitted. "I followed the lad who ran in through the postern door because I thought he should not have done so. It was only when I heard 'his' footsteps running upstairs and *your* bedchamber door shut that I realized who the 'lad' must be. However, the plain fact is that, whatever you are hearing, it is *not* Rab talking from his grave. I suspect that your conscience is shouting at you and you're imagining that it speaks with his voice. It may be some odd element of your grief. I cannot explain it, but I do know that the dead do not speak to us."

"Rab does," she said stubbornly.

"Now, look, Robby, you cannot believe that, and you certainly cannot expect me to believe it. You're too sensible for such . . . such—"

"Such madness? Is that what you think, Dev? You fear that I'm daft and that others will fear that you've married a madwoman?"

"I never said that," he replied, struggling to keep from shouting at her.

"Well, I'm not daft!" Tears welled in her eyes, and when one spilled down her cheek, she dashed it away.

"Robby," he said quietly but nonetheless grimly, "I do *not* think you are crazy. I just think that—"

"I *don't* want to talk about this anymore," she retorted. "I don't want to ride with you or to stand here and try to explain myself to you. I know what I hear, Dev. Nobody's imagination could produce a voice that sounds as if the person is standing right beside her or behind her. It could much more easily be a special connection that twins have and naught to do with imagination. Imagination takes place in one's thoughts, *inside* one's head. It doesn't float about on the air."

Striving to keep his own flaming temper in check, well aware that shouting at her would make things worse, he said with forced calm, "Dead is dead, lass."

"Blethers," she snapped. "The priests all say that our souls live on, and you don't know *how* they do that any more than I do. But since they do, *when* they do, why should they not be able to speak to those who were closest to them and are *still* closest to them. When I tell you that Rab does speak to me, and frequently, you might at least do me the courtesy of believing me."

With that, she stormed past him, flinging the door open

hard enough that it banged against the wall and nearly shut again behind her before he caught it.

But she had already run down the stairs.

His inclination was to go after her, give her a good shake to bring her to her senses, and force her to talk sensibly with him. However, experience with his sisters, as well as with Robby, warned him that such tactics would be unwise.

Granting her solitude to calm down would be wiser.

Since she'd gone downstairs, rather than up to the solar or to her old bedchamber, he decided he'd give her time to walk outside the wall to her tree, which seemed the likeliest place for her to go in such a temper.

Accordingly, he waited a few minutes before going downstairs, only to meet Coll coming in through the main doorway as he approached it.

"Sir," Coll said with a wary look, "her ladyship came out to the yard, and when she saw us with the horses at the stable entrance, she requested a leg up, mounted Corby, and rode out through the gateway at a gallop, heading southwest."

Cursing, Dev said, "Where's Auld Nick?"

"I've got him at the steps, sir. I thought you might want him close by. Um...my horse is also there. Do you want me—?"

"No," Dev snapped. "You'd be very much in my way."

～

On the landing above the master bedchamber, Benjy sat hugging himself as tears streamed down his face.

"Why d'ye talk to Beany, Rab, and no to me?" he muttered.

He'd barely collected himself enough to scramble back up to his own landing after he'd heard Beany say she wouldn't talk anymore to Dev and before she flung open the door. When he'd heard them on the stairs before then, her declaration that Rab talked to her had stunned him so much that he'd wanted only to hear more about Rab's talking. Was he still alive, or what?

Benjy overheard most of what they'd said next through the bedchamber door.

When he realized that Beany would storm out in anger, he'd fled to his own room. Had she or Dev caught him at the door, listening... He shivered at the thought.

But now, he just wanted to know why Rab talked to Beany and not to him.

Hearing Dev go downstairs at last, he followed quietly and heard Coll tell him that she had galloped Corby outside the wall.

"Good, then," Benjy muttered, wiping his sleeve across his wet cheeks so no one else would detect his distress. "I'll just go talk to our Rab, m'self."

⌒

Heading southwest to the drove road that led to Leg o' Mutton Cut, Robina urged Corby to his fastest pace on the flat part alongside the bubbling stream. Giving the big horse his head, she felt the breeze against her face begin to ease her fury.

By the time she slowed him to a safer speed, she was able to enjoy the warmth of the sun and the beauty of the new spring growth around her. Wildflowers bloomed in profusion, and the stream chuckled merrily along, lifting her spirits with its own.

*"You should not have snapped at Dev. Nor will he like your riding alone and so madly into what may now be dangerous territory. Sakes, I'd have taken a switch to you for such, myself, and so would our da."*

"I know," she muttered. "But Dev does not believe you're real, Rab. How can I persuade him?"

*"You can't."*

"But *you* said to tell him that you've been talking to me."

*"Even so, you should have agreed when he said that the dead can't speak. You should have agreed, too, that you just imagine hearing me."*

"Then you should have *told* me to say all that," she retorted. "You know I don't tell lies well. Or are you saying that he's right and I'm just imagining you?"

*"I'm talking to you, lass, but being angry with me does you nae good. You'd be wiser to look back and vow to control that wicked temper of yours before Dev does just what Da or I would have done, or what Dev did before."*

Startled, she realized that the increasing, rhythmic sound she'd thought was a new note in the stream's bubbling was really hoofbeats fast approaching behind her. Looking back, she saw Auld Nick closing the distance. She did not need to see the expression on Dev's face. His hunched posture and Nick's fiery pace told her that he was furious.

Panic stirred, and every fiber of her body shouted at her to spur Corby on.

Instead, knowing that even if he could outrun Auld Nick, she'd have to face Dev in the end, she reined in near the stream and waited for him, wondering if he'd punish her then and there and if Corby might try to protect her from him.

After all, Corby had once briefly attempted to defend her from Rab's fury, when she had ridden him without asking Rab first.

That painful memory and the fury on Dev's face, which she saw clearly now, made her sphincter muscles contract.

⌒

Having expected Robby to ride faster when she saw him in pursuit, Dev watched with grim satisfaction when she reined in at the stream's side instead. He was glad to see that Corby had not, as he had feared, run away with her but was still under her control.

The woman could ride, no question, but he yearned to take leather to her.

Her rueful smile nearly undid him.

When he was close enough to hear her, she said lightly, "Will you beat me here or wait until we get back to Coklaw?"

Suppressing a smile of his own, he realized that his anger had eased now that he knew she was safe. He was glad that she was still speaking to him, and glad to be alone with her. He'd be more pleased if she would just talk sensibly with him.

He said, "You deserve that I should make you wait and find out what I'll do."

"Ah, but that would go against your so-notorious nature, would it not?"

"It would, but I'd survive it. Your dignity might not."

"If you are going to beat me, just say so," she said testily. "If not, may we cry 'Pax' and be done with this, at least for now? I'm sorry that I—"

"Don't apologize, Robby. You won't mean it, because you were angry, and the next time you're angry, you'll likely speak so to me again. I told you that you can say what you like to me. I'll admit that I'd liefer you remain civil when you do, but I think I'll find my own head in my lap for incivility soon enough not to make a song about that."

Her eyes twinkled then. "I think you can count on that," she said.

"Even so," he said, catching and holding her gaze, "I did warn you that you'd have to suffer the consequences of your actions. Don't forget that."

The twinkle in her eyes dimmed.

Black Corby sidestepped, and as Robina steadied him, she knew that her own unease had communicated itself to the horse. Recalling how easily Dev had dismissed what she'd said about Rab's talking to her stirred her ire again.

Knowing that if Dev decided to punish her, she could do little to stop him, she kept silent and waited to hear what else he would say.

"You *heard* the threats that that Percy chap made," he said quietly.

She nodded.

"Such threats make riding alone outside our wall more dangerous now."

"Aye," she said, looking at the space between Corby's flicking ears.

"You know better than to ride madly into dangerous territory at such a time, do you not?"

"Corby is well trained," she said. "He is better than a weapon for me."

Dev looked silently at her until she grimaced.

"I do know better than to ride into dangerous territory," she admitted.

"Rab told you as much, if I remember correctly."

Since he'd used Rab's own words, she nearly demanded to know if he had heard Rab speak, too, but realized before she did just how Dev knew. "Rab told you what he did the day I took Corby out without asking him first, didn't he?"

"He did, and you'd be well served if I did the same today, but I don't want that. I don't want to fratch with you, either. I know how much you miss him, and I know you were angry with me. We'll talk more about that but not now. We must return before Sandy or Jock sends lads out in search of us."

She agreed, but she was glad he was content to walk the horses and chat about unrelated things such as the birds they saw and increasing Coklaw's stock. By the time they rode through the gateway, they were in charity with each other again, and it was just as well. They had missed the midday meal, and so had Benjy.

~

Benjy wished he'd thought to bring an apple, some cheese, or just bread with him. He'd hurried off, thinking only of where he wanted to go. Also, he'd forgotten how long the journey had taken before and how steep the last bit of Sunnyside Hill was. The weather had been cool then, too. Now the sun was high and beating down on him.

Looking ahead, he saw that he was nearing the hilltop at last and quickened his pace. A short time later, the low fence and lych-gate came into view.

Rab's grave still lacked a marker, but he knew where it was and made his way past the other graves, wondering if the dead in them could talk, too.

If they could, they most likely did so here, where they were nearest a person.

He had disliked coming up by himself before, which was one reason he had felt so grateful to Beany for suggesting a tree for Rab like her oak in the west woods. But if Rab could talk to her, then other souls must talk to their kin, too. The thought made them seem less scary, more like ordinary people.

Standing at the graveside, he muttered, "Rest in peace, Rab," as Beany had taught him. Bluntly, then, he added, "Why d'ye no talk to me but only to our Beany?"

When he heard no reply, he spoke louder, saying, "I wish ye'd talk to me. I miss ye gey fierce and I ha' questions to ask ye."

"What would you ask, laddie?"

The startling voice was all wrong, deeper and growly. But perhaps that was just a hitherto unknown trait of dead men's voices.

Benjy whirled hopefully toward it.

⁓

They searched unsuccessfully everywhere that Dev or Robby could imagine to search for the boy, and Dev unloaded his tamped down anger on more than one unfortunate person, including Ash Nixon and Coll, before it became evident to everyone that Benjy had gone farther than he'd ever gone alone before or something more dire had occurred.

When the boy had not returned by suppertime, Robby

said decisively, "Thank the Fates that the moon is full and rose before sunset, so Benjy will be able to see where he's going. But we must extend our search."

"Every man we can spare has gone out," Dev said. "They'll collect as many more as they can amongst the cottagers to help search."

"Did you send to the Douglas or to Scott's Hall for help?"

"Not yet," he said. "The laddie likely just wandered farther than usual and will return on his own. Our people know the area and are bound to find him, so to summon more men at this hour, especially Wat…"

"Aye," she agreed with visible reluctance when he paused. "It would be just like Benjy to show up the minute Wat arrives with your father and a hundred searchers."

He knew she exaggerated and that she was worried sick. But the situation was what it was, and they were doing all they could do.

A thought occurred to him. "Did you look in your tree?"

"Aye, sure," she said. "I climbed farther up than I had before, too, and found a scrap I recognize from that new tan shirt he tore. So he must have been in the tree the day after our wedding, when the Scotts and your father left. The men on the wall said he went into the south woods earlier, so I thought he might have gone up to Rab's grave again. But poor Ash and one of the other lads went up and found no sign of him in the graveyard."

"Poor Ash?"

"He is distraught, Dev. He thinks you blame him for this."

"I merely reminded him that his chief duty is to keep an eye on Benjy," Dev said, wholly unrepentant.

He ordered her to bed hours later, accepting no excuse

and pointing out that she'd be of no help to Benjy when they did find him if she did not sleep. He kept men out all night and dozed between reports but woke at the slightest sound that might herald news.

When there was still no sign of the boy when Robby came down to the hall in the morning, she demanded again that he summon Wat.

Patiently, he said, "When our search extends to Rankilburn, we'll tell Wat, so he can send men into his forest. Our lads are asking everyone they see, and no one has seen Benjy or any strangers, beyond a shepherd or two, seeking lost sheep."

"We have our own lost sheep," she replied tartly. "We must *find* him."

At midday, she asked him again to send for Wat, and Dev was about to agree when Jock and Sandy came into the hall, flanking a scraggly-looking chap that Dev recognized as Bangtail Joey, the younger of the two erstwhile Percy messengers.

His lip was bleeding, his jaw was bruised, and he walked with a limp.

"What's this?" Dev demanded, looking at Jock.

"This chappie claims to ken summat about our laird, sir, but he refuses to talk to anyone save yourself."

"What happened to him?" Dev asked, standing and putting what he hoped was a reassuring hand on Robby's shoulder.

Jock kept silent, but Sandy said mildly, "Tripped over his own feet, sir."

"I see." To their guest, Dev said, "Before I hang you, tell me why you're here and what you know about the Laird of Coklaw's absence from this castle."

"Ye'll no hang me, 'cause I ha' a message for ye," Joey said. "I'm to give it to ye alone, though. If ye want yer wee laird back alive, nae one else must hear it."

Sandy said, "Give me more time wi' him, sir. I'll ha' all he kens out o' him."

"Aye, ye great lummox, ye might," the man said. "But it'll do ye nae good. We ha' men a-watching this place. If I dinna meet one o' them afore sundown, your wee lairdie will be dead when ye next see 'im."

～

Robina gasped, and the hall seemed suddenly fuzzy as if a fog had risen within its walls. Dev's hand tightened on her shoulder, steadying her, but she believed that the Percy man spoke the truth as he knew it.

"We cannot take the chance," she said to Dev. "We must do as they ask, but I want to hear what this man says. We must talk to him together."

"Nay, then," the man said, looking at Dev. "Ye may as well hang me, for I'll say nowt till we be alone. I ha' me orders, and I'll no stray from them."

Dev said calmly, "Then it shall be as you say. Nay, lass," he added firmly when she eluded his hand and stood. "We must do nowt to endanger Benjy, so if you cannot sit here patiently, go upstairs and await me in our chamber."

She nearly objected but realized when she met his steady gaze just what he was saying to her. She said less sharply than she had intended, "I'll do as you bid, sir, but I'll demand later to know all that you know."

"You may demand all you like, but you will go now," he said sternly.

Without looking at Sandy or Jock, lest one of them see something in her expression that he should not see, she strode to the privy stairs and ran up to their bedchamber. As she left, she heard Dev say, "Show this chap into the inner chamber, Jock. Then see to it that everyone leaves us alone."

Certain that Robby had understood him, Dev watched Jock escort their prisoner into the chamber before he said to Sandy, "Tell the lads on the wall to keep their eyes sharp but to do nowt to make anyone watching us suspicious."

"Sakes, sir, how could anyone watch? We ha' men out everywhere."

"We'll take no chances, even so," Dev said. "We'll behave as if there are enemy eyes everywhere. I'm not in any mood for more surprises."

Dismissing Sandy, he entered the chamber and told Jock to stay nearby but to make sure no one disturbed them. "You must not try to hear what we say, either, Jock," he added, more for their visitor's benefit than because Jock needed telling.

"Aye, sir, I'll see to it," Jock replied. "Just shout when ye've decided what we're to do wi' this ruffian."

"Sakes, I'll tell ye that," their guest announced, squaring his skinny shoulders. "Ye'll leave me be is what ye'll do, unless ye're tired o' your lairdie."

Waving Jock away, Dev leaned against the heavy table and said softly, "You'd be wise to deliver your message before you irk me enough to make it unnecessary. You do know what they call me, do you not?"

Satisfied to see the cocky look vanish and the man's face pale, Dev kept silent, knowing that few people could let anyone's silence continue for long.

At last, the chap said, "We dinna want to harm the laddie, but we ha' our orders and we darena disobey them."

"Your orders come from Northumberland?"

"That be what I'm told, sir."

Dev nodded, saying, "I'll do whatever I must to bring that boy home safely. Tell me what I must do."

"Ye're to come alone tomorrow just afore midday to fetch him. Also, as comp…compen—"

"Compensation?" Dev supplied dryly.

"Aye, that's it. Ye're to bring a certain article what ye must ha' found recently. I dinna ken what it be, but ye'll ken that yourself or someone else here will ken what our captain means."

"I know what he wants," Dev said.

"Aye? Well, it be gey important. 'Less ye bring it, that lad willna survive the day."

"Where are we to meet?"

"It'll just be ye meeting me captain and the wee lairdie. Afore I tell ye where, I must ha' your word as a Borderer that ye'll do as ye're bid and willna reveal the meeting place to anyone. Me captain likewise promises he'll come alone wi' only the bairn."

Forcing himself to reply calmly, and belatedly wishing that he'd not sent Robby upstairs, Dev said, "You have my word as a Borderer that I'll do as you say and will tell no one what you have told me."

"Ye're also to make sure that nae one follows ye, sir. Can ye do that, too?"

Praying that he spoke the truth, Dev said firmly, "I can, aye."

⁓

Upstairs, her eyes at the squint and her ears aprick, so she could see all they did and hear every word, Robina breathed, "Blethers!"

Then, in utter dismay, she watched as the messenger whispered in Dev's ear.

*Chapter 22* _____

Benjy was miserable and wished he had not so easily eluded Ash's keen eye the day before. But he had, so his misery was his own fault. He knew that Beany would say so and that Dev would likely do more than that.

Rab would skelp him, if Rab were still alive. If only he were!

Rab had not said one word to him. Yet Beany told Dev that Rab had warned her of danger more than once, so why—?

"Art hungry, laddie?" the growly man asked, looming over him.

Benjy shrugged. He was hungry but did not want to eat their food. The four men guarding him were rough and mean-looking. But, in the graveyard, their growly leader had crept up behind him so softly that he'd had no warning until the man spoke.

By then, it was too late. The man had said they were just going for a short ride. But they'd ridden for hours before stopping by the thin rivulet in this unfamiliar forest. They'd been here for a while, too.

The sun was going down, and they'd not even built a fire to keep warm.

"Do I call ye 'Coklaw,' or do they call ye summat else?" the growly man asked.

Benjy knew his proper title was Laird of Gledstanes and Coklaw. But strangers had called Rab "Gledstanes." His friends had called him Rab even after their father died, so Benjy was not sure what to say. Still, good manners required an answer.

"Me name's Benjy," he said. "I want to go home."

"I ken that fine, Benjy. I want to go home m'self. I ha' wanted that since I were a bairn younger than what ye be."

Habitually polite, despite his anger and unhappiness with the situation, Benjy said, "Ha' ye been away from home as long as that?"

"I ha' almost nae memory o' the place," the man said. "But that doesna lessen the yearning," he added with a sigh.

"Then why d'ye no go home?"

"'Tis too far away, across fearsome seas."

"Where?"

The man glanced at their companions. "You lot, get on wi' yer work. I'll look after the bairn. Caleb, send Joey to me when he returns."

The men left, muttering to each other, and the growly one handed Benjy two small oatcakes, which the boy took without hesitation.

The man said, "I dinna talk much about me homeland. Most o' that lot doesna believe the place exists."

"What be it called then?" Benjy asked. He bit into an oatcake and chewed.

"Scots and English call it Shetland. We called it *Hjaltland*."

To Benjy's ear, the two words sounded similar but not quite the same.

"The ancients called it the Isles o' Cats," the man added.

"Are there many cats there?"

"Nae more than most places. Me mam had one, though. I ken that fine, 'cause she were sad at leavin' it behind. But had she brought it wi' her, the wee beast would ha' drooned when our ship sank."

"Then why did you not drown, too?"

"D'ye wish I had?"

Uncertain how to answer that honestly, Benjy kept silent.

~

Chukk eyed the boy speculatively and realized when Benjy bit his lower lip that the lad feared him.

"I didna mean it that way," Benjy said softly. "I was curious only because you said the cat would have drowned."

Grimacing, Chukk realized that the night ahead might be long. He dared not leave the lad with the others; yet he had to know if Bangtail Joey had succeeded. At least, Joey would not tell Devil Ormiston where the laddie was. Joey didn't know.

Chukk had twelve men at the encampment and had sent six others on ahead, so, counting Joey, they'd be a score in all. He had heard much about Ormiston, but even Northumberland admitted that, devil or not, he was a man who kept his word if he gave it. Joey would demand his word of honor before revealing their meeting place.

Not being trustworthy himself and believing that most men were not, Chukk was taking precautions to ensure that Devil Ormiston did keep his word.

The young laird was a surprise, though, having remained unnaturally calm from the outset. Although he had insisted that he would *not* go with them, he'd kept silent when Chukk forced him to go. Nor had the boy complained as they'd ridden south. In truth, Benjy reminded Chukk of himself at the same age, unhappy and homesick but doing as he was told, knowing that resistance was useless.

Chukk liked the wee lairdie and hoped he would not have to kill him.

Despite every attempt, using every wile she knew to persuade Dev, Robina failed to learn where he was to meet the villains who had taken Benjy.

"If I broke my word to the messenger now," Dev said as they left the hall after supper, "how could *you* believe that I'd not break my word to you?"

"This is a matter of life or death," she reminded him.

"However, your participation is not," he pointed out, maddeningly.

"I have a right to know, Dev. Good sakes! They are villainous Percys, who do *not* keep their word. You'll likely ride into a trap."

"Would you risk Benjy's life just to protect me, Robby?"

To her shock, a voice inside her shrieked "yes!" Her lips parted but she could not speak. Tears sprang to her eyes at the fact that she could even entertain such a horrible thought for a second. She could not bear to lose either of them.

"I can't..." Stifling an unexpected sob, she blurted, "I can't lose *anyone* else!"

He stopped on the landing, opened his arms, and held her close. She felt his breath on her hair and smelled the scent of the soap he used and the woodland scents from his jack. Its soft leather felt like a caress against her cheek. Her treacherous world steadied.

"You *must* send for Wat and your father now," she murmured.

Giving her another brief hug, he set her back on her heels to say, "I cannot send for more men, sweetheart. 'Tis too dangerous. If those villains suspect I've sent for reinforcements, they'll likely kill Benjy and slip across the line."

*"He'll need Wat, Beany! Persuade him!"*

Gritting her teeth, she muttered. "You can*not* go alone to meet them, Dev."

"Jock will go as far as—" He broke off, drew a breath, and Robina silently cursed the demon who had reminded him of his damnable promise. "I'll take Jock part way with me," he went on. "He's as skilled a man as I know for looking as if he has every right to be where he is, doing what he's doing. He'll conceal himself, keep me in sight, and be able to report what happens."

She knew that Dev was more skilled at tactics and strategy than most men, so he had to know how little aid one man, even Jock Cranston, could lend him at such a distance. The villains, having watched Coklaw unseen and abducted Benjy without a soul stopping them or reporting their presence, clearly had equally well-trained men to watch for trouble.

"'Just a few shepherds," she muttered, remembering.

Dev's eyebrows flew upward. "What?"

"What if every shepherd who was supposed to be hunting lost sheep was a villain instead?" she asked him. "Were there not several reports of such?"

"There were. But, if you think we should have questioned each one as if he were a villainous Percy, just imagine the reaction hereabouts had they all been innocent."

"They could have been Turnbulls rather than Percys,"

she said. "Having lost two cows and four sheep in return for lifting our beasts, they may be seeking revenge."

"Sweetheart, right now, who the villains are matters less than the fact that they have Benjy," Dev said. "However, as you must have heard, they want to trade him for an item about which the Turnbulls ken nowt."

"Will you give them the jar?"

"I gave my word. And its contents likely do belong to the Percys."

"Aye, perhaps," she said quietly, knowing that she'd lost any argument she might make when he'd given the messenger his word. "Promise me that you'll wear your shirt of mail under your jack and do all that you can to bring yourself and Benjy back safely."

"I'll do all of that, sweetheart. You know I will."

"I do," she said with a sigh, "but I'm so tired I cannot think. If you won't let me help, I think I'll go to bed. You'll wake me if aught else happens."

"Aye, but I'll go up with you," he said. "I don't want you to worry about me or about Benjy. Worrying alters nowt, lass. 'Tis wiser to wait and see what happens."

She agreed not to worry, and when he wanted to couple before she slept, she accepted him willingly and exerted herself to show him how much he had taught her. After all, she thought desolately, it might be the last chance they had.

Even so, she'd had to exert herself not to snort in derision when Dev said not to worry. The only people who never worried were naïve innocents who still believed that nothing bad would happen to them.

Those who knew better worried *because* they knew better.

However, agreeing with him and encouraging his

lovemaking, which she enjoyed as much as he did, meant they would waste no more time in debate. And time was vital, because Rab had said that Dev would need help.

She had realized as much herself when Dev reminded her that the villains wanted the jarful of silver. The only one likely to know its whereabouts now was the thief who had stolen and buried it or someone who had aided him. It had to have been one of Northumberland's own men just to get inside his tent.

However, once they had the money, would they really release Benjy?

Midday tomorrow would come quickly, and she had a number of things to do.

Dev was glad to see that Robby still slept when he woke at dawn to Coll's light touch. He had feared he might waken her when he'd come to bed in the middle of the night, but if they could keep from waking her now, she might sleep well into the morning.

The longer, the better, he told himself. Getting up as gently as he could, he eased the bed curtain shut to block light through the shutters and moved quietly on bare feet to the washstand to wash himself.

Coll moved as silently, gathering Dev's clothes.

"Give orders to pull our people in close to the castle," Dev whispered as he pulled on his braies and breeks by the door. "Don't ask questions; just see to it."

"I should go wi' ye," Coll whispered back. "Wherever ye're a-going."

Shaking his head, Dev opened the door and motioned for Coll to follow him onto the landing. Easing the door shut, he murmured, "I'm taking Jock, not because I trust him more but because he's gey clever about concealing himself. And he'll need to be. In a fight, I'd liefer have you and your sword. Today, I need Jock."

Coll nodded, and Dev knew that he'd obey. "Keep close to her ladyship, and see that she stays here," he added, his mind having automatically shifted to the person most likely to *dis*obey him.

"I wield no authority over her," Coll reminded him.

"You do today," Dev said. "Stuff her in a kist and sit on it if you must."

"Sir, you can't mean that, nor would *she* ever forgive me if I did such a thing."

"Then use your imagination, my lad, because if you let her do aught to endanger herself, *I* will have your head. So choose how."

Hearing Coll gulp, he knew he'd made his point, and Coll would keep Robby safe.

～

Robina waited until she was sure that Dev had gone downstairs and Coll would be busy with his usual duties. Then, aware that Dev expected her to sleep late and would tell Corinne not to wake her, she dressed as hastily as she could and went downstairs and out through the bakehouse to look for Sandy. Disconcertingly, she ran into Coll instead.

"I thought ye were asleep, m'lady," he said.

"I woke up," she replied with a smile. "Have you seen Sandy or Shag?"

"Shag's gone to help call in our lads. Sandy's yonder," Coll said, pointing. "I should tell ye, m'lady, that the master said I'm t' keep close to ye."

"Faith, why should you?" she demanded.

"To see ye keep safe, he said."

"Well, I can keep myself safe, so you need not trouble yourself."

"He said I'm t' stuff ye in a kist and sit on it if I must," Coll said desperately.

"Look here, Coll, you care about *his* safety, too, do you not?"

"Aye, sure, but—"

"Dev has gone, aye?"

"Aye, he left whiles ago wi' Jock. But m'lady, I canna—"

"Clearly, I must take you into my confidence, Coll. You see, last night…"

⁓

Chukk woke Benjy early, knowing that to reach the meeting place would take time. His men were ready. Others had gone ahead, and they all knew what he expected of them. If Devil Ormiston's sworn word was good, he'd have his treasure soon after midday.

He'd have preferred to meet at dawn, because folks in the area would still be sleeping. But they would have had to ride at night, and since their lair was two hours from Coklaw and the moon was full, they'd have risked being taken for raiders.

As it was, they'd separated into twos and threes and were keeping to woodland, away from open roads. When Chukk saw people gathering wood, he thought nothing of it. None paid heed to a man and a boy on horseback who looked like a father and his son.

Chukk led the lad's horse to keep him from trying to flee. That irritated the laddie, but his glowers would lead onlookers to suspect only that he'd misbehaved. In any event, Chukk had told Benjy he'd take leather to him if he grew troublesome.

They soon saw many more wood gatherers, and children picking flowers, whereupon Chukk realized with shock that people were gathering wood for their Beltane fires. He'd forgotten that the first of May, when folks relit their home fires from communal ones, was nearly upon them.

"Not a word, lad," he murmured to Benjy as they passed close to one group.

The boy wisely kept silent.

When someone called out to wish them good fortune, Chukk returned the greeting but increased their pace to discourage further discourse.

"Good lad," he said when they were safely past the gatherers.

"I didna ken any o' them," Benjy replied gruffly. "I didna think they'd believe aught I said. They'd ha' believed whatever ye said, instead."

"Ye're a wise laddie," Chukk said. "See that ye stay wise."

They came at last to the road he wanted, and he took it, confident that none would interfere with them there. Coklaw men would risk no harm to their lairdie, and others would assume that Benjy knew him.

He was more worried that one of his lads might err while they tried to position themselves without drawing notice. They were good lads, though, and clever.

As they rode, to pass the time, he told Benjy some of the tales his dad had told him about Shetland. When the boy asked if he thought he'd ever get back again, Chukk said, "If all goes well, I will. Sithee, me da wanted to go hisself. But he could never think how to collect in safety what I'll get today by me own wits."

"What is it?"

"Nay, then. I'll tell ye only that it be rightfully mine and I'll soon have it."

"Was it buried in the ground? Is that why your da couldna get it?"

Stunned by the question, Chukk jerked on his reins, almost stopping his horse. Urging it on, he said tersely, "Why d'ye ask me such a thing?"

"I just wondered is all," Benjy said, shrugging. "Me sister tells me tales of buried treasures, and gold that wee folk hide in the ground."

"This be real and o' greater import than any made-up tale. I swore to me da on his deathbed that I'd fetch it and go home to tell our people what became of us."

"I hope you can do that," Benjy said. "I want to go home to my people, too."

"Ye'll help us both by doing as I bid ye, then," Chukk said.

"I want to help ye, sir," Benjy said quietly. "A man must keep such a vow."

A lump formed in Chukk's throat, but he did his best to ignore it.

Leg o' Mutton Cut lay just ahead.

~

Dev approached the cut alone, as he had promised.

Bangtail Joey had said naught about weapons, so Dev had a knife in his right boot, his dirk on his belt, and a short sword in its scabbard.

He also wore a chainmail shirt under the leather jack

that he always wore in battle. Quilted and well-padded with horn and other hard objects, it weighed him down but was lighter than armor and would give some protection against arrows and sword slashes.

His head was bare, so the villains could recognize him, but he had strapped his helmet behind his saddle, atop his rolled-up cloak.

He hoped that none of his precautions would prove necessary, because if any did, Benjy might be hurt, even killed.

Robby's sorrowful face leaped to his mind's eye, but he ruthlessly banished the image. He could pray and he could hope, but he could do naught else. What happened would happen, and he would face the consequences afterward.

Jock had parted from him and gone to ground soon after they'd left. His orders had been clear: to watch where Dev went but not interfere; to note what occurred; and, if the villains broke their promises, to do all he could to aid Benjy and then report what had happened to Buccleuch and Ormiston, and to the Douglas.

Auld Nick's pace had been slow from the beginning to give Jock time to make his way, and for the benefit of any watchers. He kept it so now because he wanted to avoid having to wait alone in the cut as a sitting target for enemy archers on its slopes.

The English, he knew, were fond of archers.

He felt confident that if any were there, they'd do naught until their leader had hefted the jar and felt its weight. First, he'd want to see if Dev had it.

He did have it, in the cloak strapped to his saddle. If the silver in it did belong to Northumberland, the young earl was unlikely to see it. One of Benjy's captors was likely the thief who stole it, and would want to keep it. But Dev would give it to them, anyway.

The people of Coklaw would benefit from the gelt if he kept it, but they'd benefit more by keeping their young laird.

Auld Nick found the measured pace tedious. Well behaved though the stallion was, Dev could sense Nick's suppressed energy and his yearning to run.

Rounding the next curve, he saw the cut opening ahead. And, approaching its central and widest point from the far end, he saw two riders on trotting horses, the larger one leading the smaller one's mount. Relieved as he was to see Benjy, Dev scanned the hillsides again. He saw no movement on the slopes or sign of anyone else nearby.

Experience warned him to distrust what he saw and expect the worst, but he kept riding. He also kept Nick to a walk so the man who led Benjy's horse could choose where to stop. His choice might provide information.

When the man pulled off his cap as he drew rein, Dev recognized him as the messenger Jock o' the Storm. However, on horseback, there was something familiar...

Benjy waved, so Dev waved back and urged Nick forward. As he neared them, a score of armed men rose out of dense shrubbery on each slope, swords drawn.

Meeting their leader's gaze, Dev said, "You've broken your word, Jock o' the Storm, if that is your true name. Will you tell me why?"

"Why, me true name's Chukk Jamieson, and I've no broken me word. Them be nobbut Percy lambs grazing on rightful Percy land. Where's me jar?"

Recognizing him then and one or two of his henchmen on the nearer hillside as members of the ambush party near Chesters, Dev said, "I brought the jar, as I promised, but I expected to meet a nobleman or a gentleman spokesman for Northumberland. I did not anticipate meeting a ruffian who ambushes men going about their rightful business. I believe, however, that the contents of this jar belong to Northumberland, do they not?"

"They do *not*," Jamieson replied. "That jar and its contents are mine. Ye might call it me inheritance, to which ye've nae right at all."

He scowled fiercely at Dev as if daring him to deny it. Then, almost ludicrously, his focus shifted beyond Dev and his fierceness altered to dismay.

"Wha's this, then?" he demanded.

Benjy's mouth had fallen agape, too, so Dev looked back to see a host of mounted Borderers lining the low hill behind him and filling the mouth of the cut. Their unsheathed swords flashed in the midday sun.

He estimated that they numbered at least a hundred men.

Leading them—astride Black Corby in her breeks, boots, and jack—was Robby, waving the Gledstanes's hawk banner.

Coll rode beside her, his sword at the ready.

Just behind them, Geordie Elliot waved the crescent-moons-and-star banner of the Scotts of Buccleuch with one hand and his sword with the other. Beside Geordie sat Wat on his favorite bay, and beside Wat was Ormiston. Wat's sword remained in its sheath. His grin as the leaders reined in, however, was big enough for everyone in the cut to see.

Turning back to face Jamieson, Dev said gently, "What is that, you ask? Why those are Coklaw's sheepdogs, sirrah. As fierce as they are, they'll not stay leashed long."

"Ye broke your word!"

"I promised to come alone, and unlike you, I did," Dev said. "I promised to bring your jar, and I did that, too. I did not summon those men or know they would come. I told no one of this meeting and gave orders that none should follow me. Buccleuch, however, does not take orders from me." *Nor*, he added silently, *does my lady wife!*

"Are ye a-going to give me yon jar, then? Or is it empty?"

"It retains all of its contents," Dev said. "As to giving it to you, I have yet to understand why you think it belongs to you. But if you'll agree to return to Coklaw with me, I'll hear your tale. If you can persuade me—"

"I'd ha' to be daft to go wi' ye. Ye might listen, but ye'd hang me for taking pity on the lairdie there, all on his own-some in a graveyard, and keeping him safe overnight."

"Is that how it was?"

When Jamieson hesitated, Dev looked at Benjy.

"He did me nae harm," Benjy said.

"And you did go alone to the graveyard on Sunnyside Hill?"

Warily, Benjy hesitated. Then, drawing a deep breath and meeting Dev's stern gaze, he said, "Aye, sir, I did. Ye willna hang Chukk, will ye?"

"I cannot answer that question until I have heard his reasons. But if you mean to speak for him, likely we won't hang him."

Turning to Jamieson, Benjy yanked his own reins from the man's grasp. Then he said quietly, "Come with us, sir. I meant what I said about helping ye."

Dev grimaced at the "sir" but kept silent, watching Jamieson, who said, "Will ye let me lads go, Sir David? They ha' done nowt to ye."

"If you can assure me that they will leave Coklaw land and that I'll never find them raiding our kine, I will. I suspect they're responsible for some stock we've lost recently."

"I canna say ye're wrong, but I willna say ye're right, neither. What I will say is that I'll send 'em back to Alnwick and they willna lift your kine."

"So you do at least come from Alnwick."

"Aye, sir, all of us."

"Am I to understand, though, that *you* will return to Coklaw with us?"

"If ye'll hear me out, I will. I must."

Dev nodded. "Dismiss your men, and we'll ride together. We can talk on the way."

When Jamieson wheeled his horse and spurred it toward his men on the nearer hillside, Dev said, "I think that you and I must have a talk, too, Benjy."

"Are you going to punish me?"

"That depends on what you have to say," Dev replied. "I'd like to know why you went all the way to the grave-yard by yourself."

"To ask Rab why he talks only to Beany and see if he'd talk to me, too."

# Chapter 23 _____

Deciding that the danger was over, Robina handed the Gledstanes banner to Coll, who accepted it without looking at her. He stared fixedly at Dev, likely fearing what Dev would do to him.

Putting such thoughts out of her head, she spurred Corby forward to meet Dev and Benjy, noting with more annoyance than surprise that the raider had stayed with them.

She heard Wat shout for her to wait but ignored him. The ruffians on the hillsides had laid down their swords, and since the riders and other men-at-arms behind her outnumbered the Percy louts five to one, she knew she was safe.

*"Aye, you may think so. But take care in what you say to Dev."*

She did not argue with Rab even in her thoughts. Dev *would* be displeased to see her there, but whatever the result, she'd been right about the danger from the Percys. Moreover, she thought little of a code of honor that let any husband of hers endanger both himself and Benjy by adhering to it at such grave risk.

Rab remained silent, but common sense warned her that she'd be wise not to say *that* to Dev. She was astonished, though, to see the Percy men on the slopes walking away toward the far end of the cut. And when she neared the oncoming riders and recognized Jock o' the Storm, she had a few second thoughts about so impulsively riding to meet them.

Benjy looked unnaturally solemn, the Percy too confident, and Dev so grim that she shifted her gaze back to Benjy without hesitation.

"I'm glad to see you safe, lovey," she said, wishing she could snatch him off his horse and hug him.

He gave her a rueful smile, glanced at Dev, and sobered again.

Dev said evenly, "Take Jamieson on ahead of us, Benjy, and present him to Buccleuch and Ormiston."

Benjy spurred the unfamiliar pony he was riding, but the man, Jamieson or Jock o' the Storms, hesitated and said to Dev, "Ye did give me your word, sir."

"I did," Dev assured him. "The lad will tell them so."

Nodding, Jamieson murmured, "M'lady," and spurred his mount to catch up with Benjy's, leaving Robina to face Dev alone.

Reluctantly, she met his gaze and found it thoughtful. Taking courage from that, she said tersely, "Whatever you mean to do to me, sir, you are *not* to punish Coll. He told me what you said to him. 'Stuff her in a kist and *sit on it!*'"

He smiled briefly then but said sternly and with a more enigmatic look, "I look forward to making you wish that he'd done so, madam wife."

The bolt of fire that shot through her then from her core outward startled her, but she did not mistake it for fear . . . not really.

By heaven, she was beautiful, Dev thought, although strands had come loose from her plait and she was wearing the damnable breeks, boots, and jack again.

Her flyaway strands and the sheen on her face told him that she and her army had ridden full pelt to reach the cut when they had. It was a wonder they were not close enough on his heels for him to hear them coming.

He should not encourage such defiance of his orders, though. She deserved...Smiling again, he decided he did not know what she deserved, nor did he care.

"How did you contrive to unman Coll?" he asked as they urged their horses toward the others.

"I had only to confide to him what I'd done," she said soberly.

"You'd sent for Wat and my father against my direct order," he said.

Although she looked cautious, she said, "Aye, I did, last night. I told them to wait out of sight until you'd gone and then to follow you. Coll and I met them."

He waited for her to try to justify what she had done, but she did not.

"Would you like to know why I agreed to come alone?"

Without looking at him, she nodded.

"That jar contains a treasure by almost anyone's definition," he said. "I deduced from that fact, and the messengers' calling it something I'd dug up, that whoever would come for it was unlikely to have shared the jar's existence, let alone its contents, with his companions. Therefore, he would be unlikely to order an attack on me before he had seen the jar and examined it."

"Where did you hide it?"

"It's wrapped in my cloak, strapped to my saddle."

She gaped at the bundle. "You brought it with you?" When he did not reply, she shook her head. "Of course, you brought it with you. You promised."

"Aye, and when I met them, Benjy's attitude toward Jamieson reassured me. The boy likes him, and Jamieson seems to like him, too."

"Why did you let his men walk away?"

"Because Jamieson, whom you likely recognized as our erstwhile messenger, Jock o' the Storm, agreed to come back to Coklaw and explain *why* the jar is his."

"But what will you do with him? He deserves to hang for taking Benjy."

"He found Benjy alone in the graveyard," Dev told her.

"Good sakes, what was he doing there?"

"He went to ask Rab why he talks only to you and see if Rab would talk to him, too," Dev said. Seeing her shock and the tears in her eyes, he knew he need say no more.

~

Robina could not speak. Her throat had closed. She could scarcely breathe. It had never occurred to her that Benjy might have overheard her talking to Dev, nor that Benjy would ever know that Rab spoke to her. That her little brother *had* heard them and that his abduction occurred because he'd gone to the graveyard hoping to persuade Rab to...

She thrust that upsetting image out of her mind and ignored the tear that spilled down her cheek. She could not let herself cry in front of Wat, Ormiston, Benjy, his iniquitous captor, and all the other men who awaited them.

Collecting her dignity, she lifted her chin and decided that she deserved whatever Dev did to punish her.

Finding her voice at last, she muttered, "So what *are* you going to do?"

"I told Jamieson I'd hear him out if he came back with us."

"I want to hear him, too."

"Then you shall," Dev said.

They discovered when they reached Coklaw that Ada Greenlaw had ordered the midday meal delayed for them, and that Ormiston, Wat Scott, and the others also expected to hear what their sole "captive" had to say.

"I mean to talk to Jamieson first," Dev said in reply to demands for an immediate trial with a hanging to follow. "I told him I'd listen to him. If I decide his actions warrant criminal charges, we'll have a trial. For the present, though, Benjy has asked to speak for him, and my lady will also hear what they have to say."

"Now, see here, Dev," Wat said.

Dev stopped him with a gesture, saying, "I'm more grateful to you than I can say for your prompt response to my lady's summons, my lord, but *this* is a matter I must see to privately." Turning to Ormiston, he said, "Sir, if you'll serve as host in my stead for those of our guests who will dine in the hall, I'll meet with my ... my captive in the inner chamber. We'll join you at the table as soon as we can, but prithee do not keep the others waiting."

Ormiston agreed, and Wat kept silent, so Dev ushered Jamieson, Benjy, and Robby into the chamber. Shutting the door, he moved to the table and stood beside it, facing Jamieson, to say, "Explain yourself, sirrah."

"Call me Chukk if ye would, sir," Jamieson said, as Robby moved to stand by Dev.

Benjy stayed where he was, beside his abductor, who went on glibly to explain his actions. He was articulate, and Dev could see that he believed the tale he told and that the passion he felt about fulfilling his promise to his dying father was real. He listened until Chukk Jamieson had no more to say.

Then Dev turned to Benjy. "What do you say to this, lad?"

"I think a man who makes such a promise must keep it," Benjy said. "So I told Chukk that I'd help him keep his."

Dev nodded. "'Tis a good argument, and so is Chukk's. Yet Scotland does have strict laws against theft. Most civilized countries do, come to that. Chukk's father, Shetland Jamie, admitted stealing the coins from the English Earl of Northumberland during the siege here at Coklaw. If we aid Shetland Jamie's son now by giving him the jar, we'd all be abetting Jamie's crime. That means that all of us would be as guilty of the theft as Jamie was. Those coins should properly go back to Northumberland."

"Aye, but I doubt ye'll be returning them yourself," Chukk said scornfully. "Or that he'd believe ye if ye did. And, if ye *keep* them, then ye're the thief."

"You are in no position to accuse others or to make demands," Dev reminded him. "However, I will offer a compromise. You are innocent of the theft, so I'll accept your version of how and why you took Benjy and your assurance that we'll lose no more kine to your men. If you tell Northumberland that I have his gelt, he can request a safe-conduct from the Douglas and send a man to collect it. Meantime, I'll keep the jar and its contents secure until he requests it or for as long as I am warden here."

"Bah, ye're just keeping it for yourself, is all. I'll tell ye what, though. Ye can give *me* the jar and *I'll* take it to his lordship."

"I won't entrust you with it," Dev said. "But I *will* give you my word as a Borderer that *I'll* do as I've promised. As you must admit, my word *is* more reliable than yours."

"I'll admit nae such thing," Jamieson said. "But if ye willna give it to me, what will ye do wi' me?"

"Since you did our Benjy no harm, you are free to go."

Benjy said casually, "Then I'll walk out to the yard with him, sir. I must be sure that our lads let him take the pony I rode, 'cause it's his. I willna go any farther."

Dev nodded, put a gentle hand to Robby's back, and said, "We'll join the others on the dais then, lass."

When they reached the high table, Dev quietly told Coll to keep Benjy and Jamieson in sight until the latter had gone and the gate had shut behind him. Then, taking his seat beside Robby, he rested his left hand, under the table, on her breeks-clad thigh and gave it a gentle squeeze.

Robina's tension had eased when Dev touched her back in the inner chamber, and she relaxed more at the table when he rested his hand just above her knee. But when that hand began to stroke her and crept closer to her breeks' codpiece, she startled.

Dev smiled without looking at her. "Easy, lass," he murmured.

When she stuck her tongue out at him, he grinned.

"Davy, are you going to tell us why you let that villain

walk out of here with Benjy?" Wat asked across Ormiston, who, having acted as host, sat between them.

Giving Robina a rueful look, Dev shifted his hand off her thigh and said, "I offered him a compromise. If he'd give me an honest explanation for his abduction of Benjy and see that his men ceased their raiding, I'd let him go."

Wat cocked his head, and Robina detected a glint of suspicion in his eyes. "You want us to believe that that villain gave you an *honest* explanation?"

"Benjy supported it," Dev said.

"I'd like to hear what it was, then," Wat said.

"I, too," Ormiston agreed.

Robina held her breath, but Dev said quietly, "Benjy may tell you one day, or I may. For now, I'll say only that Jamieson did Benjy no harm and may have taught him a good lesson. Do you and your men want to spend the night here, Wat?"

"Nay, nay, we'll leave for Scott's Hall as soon as everyone has eaten. We've plenty of daylight left, and they'll be lighting bonfires tonight in my forest. I'd liefer be there to make sure no one burns it down. You're welcome to come to us, though."

Robina stiffened, and Dev gave her thigh another squeeze as he said, "I think we'll look after our bonfires here, but we'll visit soon. Father," he added, "I expect you'll be returning with them, too, since Fee is still at the Hall."

"I will," Ormiston said. "I'll expect to see you and Robina before we return to Ormiston Mains, though."

Agreeing, Dev turned his attention to his food for a short time before Wat said, "Did that Jamieson chap say how many other men he had with him?"

"No more than a score," Dev replied.

Robina saw Benjy run into the hall just as Wat said, "There were a score of them riding around this area together?"

"That's what he said. Some of them apparently avoided notice by posing as shepherds, seeking lost sheep."

Benjy took his seat, and Ash appeared with a platter of beef to serve him.

"You know," Wat said musingly, "I think I'll stop at Hawick and suggest a compromise of my own to Archie. I'll offer to let him keep my men at Hermitage if he'll tell all the men there to keep stray *shepherds* from collecting our sheep."

Ormiston, Dev, and others laughed, but although Benjy stopped eating to look at Wat, the boy's expression was more thoughtful than amused.

Wat sent one of his men to warn those outside that they'd soon be leaving, and when the time came, Robina, Dev, and Benjy walked to the yard with their guests to bid them farewell. Ash Nixon went with them, and when Wat and Ormiston had departed with their men, Benjy ran off with Ash, and Robina looked up at Dev.

"I expect you haven't finished with me yet," she said.

"We'll talk about it more tonight," he said. "I need to get men out into the hills again to keep watch. I don't entirely trust Jamieson to take his lads home."

"You said you were going to make me wish that Coll had sat on me," she reminded him. "Are you still so angry?"

"Let's say that I have mixed emotions about that," he said in the even tone he took when he was controlling himself. "Especially about riding with our men again and showing yourself to so many in those damnable breeks."

Her involuntary muscles clenched again, and Robina grimaced, certain that he'd make her rue the actions he had mentioned, at least.

Gently, he added, "I wouldn't have you any other way, sweetheart, and I love you more than I ever thought I'd love anyone. But I did warn you about consequences. We'll talk tonight, but you may want to sleep first."

That night, in bed, when he took her in his arms, he exerted himself to show her how much he cared about her, although he also realized that she might believe he had forgiven her for everything she'd done.

He took his time, enjoying himself, but concentrating more on giving her pleasure, lots of pleasure. Then, when he could resist no longer...

"Dev, Dev, don't stop!"

He stopped. "Why not?"

She wriggled under him. "Because, because I'm almost...Oh, yes, yes!"

He stopped again, although his lips and fingers toyed with her breasts.

"You devil! What are you trying to do to me?"

"I'm teaching you one of many possible penalties a husband can offer for his wife's disobedience," he murmured. "Do you mean to defy my orders again?"

"No, no! I promise! Finish it...please!"

He did not believe that promise for a second, but he willingly accommodated her, bringing her to her climax and then seeking his own.

When they lay back sated, and she grinned, he wondered when she would defy him again. Wild promises were nearly always false ones, and under the circum-stances, he could hardly hold her to one made under such duress as this one had been.

Still, she was his now, and he knew that they loved each other. He could judge each new defiance as it occurred, on its own merits.

# Epilogue _____

*Coklaw, a fortnight later*

The moon was new, and outside their bedchamber windows, the sky was black, although millions of stars blazed in it. The landscape was a sea of dark shadows, but the hawthorn bushes had bloomed. Even in the darkness, Robina could see their white blossoms by starlight as she cleansed herself after coupling with Dev.

"It occurs to me, Robby," he said from the bed, where he lay awaiting her return, "that if Chukk Jamieson and his men took your kine at Easter, the Turnbulls were innocent of any wrongdoing."

She winced but rallied gamely. "If they didn't take the last lot, they likely took others," she said. Then she added flatly, "We're keeping the cows and sheep."

He chuckled, and someone rapped on their door.

Snatching up her shift from the pile of their clothing on the floor, she pulled it on over her head as Benjy spoke from the landing: "I could hear ye talking. Can I come in?"

Scrambling back over Dev into bed, she said, "Aye, sure, lovey." When he opened the door, she raised up on her elbows, adding, "What are you doing up so late?"

"I couldna sleep," he said. "I did summat ye willna like, Dev. I ken fine that ye'll find out, so I thought I'd best tell ye m'self."

Sitting up straighter beside her in the bed, Dev reached back to pull pillows higher for both of them. "That was a wise decision," he said. "What did you do?"

Benjy glanced up at the shelf that held Rab's carved box. "I took the jar, and I buried it," he said solemnly.

Robina's breath caught in her throat.

Dev said, "How did you know where it was?"

"I'd wager he overheard us the day we talked about it under my tree," Robina said. "When I thought I'd heard a squirrel and later found that scrap from his shirt."

Benjy nodded and then kept still, attempting no explanation.

"Where did you bury it?" Dev asked sternly. When the boy didn't answer, he added, "If Chukk tells Northumberland about it, we must be able to give it back to him."

"Chukk willna tell him, though. He's a-going home to his Shetland."

Robina gasped. "Benjy, you didn't give Jamieson that money, did you?"

"Not all of it," Benjy said, looking at his feet. Drawing a breath, he looked up again and met her gaze. "I did give him some of it."

"How much?" Dev asked grimly.

"Just a handful and a bit," Benjy said. "It were a compromise, like what ye did, and what Cousin Wat's a-going to do wi' the Douglas. Chukk wants to go home to Shetland, because he promised his da he would when his da were dying, just like ye promised our Rab that ye'd look after us. Also, I promised I'd help him, so I told him to come back today and I met him. I didna ken how much he'd need to go so far, but I kent fine that I couldna give him more than just to set him on his way, so..." He shrugged.

"Then why did you bury the jar?" Dev asked him. "If you'd put it back, we might never have known that some of the gelt was gone."

"I just decided to bury it. Then I told Chukk that I had, so he'd ken fine that nae one here would ken where it was if he threatened to harm me again."

"You should never have met him alone," Robina said flatly.

"Ash were nearby," Benjy assured her. "He had his bow and arrows."

"I'll have something to say to Ash about *that*," Dev said.

"Nay, ye won't, neither," Benjy said. "Coll told Ash that ye'd said Ash wasna to share aught that I confided to him with anyone else, so I kent fine that Ash wouldna tell ye. Ye canna tell a man he must *not* do summat—like ye did—and then punish him for not doing it, can he, Robby...I mean Beany?"

"No, Benjy, he can't, and you may call me Robby if you like. I don't mind."

"Aye, then, I will, unless our Rab tells me I should call ye Beany like he did."

Swallowing the sudden obstacle in her throat, Robina looked at Dev.

He was watching Benjy, and she couldn't tell if he was angry or not. Then, in measured tones, he said, "*Where* did you bury that jar?"

"I think it should stay buried yet awhile," Benjy said, meeting his gaze. "Ye did say that the jar and its contents belong to me unless Northumberland claims it. So, since it isna ours to use, I think it should stay hid unless Coklaw be in such trouble that nobbut them coins can save it."

When Dev did not reply, and Robina dared not speak, Benjy added quietly, "I think ye should do as I say, Dev. I ken fine that ye'll likely skelp me blue for this, and 'tis likely I deserve it, but I'll still think the same as what I think now."

Dev said more gently than before, "We'll talk more in the morning, laddie. You go on to bed now, and don't fret about what I might do. You do deserve something for sneaking into this room and taking the jar from it, but all in all, I think you have acted with more wisdom than many who are much older than you are."

"Good, then I'll bid ye goodnight, Dev. Goodnight, Robby." Then, with as much dignity as he had shown throughout the discussion, Benjy went off to bed.

Robina could think of nothing to say, and Rab had not said a word.

⁓

Aware of Robby's silence and his own sense of unease because of it, Dev shifted slightly to study her expression. "What is it, sweetheart? I'm not going to skelp him blue, if that's what has put that worried frown on your face. Sometimes that laddie makes me feel younger than he is."

A weak smile curved her inviting lips. He eyed her more closely, and a memory struck him of something Benjy had said. "Is it that he's calling you Robby now?" he asked. "Do you fear that he's still waiting for Rab to talk to him?"

Bleakly, she murmured, "Do you think you can ever bring yourself to believe that I do hear Rab speak to me?"

He nearly reminded her that Rab was dead but decided to be tactful. "I'm willing to let Rab persuade me, sweetheart. Ask him what the last thing he said to me was."

"I know what it was. He made you promise to look after us."

"He said one thing more, after that. If he *is* watching us, he'll remember."

~

Silence greeted her, and Robina realized that she'd heard only a few comments from Rab since her marriage. Closing her eyes, she willed him to answer.

Still silence. Mayhap he no longer wanted to talk to her.

Dev was silent, too, waiting.

*"It's none of your damned business what I said to the man, Beany."*

Exhaling in relief, she said, "He refuses to tell me."

"You see," Dev said. "I was right."

She shook her head. "No, Rab said it's none of my business, so I know what it is now. There is only one thing that Rab would never admit to me."

"What, then?"

"He told you he was afraid to die."

Stunned, Dev growled, "I can't say that I like the thought that he may be watching us all the time. Do you think he will always be with us?"

"No, my love. I don't need him as much as I did and never when I'm with you."

## Dear Reader,

I hope you enjoyed *Devil's Moon*, the sequel to *Moonlight Raider*.

Lady Robina Gledstanes and Sir David Ormiston are fictional characters, but Coklaw Castle, details of the siege of 1403, and the jar of coins are real, as are John Greenlaw, James Gledstanes, the fifth Earl of Douglas, the Earl of Northumberland, and Walter Scott of Buccleuch.

Readers who were not already acquainted with Lady Meg Scott before reading this book might also like to read *Border Wedding*, the story of Meg and the first Sir Walter Scott of Buccleuch and Rankilburn. That book and its two sequels, *Border Lass* and *Border Moonlight*, are still in print as I write this and are available in electronic form, in most formats, from www.Amazon.com and www.barnesandnoble.com, as well as other sources.

My primary sources for Scott history are J. Rutherford Oliver's *Upper Teviotdale and The Scotts of Buccleuch* and, by the same author, *The Gledstones* (sic) *and the Siege of Coklaw*. The jar of coins was discovered at Coklaw during the nineteenth century, along with an iron horse brooch or medallion of some sort. Mrs Oliver's version of the likely source for those coins is the one I used, and I had Benjy rebury them so that the Victorians could find the jar. As knowledgeable readers (and I have *many*) will guess, the Gledstanes were ancestors of William

Ewart Gladstone (1809–98), four-time Prime Minister of England.

Other Border sources include *The Scotts of Buccleuch* by William Fraser (Edinburgh, 1878), *Steel Bonnets* by George MacDonald Fraser (New York, 1972), *The Border Reivers* by Godfrey Watson (London, 1975), *Border Raids and Reivers* by Robert Borland (Dumfries, Thomas Fraser, date unknown), and others.

My primary source for Douglas history is *A History of the House of Douglas,* Vol. I, by the Right Hon. Sir Herbert Maxwell (London, 1902). Another excellent source is *The Black Douglases* by Michael Brown (Scotland, 1998).

I extend special thanks to Corinne and Jim Shrader for the generous donation Corinne made to the St. Andrews Society of Sacramento, which resulted in the character bearing her name (and that of Corinne's flirt Jem Keith); and thanks also to Chuck Jamison for his matching donation, which resulted in the creation of Chukk Jamieson in *Devil's Moon.* I hope the result pleases all three of them. The difference in the Jamison spellings is to show readers how such a name progressed, from Shetland Jamie to Jamie's son Chukk to Chukk Jamieson to Chuck Jamison.

As always, I'd like to thank my long-suffering agents, Lucy Childs and Aaron Priest, my overworked editor Lauren Plude, master copyeditor Sean Devlin, Art Director Diane Luger and Elizabeth Turner for *Devil's Moon*'s beautiful cover, Senior Managing Editor and stressbreaker Bob Castillo, Editorial Director Amy Pierpont, Vice President and Editor in Chief Beth de Guzman, and everyone else at Grand Central Publishing/Forever who contributed to this book.

If you enjoyed *Devil's Moon*, please look for news of my next book on my website and Facebook pages, listed below. Its heroine, Lady Fiona Ormiston, who has a knack for uncovering secrets, will unexpectedly meet and marry a "barbaric" Highlander up to his devilish blue eyes in guarding secrets and issuing challenges. Thus uprooted from her comfortable life and doting family, gentle but determined Fiona will find both danger and love in the fearsome Highlands.

Meantime, *Suas Alba!*

*Amanda Scott*

www.amandascottauthor.com
www.facebook.com/amandascottauthor
www.openroadmedia.com/amanda-scott

More from Amanda Scott!

An exciting excerpt from

*Moonlight Raider,*

the first book in the Border Nights
series, follows.

# Chapter 1 _____

*The Scottish Borders, 4 November 1426*

What was she thinking? God help her, why had she run? When they caught her...But that dreadful likelihood didn't bear thought. They must *not* catch her.

Even so, she could not go any faster, or much farther. It felt as if she had been running forever, and she had no idea of exactly where she was.

Glancing up through the forest canopy, she could see the waxing half-moon high above her, its pale light still occluded by the mist she had blessed when leaving Henderland. Although the moon had been rising then, she had prayed that the mist would conceal her until she reached the crest of the hills southeast of her father's tower. After she reached the southern slope in apparent safety, she had followed a little-used track that she hoped her pursuers—for they would certainly pursue her—would never imagine she had taken.

Experience had warned her even then that the mist might augur rain ahead, but the mist had been a blessing nevertheless. In any event, with luck, she would find shelter before the rain found her, or the light of day, come to that.

Long before then she had to decide what to do. But how? What *could* she do? Who would dare to help her? Certainly, no one living anywhere near St. Mary's Loch would. Her father was too powerful, her brothers too brutal and too greedy, and Tuedy—

She could not bear even to think about Ringan Tuedy.

A low, canine woof abruptly curtailed her stream of thought, and she froze until a deep male voice somewhere in the darkness beyond the trees ahead of her said quietly, "Wheesht, Ramper, wheesht."

Terrified, knowing that she was too tired to outrun anyone and dared not risk time to think, let alone try to explain herself to some stranger, eighteen-year-old Molly Cockburn dove desperately into the shrubbery and wriggled her way in as far, as quietly, and as deeply as she could, heedless of the brambles and branches that scratched and tore at her face and bare skin as she did. Lying still, she feared that her heart might be pounding loudly enough to betray her.

A susurrous sound came then of some beast—nay, a dog—sniffing. Then she heard scrabbling and a rattle of nearby dry shrubbery. Was the dog coming for her?

Hearing the man call it to heel, then a sharper, slightly more distant bark, and realizing that he and his dogs were closer than she had thought, she curled quietly to make herself as small as possible, then went utterly still, scarcely daring to breathe.

She was trembling, though, and whether it was from the cold or sheer terror didn't matter. She was shaking so hard that she would likely make herself heard if the nosy dog did not drag her from the shrubbery or alert its master to do so.

Above the sounds of the animal that had sensed her presence came others then, even more ominous. Recognizing the distant yet much too near baying of hounds, Molly stifled a groan of despair. They were doubtless Will's sleuthhounds, trained to track people, even—or especially—rebellious sisters.

~

Twenty-four-year-old Walter Scott, Laird of Kirkurd since childhood and the sixth Lord of Rankilburn and Murthockston for a scant twenty-four hours, had just taken a long, deep, appreciative breath of the energizing, albeit chilly, damp-earth-and-foliage scented forest air—filling his lungs and trying not to think of the myriad responsibilities that had so suddenly descended on him—when his younger dog gave its low, curious woof.

"Wheesht now, Ramper," he muttered. When the shaggy pup ignored him, its attention fixed on whatever nocturnal creature it had sensed in the always-so-intriguing shrubbery, Wat added firmly, "Come to heel now, laddie, and mind your manners as Arch does. I'd liefer you disturb no badgers or other wildlife tonight."

Hearing its name, the older dog perked its ears, and Ramper turned obediently, if reluctantly, toward Wat. Then, pausing, Ramper lifted his head, nose atwitch.

Arch emitted a sharp warning bark at the same time, and Wat heard the distant baying that had disturbed them himself.

"Easy, lads," he said as he strode toward the sound, his senses alert for possible trouble.

Both dogs ranged protectively ahead of him, but seeing torchlight in the near distance and now hearing hoofbeats over the hounds' baying, he halted a few yards past the area where young Ramper had sought whatever wildlife had gone to earth there. Calling both of his dogs to heel, Wat looked swiftly around lest there be other intruders nearby.

The misty moon's position indicated that the time was near midnight, so whoever was riding his way with hounds had not come to offer condolences to the new Lord of Rankilburn and hereditary Ranger of Ettrick Forest. That they might be raiders occurred to him next, but he dismissed that thought as unlikely, too.

A third thought and a companion fourth one that brought a near smile to his face led him to shout, "Tam, Sym, to me!"

Doffing his voluminous, fur-lined cloak, he draped it over nearby shrubbery, listened for sounds behind him, and watched the torches draw nearer as he waited.

Except for the ever-closer riders and dogs, silence ensued.

It was possible, he supposed, that neither Tam nor Sym, or perhaps only one of them, had followed him from Scott's Hall, but both tended to be overprotective of him, and had been since his childhood. At such a time, it was more likely that both men were within shouting distance than that neither one was.

As the riders drew nearer, Wat drew his sword and eased his dirk forward, hoping that he would need neither weapon.

His dogs were quiet now and kept close, awaiting commands. Hearing a slight rustle behind him, Wat said, "Are you alone, Tam, or is Sym with you?"

" 'Tis both of us, laird," Jock's Wee Tammy said quietly. "We should be enough, too. It be just four or five riders, I'm thinking."

Even more quietly, Sym Elliot muttered, "Herself did send us out, laird."

At Rankilburn, "Herself" referred to only one person, his grandmother.

Wat said gently, "Are you suggesting that, had Lady Meg not sent you, you would not have followed me?"

Sym cleared his throat.

"Aye, well, I'm glad you did, both of you," Wat said, looking at the two shadowy figures as he did.

Jock's Wee Tammy, despite his name, had nearly sixty years behind him and was thus the older as well as much the larger of the two. A time-proven warrior and still fierce with a sword, he was captain of the guard at Scott's Hall. He and Sym had both served Wat's father and grandfather long before Wat was born, and he knew both men well and trusted them completely. "I was woolgathering as I walked," he told them frankly. "But Arch and Ramper warned me of our visitors."

Lanky Sym said, "Herself sent me to tell ye that her ladyship were a-frettin' earlier and restless. She said to remind ye that if she wakens—her ladyship, I mean—she'd be gey worried to hear ye was out roaming in the forest, so..."

"My mother and grandmother are both strong women," Wat said when Sym paused. "I do know that Mam is grieving, Sym. We all are."

"It were too sudden," Tam said.

"It was, aye," Wat agreed, stifling the new wave of grief that struck him. "We will miss my lord father sorely, but death does come to us all in the end."

"Not from this lot we be a-seein' now, though," Sym said confidently, drawing his sword. Tam's was out, too, Wat noted.

"Don't start anything," he warned them. "Take your cues from me."

"Aye, sir, we know," Tam said.

He knew that they did, but the riders were close. Their baying dogs were closer yet, and he hoped they were well trained. Arch and Ramper would fight to the death to protect him, but he didn't want to lose either one. He kept them close.

Seconds later, a pack of four hounds dashed toward them through the trees.

"Halt and away now!" Wat bellowed, shouting what the Scotts had long shouted to keep their own dogs from tearing into their prey.

Either his roar or his words were sufficient, because the four stopped in their tracks. Two of them dropped submissively to the ground. The other two hesitated, poised and growling, teeth bared.

Wat stayed where he was and watched the riders approach, four men in pairs, the two on the right bearing flaming torches. In the fiery glow, he recognized the two leaders and a man-at-arms who served them. He did not immediately recognize the fourth man although he looked familiar.

When the four saw him and wrenched their horses to plunging halts, Wat said grimly to their leader, "Will Cockburn, what urgency brings you and these others to Rankilburn at this time of night?"

Cockburn was a neighbor who lived at Henderland Tower on St. Mary's Loch. He was a wiry man several years older than Wat and known for leading brutal raids across the border and on the Scottish side, too. Such a reputation was common in the area, which was rife with reivers. Wat shared a somewhat similar repute.

However, the two of them had never been particularly friendly, and if Will had hoped that Rankilburn might be ripe for his raiding...

Will glowered at him. Then, exchanging a look with his brother Ned, beside him, he looked back at Wat speculatively, as if he hoped that Wat might say more.

Instead, Wat waited, expressionless, for the answer to his question.

At last, Will said, "One of our maidservants seems to have lost her way home. The hounds picked up her scent near St. Mary's Loch and led us here."

Molly nearly gasped. So she was a maidservant, was she? Not that it was far off the mark. But did they truly think that Walter Scott of Kirkurd would care about a missing maidservant? And, surely, the man must be Scott of Kirkurd if Will called him "Wat" and if they were on Rankilburn land near Scott's Hall.

"You fear that a maidservant wandered all the way here from Henderland?" Kirkurd said, his tone heavily skeptical. "Sakes, Will, 'tis eight miles or more."

"I ken fine how far we've come," Will snapped.

"Rather careless of you to lose such a lass," Kirkurd replied evenly, doubtless wondering at Will's curtness. "Do your maidservants often go missing?"

"Dinna be daft," Will retorted. "It be dangerous for a lass in these woods."

Molly could imagine the sour look on Will's face as he spoke and prayed that heaven would keep him from getting his hands on her after chasing her such a distance. He'd get his own back first. Then he'd turn her over to Ringan Tuedy, and Tuedy had told her what *he'd* do to her. A shiver shot through her at the memory.

"You won't find your serving lass here," Kirkurd said, his deep voice reassuringly calm. "My dogs would alert me to any stranger within a mile of here, just as they did when they sensed your approach."

A snarling voice that Molly identified with renewed dread as Tuedy's interjected, "So ye say! But since ye've no said what ye're doing out and about at such a late hour, how do we ken that ye didna come out tae meet some lass yourself? Ye kept them dogs o' yours quiet, for I didna hear nowt from them."

A heavy silence fell.

Molly had never met Walter Scott of Kirkurd, but her father had mentioned once that he was just six years older than she was. Tuedy, on the other hand, was older by nearly ten years. He was of powerful build, an experienced warrior, and a man ever-determined to have his own way. Would Kirkurd defer to him?

Shivering again, she hoped not.

Recalling then that Kirkurd's authoritative tone had stopped Will's dogs before they could surround her and reveal her presence to Will, she told herself she should be thankful for that one blessing and not be praying for more.

At last, in a tone that revealed only mild curiosity, Kirkurd said, "Tuedy, is that you? I thought you looked familiar, but it must be five or six years since last we met.

Do you often help others search for lost maidservants at midnight?"

Molly's lips twitched wryly, but her fear increased as she awaited the reply.

To her surprise, Tuedy said only, "I was visiting Piers Cockburn." He made it sound as if it had been an ordinary visit and not one that had turned her life upside down. "But ye've no answered me question, Wat. What be ye doing out here?"

"It is unnecessary for any Scott to produce his reason for a moonlight stroll on Scott land," Kirkurd said. "However, you may not yet have heard that my lord father died last night. We buried him today, so it has been a grievous time for us here. I came out into the forest to seek fresh air and peaceful solitude."

Robert Scott of Rankilburn was dead? Sadness surged through Molly at the news. She had met him only a handful of times, but unlike her brothers and her father, Rankilburn had treated her with the respect due a lady. He had been younger than her father, and she had thought him kinder, too. She wished she could see the men as they talked, but she was facing away from them and dared not move.

Tuedy said mockingly, "Ye come seeking peace, ye say. Yet ye come fully armed and wi' Jock's Tam and Lady Meg's Sym behind ye, also full-armed."

"Most Borderers carry weapons wherever they go," Kirkurd said.

Nay, but she must stop thinking of him as Scott of Kirkurd, Molly realized. Walter Scott was now Lord of Rankilburn and Chief of Clan Scott.

He added, "I certainly won't ask why you four are

armed or *why* you seek a missing maidservant instead of sending minions in search of her. But *you*, Tuedy, do seem over-familiar with my people."

"Sakes, everyone kens that Sym Elliot is your gran-dame, Lady Meg's, man. We also ken Jock's Wee Tammy and that he be captain o' Rankilburn's guard."

"Enough argle-bargle," Will declared curtly. "Ye willna object if we have a look through the forest here-abouts for our lass, will ye, Wat?"

Molly held her breath again.

"I do object to such an unnecessary intrusion," Scott replied, "especially whilst we here are grieving our loss." His tone remained even but had an edge to it, as if he disliked Will but tried not to show it. "Tammy and Sym were nearby," he added. "A few of my men always are. If I whistle, two score more will come."

Molly relaxed, although the thought of more men com-ing was daunting.

Another silence fell before Scott added amiably, "Methinks you should train your sleuthhounds better, Will, because they must have followed a false trail here. Moreover, you ken fine that you had no business hunting man or beast in Ettrick Forest without Scott permission. You would all be wise to turn around now and ride peace-fully back to Henderland."

"What if we don't?" Tuedy demanded provocatively.

"You are on my land, Ring Tuedy, and you must know that I now wield the power of pit and gallows. Do you doubt I'd use that power against troublemakers whilst my lady mother, my sisters, and my grandame endure deep mourning?"

When yet another silence greeted his words, Molly bit

her lip in trepidation, fearing that Will and Ned might react violently to such a threat. Then, to her deep relief, she heard Will mutter something to the others, followed by the shuffling sounds of horses turning. Calling the dogs to heel, Will shouted, "Ye'd best not be lying to me, Wat. If ye've given shelter t' the maid, ye'll answer to me."

"I am not in the habit of sheltering misplaced maidservants, Will. If such a lass shows herself here, I'll get word to Henderland straightaway."

Although Molly was sure that Will had heard him, he did not deign to reply.

She listened intently until she could no longer hear any sound of horses, dogs, or men. When utter silence reigned throughout the nearby forest, she decided that Will and the others had indeed departed. Moreover, she had begun to feel the icy chill again. Tension stirred, nevertheless. Had everyone truly gone away?

Gathering her courage, she decided to risk moving and carefully wiggled the toes of one bare, chilly foot, grateful to find that her toes had not gone numb.

"They've gone," Walter Scott said quietly. "You can come out now."

Every cell in Molly's body froze where it was.

# Fall in Love with Forever Romance

## A HOPE REMEMBERED
## by Stacy Henrie

*The final book in Stacy Henrie's sweeping Of Love and War trilogy brings to life the drama of WWI England with emotion and romance.* As the Great War comes to a close, American Nora Lewis finds herself starting over on an English estate. But it's the battle-scarred British pilot Colin Ashby she meets there who might just be able to convince her to believe in love again.

## SCANDALOUSLY YOURS
## by Cara Elliott

*Secret passions are wont to lead a lady into trouble*... Meet the rebellious Sloane sisters in the first book of the Hellions of High Street series from bestselling author Cara Elliott.

# *Fall in Love with Forever Romance*

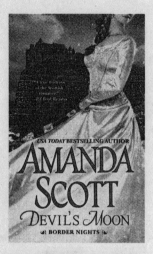

## DEVIL'S MOON
### by Amanda Scott

In a flawless blend of history and romance, *USA Today* bestselling author Amanda Scott transports readers again to the Scottish Borders with the second book in her Border Nights series.

## THE SCANDALOUS SECRET OF ABIGAIL MacGREGOR
### by Paula Quinn

Abigail MacGregor has a secret: her mother is the true heir to the English crown. But if the wrong people find out, it will mean war for her beloved Scotland. There's only one way to keep the peace—journey to London, escorted by her enemy, the wickedly handsome Captain Daniel Marlow. Fans of Karen Hawkins and Monica McCarty will love this book!

# Fall in Love with Forever Romance

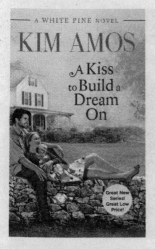

## A KISS TO BUILD A DREAM ON
### by Kim Amos

Spoiled and headstrong, Willa Masterson left her hometown—and her first love, Burk Olmstead—in the rearview twelve years ago. But the woman who returns is determined to rebuild: first her family house, then her relationships with everyone in town . . . starting with a certain tall, dark, and sexy contractor. Fans of Kristan Higgins, Jill Shalvis, and Lori Wilde will flip for Kim Amos's Forever debut!

## IT'S ALWAYS BEEN YOU
### by Jessica Scott

Captain Ben Teague is mad as hell when his trusted mentor is brought up on charges that can't possibly be true. And the lawyer leading the charge, Major Olivia Hale, drives him crazy. But something is simmering beneath her icy reserve—and Ben can't resist turning up the heat! Fans of Robyn Carr and JoAnn Ross will love this poignant and emotional military romance.

# Fall in Love with Forever Romance

### TOTAL SURRENDER
### by Rebecca Zanetti

Piper Oliver knows she can't trust tall, dark, and sexy black-ops soldier Jory Dean. All she has to do, though, is save his life and he'll be gone for good. But something isn't adding up...and she won't rest until she uncovers the truth—even if it's buried in his dangerous kiss. Fans of Maya Banks and Lora Leigh will love this last book in Rebecca Zanetti's Sin Brothers series!